The
FEUD

The FEUD

Catherine Hiller

 Heliotrope Books

New York

An excerpt from Chapter 10 of this novel appeared in *Honeysuckle Magazine* in July, 2017.

Cover Design by Naomi Rosenblatt with AJ&J Design

To Alex and Zachary and Jonathan

Prologue: The Photo

April, 1996

After Nikki got to work, she turned on her computer and scrolled through her email. Maybe a prospect had written back in response to one solicitation or another and was on the way to becoming a client. This actually happened every few weeks—but not today. Nikki's email consisted of a survey from the trade show she'd just attended, a few messages from friends (she didn't have email at home), a message from an existing client about a contract renewal (thank god), and a message with attachments from a name unfamiliar to her: *attababy@hotmail.com*.

The subject line read: "DC Souvenir." The message said, "See, these digital cameras are terrific! Hope you like the pix! Great meeting you!" Without really thinking, Nikki clicked onto the first attachment, of four, and there was the picture that Geoff had taken of her in the hotel bar. And next was the picture he had taken of her friend and colleague, Roberta, another sales rep. Quite good shots, actually, and how astonishing that Geoff could send these images across the World Wide Web without needing to physically get a print developed from a negative and send it through the US mail or via FedEx. She looked at the third photograph, another good one, of herself and Roberta, heads close. They were fast becoming best of friends.

Nikki clicked on the fourth image—and almost fainted. She was naked on a hotel bed. Geoff and Mike were naked, too.

She clicked the picture closed and looked about. No one had passed in back of her; no one had seen. Her heart was pumping hard. Then Cynthia, the office manager, came along on her way to the ladies room, swaying her hips and saying, "Good lord, girl—have you just seen a ghost?"

"What do you mean?"

"You look so pale and clammy, child—are you okay? I heard you came down with something in Washington?"

Nikki said, "No, I'm fine, I just opened a strange email."

"That email," said Cynthia, shaking her head. "It's changing everything. I can't do any work because all day long it's email, email, email. Email from Lillian. Email from Bethany. Email from you or Roberta or Yvonne." The company was largely female.

"Well, Cynthia," Nikki explained, "if we didn't have email, we'd have walked over to you or called you on the phone. This is not in addition to all that, it's instead of that."

"It's just a nuisance."

"These days my job is mainly about sending or answering email," Nikki said.

"I don't like it," said Cynthia, walking away. "And I don't like how you look. Get yourself some coffee or a Coca-Cola."

Nikki turned back to her computer and, looking around to make sure she was alone, opened the image again. Geoff must have held the camera out at arm's length to get the shot. She hadn't remembered hearing a camera, but perhaps these new cameras were silent, and she had lapsed into and out of consciousness much of the night. They must have put something into her drink. She closed the attachment; the image was burned into her brain. Why had Geoff sent it to her? Was he going to blackmail her? What if he had sent it to Roberta?

At that very moment, Roberta stopped by her desk.

"How are you?" she asked. "Recovered from Washington?"

"More or less," said Nikki. The morning after that disastrous night with Mike and Geoff, she had bolted from an industry presentation to be violently sick in the ladies room. She had spent the rest of the morning asleep in her hotel room. What a shambles of a sales trip! Nikki asked, "Did you get any email from those guys we met at the bar?"

Roberta hesitated before saying, "Yes—they sent me those photos they took of you and me."

"In the bar?"

"Yes." After a pause, Roberta added. "They also sent another image, which I deleted at once."

Nikki felt herself flushing crimson. She said, "I got that, too."

"Get rid of it!" said Roberta. "I wouldn't be surprised to learn Lillian checks our email, and you don't want a picture like that in your inbox." Lillian Watrous was their boss.

Nikki said, "I wonder why they sent us that?"

Roberta gave her a funny look.

"What?" asked Nikki.

Roberta said, "Maybe they thought you'd enjoy it." She looked around. Then she whispered, "So did you?"

"You mean enjoy the photo?" Nikki was whispering, too.

Roberta shook her head. "You know what I mean."

Nikki said, "I've never done anything like that in my life before. God, I feel so skanky!"

"Were you drunk?"

"I had only two drinks, over two hours. They must have put something into my drink. Anyway, I left the bar with Geoff, and he walked me to my room and he came in to see the view. We smoked a little pot, and soon we were on the bed. You know, it's been over a year since I've had sex at all, so I felt I deserved a good time. Anyway, after a while, Mike was in the room with us, too. I don't know how that happened, I kept blacking out. If only you hadn't left me in the bar with them!"

"I had to call Paul," said Roberta. Paul was her fiancé, and when she was out of town she always called him at eleven from the hotel room. "But you never answered my question. Did you enjoy it?"

1

Roberta

One year earlier: April 1995

Roberta Cohen had just come back from a sales call in Queens when she first saw Nikki Elkins. Lillian was parading a thin woman in a navy blue suit around the office, braying, "This is our first Westchester hire." The company was moving from Manhattan in a month's time, and Roberta knew that the company would want to hire Westchester people, who would be more loyal out of gratitude that they didn't commute, and who might work for less.

A few desks away, Lillian said something that made the new woman laugh. It was a nice laugh, Roberta thought, and she was pretty—though she should do something better with her hair. Perhaps they would be friends and Roberta would give her some tips. She guessed that the new woman was about her own age, thirty-five. Was she going to work in sales? Probably not: she had no manicure and wore strange, flat, rubber-soled shoes—very clunky and altogether wrong with the pale nylon stockings she was wearing.

Roberta was waiting outside Bethany's office to report on the sales call at Renew You, a chain of eight spas in Queens. This was one of the best moments in sales, coming back from a good meeting and talking to her CEO.

"Come in," called out Bethany from the interior of her vast office, and Roberta went into the inner sanctum. Bethany Moore, who had founded the company, was fifty-five, with a hearty smile, small, shrewd eyes, and unpredictable hair. Sometimes it was brown, sometimes it was gray, sometimes it was a dark, honey-blond. Its texture varied as much as its color, being variously wavy, frizzy, or, when she'd just been to the beauty salon, dead straight. This was a day of blondish waves. "Go on, tell me," said Bethany, leaning forward across her large desk.

Roberta smiled. She said, "They're buying the introductory package. We finally got them! And they decide on next year's supplier next month. It looks very promising."

"You genius!" said Bethany. "That's just fantastic!" And she got up from her desk to plant a kiss on Roberta's cheek. The CEO was a tall, awkward woman, with big breasts and a dromedary posture. "I've got to tell Lillian," Bethany said and pulled Roberta out of her private office to yell across the interior space, "Lillian! Roberta just bought in Renew You."

"Bravo!" shrieked Lillian. "Great job!" She turned to the new woman and said, "See how easy it is?" They walked toward Roberta.

Roberta gaped at Lillian, her boss. *Easy?* She had worked on Renew You for almost two years. She had attended a spa conference just to learn the name of their decision-maker. She had sent him personal letters with brochures. She had sent sample meals for his staff for a week. She had made weekly phone calls for the last several months just to get an appointment. Today, she had met before a committee of eight and given a PowerPoint presentation she had tailored just for them.

In fact, she had learned PowerPoint just for them.

Perhaps intuiting some of Roberta's resentment, Bethany said to her, "Roberta, you should be very proud. You're the best."

Lillian, still enjoying her role of introducing the new woman to the company, said, "Nikki, this is Roberta, our best sales rep. Nikki's taking over Marlene's accounts."

Marlene, like a number of others, was not coming to Westchester because of the commute, which was too bad because Marlene was Roberta's best work friend—in fact, her only work friend. Sometimes they had a drink together after work. Roberta herself didn't like the idea of commuting, even reverse-commuting, but she was doing much too well at Bethany Moore to consider leaving. She'd just have to get on MetroNorth every morning and afternoon. At least the company was paying for her monthly ticket. They wanted to keep her.

Lillian said, "Roberta, you can help Nikki after Marlene leaves. You're both winners," said Lillian. "I'm sure you'll get along like gangdusters."

Roberta tried not to smile. Lillian's phrasing was a source of some hilarity around the office. Lillian was a short, energetic woman in her sixties, with a cap of dark hair and a habit of walking indoors at top speed. Roberta thought Lillian's high energy and upbeat attitude were her only assets. Oh, and cheerleading for Bethany. Besides those talents, Lillian was uneducated and knew nothing about sales. Furthermore, her people skills were zero, and even when she meant to praise someone she managed to insult them. Roberta felt Lillian had demeaned her just now by calling her hard-won sales success "easy." If it's so goddamn easy, Roberta thought angrily, why do you even need a sales team? Just wait for the phone to ring—see how many clients you get! But Lillian had been with the company from the very beginning, working at no pay for six months, so the CEO was utterly loyal to her. No matter her gaffes, no matter her ignorance, Lillian's position as Vice President of Sales was secure.

Roberta went back to her desk to write up her sales report. She wondered where Nikki had worked before and why she didn't know about shoes.

2

Nikki's Journal

April 20, 1995

I got the job. It's local and it might pay well, or so they say. Didn't know what the job was when I went in for the interview, thought it was communications, but turns out it's... sales. Interviewer says more money in sales, and I need money. I've been looking for a job for three months, and I envied every woman I saw who had work of any kind—the librarian, the bank teller, the hair stylist. So it's a relief to have a job, but already I mourn my old freedom, my old life. Can I really do sales? I was introduced to Roberta, their best sales person. Very well-dressed in an overdone way. Earrings and necklaces and bracelets and rings. A beautiful pants suit and high-heeled boots. A striped silk scarf, tied just right. I did not wear high heels, never been comfortable in them, and better to be at ease than in style. But felt dowdy in my clunky flats.

What I dread about working:
Getting up early
Evening fatigue
Not knowing the industry
Not knowing how to sell
Having the job distort who I am or should be
Not getting high on sunny afternoons

What I look forward to about working:
Regular paycheck!
Buying clothes
Learning new things
Meeting new people

April 22, 1995

I had the grand room dream again last night, where between the second and third floors of my house I find a whole other floor, one huge and beautiful room. I unlock the double doors, and once again I enter the conservatory. There are ebony chairs, plush velvet couches, marble tables, silken drapes. This will always be mine, I think, flooded with joy.

April 23, 1995

Wish there was a book about women and houses. Cannot be the only female with an inordinate and perhaps unnatural attachment to my house. This might seem an innocent pleasure, but it's not. We should love people, not places.

Still, Howard's End, *that most humane of novels, is about the passion of a woman for her house.*

When David and I divided our assets, I made sure to keep the house. To do this, I gave up all claim to his pension, his business, and most of our joint assets. The house is mine: I alone must pay the mortgage; I'll be free and clear when I'm sixty-two. With only Quiana and me living here, we don't need all this room. So why is selling this house anathema, utter heresy to me? What is this bond with wood and mortar, red shingles, pocket doors?

Scarlett O'Hara's great love was not Rhett but Tara.

Before now, if I'd been keenly interested in reading a book on a subject and none existed, I would have thought about writing one. My book on women and houses would delve into women's psychology, especially in their middle years, and would examine whether we feel more bonded to certain types of dwellings (old houses?) than others. The proposal alone would entail months of research. I would interview women from every walk of life and photograph them in front of and inside their houses. If it sold, a book like this could keep me happily productive for two years, but the advance might not sustain me for three months. If I write a book like this, most likely I will lose the house I love.

So now I have this job selling frozen meals to hospitals and spas. I start working tomorrow.

3

Roberta

May, 1995

Roberta liked her job well enough, but the dread of going back to work started on Sunday night, after dinner. By then, her boyfriend, Paul, had left, and she was alone, checking on her clothes for the week, polishing shoes and ironing blouses while she watched TV and sipped a little wine. Wouldn't it be wonderful if she didn't have to work at all!

On the other hand, how would she fill up her days? It wasn't as if she was going to write the Great American Screenplay, and she had no children and no pets. Even if Paul ever proposed, she knew he would want her to work, so at least she had a job that paid well. She had bought her one-bedroom condo on the Upper East Side several years earlier, during a dip in the New York real estate market, and everything in her place was modern: marble and glass, black and white. She ate out several times a week with her girl friends. She always had enough clothes for a stylish two-week rotation (no repeats) all four seasons of the year. If only she could lose ten pounds! She wouldn't mind buying all new clothes—hey, that would be a lot of fun!—if she could only drop from an 8 to a 6. When pressed, Paul admitted that, yes, she'd look better slimmer—the bastard. Maybe if she cut down on the wine she would lose a little weight, but she wasn't going to do that. She liked where wine took her, and if she was careful, she didn't get sick. The idea was to get happy without getting a hangover.

Perhaps one day she and the new one, Nikki, would have a drink after work. Nikki looked to be a size 4. Bethany was a 14, and Lillian a 10 Petite. Roberta couldn't tell you how she knew these things, she just did, the way she knew that to her mother she would always be a failure if she didn't have children, and to her father she had always been a failure because she hadn't been a boy. She'd been the third girl of three children in a family of Orthodox Jews, and when Kenny was finally born two years after Roberta, he got all the attention. It didn't seem to matter that Roberta got all A's in school and was elected to student council, while Kenny was a mediocre student with no interest in sports or culture: her parents lavished their attention and love on the boy. When Kenny was seventeen, he began having hallucinations and was diagnosed with acute schizophrenia. Now he lived on disability in the basement apartment of their parents' house in Brooklyn, so they could keep an eye on him. Roberta never mentioned him; when asked about her family, she said she was the youngest of three girls.

At least her older sisters had gotten married and produced children. Roberta knew that her parents were not impressed with her two MA degrees and her (barely) six-figure income because she was the one who'd remained an old maid. She was the one who probably wasn't going to have children. She was the one who ate pork and sometimes dated *sheygas*, non-Jewish men. Thank God for the other daughters. No matter how hard she tried to please her family, Roberta knew she was scorned because she hadn't managed to get married.

The phone rang, and Roberta let the answering machine screen it for her. Then she heard Hevron's voice and lunged for the phone, babbling. "Hello, I'm here, hello."

"It's Hevron."

Like she didn't know. She sank into her white couch.

"Are you there?"

"Hevron, I asked you not to call."

"How are you?" Hevron asked. "I've missed you."

"You were the one to break it off."

"I just called to say hello."

"Don't call, Hevron. Don't say hello. I have a boyfriend now."

"That's good. *Mazel tov.*"

"How's your wife?"

"She's good. We're expecting a baby."

"What does that make? Three?"

"Three."

"So you got what you wanted. A younger woman who would give you lots of babies."

"You didn't want children at all."

"I might have changed my mind."

"I couldn't take that risk. And you were already thirty. If you didn't have a maternal streak by then..."

It was true: Roberta hadn't wanted children. She had never been interested in babies—repulsed by them, if truth be known—and she was appalled by what pregnancy did to the body. She suspected that if she became pregnant, she'd never lose the extra pounds, and then she'd really be a house, maybe a 10 or a 12.

After dating Roberta for a year, Hevron had left her for a younger woman with a more pronounced maternal streak. Now Roberta said, "Why are you calling me, Hevron?"

"Well, my wife's out of town, visiting her sister, and I was hoping I could stop by and say hello."

"Oh, sure. I'm going to let you into my bed and into my life because your pregnant wife's out of town!"

"Who said anything about coming into your life?" Hevron asked in that deadpan voice she had once found hilarious.

"Very funny," said Roberta.

"How's my gummy bear?"

"I'm *not* your gummy bear!" But she was smiling. "I never was."

"Oh yes you were. Are you alone?"

"At the moment, yes."

"So why don't I come over?"

"Forget it," said Roberta. And she hung up on the one man in her life who had really gotten under her skin.

She looked at herself in the foyer mirror. Her dark eyes looked very large and there were two spots of pink on her cheeks. Sometimes she thought Hevron had been the love of her life. Paul was nice, but Hevron, devilish Hevron, the Israeli-born high school teacher with the wiry black hair and intense blue eyes, was the one who could bring the blood to her face, and not just to her face. Why, even now she was aroused.

Roberta sometimes dreamed of Hevron, sensual and disturbing dreams, but she never thought of him when she was in bed with Paul. That wouldn't be right. She and Paul had a very pleasant relationship, and if it never went much beyond tepid, perhaps that was because Paul was ten years older than Roberta. He had two teen-aged girls from his first marriage, so he wasn't going to bug her about having kids. He was a handsome, easy-going lawyer, extremely eligible, and they'd been dating for two years. She was lucky she had him, she knew.

The intercom buzzed. It was the doorman. "There's a gentleman to see you, Miss Cohen. A Mister Hevron Goldman."

He must have called from the pay phone on the corner! Outrageous to come over in the face of her refusal. But Roberta didn't want to get the doorman involved in a scene, and she knew there *would* be a scene if she didn't let Hevron pay her a visit.

"Miss Cohen?"

"Fine, let him in." She had exactly two minutes to get ready for the most thrilling man she had ever known. She went tearing around the apartment, patting concealer under her eyes, trading her sweatshirt for a soft tight sweater, brushing her long dark hair to bring up the shine. He had always loved her hair, would bury his face in it, would have her shake it so it fell over his stomach, and lower.

She tipped back the last of the wine in her glass and opened her apartment door to watch Hevron in a terrible wool cap walk from the elevator toward her. "This is so wrong," she began.

"Can I at least come in and warm up? It's so cold outside."

Shaking her head, Roberta let him into her apartment.

"Beautiful place! Looks expensive," Hevron said as soon as he was in the door.

"I bought it at the right time," said Roberta. "You and your wife still in Queens?"

"Uh-huh. It suits us. Her parents live around the corner, and soon we'll have three kids under age five. We need all the help we can get."

"Sounds exciting," Roberta said flatly.

Hevron said, "You know what's exciting?" And he came across the room toward her. "Seeing you again."

Tell me about it, she thought, warmth swelling down there. But she quickly seated herself in an armchair to avoid his embrace, and he was left looking foolish. Then he sat down on the arm of her chair. "Gummy bear," he said tenderly. He reached into his pocket and actually brought out a gummy bear. He pushed it into her mouth.

She took it in, chewing and shaking her head. "You are incorrigible," she said, "but now you have to leave. I have a boyfriend and you have a wife. Go on, get up."

"That's not what you really want," he said, his fingers trying to get between her lips although he had no more gummy bears.

"Morality means we don't always do what we want." And she wrenched herself up and away from his insinuating hand and stood up, remembering to hold in her stomach. She put her hands on her hips. "You have to get out of here, Hevron. Right now."

"You look so hot when you're angry," he said.

Good, she thought. Remember me this way. But she just said, "Go now. Come back when you get a divorce." And she opened her front door and held it wide until he realized she was serious. Then he put his horrible hat back on his head and left.

She closed the door behind him and watched through the peephole as he walked toward the elevator. He did not look back.

Roberta went into the kitchen and opened the freezer. She scooped some vanilla ice cream into a bowl. Then she added blueberries, so the snack would be healthy. Since she was breaking her diet anyway, she added chocolate chips as well. Then she noticed her empty wine glass and filled it up again.

Roberta liked to get to work a little early to give herself a few minutes to brush her hair and put on lipstick in the bathroom and still be among the first at her desk. She liked to ease herself into work. She couldn't start prospecting for leads at 8:55 Monday morning, but she could sharpen her pencils, read the trade journals, and review her sales call reports from the previous week before giving them to Lillian, who never read them anyway.

At 9:15, Nikki arrived with wind-mussed hair and a wet-looking nose. She walked to Lillian's office. Roberta heard Lillian's hearty laugh as she greeted Nikki. "You're gonna do just fine, I can tell."

At 9:25, Marlene came in with a flourish. She was tall and full-figured—and with her hair dyed a violent red, she was an arresting sight. She took off her coat, dumped it on her chair and shook out her short magenta hair. Then she sat upon her desk, which was next to Roberta's, and began swinging her legs. Marlene asked, "What do you think of the new one?"

"Can't tell yet. Bad shoes." For Nikki was wearing the same clunky flats she had worn to the job interview.

Marlene said, "Lillian told me she has no sales experience. I have to train her."

Roberta shook her head. "This company. I'll never understand how it gets by. The logical thing would have been to advertise for a salesperson, but don't talk to Lillian about logical."

Marlene said, "Maybe they're saving money by hiring a beginner. But it kills me that Lillian expects me to take, what, a housewife? and make her a sales rep in two weeks."

Roberta and Marlene had each worked in sales at other companies and considered themselves to be consummate sales professionals. They were both unmarried women with cynical attitudes about life and Bethany Moore, Inc.

Roberta suddenly said, "God, I'm going to miss you, Marlene."

"Me, too. But soon I'll have the best skin in sales." Marlene had found a job selling memberships to an upscale spa, and complimentary weekly facials were part of her package. Her skin was already very good, Roberta thought: pale, smooth and luminous. Marlene said, "Uh-oh. Here she comes. Don't you think she's too thin?"

"Yeah," said Roberta, though she didn't. She'd love to be exactly Nikki's weight. Marlene eased herself off her desk as Nikki approached them.

Nikki said, "You must be Marlene. I'm Nikki."

"Yes, Lillian told me all about you," said Marlene. "Pull up a chair."

Nikki looked around and saw a gray metal folding chair leaning against the wall. She brought it forward, opened it, and sat down obediently. She asked, "Where are the computers?"

"The officers have them," said Marlene. "The rest of us share the one in the middle of the room." And she pointed to a small Kaypro in the center of the office.

Nikki's jaw dropped in astonishment, and Roberta, feeling strangely protective of the Bethany Moore Company, added, "They're getting new computers for everyone after the move."

"How can you work without a computer?" marveled Nikki.

"A lot of our work is on the phone," said Roberta. "Making calls is what we mainly do."

"Yes, but don't you need to write about the conversation? Take notes? Plan strategy? Keep records?"

"Everybody does sales differently," says Marlene. "I don't write much down, but I remember where I am with my clients, so it's fine."

"I write a lot down," said Roberta. She held out the Renew You folder, rather proud of her neat handwriting and the column of dated notations.

Nikki scarcely gave it a glance. "No computers!" she said in that wondering voice.

"Get over it," said Marlene, so harshly that Roberta was startled. "After the move, you'll have your own precious computer."

Roberta saw Nikki flinch. But she recovered quickly and asked Marlene, "How long have you worked here?"

"Eight years. From the beginning."

"Wow."

"I've been here six," said Roberta.

"Well, computers or not, if you've been here so long, it must be a good place to work."

Roberta caught Marlene's eye and they both burst out laughing.

"What?" asked Nikki.

"You'll see," said Marlene.

"No, be fair," Roberta said to Marlene. "There *are* some good things about this company."

"True," said Marlene. "No quotas. No projections."

"They're too dysfunctional for that," said Roberta.

Marlene said, "Maybe they know projections are a waste of time anyway, and why torment us with quotas? We're motivated to sell because of our commissions."

Roberta saw that during this dialogue, Nikki was turning her head back and forth as if watching a tennis match. One thing about Nikki: she seemed to actively listen. And that, Roberta knew, was crucial in sales. If she could also deliver, she might do well, despite her inexperience. Roberta suspected that Nikki was more intelligent than Marlene—and who knew? She might be able to devise a whole new selling approach from sincerity and naiveté. Perhaps a good mind and a fresh eye could trump years of sales experience. Lillian was an idiot, but she knew how to hire.

"So how does it really work?" asked Nikki. "How many clients are we supposed to sign up each month?"

"Depends on the client. If you get a chain, like Renew You, one a month is great."

"So you spend four weeks just to get one client?"

Marlene said, "You'll see how it works. It isn't as easy as Lillian pretends to believe."

"You're also servicing your existing clients," said Roberta.

"You don't have customer reps for that?" asked Nikki.

Marlene shook her head so her red hair flapped against her cheeks. "*We're* the customer reps." She stood up. "Does anyone want any coffee or a bagel?"

"I'm fine," said Nikki, glancing at her watch.

"Me too," said Roberta. She had to smile. It was only nine-forty-five, and Marlene was already running downstairs to get coffee. Marlene came in late, left early and took frequent breaks. With Marlene in the office, it was easy for Roberta to look good, but with Nikki... ? And as for Yvonne, that ditz, who could take her seriously?

At that very moment, wouldn't you know it, Yvonne came walking toward them in a tight green pants suit with black plumes at the neckline. Roberta thought Yvonne's clothes were more appropriate to bar mitzvahs and afternoon weddings than for the office or sales calls. "Here comes Mrs. Mahjong," Roberta said to Nikki, *sotto voce*. "Our third and last, and I mean *last*, sales rep."

"Hi, Marlene," said Yvonne, ignoring Roberta.

"Hi, Yvonne," said Marlene. "I'm getting coffee. Want any?"

"No thanks," said Yvonne. Marlene strode away.

Yvonne said, "I wanted to meet our new rep."

Nikki stood up to shake Yvonne's hand. "Nice to meet you. I'm Nikki."

"I'm Yvonne, and I live in Westchester, too. I'm so excited about the move! When I started working here last year, I had no idea they were planning to come into my back yard."

It was soon established that they lived in neighboring towns in lower Westchester. Nikki said, "After the move, I might go home for lunch."

"Me, too," said Yvonne. "Do you have children?"

"A twelve-year-old girl, Quiana."

"Pretty name! I've got Gillian and Gerald in college. Anyway, welcome aboard. If you need anything or don't understand something, just ask me." Plumes waving, Yvonne went to her desk on the other side of the big, seedy office.

"Why do you call her Mrs. Mahjong?" Nikki asked Roberta.

"She reminds me of those middle-aged Jewish women who get all dressed up in fancy clothes just to play mahjong with each other."

"Well, she seems nice enough," said Nikki.

Roberta said, "I used to think so, too."

"What happened?" asked Nikki.

Roberta wasn't sure whether she should confide in Nikki. Would Nikki sympathize with her if she did? She said, "I don't want to get into it."

"Tell me something," said Nikki. "Why aren't there any men at this company?"

Roberta smiled. "There are one or two. The financial officer. The tech guy. But you're right. It's almost all women here."

"No one to flirt with," mused Nikki, who was single.

"Bethany likes to give women a chance," said Roberta. "Also, she can exploit them, hire them cheaper." She handed Nikki several glossy pamphlets. "Here. Until Marlene comes back, why don't you get to know our product? These are our latest brochures." Nikki began to read.

Roberta went back to her desk, consulted a notebook, and pulled the telephone toward her. She would try to set up a meeting with Cardiology Associates in Queens and an appointment with Swedish Spas in Staten Island. And she would do serious research about Astoria Reconstructive Surgery. Who were their patients? Who was their current supplier? Astoria Recon was an eighty-bed facility, and bringing them in would make Bethany and Lillian scream with joy.

4

Nikki

May, 1995

Office politics! Nikki had often wondered about the phrase and why it seemed so important to everyone who had a job. She guessed it had to do with friendship and power: who likes you, who can help you, who can harm you, who will gain from your rise or fall. Now, sitting at the gray metal folding chair and opening a Bethany brochure, Nikki realized that barely an hour into her new job, she was coming up against office politics. Roberta and Yvonne loathed each other. Did that mean Nikki had to take sides? She and Roberta were probably culturally closer; peeping out of Roberta's large bag was a T.C. Boyle book Nikki had recently read. And Roberta probably smoked a little weed, while Yvonne probably didn't. But Yvonne and Nikki had commonalities, too: each lived in Westchester and was a mother. Then again, Yvonne, with her big smile and amusing clothes, was probably not as important as Roberta, whom Lillian had called "our best rep." Nikki would just have to be careful. She opened a brochure and read:

"Welcome to the wonderful world of Bethany spa and hospital meals! These healthy and delicious meals are prepared to please your most discerning clients. Two minutes in a microwave, and you can serve these fresh and elegant meals with pride. All of our meals are low-calorie, low-sodium, low-fat, and kosher. The Health First line is our most popular category. These meals are especially easy to digest and are recommended for patients during those all-important post-op days. For additional flavor, choose our distinctive Taste Deluxe line. Our Pretty Please line is renowned for its visual appeal and is very popular at health spas.

"Whichever line you choose, you can be proud every time you serve a Bethany meal because of it's nutritional value, exquisite taste, and beautiful presentation."

Nikki stopped reading and looked up, shocked. "Roberta?"

Roberta turned to face her. "Something wrong?"

"That apostrophe! Here, in 'it's'!" Nikki held out the brochure.

Roberta asked, "What about it?"

"It doesn't belong! It should be 'its,' without the apostrophe."

"And?"

"Well, it has to be changed! It's grammatically wrong! It's not good for the company's image."

"I guess you could tell Lillian," said Roberta, "if it really bothers you."

Nikki shrugged, reconsidering. She was getting the feeling that she shouldn't do that, at least not on her very first day. She'd make a note to consider it later. She looked around to find something to write on. On one of the sagging shelves near them, she saw a half-used legal pad underneath a stack of folders. "Can I use this?" she asked Roberta.

"Sure. Ask Cynthia for some more supplies."

"This is fine for now." Nikki opened the yellow pad to a fresh page. She wrote the word ITS and then scribbled a note about the word "meals" being used six times on one brochure page. But what other word could take its place? "Fare," "chow," "repast," "grub," "collation"? Maybe "meal" would have to do: what choice, really, did they have?

Marlene returned with coffee and donuts and insisted on giving Nikki a sugar bow-tie as a way to welcome her. It would be churlish to refuse it, so Nikki thanked Marlene and gamely ate the pastry, although it was not the sort of thing she usually allowed into her body. The first bite tasted delicious, but it soon turned into a heavy sweet sludge in her mouth. She took a second bite. She wished she'd asked for coffee as well; you needed it with a bow-tie. Marlene was taking a sip of coffee for every bite of donut and seemed to be enjoying both enormously. She finished her snack and wiped her mouth with a napkin, which was soon stained bright red from her lipstick.

"All right," said Marlene, pulling open the lid to her coffee and taking a big swig. "I'm going to make a sales call. Listen up."

Marlene pulled the phone toward her, glanced at a sheet, and punched in some numbers. "May I speak to Gena please?" she said to the person on the line. Then she told Nikki, "I always use just the first name, so the operator thinks I'm a friend."

Nikki nodded, wondering why it made a difference what the operator thought.

"Gena!" Marlene said with enormous enthusiasm. "It's Marlene from the Bethany Moore Company! How are you doing?...Yeah, me, too!" Marlene laughed heartily. "Well, it's good to talk to you. Now the last time we spoke, you said the Health First line was really delicious!... Yes, you did, I made a note! So I'm wondering if you're ready to order from us or not... Listen, tell you what I'm going to do. I'm going to fax you last year's price list. Yes, you'll see 1994 on top of the page. And if you can order by the end of this week, you can use those 1994 prices for all of 1995.... You're welcome. I always go the extra mile for my clients. So listen, I'll fax you that list and I'll call you back in a couple-three days so you can go over it with your people, and then we can lock in your rate protection—how's that? ...Not at all, Gena. My pleasure." Marlene listened a few seconds, chuckled some more, and said, "I know what you mean. Nice to talk to you! Take care now."

Marlene hung up the phone and looked at Nikki, who asked, "How did you get to know her so well?"

"Never met her in my life, the bitch."

"You seemed like good friends."

"Oh, she's been stringing me along and cadging free meals for a year. She's a pain in the ass."

"But you really seemed to like her."

"I'm an actress. You're going to be one, too."

"Are all sales people actors?"

"It helps. You have to be outgoing and enthusiastic and agreeable. And not only on the phone."

"What do you mean?"

"When Lillian or Bethany asks you anything, the answer is yes, you can, you will, it's going just great. That's the only thing they want to hear. So that's the only thing to tell them."

"What about honesty?"

"The worst policy, around here."

"But..."

"Listen to me," said Marlene, shaking out her magenta hair. "Everybody lies here. Sometimes people ask who our clients are, and I've heard Lillian mention clients who left us years ago. She phrases it, 'Bethany has provided meals for the finest hospitals and spas in the northeast, including...' Note that she says 'has provided,' which means she's not technically lying, just misleading the listener."

"Do you do that, too?"

"Sure," said Marlene. "So does Roberta."

Roberta herself was on the phone now, loudly and merrily setting up a sales appointment. Nikki knew that just getting the appointment was good, so she saw why Roberta would heighten her volume—perhaps for Lillian, who was scurrying past them toward Bethany's office.

Nikki whispered, "I heard Lillian tell someone she wanted to groom me. As if I were a pony."

Marlene snorted. "That is so Lillian."

Out of the corner of her eye, Nikki saw Roberta leave for the bathroom. Roberta had the glossy hair, smooth skin, and strong nails that often go together: the collagen triumvirate, Nikki termed it, knowing she didn't have it. Roberta was wearing that season's skirtsuit, with a snug blouse and medium heels. This was quite a different look from Yvonne and her plumes. Nikki asked Marlene, "What do you think of Yvonne?"

"She's fun, but Roberta can't stand her."

"What's *that* all about?"

"They had a fight last year, and ever since then it's been war."

"So what did they fight about?"

"The ladies room key."

"The—what?"

"The ladies room is outside, in the hall, so you need to use a key. It's on a little wooden paddle. Georgette gives it out when you need it."

Georgette was the receptionist. Nikki couldn't help smiling. "This feud is about a *ladies room key?*"

Marlene nodded. "It went missing, and Roberta found it on

Yvonne's desk and accused Yvonne of hiding it because she knew Roberta used the bathroom then. Yvonne said, 'Are you crazy? I just made a silly mistake and brought the key back to my desk. Believe it or not, I do not keep track of your bathroom habits.' Roberta said, 'Don't you *dare* call me crazy, you fat bitch!'" Marlene shook her head. "You don't want to get into a fight with Roberta. Lillian loves her, though. She's always been Lillian's little darling."

Nikki was starting to think that negotiating between the personalities at Bethany Moore was going to be more of a challenge than negotiating prices with her clients. Knowing it would get back to Roberta, Nikki said, "Well, Roberta's very impressive. Very together and professional."

Marlene gave her a flat look, and Nikki felt she'd seen right through her. Maybe Marlene wouldn't pass the message on, after all. Or maybe she'd pass it with a message of her own.

Nikki wrote on her pad, "Bethany has provided meals for the finest spas and hospitals in the Northeast, including..." Then she tore off the six or seven previously used sheets, balling up each one. She looked around for a wastepaper basket. She didn't see any in her area, so she tossed them into the first wastepaper basket she saw, which was by Dawn's empty desk. Dawn was one of Lillian's assistants, a young woman with pale hair and poor skin.

When Dawn returned, she asked, "Who put all this yellow paper into my trash?"

"I did," said Nikki.

Dawn let out a sigh of exasperation.

Nikki said coolly, "I didn't know people were territorial about their wastebaskets."

Dawn glared at her and strode away.

Marlene said to Nikki, "Bad move. You've got to get along around here. You should have just said 'sorry' instead of getting off a clever put-down. Especially to Dawn."

"Why?"

"Because she's one of Lillian's secretaries. And the officers' secretaries—or *assistants*, as we're now supposed to call them—do most of the work around here and are the gatekeepers. It's very important to treat them with courtesy. You're just lucky Dawn's not going to Westchester."

"That's good," said Nikki, though of course Dawn could badmouth her to her friends and perhaps already had. You had to watch every little thing you said—not just with your clients, but also with your fellow workers. Nikki wondered if she had the tact or temperament to be working in an office.

"Do you need any office supplies?" asked a black woman with a gentle, singsong voice. "Lillian said I should ask you."

Marlene said, "This is Cynthia, our office manager. Cynthia, this is Nikki."

"Short for Nicole?" asked Cynthia.

"Short for Nicolette," said Nikki.

"What a pretty name!" Cynthia's brown face was a serene oval, and her dark hair was elaborately styled in a bun made of braids.

"Thank you," said Nikki. "Where are you from? You have such a wonderful accent."

"I'm from St. Lucia, in the Caribbean. Come to the supply closet and tell me what you need."

Nikki followed Cynthia across the large untidy office. Cynthia was dressed very modestly, as if for church, but her hips moved back and forth as if she was walking the street. Nikki watched, fascinated. As she followed Cynthia, she tried to add a wiggle to her walk, but it didn't feel natural. They stopped at a large metal closet on the back wall, and Cynthia inserted a small key into the lock. She flung the door open as if exhibiting Aladdin's treasure, not just paper, envelopes, and other office supplies. Cynthia said to Nikki, "We're glad to have you with us."

"It seems like a great place to work." Nikki was trying her best to be bland and upbeat on the job.

"Oh, child, it is, it really is."

Child! Cynthia didn't look much older than Nikki, but she said it so warmly, Nikki knew she meant well. She took a telephone message book, a few yellow legal pads, and a couple of ball point pens. She took a box of pencils—and knocked over a stack of paper clip boxes. Several spilled to the floor, and she bent to pick them up, apologizing. Cynthia restacked them. "Whenever you need anything, just ask me," Cynthia said. And she locked the closet and walked to her desk with the wonderful hip roll Nikki envied.

As soon as she turned the corner to walk down her block, Nikki saw Taylor's old blue van parked in front of the house. She hadn't seen her sister in six months, nor spoken to her in weeks, and Nikki hurried down the street. Taylor was twenty-eight, still finding herself. She moved from one place to another every few months. Perhaps she was going to stay in New York for a while. Nikki opened the front door and called, "Hello? Taylor? Quiana?"

Quiana came down the stairs. She was twelve, tall and thin, with long chestnut hair and large semi-circular ears. "Hi, Mom. Taylor's in the bath."

"When did she get here?"

"About an hour ago. So how was your first day of work?"

"Not so bad. I'm just being trained now, but it seems all right."

"Mom, Taylor has a piercing in her eyebrow."

"Why am I not surprised?"

"Does that mean that you'd let me have one?"

"Sure. When you're twenty-one or out of college, whichever comes first."

Quiana giggled. Nikki knew Quiana didn't want a piercing, although she did want a tattoo, a subject they'd discussed several times, with Nikki always forbidding it.

Taylor padded down the stairs, wrapped in a large blue bath towel, which picked up the color of her eyes. She had cut her hair short and her face looked more angular. Nikki opened her arms and they hugged each other hard. Nikki smelled her own bath powder on Taylor's skin.

Nikki and Taylor were half-sisters, sharing a mother. Nikki had been thrilled when her baby sister was born; she'd been eight, and it seemed like a rehearsal for motherhood. Until she left for college, Nikki had helped raise Taylor: changing diapers, wheeling the stroller, and teaching her to read at age four. That had been fun: Taylor was a bright child, and she was now a bright adult. But so scattered! In the past ten years, she'd been a math major, a poet, a potter, a computer technician, and a teacher's assistant. She'd had male lovers, female lovers, and a two-year period of celibacy. She'd lived in

Boston, Austin, Boulder, New Zealand, and Burlington. She played the guitar, the drums, and the harmonica.

"You look great!" said Nikki, deciding not to mention the piercing.

Taylor said, pointing to her eyebrow, through which a silver barbell had been inserted. "You don't mind?"

"It gives me the creeps. But the rest of you looks good. Love the hair." Nikki took off her suit jacket. "How long can you stay?"

"Just a few days."

"Bummer I'm working," said Nikki. "Though more of a bummer if I wasn't."

"Has he cut you off without a penny?" Taylor was furious with David for leaving.

"No, he's been fair. But I still have to work now. What's new with you?"

"That's what I wanted to tell you," said Taylor, with a smile that showed her chipped incisor. "I'm going to get serious. I'm going to grad school."

"Really?" Nikki was very pleased. "Where? Studying what?"

"I've been accepted at Stanford, in their computer program."

"Wow. I had no idea you were even applying. Can Mom and Jack help you out with tuition?"

"I should be okay," Taylor said. "I got a fellowship."

"Taylor! That's fabulous!"

"They probably want more women in the program, so they got generous, but I ain't proud. I start in August."

"You probably got a great score on your computer GRE," said Nikki. Taylor did not dispute this. "So you think computer science is a growing field?"

Taylor smiled. "Yes, Nikki. It's a growing field."

"And are you an enthusiast about this World Wide Web?"

"Yep."

"You don't think the whole thing's been over-hyped?"

"Nope. I think it's going to change everything."

Nikki gave her sister a tolerant smile. Young people! They always believed in the next big trend. As if the World Wide Web would change the important things in life: how people did their work or found true love or had fun or worked for social change.

Now Taylor was asking, "Do you have an Internet connection?"

"Yes, I just got it through my telephone company. Believe it or not, they aren't connected at my job! They only just got computers for the office staff."

"Crazy," said Taylor. "I'll need to go online tonight."

"I've paid for ten hours a month, so don't be too long."

Quiana piped up, "I *told* her to get an unlimited plan, but no. Mom's 'watching her pennies.'"

"What do *you* do online?" Taylor asked Quiana.

"Oh, stuff."

Nikki suppressed a smile. Quiana was very secretive these days. But maybe Taylor, her hip young aunt, could coax out her secrets. Nikki said, "I'm going to make dinner. Any special prohibitions?" Taylor was often a vegetarian.

"I'd prefer no red meat."

"No problem," said Nikki. "I have chicken breasts with mushrooms." They'd each have a little less than planned, but if she made the zucchini as well as the peas... "Let me get them on."

As she was going to the kitchen, Nikki heard Taylor asking Quiana the cryptic question, "So, do you belong to a LAN?"

Nikki brought out the chicken breasts and mushrooms from the refrigerator. She had made this dish so many times before that she brought the tarragon and the thyme down from the spice rack without conscious cogitation, and her fingers flew slicing mushrooms. She was glad it was a quick meal, for she wanted to be finished eating by nine, which was when a new nature series premiered. It was hosted by Lloyd Tyson, who'd been in an anthropology tutorial with her in college, and she wanted to see what he looked like after all these years.

She'd ask Quiana to do the clean-up.

While the chicken was cooking, Nikki went up to the attic, opened a window, and stuck her head out for a pre-dinner smoke. Quiana and Taylor knew she smoked weed; they just didn't know how much, and that's how she wanted to keep it. As she toked up in secret, Nikki thought about Lloyd. Fifteen years earlier, he had asked Nikki out, and she had declined. Since then, Lloyd's career had been on a steady ascent: guest columns here, bestselling books there, even a stay at Bellagio. And Nikki? Three non-fiction books that hadn't done very well and now this new job selling frozen meals. She shook her head. Not that she would have been happy with Lloyd. Humorless drip! But his academic and now popular prominence offended and intrigued her. At nine o'clock, she would turn on the TV, and, she imagined, she'd see jowls and a balding pate, hear a pedantic drone, and she'd be glad she'd turned him down when she'd been young and hot.

She wondered if Lloyd ever thought about her. She wouldn't be thinking of him if he hadn't been so damn successful, and she took his success as a personal reproach, for she had done just as well in their tutorial, and had gotten great grades in college. Why hadn't she made more of her life? Was it because she'd fully expected to marry and have a child? Which she had, of course, done. She would have had more than one child if David hadn't been opposed, citing overpopulation and the cost of college.

Maybe she was just an underachiever: a bright girl whose promise had fizzled. Lloyd had fulfilled his early promise, while she was the one with the dreary job and the dismal divorce.

Coming down the stairs, she could hear Taylor telling Quiana something about algorithms, whatever they were. Quiana, though, seemed to know.

At nine o'clock, Nikki was at the TV, and Quiana was doing the dishes. Taylor wandered into the living room, plopped down in an armchair, feet flopped over the armrest, and asked, "Whatcha watching?"

"Shhhh," said Nikki, riveted to the screen. For there was Lloyd, soft-spoken, articulate—and astonishingly handsome. No jowls, lots of brown hair, serious eyes, and a whimsical mouth. And he wasn't in the least pedantic. Nikki couldn't take her eyes off him. It wasn't fair! How had he gotten so attractive?

Taylor said, "I didn't know you were interested in ant colonies."

Nikki said to Taylor, "That's someone I knew in college." Lloyd's name faded onto the screen.

"Lloyd Tyson? Really?"

"You've heard of him."

"Sure. Didn't he have a column in the *Times* magazine?"

"Uh-huh. Couple of years ago. He was kind of a nerd when I knew him."

"Did you know him well?"

Nikki shook her head. "He asked me out, though."

"Cool. What was he like?"

"Can we just watch for now?"

Lloyd was saying, "In many ways, an ant colony acts like a single organism." His voice imparted drama and even tragedy to this simple statement. He lived in Savannah, she knew. She had heard it was very beautiful. Why had she ever turned him down?

After the show, Nikki shook her head sadly.

"What?" asked Taylor.

"Seeing Lloyd so resplendent on TV makes me question my entire life."

"Maybe a little over-reaction?" said Taylor. "I mean, things aren't so bad for you, Nikki. You have Quiana and a beautiful house and a new job... Who knows if Lloyd even got married."

"He did. He has three children."

"Well, shoot, he still may have, oh, I don't know, heart trouble or cancer or simple chronic misery. I mean, you don't know him any more. You don't know what his life is like. You just know about his success."

"You're probably right. So young and yet so wise." Nikki smiled.

"Perhaps inside he's seething with rage," said Taylor, warming to her subject. "Or feeling profoundly alone. Or quietly dying."

"I don't know about all of that. But he's much cuter now than he was when I knew him. He used to be overweight and somehow undefined. Now he's as lean as a wolf."

"So get in touch! Write him a letter. Men never forget a woman who's turned them down."

Nikki asked, "But what would I say?" She'd have to get high for inspiration.

5

Roberta's Film Diary

May 3, 1995:
*Haven't kept a diary since I was 12 & got one as a bday present.
It was lime green leatherette book w gilt on the edge of the pages
and a lock & key. I wrote in it only 3 x: it was too grand for my
thoughts. This Moleskine book is less scary. Will try to be more
persistent here, saying how I feel about movies I see. Why movies?
Because am taking a film appreciation course, and instructor has
suggested we keep a "Film Diary," though he won't collect it and
read it. He will flip through the pages though to make sure we've
done some writing. It's supposed to make us more observant,
better viewers and critics, more insightful.*

So last night Paul & I saw Leaving Las Vegas. *Unrelenting alcoholic misery. I'm sorry, but people like the Nicholas Cage character don't inspire my sympathy. I want to grab them by the arm
and get them to rehab. Then I want to send them to refugee camps
to see real human suffering. Paul, though, seemed moved by the
film. Maybe it's more of a guy thing, self-destruction through
drink. I liked the supersaturated look of daytime Las Vegas, and
the acting was excellent. But movie monotonous, one-note: a
relentless depressing decline. Anyway, alcohol isn't necessarily so
bad. I possibly have, well, a dependence, but I'll never end up in
the gutter or embarrass myself in public. It may be three glasses
of wine every day but I have it under control.*

6

Roberta

June, 1995

When the alarm rang on Monday, she stared at the clock in disbelief before switching off the alarm. It was only 6:45, so why had it sounded? Then Roberta remembered. Westchester. It was the first workday after the move, and instead of walking just a few blocks to work (a major reason why she'd bought her apartment), she would have to take a bus to the subway, then a train to the suburbs. Roberta showered and dressed, cutting off the price tag on a new blouse with her manicure scissors and easing the short plastic filament out of the fabric. The office was supposed to be just a short walk from the station, so Roberta wore her high heels as usual. When you're five foot three, you wear heels, although Nikki did not seem to know this. Roberta had noticed that she and Nikki were the same height, and it was likely they had other things in common.

In the few weeks she'd been working at Bethany, Nikki asked good questions, Roberta thought. She had even offered up an interesting idea or two, such as a flyer showing how Bethany meals provided double the minimum daily requirements of vitamins as defined by the FDA. Not that Lillian had acknowledged any of Nikki's good ideas, but Bethany seemed to like her and had produced the vitamin flyer for their sales kits. Soon, Roberta might not be the only big fish in the small pond of the Bethany Moore Company.

Roberta lived in the east eighties, and she had decided not to go down to Grand Central Terminal but to catch the train at the 125th Street station instead, even though it was in Harlem. This would save at least fifteen minutes on her commute, but when she emerged from the subway, she wasn't so sure it was a great idea. How different Manhattan neighborhoods were from each other! 125th Street looked nothing like 96th Street, for instance. Roberta hurried along the crowded street of discount stores, fast food places with unfamiliar names, litter on the sidewalk and derelicts in the doorways. She looked straight ahead until she came to the stairs for the MetroNorth station.

Roberta was climbing up the metal stairs when she sensed someone following her too closely. She turned her head just enough to glimpse a young black man with zigzag designs razored into his hair and low-slung pants with boxer shorts ballooning above the waistband. Roberta increased her speed and then... her heel caught in the grid of the step and she pitched forward.

"Oh!" She fell hard, striking her forehead on a step and losing her grip on her handbag. She raised her throbbing head.

"Lady, are you all right?"

It was the man who had been following too closely, and he held out her handbag politely. Roberta sat up slowly and reached for her bag.

"How's your head?" he asked.

"It's okay." She put her hand to her forehead. She could feel a lump forming. He held out his hand to help her get up, but she grabbed the rail instead and pulled herself to an asymmetrical standing position. The heel had come off her shoe and was stuck in the step. She quickly bent down, pulled it out, and slipped it into her pocket. She began awkwardly climbing the stairs, pain still slicing her head.

"Do you need any help?"

"I'm fine. Thank you."

"No problem," he said, and he vaulted the stairs ahead of her two at a time and was gone once she reached the platform.

When her train came and Roberta limped into a car, she saw the back of Lillian's head. Roberta hurriedly moved into the next car before Lillian could spot her. Roberta sank into a seat. Damned if she was going to make conversation with her nitwit boss all the way to Westchester. She took off her shoe and examined the clean break, the undamaged leather. She had just bought these shoes a week ago. She put the damaged shoe back on and got out a Joyce Carol Oates novel. Soon, the pain behind her forehead receded, along with the clacketing wheels and the other commuters. She was lost in the world of fiction.

When the train arrived at her station, Roberta left the carriage and lingered until Lillian was well ahead of her. And now Roberta had a choice: she could keep limping until she got to the office or she could take off both shoes and walk in her stocking feet, which is what she decided to do. Holding her shoes in her hand, she climbed up the stone steps and onto a sidewalk. Immediately, she felt her pantyhose starting to rip. Way ahead of her, Lillian was turning left, onto a downhill street with a hair salon and a candy-store. Roberta followed, keeping her distance. Lillian turned into a building on the next corner, and Roberta did the same a little later. It was still before nine, and Roberta was alone in the elevator, which took her to the fourth floor, the new home of Bethany Moore, Inc. She put on her shoes.

The elevator door opened, and Roberta stepped out to face their receptionist, Georgette, already at her desk. Receptionists are usually young women, but Georgette was over seventy, with a raddled face, a silver beehive hairdo, and a fixed stare. Georgette had been with the company from the beginning. She had a nasal voice and a heavy New York accent. Marlene used to mimic Bethany and say, "'I've got an idea! Let's hold auditions and get the person with the very worst voice in all of New York City and make her our... *receptionist!*'" And Marlene would mimic Georgette's singsong: "Good mawning! Bethany Moore Company! How may I direct your cawl?"

Now Roberta said, "Hi, Georgette. Wow. It's really nice here."

The office stretched out behind Georgette. There were a few enclosed areas, the officers' private offices, around the edges of the large room, but most of the desks were out in the open, with only four-foot high barriers between them. All the furniture was brand new, and the walls and carpet were white. The place was elegant, airy and inviting, but Roberta worried about how noisy it would get. She did not want to hear that ditz Yvonne making sales calls, and she didn't want Nikki hearing her own calls, either.

Georgette looked down at a map on her desk. She stood up and said to Roberta, "I'll take you to your desk."

"I hope they gave me someplace quiet," said Roberta, walking carefully in her uneven shoes. "Lillian knows I work best when I have some peace."

"You got the quietest place of all," said Georgette, pointing to a desk off in a corner, under a window. "You're all tucked away like a bear in a cave."

A bear? Had she heard right? Was Georgette saying she was as fat as a bear? Roberta asked coldly, "What do you mean, a bear?"

"Off by himself in a cave. That desk in front of yaws? It's an extra: no one's assigned to it. So ya got all this privacy." Georgette began walking away. Then she turned around. "The closet's over theah."

Roberta put her jacket in the closet and turned to find Nikki waiting with her coat. "Hello," said Roberta.

"Hey, this is great," said Nikki.

"It's certainly an improvement."

"So big, so clean, so white, so *wired*! That's what really thrills me: a computer on every desk. Except that one." She pointed to the empty desk beside Roberta's.

"Where's your desk?" asked Roberta.

"Over there." Nikki pointed to the desk on the other side of the empty one. Nikki said, "I can't believe they have white carpeting here! In an office!"

"I guess Bethany wanted it," said Roberta. "It's going to get filthy."

"On the first rainy day…" said Nikki, agreeing.

Roberta began limping back to her desk. Nikki said, "Hey! What happened to your shoe?"

"The heel snapped off on the stairs to the station."

"Well, you can't go around like that all day! Give me the shoe and the heel."

Roberta handed them to Nikki. "What are you going to do?"

Nikki was at the closet, putting on her coat. "I'll take them to the shoemaker in town. He'll fix it for you."

"You don't have to do that."

"Hey, it's no trouble. My car's right outside in the lot. Just tell Lillian where I am if she asks. Tell her I'm waiting for them… and working as I wait." She grabbed a legal pad. "Tell her I'm thinking of ways to bring in that new cardiac hospital in Eastchester."

Roberta stared at her in dismay—until Nikki said, "No, I can't think about things like that outside the office. I'll really be reading *People* magazine."

"Then come back with all the gossip."

When Yvonne arrived and was led to her desk, Roberta saw that she would have to go past Yvonne's desk on the way to her own desk in the privacy corner. This was not good. She didn't like to even look at that stupid woman with the crazy clothes. Today she was wearing a red sweater with leopard-skin at the color and cuffs. Yvonne's presence was really distracting when Roberta wanted to concentrate on Astoria Recon. In the shower that morning, she had thought of an interesting presentation idea, and she wanted to write it down to see if it was viable. She turned on her brand new computer. It seemed to work okay.

Twenty minutes later, Nikki was back with the shoe. Roberta put her shoes on her feet again, and, passing Yvonne's desk but looking away, she walked to the ladies room to inspect the bump on her forehead. It hadn't risen any more, and the discoloration was mild. Still, she rubbed a little make-up on it. She walked back to her desk, exulting in her steadiness, as if she'd been deprived of it for a year instead of an hour and a half. Maybe things were looking up. "Hey, Nikki!"

Nikki raised her head.

Roberta asked, "Where's a good place for lunch around here?"

"There's Wraparound Sue two blocks away. They also have salads. We could go there today."

"Aren't you going home for lunch?"

"Not today. Not on the first day."

"Then sure. That would be great."

Nikki turned on her computer, and for a while, they were each busy. Then Nikki printed something out.

Roberta heard Nikki asking Georgette where the fax machine was. There had been only one fax machine in the old office, a source of much acrimony. Lillian had promised the sales department they'd have their own fax machine after the move. Georgette said, "Ovah theah, deah."

The fax machine rested on the lower level of an industrial cart, underneath a copier. Nikki said, "What a crazy place for the fax machine! We all use that machine a dozen times a day. And each time we fax, we'll have to bend over! Which is fine if we're wearing pants, but rather indecent if we're not..."

"I guess they don't have enough room to put it anywhere else," said Roberta sarcastically, looking around the enormous office.

"There's plenty of room," said Nikki. "I'm just going to move it."

Roberta watched as Nikki unplugged the fax machine and moved it to a higher place, on top of a waist-high steel cabinet. Nikki plugged it back in and gave a little nod of satisfaction. Then she faxed her document and went back to her desk.

Lillian speed-walked across the large office until she reached the sales department. "Nice place, huh?"

"It's beautiful," said Nikki.

"Bethany has a superb sense of style," Lillian agreed.

"I suppose the carpet was her idea?" Roberta asked mischievously.

"Most definitely," said Lillian. She and Roberta exchanged a complicit look, acknowledging how impractical it was. Still, Roberta knew, Lillian and Bethany were such a tight alliance you couldn't really mock Bethany to Lillian, nor the other way round.

Cynthia, who was passing by, said in her lilting voice, "It just looks so elegant!"

In her six years at the company, Roberta had never heard Cynthia say anything less than positive. Sometimes she thought Cynthia was just a phony: nobody could really be such a goody-goody! But sometimes she relished Cynthia's churchy good cheer. No matter what the weather or the situation, Cynthia was the company bluebird.

Lillian said, "Well, a white carpet may be elegant, but on the first rainy day..." Her voice trailed off, and her eyes narrowed. She pointed to the industrial cart. "Where's the fax machine?"

Roberta picked up the phone but didn't dial. She wanted to hear this. Nikki said, brightly, "It was really inconvenient there, so I moved it."

"WHAT?"

"I, uh, moved it. Over there." Nikki pointed.

Lillian bellowed, "It's not your place to decide what goes where!"

"But, Lillian, where it was before, you couldn't send a fax if someone was using the copying machine. And when you did send a fax, you had to bend over very immodestly. Now it's fine."

"Now it's in the entry-way, and Bethany won't tolerate that. Don't you dare move anything else!"

"I'm sorry," said Nikki. "I was only trying to help."

"You don't know *anything*," said Lillian, "so just do your job." Lillian unplugged the fax machine and moved it back to the lower level of the cart, muttering, "Now my reps think they know better than me!"

She told Nikki, whose cheeks were turning red, "You've been hired to *sell*. Not to go over my head. Stay in your place!" And Lillian raced back to her private office.

Cynthia shook her head disapprovingly but said nothing.

Roberta saw Nikki tipping back her head to hold in the tears. She looked at the list of telephone extensions and dialed Nikki's. She said, "Hey, don't let Lillian get you down. Everyone knows she's an idiot."

"Does Bethany know?" Nikki asked, with a sniffle.

"Oh, probably, but Bethany's very loyal. Lillian's just threatened by you."

"By *me?* I'm just a newcomer. She's a vice-president."

"But she sees that you're smart. And she's not. And she knows it. So she has to keep asserting her authority again and again. It makes her do ridiculous things."

Nikki whispered into the phone, "She humiliated me."

Roberta said, "That just shows how insecure she is. You did something good, showed some initiative. In any other company, you'd have gotten praised."

"Thanks, Roberta." Nikki blew her nose.

An hour later, while Roberta was still getting her desk organized, she observed Lillian sending a fax. She was stooped over the machine, and her dress rode high in the back so you could see the dark tops of her panty hose. "Georgette," Lillian called to the receptionist. "Make a note to order a stool. That's what we need for the fax machine. If we had a stool to sit on, it would be fine."

Roberta exchanged a look with Nikki, who rolled her eyes. From the way Lillian suddenly frowned, Roberta knew that she'd seen the eye-roll. Nikki would have to learn to be more discreet.

Roberta sat opposite Nikki at Wraparound Sue, on the good side of the table, facing out, toward the other tables and the window. Nikki hadn't jockeyed for the good seat, which Roberta appreciated.

Roberta ordered a roast beef wrap with chips; and Nikki ordered mesclun salad with grilled chicken. "How did you end up working here?" asked Roberta.

"After David left, I needed a job," said Nikki, "and I didn't want to commute. So I saw this ad in the local paper. The ad was vague: I thought it was something in communications or PR. Lillian kind of brainwashed me into sales. She kept saying I would sell. She said I was a natural."

"What did you do before? Were you an editor?"

Roberta shook her head. "No, I stayed home and wrote books. Non-fiction books. It's fun, but it isn't a living. I counted on David for that."

By the time their orders came, the women had already gotten to the essentials: marriage, children, men.

"What went wrong with your marriage?" asked Roberta.

Nikki put down her fork. "I *still* don't get it," she said. "I was a good wife. I was supportive and loving. I was cheerful and faithful. I adored being a mother. I cooked the meals and cleaned the house. I kept my figure and straightened my hair. I wrote interesting books. David left me anyway, for another woman."

"Younger?"

"Not significantly. When I think about all this, when I think about my shock and devastation when David told me he was leaving, I just want to scream. I want to scream so the neighbors hear me, even those across the street. I want to scream until my throat is raw and my mind is numb." Nikki's eyes were filling with tears.

"You poor thing," said Roberta. "But, please, don't scream here! You'll upset the lunch trade."

"'Lunch trade'? Did you ever wait tables?" asked Nikki, sniffling.

"For two summers during college. It's not an easy job."

"I know," said Nikki. "I was a waitress in college myself."

"They're called 'servers' now," said Roberta.

Nikki rolled her eyes. "I can't tell you how tired I am of this P.C. nonsense."

"Me, too! So did you know your marriage was headed for the rocks?"

"That's just it—I hadn't a clue! Until David told me about The Other Woman and exploded our marriage like a grenade, I thought we were fine. I miss being a wife. I miss having a partner."

Roberta said, "Of course." She had missed having a partner for a good fifteen years.

"But you know something?" Nikki continued. "I don't actually miss David! He was a perfectionist, so naturally he spent a lot of time sulking. Even after making love, he was often grouchy. It was hard to make him happy, so perhaps I stopped even trying. To tell you the truth, I have more fun with my daughter or my girlfriends than I ever did with David."

"People underestimate the power of friendship," said Roberta. "I don't know where I'd be without my girlfriends."

"You're right," said Nikki. "Friendship's so important! Yet nobody writes novels or makes movies about it. Our language doesn't even have the right words for it. Like, when a woman's interested in a man, she 'flirts.' But what does she do when she wants to be friends with a woman?"

Roberta said, "Basically, she just opens her heart."

"So true," Nikki agreed, her eyes getting wet again.

"Nothing to cry about," said Roberta. But somehow, her own eyes were wet, too.

7

Nikki

July, 1995

Dear Lloyd,

What a nice surprise it was to learn you were hosting a nature series on public television! I have seen three of your shows now, and they are beautifully written and produced—a pleasure to watch. And you are the ideal host: by turns serious, playful, curious, and compassionate. Every Monday night, I am by the box watching.

It's been so long since our tutorial with Dr. Linnear. I know she would have been proud of your success. I'm sure you know she died two years ago, at age seventy, in a mountain-climbing accident. I was so sorry to hear of it.

After getting an MFA in art history at Yale ("Available Paint: A Study of Pigment in Seventeenth Century America"), I moved to New York and took a job as an assistant at an advertising agency. Through my work, I met the man I married. When I had a baby soon after, I stopped working and started writing books. I've written books about American Communists, co-housing, and avian intelligence. Quiana is twelve now: a tall, delightful girl. We live north of New York City in Westchester County. When we moved from the city, I began to buy old furniture to fill this big house, and I've become quite good at restoration. I can upholster a couch or cane a chair or refinish a table. I've done less of that lately, as I've recently returned to the workplace in a most unlikely role.

I understand you live in Savannah. What sort of town is it? How old are your children? Have all your dreams come true?

Seeing you on TV, I was thrown back to our college years, and I became quite reflective about where I am and where I am going. I suppose everyone feels There Must Be More.

Fondly,

Nikki Elkins

P.S. Do you ever get to New York?

Nikki put the letter into an envelope and sealed it before she could reread it and change her mind, especially about that "fondly." She thought she'd done well to avoid mentioning her divorce, for that would make this letter too bluntly an epistolary come-on. She hoped she'd piqued his curiosity about her "unlikely role" in the workplace.

She scrabbled in her desk to find a non-standard stamp: not a flag stamp, but something conveying some personality. She found a festive-looking toy train stamp, left over from Christmas. It would have to do. She addressed the letter care of Lloyd's publisher, figuring that he would be more likely to receive it than if she sent it to his TV show. If Lloyd didn't reply, she could always tell herself he'd never gotten the letter. And if he did reply? They might meet for a nostalgic dinner some day. Taylor was right: Nikki had no idea about who Lloyd was these days, whether he was happy, whether she would like him in the flesh.

She mailed the letter on her way to work the next day. When she got off the elevator, she observed Georgette and Lillian opening a large box. Roberta was by Nikki's desk, watching. She gave Nikki a complicit smile. The receptionist with the bad voice held the box firmly, and Lillian tugged and tugged and emerged with... a small metal and rubber stool. "See?" She placed it on the floor, near the industrial cart which held the fax machine on the lower level. "This solves our problem! It's perfect! It's the dog's bow-wow!"

Roberta and Nikki exchanged looks, and a honk escaped Nikki. "Private joke," she gasped, but Lillian didn't seem to have noticed, thank god.

Lillian sat on the stool and demonstrated how easy it was to send a fax now. "You just sit right here, and put the paper on the glass..." Then she raced off to her office. Nikki wondered how busy she could be? Why this constant haste?

A few minutes later, Roberta phoned Nikki and whispered into the phone. "Get a look at what Yvonne's wearing." Nikki turned to see Yvonne in a yellow wool suit with a large rhinestone collar. Roberta said, "Isn't it the dog's bow-wow?"

Nikki laughed; she couldn't help it. She wasn't laughing at Yvonne and her flashy clothes: she was laughing at Lillian and her latest blunder. But she knew Roberta would choose to believe that she, too, was mocking Yvonne. Oh, well. Roberta might have her problems with Yvonne, but she was turning out to be a lot of fun, and helpful, too. Roberta had taught her about going into the conference room and making phone calls there in private, which Nikki sometimes did for important business calls, when she was nervous enough without others in the office listening to her sallies.

The fax machine incident was, perhaps, the beginning of Nikki's difficulties with her boss. After a few weeks, Bethany apparently overrode Lillian's stool "solution": one Monday, Nikki came in to find that the fax machine was on its own dedicated table at the normal height. While faxing that day, Nikki said loudly, "This is so much better than sitting on that stupid stool!" Roberta shook her head and frowned. Nikki knew she should be more diplomatic about Lillian, but she just couldn't help herself. When Lillian referred to a "mute point," hilarity bubbled up within Nikki and could not be contained. Still, when she saw that terrier-lady race across the office toward her department, Nikki's stomach clenched like a fist. If it weren't for Lillian, she might even like this job.

Nikki kept trying to set up sales calls so she could meet potential clients face to face. She had gone on several sales calls with Lillian and was convinced that she could easily do as well. Lillian, for all her energy and bustle, was not intelligent, and she was selling to educated people. Worse, she was not people-smart. She didn't notice when her audience grew bored. She didn't notice when they giggled at her gaffes. Visiting a longtime client, Lillian said, "We'll do anything for you. You're our sacred cow," and Nikki had to look at the floor so she wouldn't burst out laughing.

Before their fourth sales call, Lillian said, "I'm going to let you do the talking this time. Are you ready?"

"Absolutely." They were in the parking lot of a small community hospital in Northern Westchester. Nikki ran a brush through her untidy hair. As well as giving the standard Bethany riff, she was also going to sell competitively, against their present supplier, which Lillian did not do.

Lillian said, "They have a new purchaser, so her mind is open, I hope." Lillian had tried to get an appointment with the previous purchaser at this hospital for the past several years and had been thrilled to hear he had retired. She said, "This is a big opportunity for Bethany Moore."

"I appreciate your giving me this chance, Lillian."

"So don't screw up!"

Elegant! Empowering! But Nikki was determined to show her boss she could be trusted. She and Lillian were ushered toward a conference room, where two men and a woman awaited them. Nikki suddenly felt a little nervous. "Three of them!" whispered Lillian. Then Lillian pushed ahead of Nikki so she could walk in first. "I'm Lillian Watrous, Vice-President of Sales, and this is our new sales rep, Nikki Elkins."

"Hello," said Nikki. "I'm so glad you—"

Lillian interrupted. "It's wonderful you could see us. It's a privilege to be here. You got a beautiful office and..." Lillian spoke for the next half hour. Nikki tried to interrupt once or twice, to no avail. Lillian was like a wind-up doll, and once she started she couldn't be stopped. She ran through her spiel much as she'd done on other sales calls, only this time she ended by saying, "I virilely believe we have the most nutritious line of products in the state." Nikki saw smirks at the other side of the table.

Outside in the parking lot, Lillian said, "I think that went really well, don't you?"

"Oh, yes," said Nikki, trying to sound enthusiastic. No mention was made by either of them that it should have been Nikki's show.

The next week at the office, Nikki's phone rang, and she answered it brightly. Her voice got even brighter when she realized that Chappaqua Spa was calling her back, asking for samples. Nikki would bring them those samples the next day and hoped to deliver a presentation as well. She decided not to tell Lillian about the Chappaqua

Spa sales call until it was over. She wanted to do it alone. It was a small spa, and it was likely she'd be talking to just one person, Charlene, the owner. Nikki felt she could handle that. She went to the conference room to rehearse. "The best thing about Bethany meals is the way they *taste*, but don't they look tempting as well?" She'd go up to Chappaqua first thing the next morning, while Lillian was at the hairdresser's. Lillian had a long-standing Thursday morning hair appointment. Nikki took her samples and her brochures with her when she left work.

The next morning, she cleaned every surface, inside and out, of her microwave oven. Then she brought it to the car in a Bloomingdale's shopping bag. No doubt Chappaqua Spa had a microwave oven, but it wouldn't necessarily be located where she'd be talking to Charlene. She got into her car and drove up to Chappaqua. The spa was easy to find and Nikki parked in the lot and gathered her gear.

The receptionist, wearing gym clothes, called out "Charlene," and soon a woman of about Nikki's age came out with a puzzled look on her face.

"I'm Nikki Elkins of Bethany Moore…"

"Of course, come into my office."

Nikki tried not to mind that Charlene had apparently forgotten the appointment that had been the high point of Nikki's job so far. She saw an open wall plug near a table, and said, "May I?" She removed the microwave oven from its shopping bag and plugged it into the wall. "I haven't had breakfast yet," she confided. She wanted the sales conversation to be accompanied by the enticing aroma of a Bethany Vegetable Quiche, so she put one in the microwave.

Charlene said, "I never have breakfast."

"The most important meal of the day, or so they say." Nikki's tone made it clear that she didn't believe it.

"If I eat breakfast, it just makes me hungrier for lunch! So I skip breakfast as a weight-control measure."

"But you look very thin," Nikki said sincerely.

"I have to be thin to give the spa credibility. But it's a constant effort."

"Sometimes I wonder if it's really worth it," mused Nikki. "Maybe we should just be our natural weight and have done with it!"

"Then no one would come to this spa," Charlene noted.

Nikki backpedaled smoothly. "I guess you're right." But she couldn't resist adding, "Don't you think staying thin is just a way to be envied by women rather than desired by men?"

"That depends on the man," said Charlene. "My boyfriend Ted likes me to be really toned, so I take two classes a day."

"Admirable."

"What do *you* do to stay thin?"

"I worry," said Nikki, for a laugh. "I also have a high metabolism. The great thing about Bethany meals is they're filling without being caloric. That's why they're the perfect spa offering." She opened the microwave and brought out the quiche. The eggy smell filled the office. Nikki now placed an Asian beef entrée into the microwave.

"How many calories in the quiche?"

"Four hundred fifty," said Nikki. "And it keeps you full and satisfied for hours. Have a taste." She put some quiche on a plastic fork and held it out.

Charlene looked at the forkful longingly, "I really shouldn't."

"It's just a forkful. Take a bite."

"Oh, all right. Ted doesn't have to know."

By the time Nikki got back into her car and drove to the office, she knew all about Charlene's boyfriend, Ted; her daughter, Mimi; her dog, Jolly; and her little house near Tarrytown, a nineteenth-century millhouse, which Charlene was lovingly restoring. She had worked a lot on that house, which had a stream by the kitchen window. Charlene showed Nikki before and after pictures. Charlene would be good for the women and houses book Nikki would probably never write.

When Nikki got out of the elevator at the office, Georgette said, "Go into Lillian's office. Right now."

Nikki stopped at the closet to put away her coat. Roberta came over and said, "Lillian wants to see you."

"So I gather."

"She's hopping mad! Where were you?"

"On a sales call. She should be happy."

"She's not a normal person," said Roberta. "Good luck."

Nikki walked across the floor until she got to Lillian's office. "Hi, Lillian," she said brightly.

"So where were you? Nobody knew where you were! You absolute-ly have to call me if you're going to be late."

"But I left you a note," said Nikki. "Right here." And she fished out the pink memo slip she'd deposited deep into Lillian's in-box the afternoon before.

"Nah, that's just *junk*! Next time you gotta call me!"

"But I knew you were getting your hair done."

Lillian was frowning as she read the pink memo. "*What?* You went on a sales call? In Chappaqua?"

"Isn't that what I'm supposed to do?" Nikki asked innocently.

"Sure, maybe later. But you're not ready to go out on your own."

"Maybe not," said Nikki, enjoying her moment. "But I got the ac-count. She's ordered fifty meals a week for the next month. And I bet she'll renew for a year."

Nikki watched Lillian trying to determine what was more import-ant: disciplining her rep or celebrating the sale. "That's very good," she said at last, grudgingly. "Your first sale, right?"

"That's right. Can I tell Bethany?"

"I'll come with you," Lillian said. "After all, you're my hire."

Bethany had brown curly hair today, and when she got the news about the Chappaqua Spa, she got up and gave Nikki a hug, during which Nikki could feel the CEO's breasts pushing into her own.

Lillian said, "We strategized together." Nikki's jaw dropped open, but she didn't say a word. Lillian looked like she actually believed what she was saying. "I told her the verbage to use."

"Verbiage," murmured Nikki.

"What was that?" Lillian asked sharply.

"Yes, you told me what verbiage to use," Nikki said, as if agreeing, trying to keep the sarcasm out of her voice.

Later, Nikki told Cynthia about her first sale. Cynthia said, "Con-gratulations, child. Lord, I bet you feel good! What a blessed day for you!"

"Lillian managed to make it her personal triumph," said Nikki.

Cynthia looked around, shook her head and put her finger to her lips. She whispered, "Be careful."

She was right. There were two or three women within hearing range, any of whom might enjoy passing on what she'd just said. No matter. Nikki was happy. She'd never thought she could do sales: she had blundered clueless into the job interview. But it turned out she could listen and learn and persuade. And what a kick it was when you clinched the deal!

To celebrate Nikki's success, Roberta took her out to lunch at one of the more expensive restaurants in town. "Lillian's going to take credit for it," Roberta said, when they were seated at the table in the window.

"Oh, she already has," said Nikki, reaching for a bread stick. "She supposedly gave me the 'verbage.'"

"Don't let it bother you," said Roberta.

"It's just so weird. I can see that she's torn between congratulating me on the sale and cutting me down to size. I mean, wasn't I hired to move product?" Nikki felt that this made her sound very professional.

"Theoretically. Though in this company, it's just as important to get along and go along as it is to make sales."

"That's just weird," said Nikki. When the waiter came with his pad, she ordered the mixed salad with shrimp. Roberta ordered the lasagna.

Nikki said, "Every time I went out to lunch with a girlfriend, David would complain about my spending money. Like, he thought I was extravagant."

"Extravagant! You're certainly no clothes horse!"

Nikki realized that she was wearing her black pants for the third time that week. "See, everything I spent came out of his pocket, so he would complain if I spent too much on *anything*. Chicken breasts. A kitchen curtain. A book for Quiana."

"I could never live that way," said Roberta.

"I never will again," said Nikki. "That's the beauty of having a job."

One of the things Nikki did as a single woman was buy the marijuana, which had always been David's task. Luckily, she found a guy who delivered, Jed Monroe, a friend of her yoga-friend Patsy's. Jed lived about 10 miles to the north and the west. He charged more than David's Lucius, who dealt from a tenement in Brooklyn, but Jed was much more convenient. He was also less reliable. He would never commit to a delivery until the day itself, and sometimes she wouldn't hear from him even then. He once explained it wasn't worth it for him to come to her area for just one buyer. Given the length of the car trip and his probable markup, Nikki wondered about that, but as every user knows, the dealer makes the rules. She had learned to schedule a visit from Jed long before she actually ran dry, for she never wanted to be without pot, not even for a day.

Unfortunately, Jed seemed to have a little crush on her. Whenever he came around, Nikki was always nervous he would make an overt move, and then, perhaps, she would have to find another dealer. Recently, their mutual friend Patsy had told Nikki, "Jed tells me he thinks you're hot."

Nikki groaned.

Patsy laughed. "Guess you're not interested."

"Emphatically *not*. For one thing, he's married." Nikki had never slept with a married man, except David, and then he'd been married to her. For another, she wasn't the least bit attracted to him. Or did "least bit" even apply? A man either excited you or he didn't. Occasionally, this changed over time, and someone who was not even a candidate might become a desperately-sought love object, but that was rare. And it would never happen with Jed.

Nikki hoped her response (though not its intensity) had gotten back to him.

Now Jed was knocking at the door, and she let him in. She didn't like him coming over when Quiana was home, and she didn't like him coming over when she was alone, as now, so basically she was always uncomfortable around Jed.

"How are you?" he said as he walked into the living room. He put his backpack on the coffee table. "You're looking good."

"Thanks," she said, sitting across from him. "I have a new job. That is, I have *a* job."

"Nine to five?" he asked incredulously.

Nikki nodded. "The real deal. Luckily though, no commute—it's in the next town."

"That's good. You wanted two, right? One and one?"

She nodded. He dealt good grass and great grass, with corresponding prices. He didn't give you much description or name the strain:

you bought at either $200 or $300 an ounce.

He pulled out two baggies, pre-weighed. One had a yellow heart sticker in the corner. That was the better stuff. Jed asked, "So what's your job?"

"Sales," she said. "Business-to-business."

"No kidding! You wear a suit and all?"

At present, she was wearing a t-shirt and old, baggy jeans, the better to camouflage her form and discourage his interest. "Sometimes," she said. "When I go on a sales call."

"Wow, I'd love to see you in a suit."

There was no way to respond to this, so Nikki just opened her handbag and pulled out $500 in twenties. She hoped she could make the dope last three months. She watched as Jed counted the bills, which he always did, although her count was always correct. Similarly, after he left she always weighed the marijuana, although Jed was never off by so much as a gram.

Jed said, "Today I also have some *really* good stuff. Very expensive."

"What does that mean?" asked Nikki.

"$600 an ounce."

Nikki gasped. "Oh my God. Who can afford that?"

"There are a lot of rich people in Westchester."

"How good can it *be* to justify that price?"

"Here, let me give you a taste." Jed took out a plastic vial from which he removed a thin joint.

Nikki was torn. She wanted to get Jed on his way and did not want the intimacy of sharing a joint. On the other hand, she'd never smoked premium weed. Rock star dope. Jed fired up the joint and passed it to her and she sucked on it greedily once and then immediately again.

Jed took it from her and inhaled. Then he passed it back to her. After her second go at it, Jed put it out. "That'll do you," he assured her.

She felt a "tingly clarity," "edged with hilarity," a slant rhyme, she thought, drenched in self-consciousness. She stood up. "Thanks," she told Jed. "I feel great."

"Can I have some water?" he asked.

"Of course." She hurried to the kitchen, which was further away than usual. She thought, It's that old space/time distortion and sup-pressed a giggle. This was like her first few times getting high.

With anybody else she would have asked if they wanted coffee or tea, but Nikki really wanted Jed gone—she didn't want to waste this high on him. So she remained standing ("pointedly" she thought) as he drank the water, clattering the ice cubes until finally, *finally*, he stood up and put on his backpack and walked to the door.

Nikki waited until Jed was halfway down the front steps and there was no danger he might kiss her goodbye before caroling, "Hey, thanks for the taste!"

8

Roberta

August, 1995

Roberta didn't think that Nikki would last long at Bethany Moore. She didn't think Lillian would ever forgive her for moving the fax machine or for going on that sales call in Chappaqua on her own. She didn't think Nikki could learn to mask her scorn when Lillian said something ridiculous. Today Lillian had spoken about an upcoming conference as offering "a Pandora's box of opportunities," and Nikki had been unable to repress a snort of laughter. Roberta thought Nikki was becoming a pretty good sales person, though: her voice-mail messages were short and inviting, and she had brought in three new clients. Small clients, not nearly as big as the Astoria Recon account Roberta was trying hard to get, but clients nonetheless. But Nikki didn't seem to realize that the most important person to please was not Bethany but Lillian.

Roberta was on the subway to Brooklyn to see her parents for the Sabbath meal. As the subway train moved along, Roberta glanced down at her hands. She would definitely need a new manicure before seeing Paul tomorrow night. Paul was taking her to a very good restaurant, and Roberta wasn't sure what she would wear. She had two brand new sweaters in her closet: one made her look sexy, while the other made her look classy. If she were seeing Hevron, damn him, she'd know which to choose, but Paul wore a Rolex and liked everything upscale. Classy would probably be better with him, but he was, nonetheless, a man, and a man who responded to the usual sexual stimuli. Roberta had been with him on the beach and had seen how his eyes followed young girls in bikinis. Roberta hadn't worn a two-piece bathing suit in ten years, but she still looked very good in sweaters.

She hoped her parents wouldn't bug her about Paul. "It's high time he married you already," was one of her mother's predictable comments, and when Roberta would reply, "I'm not sure I even want to get married," her mother would shake her head grimly and say, "Bite your tongue, of course you do."

It was four blocks from the subway stop to her parents' house: not a long walk, but long enough to make her regret wearing such high heels. At the door, the usual Friday night aromas greeted her: chicken soup and brisket. The table was set for four, which meant she was the only guest. Her sisters were probably getting their own Sabbath tables ready, setting out the candles and wine, making sure that the children were presentable. Her father, Henry, now seventy-five, was watching the evening news, and he barely turned his head when she came in, merely murmuring, "Shabbat shalom." Her mother was in the kitchen, attending to the pots on the stove.

"Hi, Mom."

"Hello, honey. Do me a favor, will you? Can you make the salad dressing?"

"Of course, Mom."

"Without garlic, all right?" Her mother had apparently been traumatized by the time ten years earlier that Roberta had added crushed garlic to the dressing.

"Sure. Whatever you say."

"I'm going to get Kenny." Roberta's brother Kenny had a phone in his apartment, but he usually didn't answer because he was sure the government was listening to his calls.

"How's Kenny these days?" Roberta asked.

"Not so good." Golde Cohen, perfectly made-up and coiffed, suddenly looked old and defeated.

"Aw, Mom."

Her mother just shook her head. A few minutes later, she returned with Kenny. He hadn't shaved in several days, and his shirt was wrinkled. Roberta went over to kiss him, but he ducked and weaved, avoiding her touch. She asked, "What's new, Kenny?"

He just shook his head darkly.

"Henry?" Golde called to her husband in the living room. "Time for dinner."

They assembled in the dining room, and Golde said a short Hebrew prayer and lit the candles. Then she went to the kitchen and brought out four bowls of golden chicken soup and matzo balls.

Kenny pointed to his bowl and said, "Take that thing away."

"What's the matter, dear?" asked Golde.

He pointed to the matzo ball in the soup. "Get it out of here."

"But you love matzo balls," said his mother.

"Not that one."

It looked like all the other matzo balls, but Golde stood up and took his bowl back to the kitchen. "I'll get you another," she said.

"What's wrong with that one?" asked Roberta.

"It's got a transmitter inside it. They're listening to everything we say, and they want to listen to the insides of my body. But I can see right through their schemes."

Golde returned to the dining room with the bowl of soup and a different matzo ball. Kenny looked at the matzo ball with suspicion, but apparently it passed muster, because he began cutting it into pieces with the side of his spoon. Roberta glanced at her father, who looked like his mind was on the moon. He had learned to deal with his son by pretending to be somewhere else.

Roberta poured herself a glass of white wine, from a bottle she had brought. Her parents and Kenny didn't drink, so if she wanted any wine with dinner, she just had to bring it herself.

"Now!" said Golde with a show of enthusiasm. "Here we all are for a nice Sabbath meal. Have you had a good week, Roberta?"

"Yes, it was fine. You know that film class I'm in? They had Richard Dreyfuss as a guest last night."

"That must have been exciting," said Golde.

"Who's Richard Dreyfuss?" asked Henry.

"How did they get to you?" Kenny suddenly asked Roberta.

"What do you mean?"

"Don't pretend! I know you only too well! They got to you, all right. My question is: how? You make enough money, right? So what did they offer you?"

"*Who* got to me?"

"The government, of course!"

Roberta stared at her mother, who just shrugged her shoulders.

Kenny shook his head and said, "Great fake surprise, but you can't fool me. I'm your brother."

"Why would the government get to me, Kenny? What do they want?"

"They want the information, of course! *My* information. They think they can get it through you, but tell them I'm onto them. They can't fool me." At that point, for emphasis, he lifted his bowl and slurped the remainder of his soup down.

"Manners, manners!" said his mother.

"Roberta doesn't work for the government," Henry interjected. "She works for Bonnie Lee Moore."

"Bethany Moore," said Roberta, who thought that after six years her father might, just might, remember the name of her company.

"That's her cover," said Kenny. "But have you ever gone up to her office?" Golde and Henry were silent. Kenny said, "See? There you are. And there *she* is, the family traitor."

Golde said, "Come on, Kenny, she's your sister. Of course she doesn't work for the government."

"It would probably be better than working for Lillian," Roberta said, trying to change the conversation.

"What's Lillian's latest?" asked Henry.

"She told me in confidence that our new rep doesn't have a lot of 'charismus.'"

Henry chuckled.

"Actually, Nikki's a pretty good rep," said Roberta. "And she's also becoming my friend."

"That's nice, dear," said her mother. "I know you've been missing Marlene." Roberta had brought Marlene to a Sabbath dinner three years ago, and she had charmed everyone in the family, even Kenny.

Roberta said, "We'll probably keep seeing each other, but yes. I miss seeing Marlene at work."

Kenny said, "She probably left because she couldn't stand all the spying that they made her do."

"Actually, she left because the company moved to Westchester," said Roberta.

"There's a federal court in White Plains, right?" asked Kenny.

"I don't know," said Roberta. She poured herself another glass of wine.

"You... don't... know. A likely story." Kenny turned to his mother. "I rest my case."

Roberta said emphatically, "Kenny, I don't work for the government, and I'm not spying on you."

Golde stared at Roberta and shook her head. Roberta tried to figure out what her mother was signaling. Don't contradict him? Don't engage with him? It's useless?

"How's Paul?" asked Henry.

"Oh, the same. Busy, busy."

"But not too busy for my girl, I hope?"

"We're going out tomorrow," said Roberta, rather pleased to be called "my girl," which was effusive for her father.

"When is he going to—" began Golde.

Roberta said, "I promise you, ma. You'll be the first to know when he does."

"*When* he does? Does that mean that he might?"

"I think so," said Roberta.

"Now that would be a mitzvah," said Henry.

"Some mitzvah," said Kenny. "He's a spy, too."

Roberta reached for the bottle, but her father drew it away from her. "You're drinking too much," he said.

"Dad! It's just a little wine at dinner."

"You've had two glasses and we haven't even served the brisket."

"Are you watching what I drink?"

"I'm your father."

"Then watch this," yelled Roberta, standing up and jerking the bottle out of his grip. She put it to her mouth and chugalugged.

"Roberta!" shrieked her mother.

Roberta put the bottle down. "I'm a grown woman," she shouted at her father. "Don't treat me like a child. Don't treat me like an idiot."

Henry shook his head and said sternly, "Then don't act like an idiot. We're not a family of drinkers. How did you get this terrible habit?"

"A lot of people drink wine at dinner. It's not so bizarre. And it's not such a terrible habit. I'm not ruining my liver or anything."

"But why do you do it?" asked Golde.

"It helps me relax."

"You should be able to relax without it," her mother scolded.

"Perhaps," said Roberta. "But I'd rather have a little wine."

Kenny said, "That's because you're a wino."

Roberta looked at Golde. "Please, Mom. Can't you *do* anything about him?"

"This was a great idea," Roberta told Nikki. They were having a picnic lunch sitting on a low wall by the end of a bridge. It was midsummer and red and blue flowers were in beautiful bloom. The air was soft and warm. On one side of them lay the Long Island Sound, silvery and still; on the other ran an inland waterway, winding under the bridge past a vast house with an acre of lawn. "That house must be worth two million dollars," said Roberta.

"Try five," said Nikki. "Everyone who lives here is in finance. My village is different."

"You live how many miles from here?"

Nikki smiled. "About three. But around here, three miles is a big difference. And my village is very diverse. We even have undocumented workers."

"You mean illegal aliens?" Roberta pictured Mexicans packed into little apartments, playing loud music.

Nikki laughed. "I think 'undocumented workers' is the preferred term."

"I thought you were anti-PC."

"You got me there!" Nikki asked, "When did your family come to America?"

Roberta was unwrapping her ham and cheese sandwich. "In the nineteen twenties. And yours?"

Nikki said, "One side got here before the Revolution. The other side in the 1820s."

"So, you could join the D.A.R.?"

"If it weren't for their politics." Nikki opened a large, round, plastic container, which contained a green salad with slices of egg. She began to eat.

"Is that all you're having?" asked Roberta. Her sandwich was wonderful, and she looked forward to the chocolate cupcake she had brought for dessert.

"I don't eat bread during the week," said Nikki. "I like it too much."

"You're thin enough."

"That could change."

"Yiii!" Roberta stood up and began blinking rapidly.

"What's wrong?" asked Nikki.

"A bug just flew into my eye."

"Can you blink it away?"

"I can't! I can't! Oh God!" It wasn't a pain but it felt just awful. And... was it still moving?

"It's okay, Roberta, it's going to be fine."

"No, it's not!" There was this horrible thing in her eye! "It hurts. And it could get infected!"

"A bee once flew into my eye," Nikki commented.

Roberta was momentarily distracted. "Did it sting?"

"No, I got it out fast."

"Well, I need to see a doctor."

"All right." Nikki closed her container of salad and stood up. "Hey. Oh, don't. Don't."

For now Roberta was crying, from pain and from fear.

"You're going to be fine," said Nikki. "Come here." She held out her arms, and Roberta fell into them. "Shhhh. It's okay. It's horrible to have anything in your eye." Nikki patted Roberta's back.

After a while, Roberta stepped away. "I hate nature," she said. "Don't smile: I do!"

Nikki burst out laughing.

"What's so funny?" asked Roberta.

"I've never heard anyone say, 'I hate nature.' That's pretty funny, Roberta."

"Not when Nature's in your eye!"

"Here, take my arm." Together, they walked to Nikki's car. Once inside, Nikki asked Roberta, "How's your eye now?"

"I still feel the bug in there."

"OK. I'll take you to my eye doctor."

"Is he near here?"

"*She*—yes, in the next town."

"You know, I can go in a taxi," said Roberta.

"Don't be silly," said Nikki, starting her car.

"Lillian's not going to like it."

"I'll call the office from the eye doctor's."

After a few minutes, they pulled into the parking lot of a medical building and got out of the car. They rode up in a small elevator and went down a short hallway and into an office. Nikki's eye doctor agreed to see Roberta on an emergency basis. Dr. Kim O'Hara wore a little cross around her neck and had a soothing manner. She removed the dead insect with a swipe of a swab stick, put a few drops in the eye, and said Roberta would be fine.

"Shouldn't I get a prescription?" asked Roberta.

The doctor shrugged and scribbled something on a pad. She tore off the prescription and handed it to Roberta.

The receptionist took Roberta's medical card and asked for a co-payment of $15. Her insurance company would pay the $125 bill.

"We need to stop off at a drugstore," said Roberta to Nikki as they walked to the car. "I have to fill the prescription."

"Sure," said Nikki. She stopped at a traffic light.

"What did Lillian have to say?"

Nikki turned to face her. "She said not to worry about the long lunch, because, and I quote, 'Eyesight is our penultimate sense.'"

Roberta cracked up at that, caught Nikki's eye, and laughed even harder. She croaked, "Doesn't penultimate mean second to last? Not the very best?"

Nikki said, "Yeah," with another eye roll. "God, that woman is so ignorant. Ignorant and arrogant—a lethal combination."

"You have a way with words," Roberta said, "but she's not that bad."

"She's even worse," said Nikki.

9

Nikki

August, 1995

Dear Nikki,

Thank you for your kind words about my show. I'm glad that at least I project well—perhaps I'm a better human being on the air than I am in person. I have a few quibbles with the show's director (he cut some important material so he could include trivial footage and get a few laughs), but he chose a cameraman who lights people flatteringly.

I kept up my friendship with Dr. Linnear and saw her at least once a year, so I was devastated when I learned of her death. I spoke at her memorial service about how she helped shape my life. You may be interested to know that about ten years ago she asked me, "What happened to the girl who studied with you? The one with the big blue eyes?" And I couldn't tell her.

Savannah is a beautiful town, but I miss the crackle of the northeast. Although my dreams have decidedly not come true (I have big dreams!) I suppose I'm contented enough. Until recently, I did feel "comfortably set for life." Now I don't know. Maybe if we meet we can talk about this. I have no immediate plans to come to New York, but sometimes I spend a few days in Boston with my parents.

Sincerely,

Lloyd Tyson

"Sincerely"! Stung, Nikki began to crumple the letter. Then she smoothed it out again. The rest of the letter was friendly enough. Friendly and wary. After the way she'd treated him last, she couldn't blame him. When they'd both been seniors at Swarthmore, after their tutorial ended, he had asked her to go to a party with him, hosted by a handsome, single instructor she wanted to meet. She didn't want to go on a date with Lloyd, who looked at her with cow eyes, but she was eager to go to the party.

"Gosh, Lloyd," she had said, "Do you think we could maybe meet there?" He'd given her a look she would never forget, a look of disappointment, hurt, and contempt, and he'd said one word, "No," before turning on his heel and walking away. Her ears had burned; she'd felt discovered and ashamed. What an opportunist she had been.

Nikki returned the letter to its envelope. The rules were different now. She was the supplicant, he was the famous one. Their age, too, worked against her. Men of thirty-five were considered to be in their prime; women of the same age were past it. But maybe to him she would always be beautiful; maybe she'd imprinted herself upon him at some critical stage of his psycho-social development.

Now that David had left, she wouldn't mind cow eyes.

Nikki went downstairs and put on her jacket. It was time to pick up Quiana from soccer. As she was driving, she realized that Lloyd had responded to her letter very quickly, given that his publisher had to forward the letter to him. Maybe that was more telling than the actual content of the letter. And now she had his home address. Maybe she'd write back to him and they could start a correspondence. Maybe she would even go to Boston to meet him, to satisfy her curiosity—but wasn't Lloyd married?

On Monday when Nikki got to work, Roberta waved her over. It was a big, showy, somehow awkward wave, and when Nikki came closer, she understood. She said, "Wow! What's that I see?"

Roberta was smiling and waving her finger. "What do you think?"

"I think that's the biggest engagement ring I've ever seen."

"I know. I was really surprised."

"Well, congratulations, sweetie! You must feel just great!"

Roberta was nodding and grinning so hard her mouth looked stretched like a rubber band. Nikki said, "When's the wedding?"

"Next spring. First I have to sell my place and plan the wedding."

"How did he propose? Were you surprised?"

"Totally. I mean, the night before, I was almost expecting it, he was acting so romantic. We were at a fancy restaurant, and he just kept looking at me tenderly and touching my hand. And after dessert, he leaned toward me as if he was about to say something... and then he didn't. But the next day, we went for a drive in the country and we 'got lost.' He pulled over and asked me to hand him the map in the glove compartment. He has this brand new Audi, and there was nothing in the glove compartment except the manual and a blue velvet jewelry box. I picked up the box and asked, 'What's this?" He said, 'It's for you.' So I popped open the lid, and I saw this ring, and he looked at me and asked, 'Will you?'"

"And what happened next?" Nikki asked. "Did you cry?"

"Yes, I burst into tears. And then we went over the hill to a wonderful little inn and had a bottle of champagne and dinner. Paul had it all planned out."

"You are so lucky," said Nikki. "I'm so happy for you."

"Ladies, what's going on?" Lillian asked, striding toward them.

"I just got engaged," said Roberta.

Lillian exclaimed, "Congratulations! That's wonderful! You deserve the very, very best. You've been an exemplatory rep, and I'm sure you will have an exemplatory marriage! And that ring! That's quite a stone."

"It's an exemplatory stone," Nikki said solemnly.

Lillian turned to her and asked rather sharply. "Did you do that mailing?"

"I'll do it later today. I'm making a sales call at noon and I have to prepare."

"Where are you going?"

"I told you yesterday: Mt. Pleasant Rehab Center."

"Yeah, yeah, now I remember."

But Nikki knew Lillian didn't remember, because she had never been told. Nikki was always worried Lillian would accompany her on a sales call and antagonize the buyers with her hearty hard sell, so she continued to strategize to get out of the office without giving her boss much advance warning. Nikki was discovering that she could sell pretty well on her own. And she seemed to do best with no literature at all. She just chatted casually and offered very small tastes of a

Bethany meal now and then. When she described this to Quiana, she called it the Trader Joe's approach.

Every day, the local Trader Joe's offered customers small hot samples of their prepared entrees. Nikki often found that the sample taste was wonderful and bought a box of whatever was on offer. Somehow, knowing you couldn't ask for a second sample made your taste of the *penne pepperonata,* or whatever, maddeningly delicious, and you simply had to buy it to get more. When you could eat a lot of it a home, however, it didn't taste nearly as good. So on sales calls, she would deliberately cut off a very small piece of the entrée and put it in a tiny Dixie cup with a teeny plastic spoon. Meanwhile, the rest of the meal would sit on the desk, hot and enticing. Often, the prospect would ask to have more, and at that point, Nikki would cut off another piece, only slightly bigger than the first, while remarking about how no one could resist a Bethany meal.

Nikki began doing well enough that she thought she just might win the annual sales prize. The rep who grew her accounts by the highest percentage over the previous year would win a trip to the Caribbean. Nikki felt she had a fair shot at the prize because Roberta and Yvonne would be competing with themselves, but Nikki would be competing with Marlene, who had been a slacker.

Nonetheless, Nikki was shocked to find out that after Marlene left, she hadn't received any more commissions on the companies she had under contract. "Is she going to sue?" Nikki asked.

"Probably not," said Roberta. "She says she wants to move on, but I think she's just lazy. And lawyers are expensive."

"Maybe Paul could help."

"To tell you the truth, Paul isn't crazy about Marlene. He says she's too loud. He's more of a corporate type. He likes women to be... um, classier."

"Like you," said Nikki, because that was what Roberta wanted to hear. Roberta's eyes met hers, and they smiled. Nikki admired the way Roberta used her eyes: catching a glance, connecting, and relentlessly boring in. When Roberta gave her the look, Nikki felt like prey to a hawk—she could not move her own gaze or even think straight. Then Roberta would look away, breaking the bond... before fixing her big brown eyes on Nikki again. Nikki was sure that Roberta's eyes accounted for some of her sales success—and what was wrong with that? You had to build on your assets. She would try to use her own eyes more on her very next sales call.

When Nikki arrived at Mt. Pleasant Rehab, Daniel Roth, the buyer, wouldn't let her plug in the microwave. "That won't be necessary," he said curtly.

Nikki felt cut off at the knees. "Don't you want a taste of our meals?"

"That's pretty irrelevant. I'm sure they taste good."

"So what is relevant?" asked Nikki, sitting down and taking out her pad.

"Nutrition and price. Your line is more expensive than the company we use."

"Surely not by much," said Nikki, who was familiar with competing price lists.

"Well, we have a special arrangement with Harbor Hill."

"We can make a special arrangement with you, too," Nikki said. "As for nutrition, did you know that our meals supply twice the FDA-recommended amount of vitamins and minerals?" And now she was glad she had some literature, because this guy was one hard sell, and she was getting nowhere. "Here, have a look at this brochure."

He took it without glancing at it.

She tried to catch his gaze to do that Roberta eye-thing with him, but he didn't cooperate.

And just when Nikki was wondering what to say next and why he had even made an appointment with her, Daniel Roth said, "We're pretty happy with Harbor Hill, but some of our clients are asking us if the meals are organic. And they're not. So does Bethany have an organic line?"

"Well, it's not exactly *organic*, but all of our foods come from the finest suppliers..."

"Ms. Elkins, thank you for your time, but I have a busy day ahead of me—"

"I was hoping I could take you to lunch at Jill's Cafe," Nikki said, trying to salvage the meeting. "We can talk about this further, and I can get your input." Bethany encouraged the reps to spend money entertaining clients, and Nikki had learned that Jill's Café was the most expensive restaurant in town.

"Perhaps another time," he said, unimpressed. He stood up and ushered her out of the office. The microwave in its bag hit her in the shin.

She didn't think Lloyd Tyson got rejected like this on a regular basis.

She had lunch at home, eating the Bethany quiche that Daniel Roth hadn't even sampled. She wondered if any hospital or spa supplier had an organic line. Back at the office, she looked at the flyers from Bethany's competitors that had been collected at trade shows. When the conference room was free, she made some calls from there.

Over the next two nights, Nikki spent hours at the library and at her computer, writing a report. At home, she sometimes stepped onto the porch and took a few puffs from her pipe. It helped with her process. She didn't know anyone else who used weed to enhance report writing, but she didn't know anyone else who smoked as much weed as she did, either. When she was high, it was easier for her to begin writing, and she felt it was also easier for her to concentrate on her subject, though she suspected she might just be manufacturing this last benefit to provide her with yet another reason to say yes to the herb. At least she always woke up clear-headed, no matter how much she smoked the day before.

On Thursday morning, she dressed in her new gray pants-suit from Ann Taylor and left the house early to get five copies of her report bound at Staples. Then she went to work. Roberta was on a sales call: she had finally gotten an appointment at Astoria Recon. Lillian was getting her hair done. Nikki could talk to Bethany without anyone much noticing.

Cynthia sang, "Good morning, darling. My, you are looking good!"

"You, too, Cynthia. You look great in yellow." It was true: yellow made Cynthia's brown face seem to glow. How old was Cynthia? Nikki's age? Ten years older? Ten years younger? It was impossible to tell.

Nikki knocked on Bethany's door. "Come in, come in," Bethany brayed. Today her hair was brown and straight. A diamond pendant rested just above her impressive cleavage. "Another success story, I hope?"

Nikki closed the door behind her. "Quite the opposite," she said, sitting down opposite her CEO. "I had the most awful sales call on Monday at Mt. Pleasant Rehab. But it got me thinking. I see an opportunity for our company, a way for us to stand out from all the others."

"Some innovation in sales?" asked Bethany.

Nikki shook her head. "Some innovation in product."

"Go on." Bethany leaned back in her chair and watched Nikki.

"Organic," said Nikki. "It's become the fastest-growing packaged entrée category. It's still a tiny segment of the market, but every year, it gains market share. Organic entrees are very popular with spas, and now patients at rehab centers like Mt. Pleasant are asking for them, too. And they aren't a bunch of hippies—they're attorneys and dentists and executive wives. By the year 2000, organic is going to be very big, and Bethany could have the first organic hospital line in Westchester! That would give us a tremendous advantage."

"Do you have any idea what an organic meal would cost?"

"Yes, I do," said Nikki, handing Bethany a copy of the report, while she opened another copy herself. "Here on page 4, I've listed the cost of going organic on a thousand-unit basis for our four most popular entrees: the chicken enchiladas, the vegetable lasagna, the meatloaf, and the salmon with dill sauce. The organic meals would cost an average of $2.47 more. We'd build that into the price."

"You wrote this report by yourself?" Bethany was leafing through it. Nikki nodded.

"Has Lillian seen it?"

"She's getting her hair done this morning."

Bethany gave her a look. "Next time, show Lillian first."

"But you'll read the report and think about the idea?"

"I will," said Bethany, "You're very enterprising. I'm impressed."

"I just want to have the best possible product to sell," said Nikki, in deference to what she'd actually been hired to do. She gave Bethany another three copies of the report, one for each vice president. Nikki had been careful not to put her name anywhere on the report. She stood up and said humbly, "I just want to sell well."

10

Roberta

September, 1995

What's sadder, drinking alone in a bar or drinking alone in your apartment? Roberta pondered the question as she sat on a barstool in her favorite dim neighborhood bar, finishing her second glass of Chardonnay. Maybe neither was sad if you were drinking for celebration, as she was. She had allowed herself a special solitary... well, *binge,* because of her engagement, and if she was alone, it was because she didn't really have drinking buddies. Oh, Marlene would have wine with dinner when they ate out, but it wasn't essential to her, whereas Roberta would up and leave a restaurant if it didn't serve wine. Paul was like Marlene, a social drinker with no special enthusiasm for alcohol, but Roberta loved the stuff. Two glasses of wine on an empty stomach definitely gave her a buzz, and to better feel the buzz—to say nothing of avoiding the calories—she'd been careful to shun the peanuts.

Now she slipped a bit as she stood up and rummaged through her bag for her wallet. Bags were either too small, so you had to take everything out to find one thing, or too big, so you had to sift through many items to find what you wanted—or, like hers, too well organized, with so many pockets you could never remember what you put where. She gave a giggle of relief when she finally found her wallet, in the medium-sized zippered compartment. She took out some cash and told the bartender to keep the change. She never put wine on her credit card, so she never had to know how much she spent on it every month, either by the glass or by the bottle.

It was only two blocks to her apartment. She supposed she should get some dinner on the way home, so she picked up half a roast chicken and some potato salad. Paul was with clients tonight so she was on her own, and she intended to keep celebrating. The food would probably wait.

There was a bottle of white chilling in the fridge. She opened it and poured some into a small juice tumbler. She preferred not to use a wineglass because that would be easier to knock over. She walked with her wine to the living room and looked about. She had paid for and chosen everything her eye fell on, and it was all good. All new looking: Roberta didn't like antiques. She drank this glass of wine very fast, thinking of Paul and the moment she'd touched the little velvet box in the glove compartment. Now the fifteen-year-would-she-get-married tension was finally over!

With this third glass, she definitely felt that warm and festive confidence that wine often brought her. Alone in her glass and marble living room, Roberta felt beautiful, irresistible. Of course Paul wanted to claim her, to make her his own! She looked down at her engagement ring. She was a fiancée, soon to be a wife. When she got married, Roberta would miss some of the pleasures of living alone, including moments like this; but Paul's apartment was large enough to let them each indulge in privacy.

It was a six-room apartment in an older building on the Upper East Side, on a high floor with a good view. Roberta more or less *had* to like the apartment, because Paul would never leave it. What bound him to the place was neither sentiment nor charm but the fact that the apartment was rent-stabilized. If he paid market rates, he would be paying an extra two or three thousand dollars a month. He said that when they were married, Roberta could use one of the bedrooms as a study, and she was pleased with the idea of having one room that would be unequivocally hers. She could paint a wall mauve if she wanted.

She poured herself another tumbler of wine and took a sip and suddenly felt both dizzy and nauseous. "Stop right there," she told herself, and put the glass down. She wasn't hungry, but she knew what she had to do. She put some chicken and potato salad on her plate and flipped on the TV. She sank into the couch and tried to convince herself she was hungry. She put a bit of chicken on her fork. A commentator was discussing the ongoing O.J. Simpson trial. When would the public ever tire of it? The trial had been going on forever, and it was obvious that he was guilty. Motive, means, opportunity: O.J. had them all. And the bloody footprint. And his wife's blood on his clothes. And the DNA evidence. And the testimony of the limo driver who had taken O.J. to the airport the night of the murder. And that white Bronco, with cash and disguises in the car. And a long history of abusing Nicole. Even though the prosecution kept making huge mistakes, Roberta felt it surely must be as clear to everybody as it was to her that O.J. Simpson was the killer.

Roberta finished the food on her plate and congratulated herself on her good sense. To reward herself, she went to the kitchen and found that glass of wine she'd abandoned before.

Now she was drunk, oh yes, she was feeling sozzled. She took off her clothes, put on her nightgown, and got into bed. If her high could remain right here for a while, that would be good, but she knew it didn't work like that, soon she would start coming down, unless she drank a little more, which would probably make her throw up.

Her telephone rang and she let the machine pick it up. She heard, "Roberta? It's Marlene. I'm like two blocks from your house and I thought I'd stop by. I gotta talk to you about something."

Roberta shook her head; she was in no condition to see Marlene. Or anyone, for that matter. She did not pick up the phone. She'd talk to Marlene some other time. She fell into sleep—and woke herself up when she started snoring.

She didn't feel good the next day. She hadn't slept well, waking up twice with diarrhea. Now she was fatigued and irritable; she felt a headache would descend if she moved her head the wrong way.

By the time she got to work, the humidity had given her hair a slight wave. She hated that: she liked her hair to be perfectly straight and spent forty-five minutes most mornings blowing it dry. Entering the office, Roberta saw a pale green envelope on her desk, and this made her so curious she didn't watch where she was walking and stumbled over some cartons of literature that were resting beside Yvonne's desk. She was about to fall when she caught herself and regained her balance. Her heart was pounding. She said to Yvonne sharply, "Jerk! You can't keep those boxes there."

"And you can't tell me what to do," Yvonne replied calmly. She was wearing a black blouse with red sequins in a flower pattern on the collar.

"I almost broke my neck," said Roberta.

"Try again," said Yvonne. "I might get lucky."

"Idiot," said Roberta. Anger made her face hot. "Asshole."

"Nice," said Yvonne. "Very ladylike."

"I'll give you ladylike," said Roberta, looming over Yvonne's desk.

"Get out of my personal space," said Yvonne, punctuating this by shoving her handbag in Roberta's direction.

It caught Roberta in the side of her hip. "OW!" she screamed. "You attacked me! I'll have you arrested for assault!"

"Oh, please," said Yvonne. "Get away from me, you nut job!"

Roberta spun around and went to Nikki's desk. "Did you see that?" she asked Nikki.

"What?"

"Yvonne just hit me!"

"No, I didn't see it."

"With her bag! She used a weapon against me!"

"Are you hurt? Is there a mark?"

Roberta couldn't believe that Nikki hadn't seen the assault. She'd been sitting right there! "Yes, I'm hurt! I've got a pain in my side! I'm going to get that mahjong bitch fired!" Roberta started off to Lillian's office.

In back of her, Roberta heard Yvonne ask Nikki, "What was that about mahjong?"

Roberta knew from the anger-management course she'd been forced to take at her previous job that she should breathe deeply three times before talking to her boss. But she flung open Lillian's door and said, "Yvonne just attacked me."

"What?" Lillian lifted her terrier head.

"I was just walking to my desk and she used her bag as a weapon and drove it into my body."

"Wait a minute," said Lillian. "Go back to the beginning. Tell me the whole story. I want the whole empanada. There has to be more—it can't be just that."

"It's *exactly* that, and you better fire her or I'm quitting!"

"Well, I need to talk to Yvonne—"

"Tell you what," said Roberta, "you do that while I call the *police*. That woman needs to be locked up!"

And with that, Roberta turned on her heel. She could hear Lillian call after her, "Don't call the police, Roberta. That would be a very bad idea."

"I'll do what I have to," said Roberta through clenched teeth, breathing hard. She walked across the office. Yvonne was not in evidence, thank God. But when Roberta got back to her desk, she found she didn't have an outside line. "Georgette," she said, turning around. "Did Lillian ask you to cut off my phone?" Absently, she grabbed the green envelope she had noticed earlier and stuck it in her suit-jacket pocket.

"Yes."

"And why was that?"

"Lillian didn't say."

Roberta stood up, walked a few feet and said, "Nikki, I need to use your phone to call the police."

"Are you sure you should do that? I don't know, Roberta. It didn't look so bad."

"I thought you didn't see anything."

"I didn't."

"So how do you know how it 'looked'?"

"I just mean—oh hell, Roberta, you're not bleeding or bruised. It's not so bad you have to call the police."

"Either she goes or I do," threatened Roberta.

"That's another matter," said Nikki, "but why call in the cops?"

"Can I use your phone or can't I?"

Nikki pushed the phone over, and, standing up, Roberta dialed 911. Roberta gave her name and the address of the company, and she was explaining why an officer had to come out to make an arrest, when Georgette said to her, "Bethany wants to see you in her office *right now*."

"Good. I want to see her *right now*. I'm going to file the biggest lawsuit... Yes, officer, please send someone over at once." She put down the phone. She felt inspired by rage until she walked into her CEO's office and saw Bethany's face. Lillian was also in the room.

Bethany said, "Sit. Down."

Roberta sat and breathed three times before asking, "Where's Yvonne?" She hated the quaver she heard in her voice.

"She's gone home for the day. We'll talk to Yvonne later on."

"If she's not in jail," said Roberta.

"Roberta, calling the police was completely inappropriate," said Bethany, her face hard. "It just makes us look foolish. When the officers get here, I want you to tell them you're sorry and say they aren't needed."

"You should give them Yvonne's license plate number!"

Lillian shook her head. "You're being unreasonable—"

There was a hubbub outside, and Georgette led three uniformed policemen into the office.

Bethany said, "Officers, I'm Bethany Moore, head of this company, and I thank you for your quick response. This was all a misunderstanding, wasn't it, Roberta?"

Roberta sat silent.

Lillian prompted, "Roberta!"

The officer in charge said to Bethany, "Ma'am, we got a report about a workplace assault. Was there a weapon?"

"A handbag," said Lillian, breaking into the conversation with a smile. "Roberta and another sales rep had a hen-fight, and Yvonne nudged Roberta with her handbag."

Roberta rose to her feet, furious. "It wasn't a hen-fight! And it wasn't a *nudge*, it was a body blow!"

"With a purse?" the officer looked incredulous. "Did you sustain any physical damage?"

"I might be bruised," Roberta said. "I might have internal injuries."

"Internal injuries?" Bethany's voice dripped sarcasm. "Roberta, please sit down." Now her voice just sounded weary. Roberta hesitated just a moment before complying. "Officers, this is just one of those office feuds. It goes way back, but neither of these women is packing a pistol."

"Do you want to make a complaint?" the officer in charge asked Roberta.

"Yes, I..."

"Don't," said Bethany. "Just don't."

"I guess not," said Roberta.

"That's good," said Lillian.

The officer said, "Are you sure?"

Roberta looked down. "I'm sure."

"Then I guess we can go." He turned around. "Nice office!" It was true: the CEO's office was as big as a studio apartment, and it was flooded with sunlight. Roberta heard the cops clomp away. She saw that the green envelope was sticking out of her jacket pocket. Then she noticed the return address.

"We can't have fights like this going on in the office," said Bethany.

"Then fire Yvonne! She's the one who got physical."

"I understand you cursed her out," said Lillian.

"Who told you that?"

"Ladies, enough!" said Bethany. "Roberta, we're going to switch Yvonne's desk with Cynthia's, so that you and Yvonne aren't in each other's faces all day. And I want you to apologize to each other tomorrow."

"No way," said Roberta. "She should be fired." She eased open the green envelope and pulled out two sheets of paper.

"We're not going to fire Yvonne," said Bethany. "Get that out of your head. And you're going to apologize for cursing her out."

Roberta glanced down at the first paper. Then she looked at the second. She felt a surge of power come over her. "No, I'm *not* going to apologize. And you're not going to fire me. Because I'm damn good at my job, and that's what really matters. Here!" And she tossed the papers onto Bethany's desk. Lillian took one sheet; Bethany took the other.

One was a cover letter, and the other was a one-year contract from Astoria Reconstructive Surgery. As she left the room, Roberta thought of the perfect thing to say: "Did Yvonne ever bring in such a big account?"

11

Nikki's Journal

September 20, 1995

Quiana has her period! I'm more excited than she is! I don't think she's even interested in boys, so it's strange to think she could get pregnant. I was a late starter, so for me it was a tremendous relief when my period finally came: I was normal, at least that way.

At that age, I was terrified that people would find out I was different, odd. A few years later, I wanted everyone to know I was different, odd! And now? Now I think everyone is different, odd! Even Roberta probably has something strange about her family or her past. Whenever you get to know somebody well, you find out just how peculiar they are. Who knows? Behind that churchy demeanor, Cynthia might be a hot babe! Boy would I like to incorporate that Caribbean roll into my gait! Taylor tells me I walk like a fourteen-year- old boy. Taylor seems to be doing well out at Stanford; I just hope she's chosen the right field. How can computers get much better than they are right now?

Lloyd and I have now written several letters to each other, his somewhat stilted. Will we each be disappointed when we finally met? Possibly. As for other men, it's weird. Men of my age don't seem interested in me—only men much younger or much older. Why can't a nice, divorced forty year-old-doctor ask me out? No, it's either some bald guy of fifty or a muscular delivery boy.

I suppose I should mention that I'm probably smoking too much weed. I seem to do it every day. More than once. Apart from everything else, it's expensive. And it probably isn't good to need a substance just to get through the day. Also, it's a poor example for Quiana. I don't want her smoking pot, not for a long while. But how can I cut down on something that's so reliably good? Perhaps a first step is to practice "mindful smoking": knowing why I'm getting high and setting my direction in advance.

12

Roberta

October, 1995

It was an evening with Paul much like any other. It was ten o'clock, and they'd had dinner together at an Italian restaurant near his apartment and were going back to his place. He always wanted to make love when they saw each other, and while Roberta was glad of his continuing interest, she was less enthusiastic about that side of things than he was. This was normal, she supposed: men just had bigger sex drives than women. After she satisfied him (and, to be fair, he did occasionally satisfy her), she'd either leave or get up very early in the morning to go back to her place, twenty blocks downtown. She had to touch base at her apartment to perform her morning grooming and dressing rituals.

She and Paul had left the elevator on the eighth floor and were walking down the hall. His keys were in his hand, and Roberta saw the door next to his apartment open. Out came a good-looking brunette of about forty-five carrying a status handbag. "Hi Paul," she said, ignoring Roberta.

"Hello," he mumbled, jamming his key into the lock and turning it hastily.

"Karen says you were a real help with her paper."

"Glad to do it," Paul said, guiding Roberta into his apartment, though it felt more like a push. One of his daughters was named Karen: she was away at Vassar.

"Thanks for helping," sang out the woman.

As soon as the door closed, Roberta asked, "Who was that woman, and how does she know Karen?"

"That's Clarice."

"Clarice? Your ex-wife?"

Paul didn't answer.

"Paul? *Hello?* Was that your ex-wife?"

He nodded. "I was going to tell you." He sat down on the couch.

"When?" asked Roberta, incredulous. "After the ceremony? If we happened to run into each other by the door?"

"I was waiting for just the right moment. When you would take it the right way."

"And what way is that? *Why are you living next door to your ex-wife?*"

"It's just a practical matter," said Paul. "If I had my druthers, she'd be living in Timbuktu! I can't stand the sight of her, honestly."

"Go on." Roberta's heart was beating fast.

He patted the couch next to him, but Roberta remained standing up. Paul said, "We moved into this place when we got married, really lucking out because it was rent-controlled. And after Clarice got pregnant with Chloe, we had the chance to rent the apartment next door, which was rent-stabilized. We tore down that wall"—Paul pointed to the wall in back of a highboy— "and it was perfect. We each had our own studies, and there was plenty of room for the kids. We had one humungous apartment! We were the envy of our friends, and it allowed us to put plenty of money into the girls' college fund. So when we split up... we just put back the wall."

"How convenient," sneered Roberta.

He ignored the sarcasm. "You're right. It's really been great for the girls. I'm here next door whenever they need me."

"Or when Clarice needs you," suggested Roberta. She walked across the room to the bar. There was an open bottle of red, possibly weeks old, knowing Paul, but she didn't care. She poured herself a glass to fortify herself against the hurt to come.

"It isn't like that between us," said Paul. "Maybe that was the problem. Clarice doesn't need anyone."

Roberta said, "I wonder where she's going tonight."

"I don't," said Paul. "She doesn't interest me at all. She can do whatever she wants, whenever she wants, with whoever she wants."

Roberta brought her wine with her and sat next to him. She asked,

"Have you ever run into her at the door with a man?"

"Once."

"What was that like?"

"It was fine." Then he shook his head. "Though the guy was too young."

"Maybe it was Karen's boyfriend."

"No, the girls were at camp."

Roberta took a sip of wine. "Let me get this straight. After we get married, you want me to live next door to your ex-wife?"

"Roberta, what does it matter? You might see each other in passing twice a year!" He began scooting toward her. "Come here, baby. Let's forget about that." He put one arm on her shoulder, but she moved away.

"How can I forget it? When I think of all our nights here... why perhaps she even heard us!" Paul sometimes screamed when he came.

"No way! The walls in these pre-war apartments are very thick. Anyway, you're very quiet. Very polite. Why, I can never really tell..."

"That's not the issue," interrupted Roberta, who preferred not to talk about sex. "How can you expect me to be comfortable here when your ex and your kids live right next door?"

"I don't know. You'll get used to the idea. It's really not a problem." He began stroking her ear. "Maybe we could continue this talk in the bedroom."

Roberta shook him away and stood up. "I'm going home," she said.

"My bedroom is three rooms away from the common wall, Roberta. You have nothing to worry about. Though you do look cute when you're angry."

Who else had told her that recently? Oh, right.

"Baby, come on," said Paul. "Let me make it better."

"Like *that* will make it better?"

"Yes," he said. "It will. You'll see."

"I'm not in the mood," she said, tossing back what was left of the wine—although, suddenly, oddly, she was.

"I've got enough mood for both of us," said Paul. She let him lead her down the corridor and into his bedroom.

"Don't expect much," she muttered, taking off her clothes in the dark—by now, he knew she insisted on the dark, at least until she could lose that last ten pounds. She lay on the bed like a plank of wood. When he kissed her, she did not kiss him back. She was pretending she was inanimate. If he wanted to fuck a plank of wood, let him. She would not touch him or move or make a sound or even let her breath come hard. He didn't deserve a response. Let him feel bad. He expected her to live next door to Clarice!

He touched her down there and found she was wet, so he said "Nice" and slid right in. How humiliating! How exciting, too, but she would never let him know that. Time passed and she remained unmoving, although she was increasingly aroused. Yet she would not, she just *would* not, she tried to remember the terms of the Astoria Recon contract, she would *not*—but then she *did*, shuddering again and again.

Her voice had not betrayed her, and Hevron had once told her that a man couldn't really feel it when a woman came. So perhaps Paul didn't know. But when he came soon after, he shouted, "You see!" And she did not challenge him.

The next day, just before lunch, word spread throughout the office: O.J. Simpson had been acquitted of murdering his wife, Nicole, and her friend, Ronald Goldman. Roberta turned to Nikki. "Can you believe it?"

Nikki shook her head. "I don't understand."

"It's shocking. What an outrage."

"Imagine what it's like for the kids," said Nikki. "They'll have to live with the man who slaughtered their mother."

"How did he get away with it?" asked Roberta.

"The jury wouldn't convict. It refused to even consider he might be guilty. They deliberated for only four hours. It's pathetic."

Roberta whispered to Nikki so Cynthia couldn't hear, "If he had been white, they would have convicted him."

Cynthia now sat at Yvonne's former desk near Nikki's. She came in early, made no personal phone calls, and left late. Then she commuted to Queens, taking a train, a subway, and a bus. Roberta had heard that blacks from the Caribbean had a terrific work ethic: "they're the Jews of the blacks"—though these days, surely, Asians were more hard-working and successful than either.

Nikki called across to the office bluebird, "Cynthia, do you think O.J.'s guilty?"

"The jury has decided," Cynthia said primly.

"Yes, but what do *you* think, Cynthia?" asked Nikki.

Roberta watched Cynthia, who seemed uneasy. She opened her bottom drawer and pulled out her handbag before saying, "I just don't trust the LAPD. They could have tampered with the evidence."

"So you think O.J.'s *innocent*?" Roberta was incredulous. Was racial unity more important than personal integrity? Just because Cynthia was African American like O.J., surely she wasn't his defender. Or was she? Cynthia remained silent.

Finally, Cynthia said, "I don't know enough about the trial to give you a considered response, but the jury has decided, and that's good enough for me." She stood up, put her handbag on her shoulder, and left for the ladies room.

Roberta said, "That woman will do everything to avoid a fight. She won't come right out and defend O.J.—you never know *what* she really thinks."

"I suppose complete candor hasn't worked out for her in the past," observed Nikki.

"Yes, but how can Cynthia believe that the verdict is fair?"

"Perhaps when your race is always a disadvantage, black and white is all you see. And perhaps after years of police brutality, the jury wanted to get back at the cops."

"Oh, you're too reasonable," said Roberta. "That verdict is a fucking outrage."

Nikki agreed. "It seems to defy common sense."

The next day, the office speaker system came to life at noon. Georgette's Bronx vowels filled the air. "Attenzione, attenzione." Lately, Georgette began all her communications this way, although she did not have an Italian background. "Bethany would like everybody to come to her office right now. She has an important announcement."

"Like it can't wait until after lunch," Roberta muttered. "I'm starving." But she moved with the others to Bethany's office. In back of her, she could hear Nikki patiently talking to Cynthia about the O.J. verdict. "What about the DNA evidence?"

"That can be planted, you know," Cynthia said in her island sing-song.

"But why would they do that?" said Nikki. "The LAPD worshipped the guy. They let him off lightly all the other times they came, when he was battering his wife."

Cynthia put her finger to her lips. The CEO was about to speak.

The entire office staff except for Georgette, the geriatric receptionist who had to be at the switchboard, was now crowded into Bethany's big office. Bethany had a red suit on, matching red lipstick, and a big smile on her face. Her hair was blond and straight. "I won't make this long," she said. "I know some of you are hungry."

"You can say that again," Roberta whispered to Nicole.

Bethany continued. "We are having a very, very good year. I want to thank you all for your part in it. I especially want to thank Roberta Cohen, who has brought us an important new client, Astoria Reconstruction Associates."

Roberta felt her cheeks flush at being singled out. She saw Lillian beaming at her, saw Nikki silently applaud. She was happy to notice Yvonne frown and look away.

Bethany went on. "I've brought you here to announce an important new direction for Bethany Meals. We're going to be part of the fastest-growing segment of the hospitality industry. We're going to move into the twenty-first century right *now*, five years ahead of time. We're going to do something big!" She paused dramatically. "I've brought you all here together to announce our new line: Bethany's Organic Meals. People are asking for organic food, and we're going to give it to them! Sales team—you have a whole new product to sell, and we have no competitors! We're the only company in Westchester who can offer organic meals to hospitals and spas. I've just drafted a press release that will go out tonight. This idea is really going to put us on the map!"

"Thank you, Bethany!" said Lillian enthusiastically, and she began clapping her hands. Soon, the whole room was applauding. Lillian said, "Let's hear it for Bethany!"

Bethany said, "I want to thank Lillian Watrous for her enthusiasm and Nikki Elkins for her help with some of the research. There's pizza and sodas in the kitchen. This is a terrific day for our company!"

The meeting was over. People murmured to each other.

Roberta turned to stare at Nikki. "What research?" she demanded. "Why didn't you tell me what you were up to?"

Nikki said nothing; she had turned white and was blinking back tears.

"What's wrong?" asked Roberta.

"I didn't just do 'some of the research,'" Nikki said as they walked back to their desks. "The whole thing was my idea from the start! I wrote a ten-page proposal about the potential of an organic food line. And she gives me no credit. Bitch!"

"I could have told you that would happen." Roberta didn't go any further, didn't need to say, "You should have told me what you were doing."

By now, they had reached their computers. "Look!" said Nikki. She double-clicked the icon on her desktop that said ORGANIC and opened the report she had written. She paged down the document.

Roberta shook her head. "All that work," she said sympathetically. "If I know Bethany, by now she's convinced herself it was all her idea and *she* really wrote that report."

"You're right."

Nikki looked so miserable, Roberta said, "Hey, Nikki, look at it this way. It's a damn good idea, and now we have something unique to sell. We're going to make a lot more money. This benefits you and me more than anyone else. It even benefits that nitwit Yvonne."

Yvonne was close enough to hear this, which Roberta didn't mind at all.

13

Nikki

January, 1996

Nikki had been a working woman for nine months, and it felt like she'd always had this job. She had her work rituals, her work friends Roberta and Cynthia. Cynthia always asked about Quiana and commented on what Nikki was wearing. So Nikki learned to ask about Cynthia's children and to notice her blouse or necklace.

And Nikki was building up her own work wardrobe. Whenever she was hesitant about buying something new, she would replay Roberta saying, "Well, you're certainly no clothes horse"—and Nikki would buy whatever she'd been dithering about.

Best of all was her paycheck. Wild surmise every second Friday when they got paid: what would be in the envelope? At the Bethany Moore Company, the sales reps didn't get their commissions until their clients paid up, so they could never predict the amounts of their checks. Nikki felt she was doing quite well and also managing her money quite well, especially during the three-paycheck months. Before she went to work, she didn't even know there were three-paycheck months.

Worst of all was Lillian. She never missed a chance to insult Nikki, especially if others were around. She was probably sorry she had hired her, Nikki thought, but she was doing well enough that Lillian couldn't exactly fire her now. Plus it wouldn't be in her own financial interest. Roberta had explained that Lillian, as VP for Sales, got some percentage any time a rep made a sale.

It was the day of the company Christmas party. Nikki's work history was such that she had never been to an office Christmas party before. Roberta had told her it was dressy, so Nikki wore a silk skirt and a sleeveless black top. The young assistants wore bright, tight dresses, flaunting butt and boob, but for whom? Once again Nikki lamented the lack of men in the company. They were dressing for each other, then: to show off how they looked on weekends when they went clubbing. Yvonne wore a green satin pant-suit, trimmed with gold braid. Roberta said to Nikki, "Look at the little tin-soldier! The 160-pound tin soldier!"

Roberta's feud with Yvonne had turned bitter after the Handbag Assault. Nikki never told Roberta, but she had seen the whole thing and thought Roberta was nuts. Yvonne's handbag had scarcely touched Roberta's hip—and Roberta had called the police and now she claimed to be "frightened" of Yvonne, because Yvonne was so "tall and strong," and you never knew, Yvonne might attack her in the ladies room. Worst of all, Roberta watched Nikki closely, and if she should happen to chat with Yvonne in passing, Roberta got furious. "What were you talking about? Was she saying something about me? She's such a bitch, why do you bother with her?" It was one thing to have a feud; it was another to bring everyone else into it. Yvonne had always been nice to Nikki, who didn't see why she and Yvonne shouldn't have pleasant exchanges. Roberta didn't like Cynthia talking to Yvonne, either.

The Christmas party was held at a place called the VIP Club. "It sounds more like a strip joint than a country club," said Nikki, and Roberta laughed.

"But it looks like a country club," Roberta said, and Nikki agreed. They were in a large, elegant room, with floor to ceiling views of the Long Island Sound, which was a very bright blue on this sunny afternoon. They held full glasses of Prosecco, and Nikki clinked her glass against Roberta's. "To a great year in sales," she said.

"Especially with the organic line," said Roberta. They clinked again. "I have to give you credit. It was a great idea."

"How many organic contracts have you sold?" asked Nikki.

"Three, no, maybe four."

Nikki's heart sank. It was the casual "three, no, maybe four," that really stung, as if the sum didn't matter. She herself had sold only one. Well, the organic tide was rising—she'd sell more the next year, and the next. Still, these organic contracts just might make Roberta win the sales contest rather than Nikki, which would really be ironic. Bethany was going to announce the winner of the contest this afternoon, at the party. Nikki didn't have Marlene's sales figures, having thought it demeaning to ask for them, so she guessed (but didn't know) she was surpassing her predecessor. Roberta, however, would know to the tenth of a percentage point how much she'd increased her sales over the year before. As for Yvonne, who knew? Perhaps she'd been discreetly doing some serious selling lately.

Nikki filled her small china plate with every hot hors d'oeuvres that would fit: pigs in blankets, meatballs, stuffed mushrooms, tiny quesadillas. Even if she didn't win a Caribbean vacation (she could picture herself and Quiana, snorkeling together, parting a school of yellow fish), at least she would have a good feed.

Cynthia approached her, also with a full plate. "So, Nikki, they're announcing the winner of the sales contest today."

"Pitter patter," said Nikki, touching the area of her heart, pretending it didn't matter by pretending it did.

"Oh, you care, you can't fool me. And, girl, you deserve to win. You came here with zero experience, and now you perform like a pro! I've seen you change. If you don't win the contest today, you'll win it next year for sure."

Nikki looked around, anxious. "Don't let Roberta hear you saying that!"

"She has to expect competition," said Cynthia. "It's only right."

Soon, everybody filed into the banquet hall, where there were formal settings at every place. It was like a wedding, with numbered tables and little cards to tell you where to sit. "I would have been happy with just those hors d'oeuvres," said Nikki.

"Dial up your appetite, because you're going to need it," said Cynthia, who sat across from her. There was only one way Nikki knew to dial up her appetite, but this wasn't exactly the moment. The waiters bustled about bringing them plates of salad and murmuring, "Salmon or steak?" Between courses, the women of Bethany Meals danced in a festive mass. Nikki joined them; Roberta didn't.

After a couple of songs, Nikki slipped away from the dance floor and out the door. Shivering in the cold air, for she wasn't wearing her coat, she walked to the end of the parking lot. She still felt too visible, so she ducked behind a dumpster to take a few hits off a joint. Not the most uplifting setting, but soon she was finished and back with the others. And everything felt pleasantly strange, which usually happened the first time she got high in a new place.

As she made her way back to her seat, the mailroom guy gave her a conspicuous double sniff. Aargh! How marijuana clung to your hair and to your clothes! Nikki took out the small atomizer of perfume she kept in her bag, basically to camouflage cannabis, and gave herself several spritzes. But what about her breath? She saw that dessert was now at her place setting, and food was the best remedy, to say nothing of how much better it tasted when you were high.

After dessert, Bethany made an uplifting speech about her hopes for the coming year. She asked the people who had joined the company in the past year to stand, and Nikki and several women from different departments stood up. Then Bethany announced "employee of the year." "It's always some clerical person," said Roberta. Sure enough, Georgette, the receptionist with the terrible voice, was chosen for the honor, which came with a small check. Then Bethany said, "This whole company runs on the efforts of our sales staff."

"You'd better believe it," said Roberta to Nikki.

Bethany continued, "Without clients, we'd go out of business, so every year, we have a sales contest so we can honor, and reward, our most productive sales person. This year, our reps have been competing against themselves: who improved her gross sales by the highest percentage over last year? Next year, we'll do it by numbers: who gets the most new clients. But this year, our winner is… " And she looked across the room, smiling at Lillian, and letting her eyes rest at last on Nikki, who felt herself flush with joy… "Our winner is, once again, Roberta Cohen."

Nikki clapped hard to camouflage her disappointment as Roberta walked to the front of the room to accept her certificate and the envelope that held her vacation voucher. "Next time," said Cynthia to Nikki. "You'll see."

Nikki sat in her Boston hotel room waiting to meet Lloyd, who was visiting his parents. She wasn't sure if his wife was with him or not.

Perhaps she'd even be with him tonight. Nikki was altogether ready, sitting on the hotel bed. There were no little tasks to do while she was waiting, unlike at home, where there were always surfaces to clear, floors to sweep, dishes to put away, mail to sort. Now, because she had nothing to do, Nikki was simply waiting.

Still, when the telephone rang, she jumped as if it were a bomb. Lloyd said, "I'm here."

"I" and not "we." Nikki said, "I'll be right down." She put her winter coat over her arm and tucked the room thing into her bag, wondering when actual keys had been abolished in favor of these plastic cards. She rode the elevator down, and when they reached the lobby, the elevator doors opened and there he was.

"You've scarcely changed!" exclaimed Lloyd. "You look twenty."

She bobbed forward to kiss him on the cheek. "Well you've changed," she said. "And all for the better." In truth, he did not look as handsome as on TV, but he had indeed improved in appearance since college.

Lloyd murmured, "Fifteen years."

Nikki echoed, "Fifteen years."

"Do you like Italian food?" he asked. She nodded, and he said, "There's a good Italian restaurant just a few blocks from here."

She put on her coat.

He said, "It's windy out there," putting on a leather hat with woolly earflaps. Nikki thought it looked quite ridiculous, so she put on her own equally ridiculous headgear, a striped stocking hat long enough to also serve as a scarf. They walked out into the windy Boston night.

"I told my folks I was meeting a producer," Lloyd volunteered.

Nikki responded, "Then I'll option your next book. Are your wife and children in Boston?"

"No, they stayed home."

They walked along, into the wind. It was blowing hard enough to discourage conversation. After a few blocks, they approached a restaurant. Through the window, Nikki could see a roomful of elegant people in animated conversation. "Here we go," said Lloyd, opening the door for her.

"I was hoping this was our destination," she said. Despite woolen gloves, her fingertips were numb.

They took off their coats, and Nikki caught a whiff of stale sweat, which she hoped was not her own. A hostess led them to a small table.

"You really look great," said Lloyd. "Scarcely twenty-five. So you've been home all these years since you had a baby. I didn't take you for the homemaker type. In college."

"I didn't take you for the media type. In college."

"Lives change," said Lloyd, leaning back in his chair. "For years I was very wrapped up in my children, but that's changing now that they're older. Becky's twelve and Charles is ten."

"Quiana's twelve, too," said Nikki.

"What's this unlikely role in the workplace?" asked Lloyd.

"Let's play twenty questions," said Nikki, and he guessed "sales" in six. "I saw myself as more of a rebel," she said, "Now I'm part of corporate America."

"Can I get you something to drink?" asked the waitress, laying down menus.

"A bloody Mary," said Nikki promptly. A drink would loosen her up, which she needed.

"Club soda and lime," said Lloyd.

But maybe a drink *wouldn't* loosen her up, not if he wasn't going to join her: she'd just feel boozy and sloppy while he retained control. But she couldn't change her order without seeming like a wimp. "Don't you drink?" she couldn't help asking.

"Used to," he said. He looked up from the menu to say, "They do a nice linguini with clam sauce."

"I was thinking of the veal *piccata*."

"I've stopped eating veal since I learned how they're raised," Lloyd said.

Nikki said for a joke, "I think they're raised differently for restaurants."

Lloyd shook his head. "No, they're still kept in tiny stalls so they're unable to turn around, and they're fed a diet which keeps their meat tender but gives them constant diarrhea, and they're so starved for iron they lick the bars of their cages."

"All right, all right," grumbled Nikki. At the word "diarrhea," she had lost all desire for veal—and for anything else. "Why does everything we do have larger implications?"

"Because it does. Because we're all connected. Take the common field mouse. . ."

And before they could order (Nikki saw the waitress make a tentative dart toward their table then retreat to her station), Lloyd enumerated all the ways the common field mouse was important to the lives of human beings. Nikki suspected that he had delivered more than one lecture on the topic. Finally, during a pause, the waitress came to their table.

Nikki ordered the spaghetti *carbonara*, and after the waitress left, Lloyd remarked, disapprovingly, "How refreshing that you still eat cream."

"Gotta eat something," she said. Then, just for spite, she added, "I never trust clams unless I know exactly where they've been harvested."

This gave Lloyd pause, and he frowned.

The waitress brought their drinks, and Nikki raised her drink to his, which he had brought to his cheek as if cooling a toothache, and clinked her glass against his. "Let's drink to old friends."

"We're not old yet. Nor is our friendship. Old friendships are surely continuous."

What a pedant! "You propose a toast, then," she said.

"*Sante*. That means 'to your health' in French."

"I know," said Nikki. "I spent a month in France." Irritated at his presumption of her ignorance, she swallowed a third of her drink. Her mouth felt, pleasantly, like a pepper cave. And because he wasn't saying anything, she proceeded to describe her month in Toulouse. She concluded merrily, "In four weeks I had three lovers, each from a different country."

Lloyd frowned.

Nikki said, "Remember, this was before AIDS and after the birth control pill. In that tiny window of time when free sex was possible."

"Not compulsory, however."

"It was in the air! I wasn't a slut, I was victim to the zeitgeist." She giggled. He didn't. She said, "Of course, all that's changed."

As the waitress brought their food, Lloyd said somberly, "When the children were small, I had an offer to teach in France for a year, but Vicki didn't want to leave the states."

"Does Vicki work?"

"She does now. She edits history books. But she didn't then. I thought it would be good for the kids to learn French as children, but Vicki doesn't like to travel."

"Is this why she's not with you now?'

"Partly." Lloyd sighed. "She's also recovering."

"A cold?"

"Breast cancer."

"Jesus!" Nikki dropped her fork, which clattered against her plate. "Did they get it early?"

"Not early enough. She had to have a mastectomy. And she *elected*"—he emphasized the word—"to have it done on both sides."

"Oh, the poor thing. How hard for her."

"It's been hard for all of us," said Lloyd.

"Are the kids all right?"

"They're better now that she's home again. But they're nervous. You can see it in their faces."

"I'm so sorry," said Nikki.

"Yeah, it's pretty grim back home."

"Well, after a few months things will improve."

"To tell you the truth I don't know if I'll ever get used to... the way things are."

"But they won't stay that way. You're involved with this illness right now, but in a while your family focus will be elsewhere." Nikki paused from her happy-optimist spiel to consider the concerns of Lloyd's family. "You'll be busy deciding where your kids should apply to college. Or where you'll be taking a vacation. Or what to do on your next sabbatical. Things won't stay the same forever. They'll bounce back."

"Well, some things won't bounce back, if you'll pardon the expression." Lloyd looked her in the eye then let his gaze slip downward.

With a shock, Nikki realized he was alluding to Vicki's breasts, or their absence. But maybe she'd had reconstructive surgery: didn't most women? Either way, Lloyd's attitude appalled her. Nikki swallowed. "In your letter, you said that until recently you felt set for life. By 'recently,' were you alluding to Vicki's cancer?"

For a few moments Lloyd remained silent. Then he burst out, "She has no time for anything else any more. She spends every free moment at one healer or another. Christ, she's getting aromatherapy!"

"Good for her," said Nikki. "At least she's doing something, opening new doors."

"Doors to rooms I'm not interested in. Quite apart from the bedroom."

"Hmmmf," she said. She could hear disapproval in the sound, but she didn't care. She realized that her interest in Lloyd had collapsed around her like a hot-air balloon, and she just wanted to lift her legs high and step away from it.

Now Lloyd was asking, "What about you and... your husband?"

"Oh, he left me for another woman." Because she didn't care what effect her words had on him, she came out with the simple truth, and it was exhilarating to state it so baldly.

"Is that why you wrote to me?"

"No. I wrote you because of the show. I really like it."

"Too bad you don't live in Savannah," said Lloyd.

Nikki looked down at her empty plate, shaking her head. She wasn't going to say too bad he didn't live in New York.

"May I tell you about our desserts?" said the waitress.

"Not for me," said Lloyd.

"I'm fine," said Nikki. He offered to pay the bill, but she insisted on splitting it.

Back at her hotel, Lloyd said, in the lobby, "I hope they gave you a nice room."

"Very."

"Can I have look? In case I need to, uh..."

She looked at him expectantly. How was he going to finish this sentence? In case he needed to put up someone in Boston the next time he visited his parents?

He said nothing more and reached past her to push the elevator button. "What floor?"

"Six. Just a quick look," said Nikki. "Then you have to go. I'm pretty tired."

At her door, she put the plastic card into and out of the slot. Nothing happened. She tried it again and jiggled the door handle. Nothing.

"Let me," said Lloyd. He got it open first try. "I do a lot of traveling."

"How does your wife feel about that?"

"She's fine with it," said Lloyd. They walked into the room and Lloyd closed the door behind them and took off his winter jacket. Nikki sat in the armchair.

"Nice room," said Lloyd. Nikki had placed her overnight bag on one of the beds; Lloyd sat on the other. He bounced upon it. "Good bed." He stood up and went to the mini-bar. He took out some seltzer. "May I?"

"Sure."

"Anything for you?"

"No, I'm fine."

"They have vodka. And bloody Mary mix."

"Thanks," she said, meaning "no, thanks."

Lloyd returned to the bed. "So, Nikki. You and I have some unfinished business."

"I don't think so."

"Sure we do. Your letter came at a good time for me."

"Well, that's the problem. It's not such a good time for me."

"You have your period," said Lloyd.

She burst out laughing.

"Sorry," said Lloyd. "Come here."

In her armchair, Nikki shook her head. "I just can't," she said. "Now that I know about Vicki."

"She'll never find out." Lloyd stood up. "She never has."

"You do this often."

"Only out of town," said Lloyd, walking to her.

"It's not about her finding out," Nikki said. "It's about my knowing."

He crouched to her level in front of her chair and put his hand upon hers. "Nikki, he said, "you're so attractive—you barely look thirty. Let's catch up for lost time. Forget about my home life."

She withdrew her hand from under his. "I can't forget about it, Lloyd. It's there. She's recovering from surgery. I feel she's here in the room with us."

Lloyd stood up. He passed his hand over Nikki's hair. She smelled that stale sweat again. It was definitely his. She kept her head rigid. "Too bad," he said, and he stopped stroking her. He scooped up his jacket and stood there looking at her.

Too bad, oh, too bad! Years of wondering, months of yearning, and now they had the time and place they weren't even going to fool around! But she couldn't. Although he was good-looking now, and famous, she still wasn't drawn to him. He didn't charm her, make her laugh, engage her sympathy. She didn't want to breathe him in. You can't argue with your nose, Nikki thought: the nose knows. She held her breath and kissed Lloyd goodbye on the cheek.

After he left, Nikki rolled up a bath towel and stuffed it underneath the bathroom door. Then she turned on the fan and stood on the toilet seat to smoke a joint. Between tokes, she held the joint high above her head, by the fan. The bathroom would still reek, but the room wouldn't, and the outside hallway would definitely not smell of pot. Being a pot smoker required constant attention to these matters. By morning, the ventilation system would make the bathroom smell fine.

Now, in her new mindful mode, Nikki asked herself why she was getting high. To think about Lloyd and bid farewell to a long-distance crush? To forget about the fiasco of the evening? To feel that numbing uplift pot always brought her? To fall asleep easily and deeply in about half an hour? Yes and yes and yes and yes.

14
Roberta's Film Diary

February 14, 1996

Paul and I saw Before Sunrise *tonight. Young Americans in Europe. I thought it might be a good Valentine's Day movie, but I found it deeply unsatisfactory. What do two beautiful college-age singles have to say to me? They certainly have plenty to say to each other! Talk, talk, talk—& the dialogue neither witty nor smart. Most exciting thing that happens is he gets off the train to spend a night with her. I like movies to be more consequential! I like the stakes to be bigger! After all, if he likes her so much, why does he just let her go at the end so casually? If he loves her, or thinks he could love her, wouldn't he insist on a future meeting? These are young people with no baggage! They don't need to sacrifice anything to spend more time together, but they elect to have no future together. So it becomes like a music video: cute people moving against beautiful scenery but nothing really changes. I suppose some people wouldn't mind watching models or other pretty people doing just about anything. You could make a movie about a model brushing her teeth, having breakfast, walking the dog, buying groceries, & it would still get an audience. I prefer the traditional drama: rising action, complication, climax, resolution. Paul started sleeping by ten o'clock—long before sunrise! I had to jostle him so he would stop snoring.*

15

Roberta

March, 1996

Roberta had never told Paul about her brother Kenny. She'd mentioned her two older sisters and her nieces and nephews, but somehow she had never gotten around to telling her fiancé about the 32-year-old schizophrenic who lived in her parents' basement room. She was sure that if Paul knew about Kenny he would tease her about it. Or if they had a fight and she yelled at him, he might taunt her for being just like her psycho brother. No, she wouldn't give him the ammunition, which was why she was at her parents' house on Sunday morning, bringing bagels and lox. It was just the three of them; Kenny liked to sleep late and took naps as well. As he didn't do anything all day, Roberta thought it must be his meds that made him so sleepy. If only they made him more rational, too—but Kenny was still insisting that she was an FBI agent out to get him, a charge she couldn't defend herself against, as whatever she said just convinced him that her cover was diabolically clever. He would laugh his strange laugh and back away from her.

She rang the bell. Henry opened the door and kissed her. He had become much more affectionate since her engagement. She wondered if he expected more grandchildren. Think again, Dad.

"You look good, a nice sweater," he said, taking her jacket and hanging it in the closet.

Roberta said, "Thanks. Mom gave it to me."

They walked back to the kitchen, where Golde was measuring coffee. "You're wearing the sweater!" she announced upon seeing her daughter. "It brings out the gold in your eyes."

"Thanks, Mom. Give me a plate for the lox and I'll lay it out."

Soon they were seated around the table with full plates in front of them. Roberta loved the colors of this breakfast: the yellow scrambled eggs, the green scallions, the brown toasted bagel, the white cream cheese, the... well, *salmon*-colored salmon—all bright together on the plate. When they were on their second bagel-halves, Roberta said, "Mom, Dad. Is Kenny any better?"

"I think he is a little, don't you, dear?" Golde turned to her husband, who shrugged.

"Does he still think I'm with the FBI?" When Golde was silent, Roberta continued. "Because if he does, I don't want him at my wedding."

"He's your brother, Roberta," said Golde. "He has to be there."

"No, he doesn't. It's my day, and I don't want him blabbing to everyone that I'm a spy!"

"But he knows about the wedding!" said Golde. "He knows the date and the place. He'll want to see you get married."

"Ha!" Henry gave his bark of a laugh. "You want to know the truth, Roberta? Kenny said he wouldn't go to your wedding because you would probably poison the cake. So, fine, we'll go without him."

"That's so mean," said Golde.

"No, dear, it makes perfect sense. Roberta doesn't want him there. Kenny doesn't want to go. We'll say he wasn't feeling well. It will be fine."

Golde's eyes began to well. She stood up.

"Mom?"

But Golde was shaking her head and leaving the room.

Henry said, "Let it be. She'll be back."

A few minutes later, Golde came back to the table with a warm coffeecake.

At the office the next day, Roberta stopped at Nikki's desk. "How's everything?" asked Roberta.

Nikki sighed. "Do you ever have days when you just can't pick up the phone and sell?"

"Of course," said Roberta.

"I'm having one of those days. I'm making this a research and writing day."

"When I have those days, I go through my files, evaluate prospects, plan for trade shows. Did you ask Lillian about the Washington trade show?"

Nikki nodded. "She says since we have a booth there, the whole sales team should go. Including her."

"Damn. We could have had so much fun, just the two of us. Now we'll have to deal with the idiot and the whale."

"Yvonne's not really fat, you know," said Nikki. "Just tall and maybe a little big-boned..."

"I call that fat," said Roberta. She peeped at Nikki's computer screen and saw a document titled Mt. Pleasant Rehab. She was surprised at the amount of information on the page: statistics, personnel, notations about every contact and mailing... Nikki turned her face around inquiringly, and Roberta moved away, walking back to her desk. She supposed she should keep better records, but in sales it was the present and future that mattered, not the past. She was used to selling in the moment and sensing what would move her client. Unlike Nikki, Roberta was hyped up for selling today. The week before, she had done a mailing about the organic line, and today she was going to make follow-up calls. She wasn't going to stress the benefits of organic meals, about which she wasn't convinced. She was going to emphasize how the organic line would please clients and make the facility more appealing to them. After all, it was always good to be ahead of the crowd. As for taste, as far as Roberta could tell, the new line was more or less like the old one: quite good for frozen food. This meant she would promote it as "even more delectable than our classic line."

In the afternoon, Roberta made plans to see several prospects at the DC trade show. She would do her best to prevent clients and would-be clients from meeting Lillian, whom Roberta felt to be a disgrace not just to the company but also to the entire selling profession. She hadn't yet decided which table she would inflict Lillian upon at her wedding. Paul thought the whole Lillian thing was hilarious, but that was because he didn't have a boss himself since he operated as an independent real estate lawyer.

On the way to the mailroom to get some more envelopes, Roberta passed Bethany's large office. The door was open and Lillian could be heard saying, "Bethany, that's fantastic! And after Fairfield, maybe Nassau County!" What could they be talking about? Why would Lillian be so excited? And then it hit Roberta: Bethany Moore, Inc., was expanding its territory—first into Fairfield County, next, maybe, into Nassau County, Long Island. This had important ramifications for Roberta.

At Bethany Meals, the territory was divided geographically rather than by the type of client, such as spas or rehabilitation hospitals. Roberta had New York City; Yvonne had Rockland and Putnam Counties; Nikki had Westchester County. If the company was expanding into Fairfield County, they might have to hire another salesperson. With benefits and salary, they might not want to do that. Or they could give it to Yvonne or Nikki. Since Yvonne was a violent ditz who didn't deserve even the clients she had, Roberta would work behind the scenes to get them to give Nikki the Fairfield territory, so that the "existing rep" precedent would be established when they pushed into Nassau County, the most populous half of Long Island, just beyond Brooklyn and Queens. When that happened, Roberta knew she might well double her commissions. But she would need help if her territory were to expand like this. Perhaps she could get Lillian to spring for an assistant dedicated just to Roberta. Roberta knew that if she had a good admin, she could make a whole lot of money. For now, the best she could do was to support giving an in-house rep—Nikki—the Fairfield territory. Then she, Roberta, might be given Nassau County,

"I heard a rumor," Roberta told Nikki the next morning. They were in the small office kitchen making tea. She whispered, "Looks like Bethany Meals is going to expand into Fairfield County."

"That's good," said Nikki. "It isn't even far from here. Greenwich is about a ten minute drive from this office."

"So who'll get the territory?" mused Roberta.

"They should really get a new rep," said Nikki. "There are so many hospitals and spas around Greenwich and Westport."

Roberta wondered why Nikki was so dense. She said, "Or maybe they'll just expand *your* territory."

"I doubt it." Nikki was wringing a dripping tea bag around a plastic spoon to extract the most flavor. "I'm just getting used to the territory I have. I've finally finished my database, which will make it really easy to do mailings."

Roberta hated words like "database," and she didn't know when Nikki had taken the time to construct one. Still, she had to persist in her campaign. Roberta said, "They don't really like to hire new people. It's partly the salary, but it's also the benefits. And the space! They'd have to put her in the empty desk near me, and you know how much I value my privacy."

"Maybe they'll hire a man," said Nikki. "I think a man would be great, especially an attractive man. We would all be a lot more courteous, even Lillian, if there was a cute guy in our midst."

This was *really* getting off-topic. Roberta said, "They'll probably just give it to you or Yvonne."

"To Yvonne then. She's been here longer."

Roberta wondered: what was the matter with Nikki? She seemed utterly oblivious to her own financial wellbeing. "Yes, but Yvonne is an airhead," persisted Roberta. "They should really give it to you. You've proven yourself at this point, and with your idea of the organic line, you're probably golden."

"Yes, and I was really treated like a golden girl when Bethany made that announcement." Heavy sarcasm.

"All the more reason to make it up to you now," said Roberta, glad that at last Nikki was summoning a little passion to the discussion. "I just don't want some stranger sitting at that desk, listening to all of my calls and judging me."

"No one will do that," said Nikki.

Roberta said, "Just imagine how much money you'd make if you could get Fairfield County!"

"'Isn't it pretty to think so,'" said Nikki.

"What's that line from?" asked Roberta. "It sounds so familiar."

Nikki smiled at Roberta. "It's the last line of *The Sun Also Rises*. I once wanted to write a book called *The Sun Also Sets*."

"Ladies!" said Lillian at the doorway to the kitchen. "I must interrupt this literary conversation. . ."

"We were just going back to our desks," said Nikki.

"Relax," said Lillian. "I just wanted to tell you I've booked us all shuttle flights to Washington from LaGuardia on Delta. I think they leave from Terminal B, but you'd better check. We'll all meet at the gate half an hour before take-off. Now here's a list of exhibitors, in case you want to schedule some time with anyone in advance." Lillian handed them each a list. "At a big convention, just hoping to see one of your clients without planning ahead can be risqué."

Roberta couldn't muffle a honk of laughter.

"What?" Lillian asked suspiciously.

"I was just remembering the last time I left it to chance," said Roberta, rapidly recovering. "The only time I could talk to my prospect was on the buffet line. I still managed to wangle an appointment with him, though."

"Good girl," said Lillian. "Lemme go tell Yvonne." She race-walked through the office. All energy, no brains, thought Roberta.

"She's starting to like you," Roberta told Nikki a little later. "I heard her telling Bethany you were a barracuda."

"That's supposed to be a compliment?" asked Nikki. "To be compared to a killer shark?"

"You're in sales, dummy! Of course it's a compliment."

16

Roberta

April, 1996

Roberta looked at her watch, a Seiko Paul had recently given her, with diamond chips on the hands. Nikki was fifteen minutes late. Roberta stroked the smooth gold links of the watchband. At present, Roberta had nine working watches. If you thought of them as bracelets (for didn't they also serve as adornments for the wrist?) having nine didn't seem extreme. You had a couple of watches for the office, a couple for dressy occasions, one for sports, and a few zany ones for everything else. Her favorite was an original Mickey Mouse watch, worth a lot more than the Seiko.

Roberta was sitting at a small round table at the hotel bar in Washington, recovering from a grueling day on the convention floor and a client dinner with a woman so boring conversation had been hard labor. Now she ordered Chardonnay. The bar was in the middle of the hotel lobby, which made Roberta feel over-exposed but also allowed her to look at the elevator bank. Finally, Nikki emerged from the glass elevator in a tank top and green jeans. She slid across the table from Roberta, who couldn't help saying, "No fair! You changed!"

"I couldn't stay in those heels another minute," said Nikki, "so while I was up there, I got into my jeans."

"How was your client dinner?"

"Not great. I took two guys from Kindred to Garden," said Nikki, naming Washington's premier vegetarian restaurant. "I could tell they didn't like the food. They're probably grabbing a steak somewhere now."

"May I get you something?" the waiter asked Nikki, and she said,

"Yes, hmmm, something sweet." Since she drank so rarely, it was always hard to remember what drinks she liked. She glanced at the menu and ordered a peach daiquiri, and the waiter's eyes wandered briefly to her chest. Roberta thought that Nikki was displaying too much cleavage. About half an inch was right: hers might be an inch and a half. Why did men find that shadow, that path between the hills, so intriguing? There were many ways to dress up—but if you wanted male attention, décolleté always worked best.

"You look hot," said Roberta.

"Thanks," said Nikki. "It's been a while since I've been out and about."

"Too bad that guy in Boston didn't work out."

"Yeah, Lloyd. He's actually from Savannah. But he was wrong for many reasons." She looked over to the bar.

Roberta followed her gaze. A couple of cute guys, probably business travelers, were drinking beer from bottles. Both were in polo shirts and khakis. "Not bad," said Roberta. She observed that the guys had now noticed them, especially Nikki. Roberta, in her business blouse and pearls, knew she was at an apparel disadvantage in this dimly-lit bar—although what did it matter, she was engaged to be married. Now Nikki was flashing the men a smile. Between the smile and the cleavage, it would only be a moment before... and yes, it was happening already, the two men, maybe in their mid-thirties, were getting off their barstools and approaching their table. "Are you ready for this?" asked Roberta.

"I am," said Nikki.

"Ladies," said the tall dark-haired one. "Can we buy you a drink?"

"What are you having?" asked the sandy-haired one. His muscles stretched the hems of his short sleeves.

"A sweet drink," said Nikki.

"I'll get the next round," asked the dark haired one. "I'm Mike."

"And I'm Geoff," said the sandy-haired guy. "G-E-O-F-F."

Roberta said, "That's useful, knowing how to spell your name."

"It's such a different name," he said with comic intensity. "I wouldn't want to present myself as a mere J-E-F-F. You'd get the wrong idea." Geoff and Mike were still standing, looming over the women.

"Sit down," said Nikki.

"But we'll buy our own drinks," said Roberta. "We're on expenses—our company will pay." That always settled the issue.

"Oh, right, sure." The guys sat down, Geoff near Nikki; Mike near Roberta.

Mike asked, "So, are you from out of town?"

Roberta rolled her eyes: couldn't these guys come up with better lines? But Nikki began talking about Bethany Meals and the convention. Roberta thought Nikki was one of those women who always gained animation when talking to a man. She seemed to be aiming her smile (and her cleavage) at Geoff, which was the choice Roberta would have made if she were not engaged—although Mike, the dark-haired one, was also attractive. Roberta now asked him, "Are you here on business as well?"

"No, it's just a good bar—we live in the area," he said. Then he added hastily, "Not together."

"Somehow, I didn't think you were gay," Roberta responded. Perhaps Mike and Geoff liked to pick up women in this bar because the women would be gone in a day or two. No worries about starting a relationship, just a new woman to fuck.

Geoff was showing Nikki his new camera. "That's amazing," said Nikki. "Roberta, have you ever seen one of these?" Geoff put the camera on the table. On its back was a small screen which displayed the activity in the restaurant, as if it were a miniature TV.

Geoff said, "It doesn't use film. It's all digital."

"What does that actually mean?" asked Nikki.

"Well, first it means that you can see the image you've shot right away." Looking at the screen at arm's length, rather than putting his eye to the viewfinder, he aimed the camera first at Nikki. Roberta saw a flash but didn't hear a click. Then he took a photo of Roberta. He pushed a button or two. Then he showed them the photo of Roberta on the little camera screen. Her eyes looked red and her smile looked forced, and worst of all—was that a hint of a double chin? After the thousands she'd paid Dr. Mandelbaum to remove it?

"Delete that picture!" she said.

"Are you serious?"

"Yes, I hate it. I don't want to know it exists in the world!"

"Your wish is my command," said Geoff and he pushed another button, causing a brief buzz. He turned to Nikki and gave her the camera. "Here's your picture."

Nikki said. "Hmmm. Not bad." She pushed the camera toward Roberta, who peered at the screen. Nikki looked terrific. She had one of those faces that can look severe in real life but that almost always photographs well. Something about cheekbones and chin... no extra flesh under Nikki's chin.

"I'll take another of you," said Geoff to Roberta, and although she protested that he didn't have to, he aimed the camera at her and she raised her chin high and gave him her camera-ready smile. A few seconds later, he showed her the image on the little screen. She looked, actually, very good. "One of you two together," said Geoff, so Roberta and Nikki brought their heads close, and Geoff said "Closer," so they smiled cheek to cheek when he took the picture.

"Give me your email addresses," said Geoff, "and I'll send them to you."

"Really?" asked Nikki. "You can do that? Wow." She handed him her business card, and Roberta did the same.

"Ten years from now, nobody will be using film," pronounced Geoff. "What's so cool is you don't develop every picture you take—just the ones you like."

"Very environmental," said Nikki.

"That is cool," said Roberta, "but it won't put Kodak out of business. Too many people have regular cameras."

Geoff said, "In ten years, this will *be* the 'regular camera.' You'll see."

"What makes you so sure?" asked Nikki, tilting her face toward him with a smile.

"Track record," he said.

"What, you're some sort of futurist?"

"Actually, that's some of what I do... I work at a think tank."

Mike said to Roberta, "Your glass is empty..."

Roberta put her hand over the top of her glass and said, "I've had a long day." Remembering how she had gotten up at five to get to the airport on time, she was, in fact, truly tired.

"It's only eleven," said Mike. "C'mon. What's one more drink?"

"One too many for me," said Roberta, standing up. She saw that Mike was rising to accompany her, so she pushed down his shoulder and said, "I've got to call my fiancé." This did the trick: Mike sat down again. Roberta asked, "Nikki, you going up?"

"Soon."

Roberta said, "Don't forget, we have that industry breakfast at seven-thirty."

Nikki scrunched up her nose and mouth in a look of disgust that squished her features all together. If she had any idea what it looked like, Roberta was sure Nikki wouldn't pull such a face, but she wasn't sure she should tell her.

Nikki said, "I wish you'd stay."

"I can't," said Roberta. "Goodnight all!" And away she walked, eager to get upstairs to her quiet room, where she would call Paul. Although hotel calls were expensive, the reps were allowed one personal call a day, and this would be hers. Then she would watch a little TV.

Waiting for the elevator, she glanced back at Nikki and the guys. Geoff had his arm around Nikki, and they were all laughing.

Upstairs, after her telephone conversation with Paul, Roberta opened the mini-bar and took out a half-bottle of wine. She hadn't wanted to get sloshed downstairs, where everyone could see her. What if she acted silly, what if she lost control? But here in her hotel room, if she sipped the wine slowly and had something to eat—she went into the mini-bar again and took out a packet of pretzels—she'd be fine.

Roberta wore her new salmon-colored suit to the industry breakfast the next day and wondered if she'd match the lox that would be on the inevitable buffet. But it turned out to be a sit-down breakfast, and she nabbed the chair beside Esther Whitehall, who was the decision-maker at Allengate Spas, which had headquarters in Manhattan—Roberta's territory. Yvonne and Lillian were eating together at the other end of the table. Roberta knew she'd done well to sit by a prospect rather than a colleague, and she hoped Lillian would notice. If not, she would tell her.

There was no sign of Nikki.

An elegant bowl of fruit salad was at each setting. Roberta said to Esther Whitehall, "I'm impressed. I didn't expect to see a blood orange and pieces of fresh fig for breakfast."

"Yes, it's nicely done," agreed Esther.

"Fresh mint, as well," Roberta continued, hoping to draw in a client from this gossamer thread.

A white-coated waiter filled their cups with steaming coffee. "Are you having a good show?" asked Roberta.

"There are so many new product launches I'm getting a hernia lugging the samples down the aisles."

"I know what you mean."

The waiter asked whether they'd like a spinach omelet, a quiche Lorraine, or waffles. "Spinach omelet, no cheese, no toast," said Esther Whitehall decisively.

Roberta, who was always trying to lose weight, said, "Good idea— I'll have the same."

"So who are you with?" Esther asked.

"Bethany Moore Meals," said Roberta, and she saw Esther's face harden slightly, anticipating a pitch. Roberta knew she had to be very careful not to sell, or at least not to be seen to be selling, so she asked, "Where do you live?"

"I live in Manhattan," said Esther. And then Roberta got a lifeline: Esther continued, "88th and Second."

"No kidding! I live at 91st and First! You ever go to Paula's Pizza?"

"All the time! Excelsior Cleaners?"

"You bet!"

By the time the waiter laid down their omelets, Esther promised to stop by Roberta's booth at four o'clock.

Roberta was taking her first bite of omelet (which would have been much better with cheese) when she saw Nikki enter the hall. She looked ragged: there were circles under her eyes that her flesh-colored concealer only accentuated, the back of her hair was poufy and messy, and her blouse was creased. Roberta thought a quick pass of the iron would have made all the difference, but it looked like Nikki had gotten dressed in five minutes flat after very little sleep—and way too much drink. Or something.

Nikki sat down across the long table several seats down from Roberta. Nikki brought a piece of orange to her lips with a fork—then lowered it to her bowl again before pushing the fruit salad away. When the waiter came around, she conferred with him earnestly while he poured the coffee. Then she brought the coffee cup to her lips and closed her eyes.

Roberta, watching, missed what Esther was saying. "Sorry—what were you saying just now?"

A few minutes later, the waiter deposited a plate of dry white toast, trimmed of crust and cut on the diagonal, in front of Nikki. She picked up a toast triangle, and looked at it pensively. The room lights dimmed, and the group began listening to a PowerPoint presentation about trends in their industry. Roberta saw Nikki droop her head and close her eyes. It looked like she was falling asleep with her chin in her hand. She must have had some night.

When the speaker mentioned a trend toward natural and unprocessed meals, Roberta whispered to Esther, "We have a new organic line."

Esther turned to her with interest. "Really?"

17

Nikki

April, 1996

Her head was pounding and she was very thirsty, but she knew she shouldn't drink water. It would only make her feel drunk again, or so they said. Of course, if you wanted to get drunk, this was a cheap strategy, but getting drunk was the last thing Nikki wanted now, at this industry breakfast, with colleagues, clients, and prospects all around. She had a pounding headache, and the eggy smell in the room nauseated her. As for what had happened the night before... no, she wouldn't think about that now. Her headache was enough to occupy her completely. No wonder she drank rarely: this was only the second time she'd had a hangover. Or was it something else? She'd had only two drinks, after all. Did one of those horrible men put a date-rape pill in her drink? But was it really rape, she wondered, when she had been so responsive? She couldn't bear to think about it.

The coffee softened the pounding at her temples, and when they lowered the lights for the PowerPoint presentation, Nikki closed her eyes and let herself drift into a dream. She and Quiana were biking down a mountain trail, going fast yet in full control and there were flowers and birds...

She opened her eyes when the room lights went on. Her head had slipped past her hand and her chin was wedged into her arm. She pulled her head up, hoping no one had seen her passed out cold at eight a,m. She definitely needed more coffee.

Down at the other end of the table, Lillian was waving her hand to get the speaker's attention. Nikki exchanged glances with Roberta, who looked alert, composed, and elegant. They were both dreading the inevitable embarrassment, not to say humiliation, each felt when Lillian spoke publicly. It invariably made the company look bad; it always made selling harder for them. The moderator called upon Lillian.

Lillian, wouldn't you know it, stood up at her place. "I want to thank you and congratulate you on this delicious breakfast and the very special PowerPoint presentation you prepared. I'm sure I speak for all of us when I say you have done a rip-roaring job. I just want to mention that my company, Bethany Moore Meals, is tops in the natural and organic movement, and we have the first line of organic meals in our area. And at this moment we're lucky to have with us a person who helped develop this idea. Nikki, please stand up and tell the group why you think it's so important to go organic today."

In horror, Nikki saw a wireless mike being passed to her. She could barely hold her head upright, and Lillian, that ignoramus, expected her to get up and give an impromptu public speech! Nikki's head and heart were pounding together. She was not going to risk standing up, so when the mike reached her she looked downward and spoke slowly into it. "Going organic is important... for health and wellness care-providers... because it's important to our clients. . . It's part of the zeitgeist." (Where was she going with that? Delete!) "Our clients and future clients are the ones who are eating organic at home. . . They're the ones asking at intake if you have organic meals. . . because for them it's part of the healing process." Nikki looked up and at the others now. They seemed to think she was making sense, so she continued. "They are the new, empowered consumer, and they shop around, even for their health care. You wouldn't want to lose their business because the rehab facility in the next town provides organic meals and you don't. . . I think every hospital and spa should offer an organic line, perhaps at a higher premium... Let your clients make the choice. Let your clients show you what they want!" And with that, she passed the mike back. To her astonishment, led by Roberta, people in the room started to clap, and Nikki realized she had probably been coherent even through her headache and her nausea.

Suddenly, she was feeling physically *much worse*, and it was lucky that the moderator was continuing with the program because... Nikki knew she had to leave the room fast. She grabbed her handbag and ran for the door, but at that moment she tripped on a wire and went sprawling onto the floor. Luckily, her hands broke her fall. She pulled herself up, bolted from the room, and asked the hostess at the door, "Ladies room—where?"

She ran down the marble corridor and got herself into a stall. She pulled down her pants just in time. Stuff was pouring out from both ends at once, so she had to vomit on the floor.

Minutes later, weak, shaky, and ashamed, she went to her room, arranged for a late checkout, and got into bed.

By the time she met the others later that day in the lobby, she had recovered. As they walked to the taxi, Roberta got her off to one side and asked, "What happened?"

"I was very sick."

"Like, hung over?"

"I don't think so. Just sick, very sick."

Roberta said, "I collected some cards from your territory."

Nikki said, "Thanks. I appreciate it." Lillian insisted on seeing the business cards that they'd gleaned from trade shows, and she would get very excited to see a thick stack. The business cards were meaningless in themselves, because by now Nikki knew who did what at the companies she was targeting, but they were important to her fool of a boss.

The next day, at the office, Nikki waited until everyone had left for lunch and took another look at the threesome picture. Her eyes were closed and her hair was matted and her mouth was stretched out of shape. Mike was fondling her, and Geoff was—with a click, she deleted the picture, glad she would never have to see it again. But she could not delete what had happened.

After Roberta left to call her fiancée, Nikki had accepted one more drink from Geoff and Mike. They all laughed and flirted. Then she stood up to say goodnight. Geoff asked if he could walk her to her room, as she was sort of woozy. She was surprised: although she drank rarely, surely she could metabolize two drinks in two hours. She felt weak and clumsy. She was glad to lean against Geoff across the lobby and into the elevator. She and Geoff stumbled down the corridor to the door of her room. Fumbling in her bag, she extracted the plastic key card—and dropped it.

"Let me," said Geoff, who inserted it into the slot, followed her into her room, and dropped the card on the bureau. He strode to the window and opened the curtain. "Oh, you got the good side," he said. "The park, not the parking lot. That was very clever." He put his arms around her and stood there hugging her.

Soon they became a little unsteady, and, still hugging, they fell onto the bed. His mouth felt good against hers, but surely she wouldn't do much, she didn't do one-night stands—or did she? She liked the way Geoff kissed, waiting for her response before doing anything new with his lips and his tongue. And her response was ardent. It had been a long time, after all, and wasn't out of town a perfect time to see what sex could be like with a stranger? She didn't even know his last name! The very thought excited her and she kissed him back enthusiastically. He slid his hands under her tank top, under her bra, and his fingers were so gentle, sort of silvery light, that she just sighed and let him. "You're very beautiful," he said. "Do you know that?"

What was she supposed to say? She smiled and shrugged.

He rolled away and at first she almost panicked that their connection was broken, but no, he was just taking off his shirt, revealing a hairless, muscled chest. "Now you," he said, tugging her tank top upward.

"I don't know," she said, suddenly doubtful and tired.

"So we can be chest to chest," he explained, and this made sense, even through her fatigue, so she took off her shirt.

"Nice brassiere," said Geoff.

"Thank you," said Nikki.

"But it has to come off."

"Does it?"

"Chest to chest," he incanted, and then she remembered.

She took off her bra, which was white lace with a tiny pink ribbon bow in the middle, and felt her breasts swing free.

"You are sensational," said Geoff. "I wish Mike could see you."

Nikki shook her head.

"I'll just have to tell him," said Geoff, "what beautiful titties you have."

She hated the word "titties," but somehow she was very excited. "Don't," she said.

"Maybe I won't tell him. Maybe I'll just show him. I could take a few pictures."

"No pictures," she said. She could hear she was slurring her words and realized she was quite off balance. She lay down on the bed again. Geoff could take advantage of her, and she was so wet down there, it would be easy, he could just slide it in, and it would feel so good... she fell into a short, light doze and awoke to find him opening the zipper on her pants. Although his intention was unambiguous, she asked, "What are you doing?" Why was she so incredibly sleepy?

"I want to see if your panties match your bra."

This was an understandable wish, so she raised her hips and let him tug off her tight green jeans and throw them to one side.

"They match!" said Geoff stroking her panties with the same silvery caresses he had bestowed upon her breasts a little earlier. "White lace with a little pink bow. I like that, I really do."

It seemed okay to let him stroke her outside the panties and also it felt so good she could hardly prevent him. And just when she began to worry that he would put his hand between her legs and discover that her panties were wet... he did exactly that. "My goodness," he chuckled. "We have to do something about that."

"What do you mean?"

"Oh, sweetie, you need it, you really do."

"But I'm so tired."

"Shh. You won't have to do anything. Just lie there, baby, leave it all to me." And he worked his hand under the panties and slid a finger inside her, murmuring "Nice, very nice." He was moving his hand confidently in and out when—how was it possible?—there came a knock at the door. Geoff did not seem surprised. He moved off her and went to the door, where Mike was waiting.

"Come on in," said Geoff. "This is going to be fun. She is so ready."

Nikki grabbed her shirt and held it to cover her breasts. "You have to go," she said. "Both of you."

"Aw, don't be like that," said Geoff, approaching the bed again.

"We were getting on so well. You really liked me. Pussy really liked me. And you'll like Mike, too. Girls like Mike."

Nikki shook her head. "I'm so tired. You both have to go. I just want to sleep."

But they didn't go. They stayed for several hours. Some of the time, she was semi-conscious. She came a lot. Looking back, Nikki felt that was the worst of it, even though she knew that when it comes to sex, no one is P.C. Everybody has some private pleasure, some secret thrill, some fantasy fueled by imbalance, some hidden room they visit in the dark.

Roberta got married on a cool afternoon in May at a midtown Manhattan hotel. Nikki, in a silk sleeveless dress, was chilly as she entered the reception area. She carried a jacket, which she did not intend to wear unless absolutely necessary. Although the color went well enough with the dress, the jacket was made of wool, and now that it was too late to seek alternatives, Nikki realized that the fabric was wrong for the occasion. Ahead of her, she saw a familiar head of short magenta hair. "Marlene?"

Marlene turned. She'd gained a little more weight, but her skin was gorgeous. "Wow! It's Nikki! How ya doin'?"

"What a wonderful day for Roberta!"

"Especially wonderful because Lillian canceled out. Something about a niece in Boston."

"Whew," said Nikki. "Now I can relax a little. That woman makes me crazy."

"Apparently, it's mutual."

"Oh?"

"Roberta says you don't always mask your, uh, disrespect for Lillian."

"Disrespect! Let's just say utter scorn. The woman is a total disgrace."

"Too true. My new boss is actually smart. What a difference!"

"Does Roberta think Lillian's going to fire me?"

"No, apparently that's the problem. Roberta says you're doing far too well to be fired."

"She exaggerates," said Nikki, pleased. "But I'm getting to like my job."

"I knew you were a natural as soon as I met you."

Nikki noticed an attractive man in a navy blue blazer who seemed to be checking her out. Before she could respond, a staff member opened the double doors to the next room, and the man turned away. Guests began leaving the bar area while a string quartet played Mozart.

Marlene said, "Wait till you see Roberta's dress. It's stunning."

"I'm sure. She's a terrific dresser."

"She spends a fortune on clothes, so it's good that she's marrying Paul."

"Is he very successful?"

"Oh, yeah. And now she won't be paying mortgage and maintenance, phone and electricity, she'll be better dressed than ever." The bar was emptying fast. Marlene said, "We'd better move in with the others."

Nikki and Marlene found seats in the middle of the hall. Predictably, the wedding procession made Nikki teary, brought her back to her own wedding day and the marital joy she thought lay ahead. She felt envy and pity for that younger self. A flower girl and flower boy came down the aisle, strewing pink rose petals. Then members of the wedding party walked up the aisle and assembled up front, under a fabric canopy held up by wooden poles.

Now the quartet segued to "Here Comes the Bride," and Roberta came down the aisle on the stout arm of her father. Her wedding dress was both sophisticated and bridal: a floor-length, white satin sheath, with white net sleeves and a white net back. Roberta had been dieting, and the dress hugged her curves, emphasizing her small waist. Her glossy dark hair was piled on top of her head, and there were diamonds in her ears. "Wow," said Nikki to Marlene. "She looks gorgeous."

"Vera Wang," said Marlene.

Roberta and her father joined the wedding party at the front of the hall. The rabbi, a fifty-year-old bearded man, spoke about the wisdom that comes in the middle years, and the joys that ensue from maturity. "These are not high school sweethearts; they are adults in the middle of their lives, who have come together because they find happiness in each other." Nikki made out a navy blue blazer ahead of her and wondered whether it was that guy. Then he turned, and it *was*, and he caught her eye and they shared a small smile. "This couple," intoned the rabbi, "know the pleasures of conversation and enjoy cultural events together. This couple..."

A disheveled man in a gray sweatshirt and blue jeans burst into the hall and hollered, "This couple can never be married!" He ran up the aisle.

"Kenny!" shrieked Roberta's mother. "What are you doing here?"

"Kenneth," said Roberta's father. "Come stand with us under the *chuppa* and be part of the wedding ceremony."

"I gotta warn her fiancé," said Kenny. "I can't let an innocent man fall into her clutches." He pointed at Paul. "You're the groom, right? Do you have any idea who she is?"

"Of course I do!" said Paul. "She's the woman I love." And he reached for Roberta's hand.

"She's also an FBI agent," said Kenny. "I bet that you didn't know that!"

"Dad," said Roberta. "Get security to take him away!"

"I'm your brother," said Kenny. "You can't send me away."

But the rabbi was already signaling a waiter. Then he said, "Son, either stand here with us or sit down with the other guests."

"You don't understand. This wedding must not happen! I'm here to let everybody know the true story of my 'sister,' Roberta so-called Cohen!"

"Get him *out* of here!" yelled Roberta.

Two well-muscled waiters came forward and positioned themselves on either side of Kenny, who was addressing Paul. "If you marry that woman, you'll be sorry for the rest of your life!"

"That's enough," said Paul. And he gave a small nod to the waiters, who held Kenny above the elbows and frog-marched him down the aisle.

Kenny gave them little resistance, but he never stopped warning Paul. "First she'll spy on you, then she'll report on you, and if you confront her with it, better watch out for the pistol she carries in her purse!" And with that he was gone from the room.

"Who was *that*?" asked Nikki.

Marlene said, "Didn't she ever tell you about her brother Kenny?"

The guests were standing up and craning their necks and talking to each other.

"Everybody, please settle down," said the rabbi.

At the front of the hall, Paul demanded, "Who *was* that?"

"That's our son, Kenneth," said Henry Cohen.

"You never told me you had a brother," Paul said to Roberta.

"Can you blame me? With a brother like that?"

"Please forgive us," said Roberta's father. "Kenny's not in his right mind."

With all the dignity she could muster, Golde Cohen said, "My son has been diagnosed with acute schizophrenia. You must excuse him."

The rabbi said, "Let's attend to the business which brought us here, the marriage of Roberta and Paul." When the chattering finally died down, the rabbi continued. "These are people who have committed to love one another no matter what, even through disturbances like the one we've just had here. These are people who are experienced enough in life so that their commitment has value and meaning. These are people... " and he was back on track, giving the speech he always gave, Nikki suspected, whenever he married people he scarcely knew who were over age thirty.

When the bride and groom said, "I do," Nikki's eyes got wet again. Maybe marriage and the steady love it could bring would be good for Roberta, would give her more to think about than how much she hated Yvonne.

Marlene said, "Bet she never speaks to her brother again."

"Who could blame her?"

When Nikki came to Roberta on the reception line, Nikki said, "I'm sure you'll be very happy together. And—more important—you look absolutely stunning."

"I haven't eaten a carb in three weeks," said Roberta, with pride.

Marlene said, "Congratulations, baby!" She threw her arms around the bride.

Roberta said, "I could kill that Kenny!"

"Look at it this way," said Marlene. "This is one wedding no one will ever forget!"

Roberta gave Marlene a long look, and Nikki felt her stomach clench, anticipating trouble. Then Roberta threw back her head and laughed, and Marlene laughed, too, and soon they were hugging and shrieking and crying.

Nikki found her table and sat down. From her seat, Nikki had a good view of the man with the navy blue blazer, who was seated two tables away from hers. He had bright blue eyes, regular features and straight brown hair cut very well. It didn't seem like he was part of a couple. She had observed earlier that he was maybe five-foot nine, a height that pleased Nikki. Although height didn't much matter for making love, it was easier to hold hands and kiss and dance with a man who wasn't tall. What excuse could she possibly have for barging up to him, now that people had settled into their chairs around the tables? No excuse. The waiters served salad with walnuts. The woman to her right was asking how she knew Roberta. The man to her left spent his entire time talking to his date. From what Nikki could hear, he was asking such basic questions it had to be their first date.

The dancing began after the entrées were cleared. Roberta and Paul danced gracefully together before the bandleader urged the guests to join them. Nikki watched as couples around the room stood up and joined the newlyweds on the dance floor. She felt a tap on her shoulder and looked into the very blue eyes of the man in the navy blue blazer. "Would you like to dahnce?" he said.

She stood up eagerly. "You're English!"

"This is true." He held out his arms, and soon they were on the floor dancing, if you could call it that. They lurched around together, feet colliding. "I'm not much of a dancer," he said, "but I couldn't figure out any other way of meeting you."

"That's so sweet," Nikki said. "Dancing's not hard. This is a slow song, a one-step. Let's just take some very small steps."

"Small steps? My name is Ian, by the way."

"I'm Nikki. Yes, small steps, little more than rocking back and forth. Like this. Doesn't that feel better?"

"Oh, yes," said Ian.

"Now get a little closer and close your eyes," said Nikki.

"Close my eyes?"

"So you can really hear the music and feel what I'm doing, really feel it. Closing your eyes helps you concentrate." Ian closed his eyes, and they moved together for a while. Nikki said, "See?"

"Oh, yes. This is utterly delightful."

Utterly delightful! Nikki wondered if he was gay. But if Ian was gay, why had he been so eager to meet her? No, he was just eloquent and enthusiastic and adorable. When the song ended, he said, "I haven't quite got the hang of it yet. Do you think we could have another go at it?"

18

Roberta

August, 1996

Roberta loved living in Manhattan, the best borough of the best city of the best country in the world. But on muggy summer mornings, she came to enjoy getting on the train and riding up to Westchester, where it was cooler, breezier, leafier. The company was still paying for her monthly MetroNorth ticket, and she was no longer bitter about her commute. Indeed, it gave her a good excuse not to shop and make dinner: how could she be expected to do all of that after a day in the office and a trip on the train? Paul made his own hours, and he was on an early schedule, so he either cooked for them or got them take-out. Paul was proving to be very easy to live with, although he had scolded her about not telling him about Kenny. She would never forgive Kenny for having spoiled her wedding—never!

Roberta looked out of her window at the office. It was a sparkling morning in August, and she watched two squirrels chase each other, racing up the trunks of trees, springing from branch to branch. Her phone rang; it was Nikki, from twenty feet away. They waved at each other.

"Hey," said Nikki, "I was thinking. Why don't you have lunch at my house today? I've got this salmon from last night. We can put it in a salad and eat in the garden. It's such a pretty day."

They ate on a wrought iron table on a slate stone patio. Instead of an umbrella, a tall Norwegian pine tree shaded the area. Roberta had to pull her chair out to feel the sun on her face. She leaned back and said, "Ahhhh. The sun."

Nikki asked, "How can something that feels so good be so bad for you?'

"What about Vitamin D?" countered Roberta.

"That's the good part. I was thinking melanoma."

"I'm okay," said Roberta. "I'm naturally dark. I get a good tan."

"You're lucky. I'm pale; I burn."

"It's that WASP heritage of yours," said Roberta.

"It's true—we wrinkle."

"Blacks have it best of all," said Roberta. "How old do you think Cynthia is?"

"Well, her kids are twenty-four and twenty-two, so she's probably... fifty?"

"Right. And she could be thirty. Except for those matronly clothes."

"You're right. She dresses like a preacher's wife. But with that Caribbean roll to her hips, she could make a housedress look sexy."

"Speaking of sexy," said Roberta, "how are you and Ian getting along?"

Nikki said nothing.

"Oh, my goodness, Nikki, you're *blushing!*"

"It's this thin, pale skin. I have nothing to blush about. Ian and I are getting on fine. Really fine."

"He's not kind of, oh, I don't know... metrosexual?"

"No! That's just his outward demeanor."

"So he's good in bed?"

"Oh, yeah. He's lusty and sensual and affectionate, too. He massages my feet while we watch TV. Then I massage his."

"Wow," said Roberta. Ian was a friend of Paul's, and she had only met him a couple of times before the wedding—never with a date. She couldn't imagine Ian relating physically to a woman, yet apparently he was good in bed! Of course, Nikki was a little man-crazy, so perhaps she was easily pleased. Now she watched as Nikki put the used lunch plates on a tray and carried them into the house. Because it was casual Friday, Nikki wore jeans: snug ones tight against her little butt. And a white cotton top with short lace sleeves. She was definitely dressing better lately. It was pleasant here in Nikki's garden, waiting for the coffee. Several small brown birds were pecking at the crumbs that had fallen under the table, and the yard was so densely forested you couldn't see the neighbors' houses. Lillian had left early for the weekend, so they were in no particular hurry to get back to work. Roberta considered herself a confirmed Manhattanite, but on days like this, in a garden like this, she could see the appeal of the suburbs.

"It sure is nice here," she said to Nikki, who was coming out with a red wooden tray.

"Maybe you should move."

"No, we could never leave the apartment. It's rent stabilized. Paul says it's like winning the lottery."

Nikki put the tray on the table and asked, "Aren't there income limits on rent stabilized apartments? You told me you make six figures, and a real estate lawyer like Paul must surely be doing quite well."

Roberta said mischievously, "Perhaps they don't know I've moved in." She glanced over at the tray, which contained a pot of fresh coffee, two cups, two spoons, a sugar bowl, a creamer, a cigarette lighter and... a joint. Roberta said, "Interesting coffee service."

"Are you interested?" asked Nikki.

"God, it's been years, I don't know."

"I smoke a lot," said Nikki.

"You're not frightened of getting caught and going to jail?"

"That doesn't happen these days. I think they just give you a fine. Anyway, sometimes I'm scared, but not on home territory." She lit the joint and inhaled deeply. "Casual Friday," she said after a while. "I often come to work high on Friday afternoons. You never noticed?"

Roberta shook her head.

Nikki continued, "I do my best planning Friday afternoons. Nobody phones and I've got my inspiration." She waved the joint and held it out to Roberta.

Roberta said, "All right. Just one hit."

"With just one hit you won't even feel it," complained Nikki, but Roberta felt it right away and was glad she had stopped at just one. She wasn't crazy about feeling high; she didn't like to be out of control. Meanwhile, Nikki was sucking it down greedily, again and again, as if it were pure oxygen. "I don't do other drugs," she said, "but I sure like my grass."

"And pharmaceuticals?" asked Roberta, who took Prozac every day.

"No. I'm naturally pretty cheerful. Pot just helps me relax. And it helps with the creative process. For instance, when I get back to the office, I'll probably work on a new general pitch to rehab facilities. Later, I'll just tweak it for each one."

Roberta was dismayed. She never worked on a general pitch; she sold based on her relationship with the decision maker. Her last sale had been to Allengate Spas, after several lunches with Esther Whitehall, whom she had met on the Washington trip. A real friendship was growing between them, for they were both considering adopting babies. Paul was keen to have a little boy, and when Roberta said she probably couldn't conceive, he suggested adoption and a full-time nanny. So Roberta began to get interested in the project. A little boy might be a lot of fun.

Roberta closed her eyes and let the sun warm her face.

Nikki asked, "So what are you guys doing this weekend?"

It seemed to Roberta that Nikki's voice came from far away. Roberta said, "We're meeting friends at a restaurant tonight. And tomorrow we're eating at Bouley."

"Wow. You guys eat out a lot."

"Well, sure. Don't you?"

"Almost never. It's so expensive. Ian has all this child support."

"Does he always pay for the meal?" asked Roberta.

"We sort of take turns."

"Well, don't you deduct your restaurant meals from your taxes? As a business expense?"

"No, Roberta—I'm not entertaining a client! Besides, Bethany always reimburses us for our entertainment expenses, so it's a wash—I couldn't deduct them."

Roberta was astonished at Nikki's naiveté. Roberta always deducted her meals when she ate out, no matter who she was with: client, friend, or Paul. Who would ever check on her? Last year she had deducted $12,420 in so-called business expenses, with credit card documentation for every penny. Roberta and Marlene sometimes cackled about the restaurant benefit of being in sales—usually during restaurant meals they would each deduct.

Nikki said, "Besides, I'd worry about getting caught."

"You smoke pot in your garden—and you worry about your business deductions?"

"I guess we worry about different things."

Roberta helped Nikki bring the lunch things to the kitchen. "Who's that?" she said, of the striking, androgynous photograph held by magnets to the refrigerator. It looked like a young, blond Patti Smith.

"That's my sister, Taylor. She lives out west."

"What does she do?"

"Something with the World Wide Web, I think. She's been working on something huge. She hasn't had a day off in months."

Roberta looked at her watch and jumped up. "Oh my God! We've been here almost two hours!"

"Yeah, I guess we should get back."

"Will you be able to drive?"

"Sure. I've taken the trip hundreds of times, and it's less than two miles."

"Maybe you should brush your teeth to get rid of the smoke smell," said Roberta. "You had a lot more than I did."

"I most certainly did," said Nikki. "Actually, before going back I'll do my six."

"What do you mean?"

"Tell you in the car."

Nikki put the long roach into a carved wooden box on the mantelpiece, and Roberta used the downstairs bathroom. She could hear Nikki above her using the upstairs bathroom and moving around quickly from one room to another. Nikki came downstairs, and they left for the car. After they'd strapped themselves in, Roberta asked Nikki, "So what are the six?"

Nikki slowly backed out of the driveway. "The six things I do after smoking pot so others won't know."

"And they are?"

Nikki drove down the street. "Brushing my teeth and eating a mint or some food. Washing my hands and putting on perfume. Squirting eye drops and taking an ibuprofen to avoid bloodshot eyes."

"Wow. You've got it down to a science. How does the ibuprofen work?"

"By constricting blood vessels to avoid inflammation. And some of those vessels are in the eyes."

Roberta was surprised by the random bits of science Nikki knew. She glanced at her friend. She knew Nikki was stoned, but there were no outward signs. Nikki drove them to work without incident, and as soon as they got to their desks she turned to her computer screen with real interest. Roberta, bored, glanced over from time to time. No doubt about it: Nikki was mesmerized, in the flow, high on her new pitch to the rehabilitation facilities.

19

Nikki's Journal

September 15, 1996

Once I was stoned when Ian unexpectedly stopped by, and I felt estranged from him; he seemed fussy, effeminate and short. I had the good sense to pretend I was my usual self and hoped he didn't notice how distant I really felt. We went for a moonlit walk by the harbor, and by the time we got home, I had come down, and Ian was dear to me again.

So I must never get high before seeing him. And I'm going to smoke less in general, maybe get my habit down to once a day. I want Ian and me to be on the same level, on the same wavelength, on the same plain. And he's not into weed, although he used to smoke a bit when he was "at university."

Oxford University.

What's so great about the Brits is their quick wits. They can think on their feet and find just the right word. They speak in graceful sentences. They make jokes. They are self-deprecating and funny. They are well educated. They recite poetry to you, and the lines are always apt. They know about current events. They don't natter on about their personal problems, yet they appear fascinated by yours. They wear quality clothes and get good hair-cuts. They like complicated kisses. I guess I'm not talking about the Brits—I'm talking about Ian. I'm really falling, I haven't felt like this in years. I can't think about him without smiling. Ian. Thank you. Sweetheart.

20

Nikki

October, 1996

When Nikki's sales commissions began exceeding her salary, she began liking her job a lot more, and when some paychecks reflected commissions twice the size of her salary, she exulted. She was ashamed to admit that being well paid made her enjoy her work more, but it was the truth. And it was wonderful to come home for lunch. She felt restored by this time in her house, with the afternoon sun flooding into her dining room. She often ate her salad there while reading the *New York Times*. How many people got to come home for lunch? Just she and Yvonne: it was their quiet bond. They'd sometimes ride the elevator up together after lunch, exulting in their fortune as non-commuters. Of course, they could never chat easily or even at all when Roberta was around.

Ian loved hearing about the conflicts at work. He'd say, "What's new at the office?" and listen with great interest as she described various squabbles and intrigues. And he adored hearing Lillian's malapropisms, especially "penultimate." "Write them down in a notebook," he told her. "They're too funny."

Now he patted the place beside him on the bed and said, "Get over here, wench." Nikki snuggled next to him, her back against the padded headboard. She sniffed him appreciatively; she had forbidden him to wear after-shave. He was in a tee shirt and pajama bottoms, and she wore a white cotton nightgown. Quiana was with David for the weekend, and Ian's ex was taking care of his three children, so Nikki and Ian were temporarily child-free. It was their first sleepover date, and she had laid out candles and changed the sheets, even though she knew men paid scant attention to such matters. Before now, no man except David had spent the night in this bed. She would have to stop thinking about things like that.

Ian took Nikki's foot in his lap and tenderly pulled her big toe. She smiled at him, and their eyes fused. She gazed at him. What if? What if he cares about me as much as I care about him? What if it's always like this between us? What if we get married? Bad, bad, don't think about that, it's much too soon for that. But don't you love kissing him like you are kissing him now, his fingers brushing your hair off your forehead and—

Nikki heard the front door unlock. Someone was in the house. She pushed Ian away. "Hear that?"

More noise downstairs.

"Who's there?" Ian asked Nikki.

"I don't know." Nikki jumped out of bed and put on her robe.

"I'll come with you." Ian pulled on his sweatshirt.

They left the bedroom and looked downstairs. The hall light was on, and Taylor was putting her jacket on a hook in the closet. Nikki said, "Taylor?" and motioned Ian back into the room. "It's just my sister," she said, but he didn't move.

"Nikki?" Taylor called up. "Sorry to barge in like this... " Her eyes took in Ian, and she said, "*Really* sorry to barge in like this, but my other arrangements... didn't work out."

Nikki said, puzzled, "You can come here any time, but why didn't you call?"

"I didn't want to wake you. I was visiting a friend near here, and I had a quarrel with them, so I thought I'd sleep here."

"*Them*?" asked Nikki. "Your friend is now a 'them' so you don't have to reveal 'their' gender?"

"Totally." Taylor looked up. "Shall I make us some tea?"

Five minutes later, they were sitting around the kitchen table. Nikki thought Ian looked adorable with his hair all mussed up. Rather like Hugh Grant, though not as obnoxiously good-looking.

"What are you doing in this part of the world?" Nikki asked.

"I was at this conference in New York." Taylor swallowed a little tea.

Nikki sighed. "You might have told me you'd be coming east."

"I'm only here for three days. And I thought I'd be... busy."

"The mysterious lover!" said Ian.

"No more mysterious than you are. Just a person."

"What conference are you attending?" Ian asked.

"TechnoWorld at Javits."

"Oh, really?" Ian sat up straighter. "I need to know more about that."

"Why?" asked Taylor. Nikki was curious herself.

Ian said, "I produce industry sector reports for big corporations, and from what I can tell, the World Wide Web is going to change every single industry, from publishing to manufacturing to hospitality to medicine. So I need to understand the technology, what's ahead. What's your interest?" he asked Taylor.

"I'm a computer science geek at Stanford," she said. "I want to see the latest stuff."

"What are you working on?"

"A few classmates and I are working on a way to organize the Internet. So you can find what you need."

"Think big!" said Ian.

"Why not?" said Taylor. "You see, right now, the user is just dumped into a world, but there's no map to it, no good way to get around."

"There's Lycos," said Ian.

Taylor wrinkled her nose. "We're doing a much better map."

"Hurry up, please," said Nikki. "I don't see why we're even connected to this web when it's so hard to navigate. And the load times! Just waiting for a page to appear on your screen can take minutes! I think the Internet is just a big hype."

"Trust me," said Taylor, with a smirk. "It's not."

"She's right," said Ian, putting down his mug of tea. "Remember how computers changed things? The Internet will change things even more. Just think how dependent on email we are. And that's just in the last couple of years! Who gets a personal letter through the U.S. mail any more?"

"You mean 'snail mail,'" sneered Taylor.

Ian said to Nikki, "It's the biggest societal change since the sixties counterculture."

"And you don't want to be left behind?" Nikki asked Ian.

He shook his head. "I *can't* be left behind. Among other things, my livelihood depends upon staying ahead. It's exciting. That's why I like what I do."

To Nikki, the business reports he produced were dry stuff, but Ian had enormous enthusiasm for his job. That was another thing about the Brits. They felt or feigned great enthusiasm, while New Yorkers usually affected ennui. This was the reverse of what one might expect, and Nikki thought it helped explain why New Yorkers found Britons so charming.

Soon, Taylor gave a big un-camouflaged yawn, and Nikki said, "Yes, it's that time." She stood up and began clearing the cups.

Taylor stood up and kissed Nikki. "'Night, big sister. See you in the morning." Then she said in a loud stage whisper, "I like that guy."

"That was an interesting interruption," said Ian, when he and Nikki returned to bed. "You don't look anything alike."

"Different dads," said Nikki.

"She's cute all the same," said Ian. "Well, not cute exactly, but appealing."

"She's very young, you know," said Nikki.

"You look about the same age."

"You're sweet."

"So she bats both ways?" Ian asked.

"I guess. Probably not simultaneously."

"Have you ever... ?"

"Had a threesome?" asked Nikki. "No." Then she remembered Washington. She added quickly. "A man and a woman at once—that would be weird." She snuggled up next to him. "I'm afraid I'm pretty sheltered. You know, I was married so long," she said, in mock apology.

"Have you ever had sex with a woman?"

She shook her head. "You with a guy?"

"Only in boarding school. A much younger boy. We, ah, just petted. He had flaxen hair."

"Well, in that case, who could resist?"

They began kissing again. After a time, Ian pulled away. "And one night stands?" he asked.

Nikki shook her head. "I don't find the idea exciting." She had waited more than a month before making love with Ian. "It's so much more interesting when there's a build-up, and time for speculation, and the friction between expectation and reality. Don't you think?" She raised her eyebrows coquettishly.

"I'm a guy," said Ian. "I'm fine with just the friction."

21

Roberta

October, 1996

Roberta was at the sink, helping her mother wash up. At the end of a meal, Henry simply rose from his seat and walked to his armchair in the den. Roberta felt washing up in someone else's kitchen was mildly interesting, for you got to use new varieties of sponge and soap and dishwasher. Her mother now bought yellow sponges backed by blue abrasive pads and an environmental liquid detergent that didn't seem to be very effective.

Golde swept the floor and asked, casually, "So are you going to make me a grandmother again?"

"Maybe," said Roberta.

"Have you missed a period?"

"No, Mom. I'm not pregnant. And I probably won't be, you know. But we're thinking of adopting."

"Paul wants to do this?"

"If we can get a baby boy. He has two daughters, and he's always wanted a son."

"You could try in vitro," suggested her mother. "And then test the embryo."

"I don't want to subject my body to all that. You need to take a lot of hormones." Truth was she didn't want to subject her body to *pregnancy*, even if she did manage to conceive. Adoption seemed an altogether better option, and this way, Paul would get a boy, guaranteed. She had to find out about adoptions from Russia and Guatemala. Forget China: they only had girls. And forget the United States. With Paul already forty-five, they were not likely to impress adoption agencies. Furthermore, Roberta would have to admit that she planned to get a nanny for the baby and go on working, because she liked what she did. But things might be different abroad. If you gave a big donation to the orphanage... Maybe she should investigate Vietnam, but—no, she was hoping she could adopt a baby who could pass as her natural child.

"Adopting a baby is expensive," said Golde.

"Mom, I save forty thousand a year living with Paul! We can afford to adopt."

"Then do it! No woman's life is complete without a baby."

"That's not true," said Roberta, "but I've come to think a baby boy would be good for me and Paul." She turned off the faucet and squeezed the sponge dry.

"Then do it," said Golde. "Paul's a good man. I'm sorry he couldn't be here today."

"He had to visit his father."

"See, that's what I mean. He's good, responsible. You know, Roberta, I didn't think you'd get ever married."

"Thanks, Mom."

"Oh, you're attractive to men, anyone can see that, but I've seen you get angry over nothing, exploding like a volcano! So I thought that you'd drive all the good men away. But Paul stayed with you. He saw your quality. He's a *mensch*."

"I almost never get angry at Paul," said Roberta. "Maybe that's why I married him. He doesn't do anything wrong." Except living next door to his ex, she didn't say. Golde had no idea about that.

"You wouldn't consider saying hello to Kenny?" asked Golde. "We could just go down and—"

"Mother, I never want to see him again. How many times must I tell you?"

"I'm sure he's sorry..."

"No, he's not. You're in denial, Mom. Kenny's not sorry for anything he ever does. That's part of his 'disorder.' He ruined my wedding, and he's proud of it. Stop asking me to forgive him."

"Your father thinks you should forgive him, too."

"*Dad?* Since when has Dad had any interest in my life?"

"Roberta, really! Don't say things like that."

"Yeah, never tell the truth," Roberta muttered. But her mother looked so distressed Roberta relented. "I know, I know, Daddy loves me. He just has an odd way of showing it."

22

Roberta's Film Diary

November 16, 1996
The First Wives Club. *I'm glad I saw this movie with Marlene & not Paul, because it's so anti-male. The unlikely premise is that four friends from college, now in their mid-forties, are all left by their husbands in the same year for younger, skinnier women. When one of the friends commits suicide, the other three get together after the funeral, joking that "this is a terrible excuse for a reunion." (Thru the movie, there's this great, peppy dialogue.) The ladies have lunch & decide to damage their exes. Their motto: "Not revenge, but justice!" Now it's true I can't perfectly relate to this scenario, as Paul is ten years older than I am, so I suppose I'm the "younger woman" (although Paul left Clarice long before meeting me, & she looks thinner than I am). But I can certainly relate to the idea of punishing people who do you wrong. The Diane Keaton character buys out her husband's ad agency & fires him. Bette Midler kidnaps her ex with the help of some thugs and has him sign his business to her. Goldie Hawn, playing a movie star insultingly cast as the mother of the ingénue her producer-husband is fucking, finds out the ingenue is only 16 years old & threatens to send her husband to jail for statutory rape. I liked that one, but I can think of other punishments for the others. Physical punishments. I would have arranged to have them beaten up. Maybe I'd have kicked them in the crotch. Or cut up all their clothes. Maybe I'd have keyed their cars, cut the brake-lines, sunk their boats. With them on board! Now that would be justice!*

23

Nikki

November, 1996

Ian got a promotion at work and decided to celebrate with Nikki, Paul and Roberta at Windows on the World. Nikki would have preferred going to a trendier place with better food, but Ian remained impressed with New York skyscrapers and New York views, and it was his night, his choice, his treat. Nikki and Ian emerged from the subway onto the World Trade Center plaza: they were meeting the others upstairs, on the 106th Floor. Nikki thought the concrete plaza looked cold and sterile, but Ian seemed enchanted. He bent backward to stare at the towers stretching above him. "Such power, such force!" he exulted. "Like a cathedral!"

"But cathedrals are beautiful. These are just concrete and glass monoliths, stark and brutal."

"To me, they're the thrusting manifestation of human mastery, stretching to the heavens."

"Not me," said Nikki. "Architecture like this leaves me cold. It's engineering, not art. There's nothing to delight the viewer."

"I find the Twin Towers inspiring. Awesome." He kissed her. "Almost as awesome as you."

"No, you," she said softly, kissing him back. She held his arm, and they entered the North Tower.

Upstairs, they checked their coats and walked to the reception desk. Nikki was wearing new high-heeled boots, and she was conscious of the little clicks she made with every step. She liked how the boots made her hips sway, not Cynthia's full Caribbean roll, but she could feel each hip go up/down, up/down. She wouldn't want to walk a mile in these boots, but they were fine for an entrance.

Paul rose, murmured "Wow," and sat down again, and Roberta said, "We got here early." She and Paul were drinking margaritas.

Nikki was about to sit opposite Roberta when Ian deftly guided her to the other seat, opposite Paul. He himself sat across from Roberta. "That's better," he said. "Man woman, man woman." Ian looked about him. "This is fabulous!" They were in the highest building in New York, and the windows gave onto the spires of Manhattan, the silvery rivers, the outer boroughs, and New Jersey. "We don't have anything like this in London."

"It is impressive," said Roberta. "Tourists love it."

"I guess I'm still a tourist," Ian said with a laugh.

Roberta touched the little golden ball that hung on a chain against her red silk blouse.

"That's a nice necklace," said Nikki. "I haven't seen that before."

"A birthday present from Paul," said Roberta.

The men were talking about which wine to order, a decision Nikki was glad to leave to others. She never understood this great fuss over wine. Even a fine wine wasn't as delicious as a glass of freshly-squeezed orange juice. To say nothing of the inferior high wine produced, compared to marijuana.

"Lillian's coming back on Monday," said Roberta. Their boss had been out sick for over a week. Rumor had it that she'd had a small stroke.

Nikki gave a sigh. "It would be so great if she never came back at all. It's a daily ordeal to be bossed by a woman as stupid and insulting as Lillian. How do you manage to get on with her?"

"I play her game. I tell her what she wants to hear. And I don't go around moving fax machines!"

Ian said, "What's this with fax machines?"

"Nikki never told you?"

Ian shook his head.

"Oh, it was Lillian at her finest." And Roberta gave a spirited account of the fax machine saga, complete with the arrival—and removal—of the rolling stool.

When the tale was over Paul said, "We'd better decide on our meal." They studied their menus. It was not an adventuresome offering, thought Nikki, but when the food arrived it was delicious, and it was thrilling to gaze down onto skyscrapers and out upon a million lights.

Ian told them about his new promotion, to vice president for publications, and they toasted his success. They finished one bottle of wine and were well into a second as they awaited dessert. Roberta reached for the bottle.

Paul put his hand over hers and said, "Are you sure?"

Roberta gave him a cold look and he removed his hand. She poured herself the last of the wine.

"Whatever happened to genre jokes?" asked Ian, breaking the silence. "You know, like knock-knock jokes."

"Yeah, or light bulb jokes," said Paul. "Like 'How many philosophers does it take to change a light bulb?'"

"How many?" asked Roberta.

Paul said, "It depends on how you define 'change.'"

They all smiled. "Wait, I have one," said Ian. "How many theologians does it take to change a light bulb?"

"How many?" asked Nikki.

Ian said, "God knows." They laughed, and Ian, pleased, said, "I made that up on the spot."

Paul said, "How many epistemologists does it take to change a light bulb?"

"How could *any*one know?" suggested Ian.

"Correct!" said Paul. "I made that up, too."

Nikki and the men laughed, but Roberta did not. Nikki said, "I'll rise to the challenge." She paused, her eyes faraway, seemingly over Brooklyn. Then she grinned. "OK! So how many chaos theoreticians does it take to change a light bulb?"

"How many?" asked Paul.

"None," said Nikki. "They just get the butterfly to flap its wings a second time."

There was a moment of silence—then Paul and Ian burst into laughter. When Nikki caught Ian's eyes, he gasped, "The butterfly!"

Roberta wasn't laughing. "I don't get it," she complained. "What's so funny?"

"Never mind," said Paul, "If it has to be explained, it's not funny."

"What, you think I won't understand it?" She glared at them all. "Will somebody please explain?"

There was an uncomfortable silence, into which Nikki finally plunged. "Well, okay. Chaos theory holds that the world is so complex and interdependent that it's simply impossible to predict the consequences of any single action. The most minuscule acts can have large-scale results. So, in the classic example, the flap of a butterfly's wings in Brazil might create tiny changes in the atmosphere that would ultimately set off a tornado in Texas."

There was a stony silence before Roberta said, "And that's supposed to be funny?"

Paul said, "Sweetheart, what's this all about?"

Roberta's voice was loud and angry. "You all think you're so superior because of this chaos theory? And epistemediology!"

"Oh, come on, Roberta," said Nikki.

Ian said, gallantly, "I, for one, confess I *am* superior! I've half a mind to join Mensa, but... they probably wouldn't take me, with only half a mind!"

The sheer silliness of Ian's joke set Nikki and Paul laughing again.

"Excuse me," said Roberta, standing abruptly. "Ladies room." And she left in a hurry.

"Is she okay?" Nikki asked Paul.

"Sometimes she gets moody. If she's been drinking, any little thing can set her off."

"But it was just a joke," said Nikki. "Not even a funny one. All the humor derives from the set up, the epistemologists or chaos theoreticians scratching their heads at the light bulb..."

"I like your theologians," Paul said to Ian. "God knows why."

Nikki stood up. "I'd better see how she's doing."

She opened the ladies room door. She expected to see Roberta by the mirror, brushing her lustrous dark hair or applying more lipstick. But she didn't see her friend anywhere. Then she heard someone crying behind a locked stall. "Roberta?" she called.

"Go away!" said Roberta.

Nikki said, "If you don't mind, I have to pee."

"Go yuck it up some more with Paul and Ian." More sobs. Then from the stall: "This is just what you like, isn't it? You and two men!"

"What are you talking about?" said Nikki, knowing full well and rushing onward. "Why are you getting so upset just because you didn't get some stupid joke?"

"Because the whole idea was to humiliate me," said Roberta. "Now get out of here."

"Roberta, it wasn't about you at all." Nikki entered the stall next to Roberta's and pulled down her pants and panties. "No one was trying to humiliate you! You're being paranoid. Don't spoil such a nice evening."

"*You're* the one who spoiled the evening with that joke about chaos theory." Nikki could hear Roberta opening the door of her stall.

Nikki called, midstream, "What about Paul's joke *first* about epistemologists? We were all just goofing around."

She could hear Roberta washing her face at the sink. Then Roberta said, "Well, goof around without me."

Nikki tore off some toilet paper from the roll and wiped herself. "Come on, Roberta. Let it go."

Roberta didn't answer. By the time Nikki flushed the toilet, drew on her panties, pulled up her pants, zipped her zipper, buckled her belt and left the stall, Roberta was nowhere to be seen. Nikki washed her hands, renewed her lipstick, brushed her hair, and spritzed on perfume. She was not looking forward to returning to the others. Why was Roberta so touchy?

Finally, Nikki went back to the table, click-clicking in her boots. Roberta and Paul were gone, their desserts untouched at their places. "What happened?" asked Nikki, sitting down at her place.

"Roberta made him leave," said Ian. "She said she had a terrible headache. She apologized to me and said to tell you goodnight."

Nikki said, "I wonder what brought it on?"

"Perhaps those jokes made her feel intellectually insecure."

Nikki said, "Even if I felt that way—"

"Which you never would," interjected Ian.

"But even if I did, I'd never let it show. I have too much pride for that."

"She'll probably forget about it by Monday."

"Roberta? Are you kidding?"

Nikki dreaded going to the office Monday morning. Not only would Lillian be back, but Roberta might not be speaking to Nikki after the Windows on the World debacle. Nikki hated the silent treatment and was fully prepared to eat humble pie to make peace. Immediately after taking off her coat, Nikki went to Roberta's desk. "How are you feeling?" she asked. "Headache gone?"

"Yes," said Roberta. "I'm sorry I had to run out on you like that."

Good! Roberta was still talking to her. "Oh, that's okay," said Nikki. "These things happen. Ian took home Paul's dessert."

Roberta gave a small smile. "What about mine?"

"Girl, I scarfed down that crème brulee right on the spot!"

"Perhaps I drank a bit too much," admitted Roberta.

"It happens," said Nikki, returning to her desk, relieved to buy into the headache and drinking story. She couldn't cope with the meltdown that might ensue if she suggested that Roberta had over-reacted to a couple of innocent jokes.

Then again, mused Nikki, how innocent were those jokes? In a way, they were smug, because they relied upon your sudden feeling of triumph when you understood them, and, according to the English philosopher Anthony Ludovici, this sudden feeling of superiority is the main cause of laughter. There had been that two-second silence before Paul and Ian had laughed at her chaos joke, and in those seconds, they had made a leap, as across a synaptic void, and they had landed safely on the other side and were laughing in relief and validation. So perhaps the joke that makes you laugh is the one you have to work at a bit, which is why when you comprehend a joke in a foreign language, it seems uproarious.

"Lillian's already here," said Roberta. "We should go into her office and welcome her back."

"Must we?" asked Nikki.

"We must. She's our boss. Come on."

Lillian was at her desk, on the phone. She held up one finger and continued babbling into the phone. There was only one empty chair in her office, and neither Nikki nor Roberta wanted to claim it. Nikki began creeping away, but Lillian said, "Wait, I'll be there in a moment," and Nikki was trapped.

24

Roberta

December, 1996

This year, the Christmas Party was held at a high-end Italian restaurant in a loft building with windows overlooking the throughway. A deejay was playing a Joan Jett song as Roberta and Nikki got drinks and milled around, trading bonhomie and assessing everyone's clothes, including each other's. Roberta was wearing a black cocktail dress, and Nikki was wearing a slim blue shantung pantsuit with no blouse. Once again, Roberta thought, Nikki was displaying too much cleavage. Cynthia wore a modestly cut red dress with a green necklace.

Nikki nudged Roberta. "Over there. The guy I was telling you about." He was tall and pale with dark hair, badly cut. Right now he was trying to hold a glass of wine and cut a slice of cheese at the same time. "They just hired him. We should go say hello, make him feel at home."

"You are so man-crazy," said Roberta. She was on her second bloody Mary and intended to have three.

"If I were man-crazy," said Nikki, "I wouldn't be working at Bethany! He's the only possible candidate in the company." They walked across the room toward the new IT hire. "Hi! You're new here, aren't you?"

He nodded. He was chewing cheese on bread.

Up close, Roberta saw that he was probably about twenty-five. Hardly a candidate!

"Welcome to the Bethany Moore Company! I'm Nikki, and this is Roberta. We're both in sales."

"I'm in IT. I'm Vlad." He had a Russian accent. Roberta listened more attentively. "Just started work here two weeks ago."

"Do you live nearby?"

He shook his head. "Live in Brighton Beach, Brooklyn."

What was it about accents? Hevron's accent had been part of his charm. Roberta found Vlad's accent, and only his accent, quite exciting. "That's a long commute," she said.

Nikki chimed in about how lucky she was to live so close to work. Next thing, thought Roberta, she'll be asking him over for lunch. And sure enough, Nikki said, "You really should..." and Roberta waited, but Nikki continued, ". . . get to know this area a little. Walk to the water or have lunch in the park. Who knows? You might want to live here and have no commute."

"Would be nice," he agreed, "but I live with family."

"Are you married already?" asked Nikki.

"No, I mean mother and father."

Roberta saw that he was not unhappy with that situation, the way American men of that age might be. How would she feel if the child she adopted with Paul grew up and kept living with them at twenty-five or thirty? She had to smile: she hadn't even met the baby she would adopt, and here she was worrying about him returning to the nest after college. She wondered if Nikki wanted more children, and whether this would be a problem for Ian, who already had three.

"Well, Vlad," Nikki was saying, "any time you get bored in IT, come visit us in sales! We can have a glass of tea in the kitchen. Russians drink tea in glasses, right?"

"Is true," said Vlad, darting a glance at her cleavage.

"Merry Christmas," said Nikki, turning away to talk to Yvonne.

Roberta noticed that they walked across the room for their chit-chat. Like I care, she thought, trying to keep Vlad talking so she could isolate what it was about his accent she found so attractive.

After dinner, there were the usual speeches. Then Bethany stood at the front of the restaurant to announce the awards. The Employee of the Year award went to Pedro Ramirez in the mailroom. "And now," said Bethany, "It's time to announce the winner of the sales contest, and the prize is, as usual, a trip to the Caribbean. Folks, you know we have a crackerjack sales team. And this has been a year of great growth. Our organic line now comprises 12% of our business. Next year, we expect that segment to grow even more. And our classic line is also doing very well. We may have to hire another sales person."

Now Roberta was *sure* they were expanding into Long Island, the territory she coveted. As Bethany rambled on, Roberta realized she would have to speak to Lillian about how it would be cheaper to hire an assistant than another sales person. This should be easy after the announcement tonight: the contest was for who'd brought in the most new clients, and she'd brought in four since September alone. This would be her third win in a row, and she didn't see how Lillian could deny her at least the chance to show that she could handle Nassau County in addition to her present territory, as long as she had a good assistant.

It would be great to be the only sales rep with her own assistant.

"And the winner of the sales contest is... Nikki Elkins!"

Nikki! Roberta couldn't believe it. How was that even possible? Nikki hadn't mentioned any new clients lately, that sneak. Roberta stared as Nikki walked to Bethany to get her kiss and her certificate.

"We're very proud of you," said Bethany. "You have real talent. And intelligence. And charm."

Had Bethany said anything nearly as nice to her when she had won last year? Roberta didn't think so. When Nikki stepped back to their group, Roberta heard Cynthia tell Nikki, "You see? I knew you would win it this year."

Nikki said, "I've never been to the Caribbean! I'm so excited."

Roberta said, flatly, "Congratulations." She tossed back what was left in her glass.

Nikki said, "Thanks. I'm glad they counted new clients, not sales, this year. You have the most sales, Roberta. You take home the most money, and you always will."

"I don't care about the stupid sales contest," said Roberta loudly, "so you don't have to console me."

Lillian barged into their group. "I hope you two aren't quarreling? We can't have our biggest stars fighting at our Christmas party."

"We weren't quarreling," said Nikki. "We're friends."

"Work friends, anyway," murmured Roberta. She just couldn't help herself.

"Work friends?" asked Nikki.

"We're not *real* friends, you know."

Nikki looked like she'd been whipped, and Roberta added, "Don't look so shocked!"

"Whatever," said Nikki, her eyes filling with tears as she turned away.

Good! This shouldn't be a perfect day for skinny Miss Superior. Roberta heard Cynthia tell Nikki, "Don't fret about her. You know what a temper she has."

"But I didn't do anything. Why is she acting like that?"

Roberta heard Yvonne respond loudly, "Jealousy, just jealousy."

That was the last straw, and from that cow. "Jealous?" yelled Roberta. "You think I need to win a sales contest to know how good I am?" Conversations stopped as Roberta went on, a righteous rage emerging. "Why would I be jealous of that la-dee-dah bee-atch?"

"Why are you attacking me?" asked Nikki. "Why don't you calm down?"

"Oh, I know your game, Miss Snob! Trying to make me look stupid and crazy!"

For a moment, Nikki was silent. Then, and it was as if a dam had finally burst, she yelled back, "No one has to *make* you look crazy. You *are* crazy. Crazy and paranoid, just like your lunatic brother!"

Roberta felt her heart go white. She had never told anyone at the office about Kenny.

Nikki was telling everyone, "Her brother's so nuts he tried to stop her wedding! Said she was an FBI agent. They had to take him away, raving. Well, these things run in families. Everybody knows that."

"Shut up your bony face!" screamed Roberta as she ran out of the room and down the restaurant stairs. There was silence in back of her. Silent Night, Roberta thought. Merry Christmas to all!

She called a taxi to get to the train station. She felt waves of nausea. Perhaps that last drink had been a mistake.

At home, she took one look at Paul and burst into tears.

He held her to him and said, "What happened, sweetheart?"

"I hate that woman, I just *hate* her," sobbed Roberta.

"What did Lillian do now?" asked Paul, with just enough amuse-ment in his tone to inflame Roberta. She pulled back to look him in the eye.

"Not Lillian, you dodo, *Nikki*."

"Nikki? But she's your friend."

"Not any more! She told everyone about Kenny and called me a lunatic, too. I'll never forgive that bitch, never, never, *never*." She began sobbing anew.

"Take me back to the beginning," said Paul, holding out a tissue. "What was the first thing that happened?"

When he had heard the whole story, Paul asked, "Would any of this have occurred if you hadn't been drinking?"

The bastard! "What, now it's my fault, I'm a drunk?"

"I just asked a simple question. You got all paranoid at the World Trade Center when we had dinner with Ian and Nikki, and now you got enraged because for once you didn't win the sales contest or Yvonne taunted you or something, and both times you'd been drinking."

Roberta was silent.

Paul went on, "I *know* you've been drinking today because I can smell the alcohol coming off your skin. Roberta, you're drinking too much, and it's damaging you."

She sniffled. "What do you mean 'damaging'?"

"It's not good for your image to get into a shouting match at the company Christmas party."

"She was much more abusive!"

"It's not good for her, either, but you're the seasoned professional. You have to stay in control. And you have to stop drinking like this."

"What, I should go to AA?"

"That's a good idea," said Paul.

She wanted some wine at the very thought of it, but obviously she couldn't have any here, in front of Paul. It would only confirm his stupid belief that she was an alcoholic or something. Luckily, she had a secret bottle of vermouth in the back of her closet, about a quarter full.

Paul kept at it. He found a schedule of AA meetings in the neigh-borhood and nagged her until she agreed to go to one. By then, after finishing the closet vermouth, she had gone five days without drinking: surely the longest time since she had left—or maybe started—college. She missed the lift wine gave her, but she didn't feel bad. No heebie-jeebies, no spiders! She was doing okay. She didn't have to or want to talk about drinking or abstaining with a bunch of strangers, but she finally told Paul she would go to a meeting just to get him off her case.

He walked her to a nearby church, where the meeting was held in the basement. She thought this was a gallant gesture, and she kissed him goodbye fondly until she realized he had walked her to the door to make sure she would really attend the meeting.

Roberta looked around. There were twenty or so people in folding chairs, waiting for the meeting to begin. It was a seven o'clock meeting, so many of them were still in their work clothes. Young, older, black, brown, white, gay and straight: it seemed a reasonable cross section of the city, perhaps skewed to the young. She was dreading the moment she would have to introduce herself as an alcoholic, as if that was her defining characteristic, but she would take the plunge and see what came next. At least she didn't know anybody here.

"How did it go?" asked Paul. He was waiting for her at a local restaurant, one which didn't have a liquor license yet. She sat down across from him and shook her head.

"What?"

"It's just not for me," she said. "All that storytelling, all that confessing."

"Did you say anything?"

She shook her head again. "Introducing myself was bad enough—even though I gave a false name."

"Roberta! It's supposed to be based on honesty!"

"Well, I'm not going back, so it doesn't matter."

He stared at his plate, downcast.

"You really think I need to stop drinking?" she asked.

He nodded. "It's just you sometimes fly off the handle when you're drunk."

"Maybe I need to fly off the handle."

"Maybe you need therapy," said Paul.

Roberta thought this conversation was really going astray. "Tell you what. I'll stop drinking completely for a month, and then go back to drinking less."

"You can just do that?" he asked.

"Yeah. I haven't had a drink in five days, not a problem, I can stay sober. I just don't want to go to meetings."

"And if you lapse? If you take a drink before the month is up?"

"Then I'll go to a meeting," said Roberta. "But meetings will only remind me that I'm not drinking, and I'd rather do something else, really anything else, even a Pilates class!"

"I see your point," said Paul. "All right. Tell you what. I'll keep you company. I won't drink for a month, either."

"Really? But why?"

"I love you, babe," he said. "I want to make your life easy and good."

25

Nikki

February, 1997

Nikki and Ian had removed the armrest between their two seats and were pressed together aloft. He was reading an article about how Dolly the sheep had been recently cloned from a single mammary cell that had somehow been reset to become an embryo again. She wasn't reading the open paperback novel she was holding. She was too happy to read. Here she was with this wonderful man, on their way to Guadeloupe, away from the miserable cold and dirty snow of February; away from the office, where Roberta had become enemy number one: there was just no appeasing her. One week away from all that: a week of being with Ian, day after glorious day, Ian who was stroking her ear even as he was reading about the implications of cloning as a technology, Ian her beloved. It was getting harder and harder not to tell him she loved him.

She felt, once again, a stab of guilt regarding Quiana, whom she'd left with David. Another year, she'd have gone to the Caribbean with her daughter—but now, she had chosen Ian, and here he was beside her on the plane. Her vacation voucher permitted them a few days at each of two hotels on the island, in the north and in the south. The north was the tamer part, with sandier beaches, better snorkeling, and more tourists. The south was more luxuriant, with mountains and jungles and deserted beaches. She had once told herself she'd be happy to be with Ian for a week anywhere: say, in a basement in Hoboken or a motel room in Des Moines. Instead, Guadeloupe lay ahead.

They were both fair, so they diligently applied sunscreen to themselves and each other several times a day: before breakfast, which was outdoors under a thatched roof; before going to the beach; after swimming. She liked that Ian was only a few inches taller than she was: it made it easy for her to reach his shoulders with the sunscreen, easy to hold hands as they walked along the beach, easy to wear each other's clothes. He looked very good in her blue sweatshirt, and she liked to wear his faded jeans, cinching them with a leather belt. Nikki loved that, unlike David, Ian was never rattled or ill-tempered, not even on the first night, when they napped past dinner time and had to concoct a meal from food at the gas station mini-mart. She adored looking up at Ian when they made love to see his eyes closed, his mouth parted in bliss.

On the second day, they drove to the northernmost part of the island, where they parked on a hill. A long, uninhabited isthmus stretched out before them, receding into the distance, with sandy coves on either side, lashed by the ocean spray. The strip was perhaps a quarter mile wide and ten miles long: a gray-green ribbon with beige, scalloped edges, pounded by the surf. She had never seen geography like this before, and Ian took out his camera and posed her in the foreground. Then she took her camera out and posed him. A young couple from France soon joined them at the view spot, and Ian, who spoke good French, held out her camera so that they would have a picture of the two of them together in this spot. When Nikki developed the film, the photo would show them with windswept hair, sunglasses, pink cheeks, and broad smiles. She would keep that picture always.

The next night, there was a festival in a nearby market town, and the street was cordoned off. Nikki and Ian ate *boudin* and rice on paper plates and drank rum drinks outdoors. When a steel band began playing and people began dancing in the street, Nikki stood up. Ian joined her. They began dancing apart, which was good, Nicole thought, because Ian was game but awkward. His movements were unnatural, contrived. "Just let the music flow through you," she said.

"I am."

A sleek and graceful black man of thirty was dancing alone near them. His eyes caught Nikki's, and he held out his hand. She meant only to shake his hand, to be part of a merry, egalitarian scene, but he took her hand and drew her into him so they were partner-dancing to the steel drums. He spun her out and she turned and shimmied back. Oh, this was fun, dancing with a man who knew the moves. All you had to do was be attentive and respond to a pressure here, a look there. From the corner of her eye, Nikki saw Ian sit down. Then her new partner held out his arm and sent her out and she was laughing into his eyes before she spun around. Then—how did he do this?—he put her hand around his waist and turned so they were promenading to the reggae beat. She began to sweat but was too euphoric to stop. This was why you traveled: to have unexpected, festive encounters. She saw Ian watching her, and she smiled at him. The lively song segued into a slow number, and Nikki's partner pulled her close to him to dance. This was not so nice, and she pulled away so there was some space between them, but a few bars later, he pulled her to him again and murmured *"Doudou"* into her ear. At least, it had to be spelled that way, didn't it? He couldn't be saying "Do, do," or "Doo-doo."

"C'est quoi, ce doudou?" she asked: what is doudou?

Perhaps he hadn't heard; perhaps he was saying "doux-doux," or soft-soft. What would that be, her skin? She pulled away again, and he held out his arm so she could twirl under it, but on her return, he pulled her against him again, and she was tired of fighting, she let him press her against him, and, once again, he said into her ear, *"Doudou."* Finally, finally, the music ended and Nikki pulled away to sit next to Ian. "Whew," she said. "I need another drink."

"Then let's get you one." They bought another round of rum drinks at an outdoor bar.

"I got so hot dancing," she said, when they sat down again.

"I noticed."

"You don't mind?"

"No," said Ian. "I'd just like to know what he said into your ear."

"So would I. It sounded like 'doudou, doudou'—I don't have a clue." Nikki asked a young woman sitting at a nearby table. *"Ca veut dire quoi, doudou?"*

"Sweetheart," the girl said. "Lover."

Nikki blushed and hoped that Ian hadn't heard.

The band began playing another reggae number, and, suddenly, there was the man again, with his white smile in the night, holding out his hand.

Nikki shook her head and said, *"Merci, non."*

"Merci, oui," he said, holding up one finger solemnly. *"Un fois plus."*

"Just one more," she said to Ian, "OK?"

"Whatever you like."

And Nikki and the stranger were in perfect synch again: he led her through one new move after another, and she never missed a beat. If I were a man, she thought, the first thing I'd do is learn how to dance—such an easy approach to physical contact with strangers, such a fine way to establish rapport. Her hands were getting slippery with sweat, and not only her hands. The song seemed to last half an hour, or had there been three or four songs all melded together? *"Merci,"* she said at last. *"Je suis fatiguee."* And she sat down again beside Ian. The ice in her drink had melted, which was good because there would be more liquid to drink, and she was very thirsty. She downed the drink in several swallows, as if it was water, while Ian watched.

"We'd better get you back while you can still walk to the car."

"You exaggerate, darling," said Nikki, but she stumbled on the cobblestone street. She gripped his arm, stumbled again, giggled. "Wow, those rum drinks sure make you feel good! Maybe we should drink rum more often."

"Maybe not," said Ian. "We can't have you falling down in the street." He helped her into the car, and she sang as they drove. She thought she sounded pretty good.

He pulled into a parking space at the hotel. "You wait there while I come around."

So she sat there smiling, and then he was opening her door, and she got out and once again leaned against Ian, this wonderful man. They walked down the path to their stairway and up the stairs to their room. She moved to the bed and, lay down, facing the ceiling, spreading wide her arms and legs. Truth to tell, she wasn't feeling so good any more. "Ian? Could you get me some water?"

"In a jiff."

It wasn't only this thirst, it was that with her eyes closed she was very dizzy, so she opened them to steady herself, only to find that the ceiling was moving in an arc, and when she looked at the walls, they were moving, too, back and forth, back and forth, and this was so frightening she closed her eyes again, which did not stop the dizziness, nor the nausea.

Ian was beside her, holding the glass of water. She managed to sit up and grasp the glass. She took a few swallows, then handed him back the glass and fell back against the pillow.

"I think you had too much to drink," he said.

"It felt so nice... for half an hour."

"And now?"

"I'm not thirsty any more, I'm..." Nikki leaped out of bed and made it to the bathroom just in time. She vomited into the toilet, eyes closed, because she didn't want to see any part of the dinner they'd eaten. *Boudin*. Blood sausage.

"OK in there?"

She was gasping and shuddering. "I'm getting it out," she called. Then another spasm wracked her. No question: alcohol was poison to her particular system. She would definitely stick to marijuana. She never wanted to feel like this again.

She washed her hands and face and brushed her teeth. She opened the window. She searched under the sink until she found a square plastic container designed to hold ice for drinks. She brought this back to her nightstand and lay down.

"Do you feel any better?" asked Ian.

"Not much. I'm afraid I just can't drink. If I drink enough to feel good, I get sick."

"Were you always like this?"

"More so lately. My substance of choice is pot, of course, but I didn't want to bring it across a foreign border."

"I should think not."

"It's just so unfair!" said Nikki. "Alcohol is far more dangerous, yet there are bars and liquor stores everywhere. And I'm made to feel like a criminal because I smoke a little grass. Oh. *Oh*. Ian, please leave the room," she gasped, and she reached for the square plastic container and retched into it. Another half pint came out. When she was finished, she tottered to the bathroom and poured the vomit into the toilet. Once more, she cleaned herself up and returned to bed. She was relieved to find the room was empty, and she got into bed once again. Now the ceiling scarcely moved.

When Ian came back, she said, "I'm much better now. I'm so sorry."

"It could happen to anyone," he said, but she thought he sounded cold.

"I just have to remember my limited capacity."

"Cheap date," said Ian, on his way to the bathroom. Then he murmured, "In more ways than one."

He closed the door, and Nikki waited. When he came out of the bathroom, she was sitting up in bed. She asked, "What do you mean about cheap?"

"Oh, never mind."

"No, really!"

"The way you were carrying on with that guy! All that exuberant movement. And letting him press up against you."

"I tried to stop him doing that! Hey, I'm flattered by your jealousy, but I was just having fun dancing with a stranger in a foreign land. I had no idea you'd take it this way."

"Well, I had no idea you don't know your own limits!" Ian was staring out the window. He muttered, "If you can't drink, *don't* drink."

"Well, aren't you Mr. Uptight!"

"It's not exactly pleasant seeing my girlfriend barf into a carafe."

"I said I was sorry. My body's punishing me enough—you don't have to add to my misery." She glared at him, tears in her eyes.

He stared back at her. She knew they were having the same thought: they were having their first fight.

"I'm sorry," said Ian, pulling them back from the slope. He sat on the bed beside her. "I'm being beastly."

Relief washed over her. "You are," she said. "Why?"

"You danced so well with him. I'll never move like that."

"Maybe not. But you have all the right moves where it counts."

He touched her neck. "Is that a come on? I hope."

"Can you wait until morning?"

He looked at his watch. "How do you define 'morning'?"

The next day, they packed up and went to the south side of the island. Their new hotel had Internet access, and after they checked in and put down their luggage, Ian went down to the lobby to check his email on a computer in an alcove to one side. "We're on vacation," said Nikki. "I'm not going to bother."

"There may be something important for me," said Ian.

"Go on, then. I'll go down with you to get a map."

A couple about her age was checking in, and Nikki chatted with the woman. "What are your plans?" Nikki asked.

The woman, whose hair had been braided into forty blond braids, said, "My basic plan is to get loaded after breakfast and loaded after lunch and loaded after dinner!"

"I'll drink to that!" said her boyfriend or husband. They followed the bellboy out of the lobby. Nikki stared after them, imagining what it would be like to tell a stranger, "My basic plan is to get high after breakfast and high after lunch and high after dinner." Why was it considered okay (perhaps comic, but also commendable) to brag about drinking, which damaged your liver and made you aggressive, but a terrible faux pas to allude to marijuana, which was healthy for the body and made you calm? It was so unfair.

Nikki returned to their new room. The hotel was in the mountains, and from the private balcony, you got a splendid view of the sea far below. Nikki put on her bikini. She loved the feeling of the sunlight and water on as much of her skin as possible. Completely naked was the best way to experience the sun and the sea. Perhaps one day she and Ian would go to a nude beach, though she didn't think nudism was his cup of tea. But maybe if they found themselves on some isolated beach they could put their entire bodies into the elements... She put her beach dress over her bathing suit, changed her earrings, and picked up her the second of her Guadeloupe novels. Days were so much longer on vacation!

Twenty minutes later, Ian was back. Nikki said, "You must have had a lot of important mail."

"Nothing important," he said cheerily. "But I found myself opening it all. What's next, my beauty?"

"I thought we'd go to one of those secluded beaches," said Nikki.

She held out the map. "Like this one." She pointed to a spot a few miles from their hotel.

"Sounds good," said Ian. "Let me change."

The beach wasn't entirely deserted: a young tourist couple was frolicking in the froth of the waves, and a local family was having a picnic under some small trees. But soon, the young couple left, chattering in French about where to have lunch. A little after that, the family left, too.

"Shall we go for a swim?" Nikki asked Ian.

"Let me this finish this chapter."

"Well, I'm hot. I'm going in." She hoisted her beach dress over her head and checked to see if her bikini top needed adjusting. She took off her watch and tucked it into her handbag. Then she ran to the water and made a shallow dive into the curl of a wave.

Ahhh. With water this warm there was no entry shock, just the feeling of slipping from one medium to another in effortless immersion. She had her diving mask on, because you could sometimes see fish in these amazingly clear waters, and, yes, even now, there were six or seven iridescent blue ones, each perhaps eight inches long, swimming together. Then she felt herself rise on a new swell of wave and brought her head out of the water. She was further out than she'd thought. The swell subsided, and she reached for the ground with her feet but she was over her head, which wouldn't usually bother her, but she had heard that some beaches here had a riptide. She began swimming strongly toward shore. She kicked hard and did ten crawl strokes before looking about. She was out even further than she'd been before. She was rising up and down with the swells and getting carried out to sea. She couldn't seem to make any progress toward shore, and she was getting tired. She called, "Ian. Ian."

He was immersed in his book.

"Ian! IAN!"

He looked up and gave her a merry wave.

"Help! HELP ME!"

He waved again.

"HELP!"

He leaped up, dropping his book, and ran to the water's edge. He plunged in, still wearing his shirt, and began swimming toward her.

She headed toward him, this time on a diagonal toward shore to meet him. She used all the strength in her arms, in her legs, and it seemed she made a little progress now, and he was coming toward her. She kept flailing toward him, and after a time, she put her foot down and felt the ground beneath her feet, before being lifted on a swell, but afterwards she felt the ground again and knew she was safe. Less panicky now, she swam the last strokes to Ian who was standing up in the waves. She grabbed his shoulders, and he took her in his arms.

"There's a riptide," she gasped.

"I felt it," he said. They held each other for a moment. Then they walked against the water toward shore, fighting the undertow. They came out of the water.

The sun was so strong they were practically dry by the time they reached their towels. Nikki said, "Thank you for saving my life."

"You saved yourself," Ian said. "You would have made it."

"Maybe not. There was that terrifying moment when you were just waving at me when I was yelling 'help'!"

"You were smiling when you called. I thought you were joking."

"Smiling? I was terrified."

"How about I put sunscreen over you and you put it over me?"

Nikki looked about. They were still alone on the beach. "*All* over," she suggested. She reached for the bottle of sunscreen.

He said, "Someone could come."

"We'll cover up then," she said. "I want to feel the sun all over."

"You want to show off that great bod."

"Just to you." She took off her bathing suit top and her bathing suit bottom.

"You bold wench!" said Ian, pulling down his bathing suit.

They oiled each other up, with special attention to the newly exposed areas. They lay back on their towels, she with her dress on hand, he with a shirt, in case they needed to cover up fast. The sun warmed them all over; it was a sunbath. She closed her eyes and was drifting off to sleep, when Ian shook her shoulder and said, "Darling. We have to get dressed. People are coming."

She looked over the rise to the end of the road, and sure enough, another tourist couple was approaching. Nikki had an easy time of it, just pulling the dress down over her head, but Ian was still hopping into his suit as the others drew closer. The man of the couple said, in French, that they didn't have to get dressed for them, and Ian said they were leaving anyway and warned them about the riptide. "I'm really hungry," he told Nikki.

"Me, too. I hope they're still serving lunch somewhere." They packed up and walked to the car. They ate grilled fish at a tiny restaurant, with only five tables. They drove back to the hotel with the windows open so they could feel the warm breeze on their arms. He had his right hand on her thigh. She had her left hand on his neck. They were singing, "Riding on the City of New Orleans."

Back at the hotel, Ian said, "I'll just check my email."

"Leave it behind!" she said. "We're on vacation."

"Quick look," he said, and although she knew there was no such thing, what could she do? She went upstairs without him. Why was it so important to be connected to the office all the time? She certainly wasn't, never would be, not while Lillian was her boss and not until Roberta ended her ridiculous vendetta.

Nikki wondered whether she'd have enough time to write in her journal, then decided she wouldn't take the chance of being caught in the act. Despite her best precautions, over the years, her journal had been read by others several times, never to happy results. When she was fourteen, her mother had read about a petting party "because your diary was lying open on your desk." When she was sixteen, her best friend Beth read all about a recent fight they had had and Nikki's thoughts about why their friendship should end. When she was twenty-five, her husband David alluded to an incident about nose-picking she was sure she'd confided only to her journal, and she'd been embarrassed and indignant.

With Ian, the problem would be he'd see how often she thought of him, how much she loved him.

The door opened, and he walked in. He put down his beach bag and went to the window. He just stared out.

Nikki said, "Ian? Bad news?"

He nodded.

"What is it?" She moved to where he stood at the window and touched his arm. He drew violently back from her. Startled, she said,

"Hey!"

"Don't touch me," he said. "OK?"

"For God's sake, what is it?"

"I got an email from Roberta," he began. He looked white. "She said you..." He shook his head, he couldn't go on.

"Ian, you can't believe anything she says. You know she hates me."

"She must hate you a lot," Ian said, "because she sent me a photo."

"A photo?" asked Nikki numbly. She knew just what photo.

"She said you picked up men on all your business trips. Sometimes more than one at a time. And she sent me a photo," he repeated. He gave her a look of pain. "How could you?"

"Ian, it was just that one time, I swear. They must have put something in my drink and I'm not really sure what happened next. I let one of them walk me to my room, and I don't know how the other got there."

"What a convenient excuse: 'They must have put something in my drink.' And then you fuck two complete strangers! And you tell me one-night stands aren't 'interesting' because you like 'anticipation.' What a liar!"

"Ian, I'm not. That was just one horrible time. And they did put a pill or something into my drink—I've never felt like that before, in and out of consciousness. They were such *creeps*! This awful guy took that picture and sent it to me and Roberta. She told me she'd deleted it, but I should have known she would keep it in reserve. She's such a vicious woman."

"This isn't about Roberta. It's about you."

"Ian, you *know* me. I'm not like that."

"Yes you are," said Ian. "*Doudou.*"

"I thought we were finished with that."

"It's part of the pattern," Ian said. "I'm going for a walk."

"I'll come."

He shook his head. "I'd rather not look at you right now, if you don't mind. That image is seared on my brain."

26
Nikki's Journal

February 3, 1997

So he's gone. He came back from his walk and began to pack,
stuffing clothes into his suitcase willy-nilly. He went to the bathroom and swept his toiletries into his travel case with one hand.
Nothing I said made any difference. He took a taxi to the airport
and left two days early, leaving me here in our heaven, my hell.

I can't even tell anyone about what happened because then
I'd have to say what was in the photograph. R chose her timing
deliberately, letting me enjoy a few days with Ian, just so I'd know
what I'd always be missing. She wanted him to leave early, so I'd
be totally humiliated.

But I'll find a way to get even. I'll make her sorry she started
with me. She's not the only one who can play dirty.

Yesterday in town, I saw the man I danced with, the man who'd
called me "doudou." He was walking toward me, and I ducked into
a shop until he passed. Then I thought, wait, he might be able to
help me, and I followed him until he turned around, and I told him
what I wanted.

Half an hour later I was getting high alone on the balcony of my
hotel room. I bought an eighth of an ounce and I intend to smoke
it all up in two days. Now that Ian is gone I'm going to stay stoned
till I leave the island.

I dreamed of the grand room last night, but now it was empty
and cold. Where were the couches and draperies, the fine paint-
ings, the marble tables? The room had been looted by hoodlums,
and the floor was concrete, blotched with oil.

27

Roberta

February, 1997

"That's a beautiful watch," said the very old lady, leaning on her walker.

"Thank you," said Roberta, glancing at her wrist to see which one it was. "A present from my husband." They smiled at each other, the old lady's smile revealing a gap in her front teeth. She was less than five feet tall, with a face full of wrinkles and something like a small grape on her lower lip, as if a pimple had turned purple.

The elevator reached Roberta's floor, and the old lady stepped out, walking so slowly Roberta pressed the "open" button to give her time to clear the threshold. Then Roberta left the elevator as well. She watched the tiny figure continue down the hall, lifting her walker and putting it down, advancing by ten-inch increments. At her apartment door, she took out her keys—and dropped them. Roberta was by her side in a moment. "Let me," she said, picking them up.

"Thank you, my dear. That's very kind of you." She unlocked the door and said to Roberta, "You're new here, right? Would you like to come in for some tea?"

And although Roberta didn't much like tea and certainly didn't have time on this chore-filled Saturday to sit and chat, the old woman looked lonely, and Roberta found herself saying, "Why, thank you. That would be lovely."

"I'm Gloria Melman," said the woman. They entered the apartment, and she put the walker against the wall. "Please—take a seat."

Roberta sat on the couch. The living room was clean and bright, with an Oriental rug on the floor and polished furniture. There were photographs in frames on the piano. Gloria made her slow way into the kitchen. Sometimes old people's apartments had an unpleasant odor, dusty and medicinal, but Gloria's apartment smelled like lemon wax.

Gloria called, "Would you like regular tea or the herbal kind?"

"Herbal, thanks—any kind." Roberta had noticed that black tea, seemingly so benign it is routinely offered to the sick, often gave her a low-burning pain right between her breasts. The tannins, perhaps, though she'd never met anyone else afflicted exactly this way. Each body was different. That was something she kept learning over and over again. Paul, for instance, broke out in hives if he ate strawberries.

After a while, Gloria carefully entered the room with the tea tray, shaking the cups in their saucers. Roberta jumped up and took the tray from her. She placed it on the coffee table.

"Thank you, my dear. I always forget that I'm just not as strong as I was. You know, I'm going to be ninety years old in two weeks!"

"That's wonderful."

"Not so wonderful. Old age isn't for sissies." Gloria proceeded to enumerate her ailments: arthritic knees, poor eyesight, bad hearing, frequent indigestion. As she went through her litany of distress, Roberta's mind began to wander. Why did people assume you were interested in a subject just because it was important to them? Why couldn't they gage when a listener was bored? When she had client meetings, she always knew when the decision-makers were interested and when they were not. That was one of her strengths, knowing when to abandon one avenue and embark on another.

"So you see," Gloria was saying, "I can't go out now because of the ice on the sidewalk, and I really miss that Korean fruit store on Second. They have the best papayas, nicely cut up and always perfectly ripe." She took a sip of her tea.

Roberta said, "My husband says they taste musty, but I love a ripe papaya myself."

"They're very good for your digestion, too. At least they work for me. Some kind of enzyme..."

"Well, I'll pick up a papaya for you next time I'm out," said Roberta.

"No, I can't let you do that."

"Of course you can. It would be a pleasure." Roberta put her cup down into the saucer, thinking how rare it was to see a saucer nowadays. Everyone preferred mugs.

"Well, that would be wonderful, dear. You see, they don't deliver…"

"Don't give it a second thought."

"When did you move in?"

"Last May. After I got married to Paul Eisen, in 10D."

"Oh, that nice Mr. Eisen and those sweet little girls."

Roberta smiled. "They're young women now."

"Do you have any children?" Gloria asked.

"No. We're trying to adopt."

"A Chinese girl?"

"No, Paul wants a boy. We're hoping to get one from Guatemala."

"With your hair and skin, everyone will think it's yours."

"He will be ours," said Roberta, "whatever he looks like."

"Of course, of course," said Gloria. "I didn't mean to imply otherwise."

"I suppose you know Clarice, too? Paul's ex-wife?"

Gloria nodded. "I see her now and then, in the elevator. Sometimes with a young man. She never acknowledges me. I don't think she knows who I am."

"But you've been living on the same floor for, what, twenty years?"

"I've been here fifty-five years."

"Fifty-five years!"

"The landlord wants to get me out of here," said Gloria, "so he can quadruple the rent."

"I bet." Roberta finished her tea.

"He's offered me fifty thousand dollars to move out, but where would I move to? And how would I get everything out of here?"

Roberta shook her head in sympathy. "You just stay put. This is your home." She stood up. "Thank you for the tea. It was delicious."

"I'm glad you had some time to spend with an old lady."

Roberta waved her hand, dismissing the "old lady" characterization and refuting the notion that having tea with Gloria had been the slightest imposition on her time. She said, "Please call me at any time if you need any help." She took out her business card and wrote her home telephone number on it. "And I'll come by tomorrow with that papaya."

"You're a sweet girl," pronounced Gloria.

When she got home, Paul came to the door, jubilant. "The adoption agency just called. They're making a home visit on Monday."

"Great!" Roberta looked around. They had a cleaning lady twice a week, and the surfaces shone, the rugs were immaculate, the kitchen floor sparkled. The room that would be the child's (and now functioned as Roberta's home office) was a bright corner room with a view of the East River.

"Be sure to stock the fridge," said Paul, as he went through the mail.

"How do you mean?"

"It's gotta have stuff in it like fruit and yogurt and chicken."

"Chicken?"

"You know, a partially-eaten home-roasted chicken. It's part of the classic American open-fridge paradigm, along with half a chocolate layer cake."

"I can buy a rotisserie chicken," said Roberta, "but these days? A chocolate layer cake? I don't think so."

"How about a bowl of fruit salad?"

"I'll pick some up."

"I think it's all about doing it yourself, demonstrating domesticity."

"Don't worry—I'll hide the plastic tubs."

The next morning, Roberta made sure to be on the early train so she could see Nikki arrive at the office after her vacation. She expected Nikki's cheeks to be pale and her eyes to be red, with dark circles under them. But Nikki breezed in with rosy cheeks and a smile on her face. She hugged Cynthia and Yvonne, and Roberta heard her say how she'd had a wonderful time, and that Guadeloupe was a splendid island, off the beaten track—but it really did help to know French. Which luckily Ian did. And babble, babble, on and on.

Then Nikki went into Lillian's office, with a package, the sneak. What—now she was bringing back souvenirs for the boss she hated?

After a few minutes, Lillian stuck her head out of her office and yelled for Roberta. Nikki was still in the office, and Lillian, as if unaware of the vicious feud between her two best salespeople, said, "Come join us, sit down."

Roberta had to sit right next to Nikki, their legs almost touching.

Lillian said, "Look what Nikki brought back from the island." She held out a small ebony bowl.

"Did you call me in just for that?" asked Roberta. She intended it to sound playful, that is, if she intended it at all, for the words had just popped out unbidden, but she knew she'd sounded bitter. And bitter equaled negative to Lillian. Roberta had to turn the dial. "Is there some company news?"

"What, you're a mind-reader?" Lillian asked, beaming at her. "You bet there's company news, and it's big news for you gals! Bethany has decided to grow her operations, to maximize the potential in the organic line. That was some brilliant idea she had about organic! Anyway, she's been going back and forth about expanding for months, and last week she had a meeting with Maury, and he said she should do it." Maury was the company CFO who dropped by the office every few weeks, a bulky man with a gruff, no-nonsense, no-charm personality. "So Bethany's expanding her field of operations. She's moving us into Nassau and Fairfield counties. But instead of hiring another two sales people, she's going to let Roberta get Nassau and Nikki get Fairfield. You're going to make out like panthers!"

Panthers? Oh, bandits! Roberta held back a snort. Nikki's lips twitched.

"Wow!" said Roberta. "That's wonderful."

"Are you sure, Lillian?" asked Nikki, that idiot. "My territory keeps me quite busy already."

Roberta jumped in quickly. "I'm sure *I* can handle it. But I'm going to need some admin support."

"We're a step ahead of you on that," crowed Lillian. "We've already gotten you gals an assistant to help out."

"That is exciting news," said Nikki.

"Wait a minute," said Roberta. "About the assistant. We each get one?"

"I didn't say that," said Lillian. "You'll have one assistant between the two of you."

"I'm not sure that's such a good idea," began Roberta.

"It's an *excellent* idea," said Lillian. "Bethany thought of it. And we'll put the assistant at that empty desk between you, so you can each have easy access."

"I need to talk to you, Lillian," said Roberta.

"Go ahead."

"I mean, alone."

"If you're going to talk about some silly hen fight between the two of you, I don't want to hear it. We're supposed to be grown ups here, and you used to be friends. Maybe sharing an assistant is a good way to bury the matchstick."

"The what?" asked Nikki. She looked genuinely puzzled, the jerk.

Apparently realizing she had said something wrong, Lillian suddenly looked flustered, vulnerable. "Whatever you're fighting about," she said, "it's high time you stopped. It's highly unprofessional."

"I agree," said Nikki in an insincere voice.

"Oh, barf," said Roberta.

"Can I see you shake hands?" asked Lillian.

Nikki paled, leaning back in her seat.

"Not going to happen," said Roberta, standing up. "But thanks for the territory! Great idea!"

"Yes, thank you," murmured Nikki, standing up as well.

"Sit down, both of you," said Lillian. "We're not finished."

Roberta sat back down. Nassau County! She was going to have a very good year. Lillian was on the phone, saying, "Bring him in."

Nikki straightened in her chair. Roberta wondered whether she had any idea that the mere suggestion of a man made Nikki alter her posture so that her head was higher and her bosom more prominent. Roberta felt her own spine straightening in response, for she didn't want to look shorter than Nikki.

Bethany, in a tiger-print dress and wavy brown hair, opened the office door. She had a young man in tow. He was about twenty-five with pale orange hair and a splash of freckles on his pink face. He wore a white shirt, a brown tie, and a tan corduroy jacket. His eyes were small and gray. "This is Andy O'Brien," said Bethany. "He's going to be your assistant. And this is Nikki Elkins and Roberta Cohen."

"Welcome aboard," said Nikki.

"So glad to meet you," said Roberta, extending her hand. Andy's handshake was firm.

Bethany said, "With Andy as support, I know you ladies are going to take every advantage of your wonderful new opportunity."

"Absolutely," said Roberta.

"We'll meet in two weeks to talk about your progress with the new territory. And be nice to Andy. He's the son of my close friend, Pam."

Andy blushed so his freckles disappeared.

"We'll be gentle and kind," said Nikki. "That's who we are."

"You'll have to teach him the ropes," said Bethany, "but you'll find he's a quick learner. He graduated from Fordham last June, *magna cum laude.*"

"Impressive," said Roberta.

Andy's flush deepened. He said, "I'm happy to be here."

"Let me take you to your desk," said Bethany, "and then these ladies will tell you what they'd like you to do."

Bethany led Andy out of the office. Lillian said, "Nice young fella, right? He's going to help both of you sell well. OK, meeting's over, back to work!"

Soon, Roberta saw Andy getting settled in his desk, turning on the computer and opening empty drawers. Cynthia came by to introduce herself and ask what office supplies he needed. "First of all some floppy disks," said Andy. "And legal pads."

Cynthia said, "Make a list, and we'll go back to the store-room."

Nikki said, "Andy, when you're free, I'd like to talk to you about Fairfield County."

"And I need to talk to you about Nassau County," said Roberta.

He looked back and forth between the two of them.

Nikki said, "First, I'd like you to develop a database for me."

Roberta said, "I want a list of the ten largest rehab hospitals in Nassau County. By number of beds."

"My request came first," said Nikki to Andy.

"A database could take weeks," said Roberta. "I need my information by Thursday!" She didn't know why she said Thursday; she could as easily have said Wednesday, or Friday.

The women glared at each other.

"Wait a minute, wait a minute," said Andy. "I'm happy to do whatever you need, but I can't work for both of you at once. So I'm dividing my day. From nine to twelve-thirty I'll work on Nikki's projects, and from one-thirty on, I'll work on Roberta's. Okay everyone?"

The women nodded. It was a good solution, thought Roberta. Still, she wondered why Nikki was going first. Did Andy prefer Nikki to her?

Soon, she saw them going into the conference room. For privacy, Roberta knew. Her own privacy was ruined now that Andy was established at his desk: the price she paid for getting Nassau County. She opened a new computer file, calling it "Ideas for Andy," and began listing all the tedious sales tasks she would have him do, including follow-up calls, which she hated above all.

When Andy and Nikki returned, they were laughing about something—probably laughing at her, Roberta thought. She saw Nikki open her desk drawer and bring out a book. She gave it to Andy, who put it on his desktop. That was really too much, Nikki giving him presents! And what could the book be? When they left for lunch, Roberta took a look at the title: *The Little Red Book of Selling*. Roberta had seen this book at airport bookstores, and she wondered what it contained. If it was useful at all, it would help Andy's efforts in Nassau County as well as in Fairfield County, so she had only to gain by Nikki's gift or loan.

After lunch, it was her turn to bring Andy to the conference room, only now it was occupied by Bethany, Lillian, and Maury, so she had to take him to the kitchen. Roberta turned this to her advantage, offering Andy a cup of hot chocolate from her stash, as well as some cookies from her emergency supply. Was she reduced to this, bribing the assistant with snacks to gain his allegiance? While the water was heating, she asked him about himself, where he lived (Forest Hills, with his parents), what he hoped to do in life (not sure), why he'd taken the job (needed a paycheck). She found herself telling him why she'd started in sales. "I have two masters' degrees," she said, "and I was working for the state, but I couldn't bear to be in an office all day. I need variety, change, getting out and meeting people, closing the deal! Maybe you can come on a sales trip with me. And afterwards, we can go out for a glass of wine."

"I don't drink, but that sounds great," said Andy, "if Lillian agrees."

"What do you think of Lillian?" she asked, curious.

"Hey, I'm new here, I haven't had time to form an opinion."

"You're a smart boy," said Roberta. A look of irritation passed over his face, and she amended, "Smart man. But you can refer to me as a girl whenever you like."

Now he was blushing again, so she busied herself pouring hot water over the purplish pink hot chocolate powder. She said "Let's talk about the selling process and how it usually begins: with research—a list of prospects."

She raised her eyes and saw he was watching her, listening attentively.

28

Nikki

March, 1997

Taylor sounded rushed, but she always sounded rushed. She had been working on her Internet map, or whatever it was, non-stop for the past year.

Nikki said, "Is this a good time?" She was calling from home.

"I can talk for a couple of minutes," said Taylor. "How's Ian?"

"He broke up with me in Guadeloupe."

"Oh, no! You seemed perfect together! What happened?"

Nikki found she couldn't speak. Her throat was thick and she made squeaking sounds.

Taylor said, "Sweetie, I'm so sorry. Go get a tissue and a glass of water. I'll be here. Tell me everything."

So Nikki told her the whole sordid story, ending with Roberta sending Ian the photo.

Taylor said, "That fucking bitch! What are you going to do now?"

"I tried calling Ian, but he won't pick up. He won't answer my emails. It's over—that photo did it. So what I really want to do is get even. Wreck something big in Roberta's world, like she did to me."

Taylor was silent. Finally, she said, "Are you sure about that?"

"Totally."

"Wouldn't it be better karma if you didn't go down to her level?"

"No, Taylor. It would be better *karma* if I could get revenge. I wanted to *marry* that man."

"So what are you going to do?"

"I'm not sure yet. I need to get into her email. I thought, like, you could find out her password."

"That's against the law."

"I figured as much."

After a pause, Taylor sighed. "OK. I'll try. It may not be easy."

The next evening, Taylor called Nikki to tell her that Roberta's password was "hevron," no caps.

"'Hevron,'" said Nikki. "I wonder what it means."

As soon as Nikki hung up the phone, she was at her computer. While waiting to get connected to the World Wide Web, she opened a poetry anthology she kept on her desk. She could usually read and sometimes analyze a short poem by the time she got online. She would open the book at random and use the wait time for poetry. She wondered if a poetry program could be written so that a random poem appeared onscreen during the wait.

Finally, she was connected. Finally, she was at her company website. Finally, she was in Roberta's email. First, Nikki went back many months, to find and delete the original email from attababy with the photo. Possibly Roberta had made no other copies and it could do no further damage. She also deleted the recent sent message to Ian with the photo attached. (It seemed Roberta had forwarded the original email to Ian, which indicated she might not have saved it elsewhere.) Then, just to be safe, she deleted the recent deletes in the trash folder as well.

Then Nikki began reading Roberta's recent messages, both incoming and outgoing, starting from four weeks earlier.

Quiana poked her head into Nikki's office and asked, "When's dinner, Mom? I'm hungry!"

"Soon, dear. I'll be down in a jiffy."

"That's iffy," said Quiana.

Nikki turned to smile at her daughter. Was she wearing mascara or were her eyelashes really that long? "Why 'iffy'?"

"I know what happens when you sit at that computer."

"Ten minutes," said Nikki. "Time me." She kept reading, getting to the previous week, until she heard the kitchen timer go off. She hadn't come across anything, but it would surely be useful to have Roberta's password. Before Quiana could nag her, Nikki went downstairs, admiring the graceful staircase with its rich mahogany steps and bright white newel posts and glossy brown banister, as she did almost every time she used the stairs. How could you measure the pleasures a house could yield?

"Mom," asked Quiana, once they were at the table with their plates of pasta primavera, "How can I make this guy know I'm alive?"

"Oh, honey—who is he?"

"Just a boy," said Quiana, blushing.

"How do you know him?"

"He's in my math class."

"Is he smart?"

"Very."

"You could ask for his help with the homework."

"Mom, in case it's escaped your notice, I'm very smart, too."

"It hasn't escaped my notice, sweetie. Do you sit near him?"

Quiana shook her head. "We have assigned seats, and he's in the front and I'm further back, to the side."

"Hmmmm. Well, maybe sometime if he answers a question, you can follow it up by saying there's another way to get the answer."

"That would make the *teacher* notice me, but maybe not *him*."

"Does *him* have a name?"

"I'm not telling," said Quiana.

Nikki shot her a look and Quiana finally said, "OK," and something that sounded like "Ja-eer."

"What? How's it spelled?"

"J-A-I-R."

"Interesting," said Nikki. African-American. "Well, you've got unusual names in common."

"That's not enough," moaned Quiana.

"Just be his friend," said Nikki. "Talk to him about anything at all as if you were talking to a girl." She finished the last of her pasta.

"What would I talk to him about?"

"Well, say you meet at the lockers, you could say, "So what do you think of Mr. Smith or whatever your math teacher's name is."

"Myers," said Quiana. "Mr. Myers. Don't you think that's too obvious?"

"It's ordinary but not obvious. It's the kind of thing you could say to anyone, like 'when's the weather going to warm up?' Really, it doesn't matter *what* you say as long as you say something, in a natural, friendly way. You just want to make contact, establish a tie, let him know you're alive."

This was true with adults as well. Nikki had read that whether or not a person will encourage a flirtation is decided upon the first glance, in less than a second, so people shouldn't fret about being original. If you like the looks of someone who asks, "Come here often?" you'll respond with a smile.

After dinner, Nikki went back to the study. First she called her dealer, Jed, but once again he didn't answer. Then she returned to Roberta's email, which was mostly business. Emails from her friends were mainly about setting up dinner dates, and Roberta occasionally sent her husband a message about what to buy or cook. Nikki was surprised that Paul did the shopping and cooking, because she knew he, too, had a fulltime job, though perhaps more flexibility. Nikki saw an email from *susant@allforchildren.org*. What could that be, some charity? She clicked it open. After reading a few lines, she closed her eyes in relief. She had found what she was looking for.

Nikki hit the reply button and began composing a new message from Roberta's email account: "Hi Susan…" She made sure that the message was in Roberta's style. "It was so good to meet you last night. I hope you got a good impression of our home. I think it's just ideal for raising a child. Looking into the future, there's even a good school across the street." Yes, Roberta would use the word "good" three times in four sentences. "My husband and I are just longing to have a baby, and adoption is the best option for us, because my brother is schizophrenic and I know that it's often hereditary. Paul and I sure don't want to bring another loony into this world! God knows even one in the family is plenty!" Surely using the word "loony" and the mild blasphemy "God knows" would make the letter writer unsympathetic, and Nikki was just getting started.

"Mom?"

Nikki turned to look at Quiana, who was dressed for bed in a T-shirt and flannel pajama bottoms. She looked especially young and vulnerable.

"Yes?"

"Could I join the debate club?"

"Why, sure."

"I'll need a ride home from school at five-fifteen, Tuesdays and Thursdays."

"No problem."

"Great!"

Nikki asked, "Is Jair by any chance in the debate club?"

"Mom!" Quiana stalked out without answering the question. Nikki smiled, feeling that warm glow Quiana could give her even when she was walking out of the room pretending indignation. She couldn't imagine her everyday life without Quiana, although in a mere five years, she'd be away college.

Nikki turned back to the email. Now what would she add? Some slick justification about leaving childcare to a nanny because she was a consummate sales professional? Or some nonsense about how being in sales was really a lot like being a mother because you had to smile a lot and service the client's needs? How about needing to work because it was important to provide a child with a private education and horseback riding lessons? Or how she sometimes had these irrational temper tantrums, and at one job they had said she had anger management issues, but she was sure that having a child would calm her down.

There were so many ways this letter could go, and any way Nikki chose would probably work fine.

Then why were her fingers quiet on the keyboard? Roberta had ruined Nikki's chances with Ian, so why shouldn't she wreck Roberta's hopes for adoption? "In my case, a baby will work like a therapy pet, easing the tension from my life and providing me with inner peace." Yet although it was formed in her mind, Nikki found she couldn't type the sentence.

Nikki sat there for ten minutes, furious at herself. You have every right to ruin her life, she told herself, because she's doing her best to ruin yours. Go ahead. Do it. Just do it. Yet with every minute Nikki knew with greater certainty that she wasn't going to do it. She shouldn't have any scruples at all when it came to Roberta, her sworn enemy; she should actively work for her downfall. But here she was, hitting the cancel button. Nikki would find some other way to hurt Roberta.

Let her have her damn kid.

The next day, from the conference room at work, she called Jed again. She'd been leaving messages all week, and now she was down to two joints. What was the matter with the man? Why was he avoiding her like this? Just because he found her attractive and she had indirectly turned him down? Oh, the frail male ego...

This time, Jed picked up.

"Hi," Nikki said, "I've been calling you."

"Hey, sorry about that. We're getting ready to go on vacation. I've been busy."

"When are you leaving?" she asked ungraciously. (Who cared where he was going, but *when* was he going?)

"Tomorrow."

"Can you see me before then?"

"Sorry," said Jed, sounding not the least regretful.

"Like, I'm all out."

"Not my problem," said Jed. "I'll be back in three weeks. I'll give you a call when I get back." And he hung up on her, before she could say, "Don't bother," which was probably a good thing.

Now she was in a real fix. None of her friends smoked pot, except when they were with her, so they didn't have dealers. She'd have to go back to Lucius, whom she hadn't seen in five years, since before the divorce. She supposed her ex still used Lucius, if, in fact, he still used marijuana. David had married a yoga instructor who frowned on recreational drug use. Nikki's own cannabis consumption had greatly increased since her divorce, and she didn't want David to know that. She wanted him to think her life was fine now without him, and he'd term her pot smoking excessive, an obvious sign that something was wrong. Nikki thought her pot smoking was an obvious sign that she loved smoking pot.

On the way home, Nikki noted that the forsythia was early this year. Was this an example of climate change? On her short trip home, she saw the yellow flowers in all their variety: as great sprays of trailing branches, supple as weeping willows; as neat little hedges, tidy as privet; and as ornamental bushes, placed as carefully as sculpture on lawns that were just turning green. There were even a few straggly forsythia branches by the side of her driveway.

After dinner, she got into her car again. Lucius lived in Green-point, Brooklyn. Nikki had his address from the old family phone-book, but there was no telephone number. Anyway, you didn't call Lucius: you just dropped in between eight and ten, weeknights. At least, you used to. For all she knew, he had left the business, but anyway, she was on the Brooklyn-Queens Expressway, with cash in her purse and worry on her mind. Back when David used to get the grass, he had his own key to Lucius's front door, as did all of Lucius's clients, because for safety reasons, Lucius never answered his bell. Now Nikki wondered how she was going to get inside the downstairs door. She turned onto his block, which was in an industrial area. Lucius worked in a nondescript four-story building, and tonight, as usual, she was able to park nearby. Now she sat in her car and wait-ed. When she saw a long-haired guy of forty turn into the building, a likely customer of Lucius, she left her car and followed him in. He opened the downstairs door with his key and held it open for her. She thanked him, and he asked, "Do I know you?"

She said, "I'm a friend of Lucius." He gave her a blank look, and she added, "On the fourth floor."

"I'm new here," he said. "I don't know my neighbors." He took to the stairs, and Nikki followed him. He said, looking back, "I was kind of hoping you were my neighbor."

"Neighbor from Westchester," said Nikki. "But thank you." He turned off on the second floor, and she kept climbing.

She knocked at the door to 4A. Then she knocked again. She was about to knock a third time when she noticed a card scotch-taped to the wall beside the door. The name on the card was "S.E. Curtis." Not Lucius Brown.

Bummer, bummeroo, bummeroonie. She descended the stairs and got into her car for the long drive back. When she got home, she was definitely going to smoke a little bit for consolation, even though it was, *pace* Lillian, her penultimate joint.

Nikki managed to make her two joints last four days (retaining a roach for a dire emergency), and then she started doing without. At the very least, she told herself, a little detox, a cannabis fast, would mean she'd get higher more easily when she resumed. It would show she could do without marijuana. It would show she could just say "no."

But *living* with no was more difficult.

No reliable unwinding after a day at the office, bringing dinner to a higher level. No couch lock in front of the tube or a book. No passport to insight and pleasure and fun. Or so it felt to her. That first week without pot, Nikki thought about it constantly.

And her eyes hurt. Her eyes always ached when she went on a pot fast. After a few days, the ache went away, but not the insomnia, which seemed to be getting worse. She never had problems with sleep when she was getting high, but tonight, on day eight of her mandatory fast, she was wide awake, staring at the ceiling. No position was comfortable: her hands felt heavy and her back felt sore. She had already been in bed an hour, and sleep seemed as distant as ever. Purely as a palliative measure, for she wasn't feeling sexy, she began touching herself. It took a while, and the orgasm was insipid. Sleep did not carry her off as it usually did after she came. Maybe a utilitarian orgasm didn't work. Nikki lay in bed another hour, waiting for Morpheus to arrive. Then she went to the kitchen and made herself a glass of warm milk with honey.

Back in the bedroom, she found a dense novel she'd abandoned months earlier. She opened it to the bookmark 50 pages in, but it was as if she had never read it at all, so she started in the beginning, on page one, hoping it would bore her once again and leave her ready for sleep. But this time around, the novel proved absorbing, and she read on and on. Finally, at five-thirty, the book slipped through her fingers and she slept.

She was exhausted and haggard the next day. Doing without pot was apparently bad for her health and bad for her looks.

After dinner that night, Nikki went to a bar two towns away that was famous for its young and rowdy crowd. She parked in the lot and saw several people smoking by the door. Wouldn't it be wonderful if one of them were smoking a joint... but no such luck. By now, Nikki was so eager for the feel of smoke in her lungs that she inhaled sharply the tobacco smoke in the air before going into the bar.

She opened the door, which was already quite full. Nikki wore jeans and a T-shirt, but who was she kidding? She looked older than everyone here. She took a seat at the bar. If the bartender looked cool, perhaps she could ask him where she could buy a few joints, but the bartender was a clean-cut and preppy young woman, so Nikki just ordered a beer. Then she looked about, hoping for a sign: dreadlocks, a peace sign tattoo, perhaps bloodshot eyes. Nothing. She finished her beer and left. She'd just have to wait until Jed came back from vacation.

29

Roberta

April, 1998

Benjamin was, everyone agreed, an exceptional baby. At thirteen months of age, he was bright-eyed, curious, and calm: a happy fellow who almost never cried. He had smooth, toasty skin, which matched Roberta's own when she was tanned; large, almond eyes; and thick black hair—Amerindian hair, but also, conceivably, Jewish hair! Benjamin was beautiful and bright and altogether delightful. Sixty Gs and a lot of luck had brought them a wonderful baby, and Roberta and Paul were going to do their very best to give this Guatemalan foundling a wonderful life.

They hired Grisella, a cheerful, plump woman, as their nanny. At first, Paul did all the baby care when Grisella was away, because he had done it before. Roberta watched closely, and soon she was doing some herself. Bath time was especially delightful, and she asked Grisella not to bathe Benjamin so she could do it herself when she got home from work. If she made her usual train, Benjamin might be asleep by the time she got home, so Roberta had gotten Lillian's permission to take the 4:50 train to Manhattan instead of the 5:20. Before boarding her train, she had to visit the ladies room, put on her outerwear, and walk to the station, so she effectively ended her workday half an hour earlier than other people. She knew it bugged Yvonne and some of the others when she turned off her computer at 4:30, but hey, let them make their own deals. Let them make as much money for the company as she was raking in.

Nassau County had proved every bit as profitable as she had hoped, and with Andy sending out mailings and e-blasts to potential clients, Roberta was able to concentrate on what she liked most about sales: getting up close and personal, persuading other people to buy through the sheer force of her personality. It was like a sport—there was that moment when the person paused, on the brink of becoming a client, and you had to make the putt, a gentle tap, and get him or her safely into the hole. Usually the decision-maker was a guy, but that was changing, which was good. She felt she could bond more quickly with women than with men (unlike that slut Nikki).

Roberta liked to bathe Benjamin in a plastic tub on the kitchen counter, and while Grisella got the water ready, Roberta undressed the baby. He flapped his arms and said, "Ba-ba-ba." She wrapped him in a towel, head to toe, which made him look like an Arab, and brought him into the kitchen. The yellow rubber ducky, the clear plastic rattle containing colored balls, and the blue plastic boat were already floating in the water.

"Okay, Miss Roberta?" asked Grisella.

"That's fine. Good night."

"Good night then." Grisella walked to the door. "See you tomorrow."

Roberta settled Benjamin into the bath. He sat very straight in the water, beating it with his hands and crowing when he splashed. He declaimed, "Ba-ba-ba-ba-ba" and splashed a little more. Oh, how joyful he was, this baby, her baby Benjamin! Really, you had to feel happy near him, he was so delightful, such an adorable baby, so thrilled with going bye-bye and his bottle and his bath. Roberta had read about adopted children from Russia who had grievous psychological wounds, and she knew she was fortunate to have gotten an infant so healthy and happy.

Benjamin flung the rubber duck to the floor. "No!" said Roberta. Then he threw down the rattle and gurgled. "No," she said again, but the plastic boat was next. "*Be* that way," she told him. "Now you don't have any toys."

He looked down to where the toys had landed. "Unh, unh," he said, straining toward them.

"All right," said Roberta, "but this is the last time." She bent down quickly and retrieved the toys. She put them in the bathtub again, and immediately, he threw out the duck, gurgling. "No!" said Roberta, but she couldn't help laughing herself, and at that moment Paul walked into the kitchen.

"I'm glad somebody's having a good time," he said.

The baby shrieked with joy.

"What's wrong?" asked Roberta.

"We're getting audited by the IRS," he said. "Prepare for a nightmare."

"We haven't done anything wrong, have we?"

"God damn it!" Paul yelled.

Benjamin stopped smacking the water and stared at him, openmouthed.

"What?" Roberta asked.

"It takes *weeks* to prepare for an audit, I'll have to go back and find a written record for every expense, it's god-awful boring and tedious. I could *scream.*"

"You just have," she rebuked him. "You frightened the baby."

"And they always find something," Paul went on. "They have to. So you have to pay up *and* pay the penalties. It happened to me once before, in '86. It's a fucking disaster."

"Language," she said. She hated when he cursed, especially in front of the baby.

"Amazing," Paul said flatly. "You just don't get it, do you? They're auditing us *for the last two years!*"

"All right, all right, I get it." She began splashing water on Benjamin's head to wash his beautiful hair.

Paul said, "I hope you have documentation for all your business expenses."

"Of course I do." Her credit card statements were proof of her expenses, and who could ever tell which of her restaurant meals were legitimate and which were personal? She rubbed Benjamin's head to bring up the bubbles in the shampoo. Surely the auditors would have no way of knowing that Bethany reimbursed her staff for all their business expenses. Roberta always cashed those reimbursement checks promptly, never depositing them into her account, thus averting, she thought, a paper trail. So the IRS couldn't possibly know about her restaurant scam, unless someone had told them.

A chill went through Roberta when she realized who might have told them.

"How does the IRS work?" she asked slowly. "Is there a bounty system?"

"Why? You think someone reported us to them?"

"Maybe. Would somebody get a reward?" She spoke carefully because Paul always dismissed her when she accused Nikki of anything. With a plastic pitcher, Roberta sluiced warm water over Benjamin's head to rinse him off. He scrunched up his face and let out a moan. He didn't like this part of the bath.

Paul said, "If informants provide the IRS with new information they get, like, 15 to 30% of what the IRS recovers. In our case, it would hardly be worth it for anyone to inform on us because the IRS isn't going to find much. We've been pretty straight with them."

But reporting them would be worth it to Nikki, Roberta knew. Just riling up Roberta and Paul would be enough for her: bounty money would be the cherry on the cake.

Now that the rinsing was over, Benjamin recovered his good humor, and he threw the blue boat to the floor, crowing in triumph.

For the next two weeks, Paul worked intermittently on the taxes. He and Roberta disassembled Benjamin's room and made it look like a home office again, because they had deducted a sixth of their apartment rent, utilities, and cleaning expenses on the pretext that Roberta used that room exclusively for work. The crib and the changing table and the diapers had to go into their bedroom, and Benjamin's white chest of drawers was moved to the dining room, where it looked out of place. Benjamin's toys and books (he already had a surprising number of books) were put into their storage area in the basement. "We'll move everything back after the audit," said Paul. "Can you bring some of your work things in here to make it look like a real office? Like call reports or price lists?"

They were at the table, having thin-crust pizza with chicken and broccoli from the terrific pizza place a block away, and Benjamin was asleep in their bedroom. Roberta made a face. "I come home to get away from all that. The great part of my job is I leave it at the office every day at 4:40."

"Just for the audit," said Paul. "A home office is the first thing they go after."

"What's the second?" asked Roberta.

"Business expenses."

She felt cold.

Paul said, "I'm going back to my diary to note or write exactly who I was entertaining on every day. And I recommend you do the same."

She could do it, or fake it, convincingly. With the help of her Xeroxed call reports and credit card statements, she'd fill up her datebook with clients real or imagined.

Finally, two days before the auditor was due to arrive, Paul visited his accountant. He came back less anxious and angry than he'd been for weeks. "Jerry says we're in good shape," he announced, "as long as your expenses are legit."

"Good. Then that's fine."

"I certainly hope so. Once the IRS gets you into their maw they want to swallow you whole. Have you arranged to take Friday off from work?"

"I'll do it tomorrow."

The next day, she went into Lillian's office and explained she would need to take the following day off because of the IRS audit. Lillian was happy to give her a personal day, and as further proof of her complete support for Roberta, as she rushed by near Roberta later on, Lillian hollered, yes, *hollered*, "Good luck with your audit tomorrow!"

Roberta couldn't help it: she looked at Nikki. And, make no mistake, Nikki was smiling, the evil bitch. Evil and perverse. Why only yesterday, Roberta had heard Nikki holding forth to Yvonne and a scandalized but delighted Cynthia about how people should forgive Clinton and Monica, for perhaps they had fallen in love. And Clinton was right, they hadn't really been having sex, and the whole thing was trivial, yadda, yadda, yadda. Nikki said, "Only you have to wonder why Monica didn't clean the semen-stained dress. Is she intending to donate it to a museum? Like—the Costume Institute at the Met? Or maybe that new Museum of Sex?"

Trust Nikki to know about a museum like that.

The auditor was an impassive Asian woman of thirty-five named Marilyn Ming. She wore a gray skirt suit, a white shirt, and low black pumps. She didn't smile on saying hello nor on seeing Benjamin in Grisella's arms, nor when offered a cup of coffee, which she declined curtly. "We'll work in the home office," she said. Was that a tinge of derision in her tone? She spread their tax forms out on the desk and sat in the chair behind the desk. Paul brought in two dining room chairs. The auditor and Paul discussed his income and expenses first, and Roberta became fidgety. "Call me when you need me," she said. "I'm going to run some laundry."

A little later, Paul called, "Roberta!"

"Have a seat," said the auditor. "You can help us here."

Roberta's heart began to pound.

"So you use this room for what exactly?" Ms. Ming asked Roberta.

Whew! Just the home office! And it certainly looked official, with various Bethany Moore materials and notebooks in piles on the shelves.

Roberta said, "As you can see, I use it when I work at home for sales-related business. I make follow-up calls and coordinate strategy and email my clients from here. We've just gotten a fast new Internet connection here, and that makes all the difference."

"So you use this space only for work?" asked the auditor.

"Yes."

"I'm just wondering because of that decoration," said the auditor, pointing to a band of trim that ran around the walls of the room near the ceiling, which showed giraffes and elephants and zebras in a happy circus parade. The auditor said, "Do you use this as the baby's room?"

Roberta recovered quickly. "We're going to do that when Benjamin turns two," said Roberta, "but for now we like to keep him in the bedroom with us."

"We're transitioning," said Paul.

"May I see your bedroom?" asked the auditor.

Roberta led the way. The room looked rather cramped with the crib and the changing table in it. Ms. Ming walked to the crib, and to Roberta's surprise, she pulled a tape measure out of her pocket. She measured the width of the crib from leg to leg. "Thirty-two inches, wide," she said to herself. She measured the length. "Forty-four inches long. Okay, let's go back."

Roberta looked at Paul in bewilderment, and he gave a slight shrug.

Back in the "home office," Ms. Ming said, "You're probably wondering why I measured the crib."

"Sure," said Paul.

"See, I noticed those depressions on the rug." They all looked down. There were four shallow pits on the floor.

She lowered herself to the floor and pulled out the tape measure. "Thirty-two inches, wide," she said again. "Forty-four inches long. The baby's been sleeping in here. I'm going to disallow your home office expenses."

"Hey, wait a minute!" said Paul.

"Yes?"

"We adopted the baby last August. At least grant us the home office credit for two-thirds of the year!"

"Can you show me his adoption papers?" asked Ms. Ming.

Paul reached into the file cabinet.

At lunchtime, Ms. Ming went out to eat, returning half an hour later.

"Let's go over your entertainment expenses," she said to Roberta. "They're surprisingly high."

"I have to entertain my clients," said Roberta. "That's part of my job. I can break it all down for you." She took out her credit card statements. "Let's start with January. There's the bill for Da Silvano on January 4: I took Harry Therlow of Rockwell Rehab out for dinner. Then on January 7, I took Merrill Brown and Thomas Casey of Red Door to La Caravelle." She declaimed dates and companies through the third week in January.

Marilyn Ming listened to this recitation unimpressed. "How do I know you're not just going out with your husband or girlfriends?"

"I can show you my datebook," said Roberta. Indeed, she wanted to show her the datebook, created especially for this moment, using a variety of pens and pencils for greater authenticity.

"Perhaps later," said Ms. Ming. She made some notes on a pad, and then raised her head. "What I don't understand is how you can claim these as expenses when your company reimburses you for every meal."

Roberta felt the blood drain from her face. "I don't know what you're talking about."

The agent brought out a sheaf of papers and held them out. They were copies of the Bethany Moore expense logs that Roberta had submitted, with receipts, to get her reimbursement checks. "This is for January of last year," she said. "And there's your Da Silvano bill. And it was paid in full. So how can you claim it as an expense?"

Paul was staring at her, incredulity turning to anger as she watched. She didn't know what to say.

Ms. Ming went on. "I'm wondering why I don't see La Caravelle at all on the Bethany January expense forms. This leads me to believe that your meal there wasn't a business meeting at all. What with one thing and another, you're systematically engaging in tax fraud."

"Now wait a minute!" said Paul. "People make mistakes, you know."

"I thought I could deduct my business expenses," said Roberta, with feigned indignation.

"How could you think that when you were being reimbursed?" asked Ms. Ming.

"I didn't think it made any difference."

Paul looked at her as if she was a moron, but better a moron than a felon.

Ms. Ming was tapping at her calculator. "This is all taxable income," she said. "At your income level, you owe the Federal government $4,560, plus $228 in interest. The penalty for hiding a sum like that is $2,500, so altogether, you owe the IRS $7,288 for that particular category. I imagine we'll find other irregularities, as well."

She went over every line of the tax form, and found they owed another $323. Then she turned to the tax form of the year before. She allowed the home office deduction in its entirety and eliminated the restaurant expenses in their entirety. So they owed another $8,548. Ms. Ming said, "I'm going to recommend to my superiors that we review all of your taxes since you started working at Bethany Moore, with special attention to the entertainment deductions."

That would be another five years of disallowed restaurant expenses, and interest, and penalties. Altogether, she was going to owe some $38,000.

"Does your little snitch get a percentage of the interest and penalties?" asked Roberta.

Paul was frowning at her.

"I don't know what you mean," said Ms. Ming.

"Oh, come on. What made you get my expense reports from Bethany?"

"It's standard procedure when we investigate business expenses."

"My wife is referring to the bounty program," said Paul. "And if somebody suggested that you investigate her? What would the reward be?"

"At this recovery level, that person would get 15% of the funds but no part of the penalty."

"That's several thousand dollars," said Roberta. "She'd better report it on her taxes!"

Ms. Ming did not smile. "We share our audit information with the state," she said sternly, "so you should be prepared to pay New York State back taxes, interest, and penalties, too."

When Ms. Ming finally left, Paul glared at Roberta. "You make a very good living," he said. "Why the fuck did you claim those expenses?"

"Everyone in sales does it," she said. "I just got caught." But she felt his stern eyes upon her, and she knew he would always resent and mistrust her because of what she had done. Nikki had won this round.

The only way Roberta could come up with what she owed was by raiding her 401k plan, and that carried a penalty, too. She shook her head and walked to the refrigerator to get some white wine. Paul gave her a look, but he didn't say anything. He couldn't. She'd gone a month and more without a drink, and she had resumed again, as she said she would do. Who could really fault her? We all have our ways to de-stress. Paul used the gym. Nikki used pot. Roberta used wine.

"At least the audit's over and we won't have to do jail time," muttered Paul.

And that's what gave Roberta the idea.

30

Nikki

August, 1998

It felt like a force field of hate emanated from Roberta's desk, and Nikki dreaded coming to work. One morning, Nikki was leaving the ladies room just as Roberta was entering, and they almost collided head on. Roberta stuck out her tongue, and Nikki was so surprised at this childish gesture that she actually laughed. "Roberta," she heard herself saying. "This has gone on long enough. Let's end it already."

Roberta tossed her splendid dark hair and flounced away without saying a word.

"All right, have it your way," said Nikki after her.

Roberta turned and said, "Fuck you."

Nicky said, "Aren't you the eloquent one! Elegant, too."

That afternoon, Lillian sent the office staff an email.

Dear Employees of Bethany Moore,

As you know, we are coming upon the 10th Anniversary of the Bethany Moore Company. Save the Date! On October 20, we will celebrate with a gala lunch at Tavern on the Green. Our company is growing fast, and I'm sure you appreciate how great it is to be working for a CEO as dynamic and creative and generous as Bethany! We are collecting donations for a company present: a slab of crystal specially ordered from George Jensen. Please have your donation ($25) ready by Friday morning. Georgette will come around to collect it and get your signature for the card.

Lillian

Nikki went to Cynthia's desk and sat at the chair nearby. "What do you think about this latest email from Lillian?" she asked.

Cynthia was immersed in a spreadsheet. "Always the email," she complained.

"Just read it," said Nikki.

Cynthia clicked her way to her inbox. After reading the email, she said, "I like the part about Tavern on the Green."

"But..." prompted Nikki.

"But I don't think it's right to tell people how much they should 'donate' to a gift. A donation should be voluntary. And $25 is a lot of money."

"My feelings entirely," said Nikki, relieved. "We don't have to give Bethany a thousand dollar piece of glass. We could choose something less pricy."

"What do you think, Andy?" Nikki asked.

"First, it's a lot of money. And second, I don't like the bit about signing the card. So Bethany can see who gave and who didn't."

Roberta called out. "Makes sense to me! If you don't want to contribute, you can't sign the card."

"It's a lot of money," protested Andy.

"She's given you a *job!*" said Roberta. "If she didn't have a business, who knows where you might be. Or me. Unemployed, maybe. $25 is no big deal."

"Maybe not for you or me," said Cynthia. "But there are people working here who can't afford it. And they're not going to be happy."

"For Chrissake," Roberta called. "It's a one-time contribution. What's the big deal? Bunch of whiners."

Nikki stood up and looked across the office. Little knots of people had gathered here and there, probably talking about the forced donation. She decided to go for a tea break. In the kitchen, she found Yvonne eating a yogurt. "What do you think about that email?" asked Nikki.

"Nice," said Yvonne. "Tavern on the Green. I love it there."

"How about the $25 per person donation to Bethany's gift?"

"It's brilliant," said Yvonne. "Bethany's going to love that lump of glass—it's just the kind of thing she goes for."

"But isn't it a lot of money to ask of some of the people who work here?"

"Well, if it wasn't for Bethany they wouldn't have a job at all."

"That's exactly what Roberta said," Nikki murmured. Yvonne blanched. Nikki continued. "I think it's coercion. And that bit about signing the card! So she knows who gave and who didn't!"

"I see your point," said Yvonne. "That's not right."

"I think it's okay to have a 'suggested contribution,' but people should give what they want. And everyone should sign the damn card! Or no one!"

"I agree with you," said Yvonne. "Absolutely."

Nikki finished her tea and walked to Lillian's office. She knocked on the glass door. Lillian looked up, and on seeing Nikki her face hardened. "Yes, what is it?"

"It's about this gift for Bethany."

"You have a problem with that?"

"I do," said Nikki, and she detailed her objections.

"Well, I make those decisions around here," said Lillian, "and while I appreciate your input, I've made up my mind."

"What if people just can't afford it?"

"That's their choice. How they prioritize their money is their choice."

"Not if they're just making ends meet," said Nikki. "Look, at least rethink signing the card. Either everyone should sign it or it should just read, 'The Staff of Bethany Moore Meals.' It's the signing that's coercive."

"If everyone doesn't contribute, we won't reach our goal."

"I'm sure some people could give a little more. In fact, I'm happy to."

"So why are you yelling and screaming about this?"

"Yelling and screaming?" Nikki's voice lowered to a whisper. "Lillian, I haven't even raised my voice!"

"Get out and sell," said Lillian. "That's what we hired you for."

By the next morning, the office was polarized. Half the people (those who liked Nikki) were opposed to the contribution and the card, and half (those who liked Roberta) thought it was a perfectly fine idea. On Thursday afternoon, Lillian sent an email reminding everyone that the next day they should bring in "$25 cash—exact change would be appreciated—for Bethany's present."

When Georgette stopped by Nikki's desk the next day, Nikki pulled out two twenty dollar bills. "I don't have change," said Georgette.

"I'll contribute $40," said Nikki. "Be sure to tell Lillian."

"Okay," said Georgette.

"Where's the card?" asked Nikki.

Georgette said, "Lillian changed her mind about having contributors sign the card. It will be signed by 'the staff.'"

"Really?"

Georgette said, "She realized you were right. She's not so bad, you know."

Nikki told Andy about Lillian's retreat. "I'm really surprised," she said. "She almost never changes her mind."

"You must have convinced her," said Andy.

"Maybe. At the time, she made me leave her office—'Go out and sell!' But sometimes a message needs a little time to sink in and be absorbed."

"That's true," said Andy. "Like, people will say you're all wrong and the next day they'll say, 'I was thinking about what you said, and it makes a lot of sense.'"

"If only it happened more often in sales," said Nikki, reviewing her plans for the day. She had a fair amount of autonomy as to what she did when, which was one thing she liked about sales. She actually liked a lot of things about sales—except the actual selling part.

At lunchtime, she and Andy rode the elevator downstairs alone together, and suddenly Nikki had a great idea. "Andy," she said, "I was just wondering. Do young people still smoke pot?"

"Some do," he said. "I don't. Why do you ask?"

I thought maybe you could score me some, she didn't say. "Just curious. I used to love it."

Every day at home, Nikki checked Roberta's email. She wasn't sure how the system would react if two people were simultaneously logged into the account, so she did this late at night, figuring that Roberta would probably not be using it then. In the days when they'd been friends, Roberta had said—no, bragged—that she left work at work and never thought about it after she left the office, and Nikki had to hope this extended to email. So far, Nikki hadn't done much mischief from Roberta's email account: if she did anything obvious, Roberta would get suspicious and change her password. But Nikki had ruined a deal with LIC Rehab by writing that Bethany Moore Meals had been forced to impose a 15% price increase on the organic line. And she had abruptly and rudely canceled a client meeting so that Roberta had waited and waited in vain outside Balthazar for Maggie O'Donnell. Nikki heard Roberta complaining to Andy, "Maggie just stood me up and now she won't take my calls!"

Tonight, Nikki was ready for bed before she remembered her nightly ritual. And there in her inbox was a message, subject line "Hello Again," from one *hevronlampart@yahoo.com*. It had already been opened, so Roberta would never know if it was read again. Nikki saw:

Darling,
It was great running into you in SoHo last night. You look wonderful: marriage must suit you, and motherhood, too! My mouth still burns from our goodbye kiss. When can we meet again? H

Nikki stared at her computer screen, dazzled by the opportunity. She could forward the message to Paul. She could make it even sexier, for you could alter messages you forwarded, and *then* forward the message to Paul. The trouble with such a scenario, however, was that the forwarded email would originate from Roberta's email address and Roberta would never forward such a message to her husband, so the sting of possible adultery would be muffled by the issue of how and why someone had hacked into Roberta's email. Nikki smiled. No, she wouldn't forward the message—she'd respond to it. Just imagining the possible consequences made Nikki's fingers dance as she typed:

I want to see you, too. We can be alone on Thursday night at 6:30 in my apartment. Just come, don't confirm, don't 'reply' to this email, too dangerous. Love, as always, R.

She pressed SEND, and moments later she erased the email from the SENT box.

Nikki finally understood why Roberta had chosen "hevron" for her password.

31

Roberta's Film Diary

August 15, 1998

Life is Beautiful. *Paul and I fought about this one. The main character is a clownish waiter, & the first half of the movie shows his playful, rather silly pranks—& the beauty of the lush Italian countryside in the 1940s. Because of his tricks and surprises, he wins the love of a beautiful woman, & they get married and have a son. The little boy has the most wonderful face, but the movie is slow & not too funny—until father and son (about 4) are rounded up because they are Jewish. Then the movie gets darker and more implausible. To protect his son, the father insists that everything is a game: the box cars, the concentration camp, the suffering. If we get one thousand points, he tells his son, then we will win a tank. Even the son doesn't quite believe it, but the father insists that if the child doesn't complain about his hunger, for instance, he will win 10 points. When the son says he's heard that the Nazis will burn them and turn them into soap and buttons, the father pooh-poohs this information & begins jokingly addressing the buttons on his shirt, "Hey, Guido! How are you?"*

I found this beyond tasteless—appalling, even. But Paul agreed with my film teacher that this is a wonderful film, showing the resilience of the human spirit, because through the father's strategies, the little boy survives & is reunited with his mother. I told him you don't make jokes about the Holocaust. Perhaps I shouldn't have stormed out of the café, but I just couldn't bear the notion that <u>anything</u> can be the subject of comedy. I lost several relatives to the Nazis, & I don't think you should make a movie about that era with the title, Life is Beautiful. *Irony & humor are the wrong way to confront the evils of the Nazi regime.*

32

Roberta

August, 1998

On her way home from the subway, Roberta picked up a package of cut papaya, as she did twice a week for Gloria. It had been an exhausting week, with many sales calls per day and no signed contracts. Today had been especially frustrating: she didn't feel optimistic about Glendale Rehab, and she'd gotten caught in bad traffic back to Manhattan. Luckily, she had a good book on tape from the library in her cassette player; unluckily, it was damaged, and from time to time the cassette had to be extracted from the player, and long brown loops of tape had to be wound back into the cassette, using a hexagonal pencil as cranking device. Under normal highway conditions, this would have been a significant challenge, but traffic was moving slowly enough for Roberta to make her repairs.

When Gloria opened her door, Roberta said, "I can't stay stop and chat tonight, but here's your papaya."

"You're a good girl," said Gloria. "Come give me a kiss! And bring the baby with you next time."

"I will," said Roberta. And she bent way down to kiss Gloria's wrinkled cheek.

Not for the first time, she observed that Gloria had surprisingly long lashes for an old woman. Roberta's own lashes were already shorter and sparser than they had been in her twenties.

When Roberta opened the door to her apartment, it was 6:25, and Benjamin was asleep. Paul was in the kitchen, slicing vegetables for a stir-fry. For this task he wore the grubby white chef's apron he favored. Roberta thought: whatever, as long as *he's* cooking dinner, not me! She got into her loose, comfortable blue jeans and a soft, frayed sweatshirt, for they were staying home, and she didn't have to impress anyone. She was looking forward to that first glass of wine on an empty stomach, to the warmth and confidence it always imparted. She removed her earrings and was about to brush out her hair when the upstairs doorbell rang.

Paul asked, "Expecting anyone?"

"No." Roberta went to the door and opened it cautiously.

There, on the threshold, was Hevron.

Roberta's heart descended in a roller coaster swoop. She said, "What are you doing here?"

"You told me to come!" said Hevron.

"No, I didn't!" Then she whispered, "My husband's here!"

"You sent me an email," Hevron protested.

"I did not!" said Roberta.

Roberta heard Paul's footsteps approaching. Paul said to Roberta, "What's all this?"

For Hevron was holding the traditional gifts of seduction—a bottle of wine and a single long-stemmed rose.

"I don't know," stammered Roberta, "I can't imagine..." Even in her alarm and fear, Roberta wished Paul wasn't wearing the apron.

Paul asked, "You are...?"

"Hevron Lampart. An old friend of Roberta's. I was in the neighborhood, and I thought I'd drop in and say hello."

"Haven't you heard of the telephone?" Roberta said brusquely. "This is really not a good time."

"All right, I'll go," said Hevron. Ever dramatic, he flung the rose to the floor. He did not, however, toss the wine.

Roberta closed the door and leaned against it.

"What was that all about?" Paul asked.

"I have no idea. He said I sent him an email, and I would never do that."

"Are you sure?"

"Of course I'm sure! Why would I ask him to come for a visit while you were making dinner?"

"But otherwise it would be okay?"

"Of course not! I'm just talking about today, explaining that it wasn't me who sent him any email."

"So is he an ex or something?"

Avoiding the question, Roberta said, "I'm wondering if a certain someone got into my email…"

"You think *Nikki*…?" Paul asked skeptically.

It was infuriating that Paul never took her feud with Nikki seriously.

"If you're worried about your email," said Paul, "just change your password. But tell me about this guy and why he thinks he can just drop in on you with a bottle of wine. And a *rose*. Is he an ex or something? Is he married? You never mentioned a 'Hevron.'"

Roberta sighed.

"What?" asked Paul. "You don't think I have the right to ask these questions?"

33

Nikki

October, 1998

Nikki's house was not one of the grander ones in town: indeed, it was the smallest on her block. She had only 1.5 baths and neither a family room nor a finished basement. Yet she felt her house was exceptionally charming, with its beamed living room and etched glass windows and built-in bookshelves on the stairway, framing a Palladian stained-glass window. Now she went about the first floor, lighting candles and distributing flowers onto the mantelpiece, the coffee table and the .5 bath. The drinks and ice were laid out on the dining room table; the cheese puffs and miniature quiches were in the oven; and the coat closet had plenty of room and plenty of hangers.

She called "Quiana!" and her daughter came thundering down the stairs. It amazed Nikki that her daughter, who weighed 95 pounds, could make so much noise in descent.

"What is it, Mom?" She wore cut-off shorts and a tight T-shirt.

"Do you want to change?" asked Nikki.

"Do I have to?"

"That would be nice. I just wanted to ask if you'd bring out what's in the oven when the timer goes off. I might be busy and not hear it. And lay them out on the platters I've put on the counter."

"Sure. You look different than usual. Like you're going to church or something."

"Well, I may be overdressed for the occasion, but the hostess can't go wrong."

"Is that, like, a rule?"

"Kind of."

The doorbell rang. Someone was ten minutes early. Someone was always ten minutes early. That, too, was, like, a rule.

It was Jackie Schmidt from across the street, in the jeans and sweatshirt in which she'd been gardening all afternoon. Nikki was pleased to see she had her handbag on her shoulder because a handbag might hold a checkbook. "I love your house," exclaimed Jackie Schmidt.

Old Raymond Spitzer from the house on the corner was next. He had profound osteoporosis and walked very slowly with a cane. "Please sit down," said Nikki, "and my daughter will get you a drink. Quiana!"

Quiana descended the stairs more quietly, as if her attire, a striped T-shirt dress, had affected a change in her gait. "Please ask Mr. Spitzer what he'd like to drink."

The doorbell rang again, and it was Cindy MacKenzie, the candidate, and her husband, George. "I can't thank you enough," said Cindy, who was running for Village Trustee.

"No, it's my pleasure," said Nikki. "Have a glass of wine."

"I need it," Cindy said. "I'm nervous."

"Sweetheart," said George, "you have nothing to be nervous about. The Party already nominated you. Tonight, you just have to encourage these nice folks to show their support with a check."

"These are all your friends and neighbors," added Nikki. "They want you to be their trustee! You'll be fine."

People kept arriving at the door. Nikki guessed some of them had come just to see the inside of her house, because it looked so appealing from the outside. Shabby, but inviting. Same as inside, actually. One day she'd have enough money to renovate, or at least repaint, but in the meantime, the shape and flow of the rooms and the period details, the battered brass doorknobs and old chandeliers, gave the house authenticity and charm. Over the years, a dozen people had told her, "If you ever think about selling this house, call me first."

Nikki had no intention of selling her house and was proud to display it on an occasion like this. Now that Quiana was getting around by bike, Nikki saw less of the other parents, and she had decided to play a larger role in community affairs just to stay connected to her village. When Cindy MacKenzie had asked if she would host this fundraiser, Nikki had been happy to oblige. And really, it was good to look around the room, which was filling with Cindy's friends and political connections, among them a popular novelist and a minor film director, both of whom Nikki had wanted to meet for some time. It was a fine turnout, and the borrowed folding chairs were all in use. Two of the other trustees were now here, along with the Mayor, who would be introducing Cindy and explaining why she'd be an asset to the village government.

The mayor stepped to the front of the room and tapped his wineglass. "May I have your attention?"

And at that moment, the doorbell rang. Nikki's first thought was that it was odd, because she'd left the door not only unlocked but a little ajar, so people could come in without ringing the bell. Then she went to the door and saw the two policemen. Had there been a noise complaint? Impossible. The policemen were probably here in connection with the mayor. "Come on in," Nikki said merrily. "We're all in the living room."

"You heard that, Joe?"

"Yes, Captain, she asked you to come in."

Joe was paunchy and dark-haired, perhaps of Italian origin; the captain looked athletic and Irish: tall, blond, pink-cheeked.

Later on, she wondered what would have happened had she not invited them to come in. Did they have a warrant? Would they have bothered getting one?

"The living room, you say?" asked the captain, giving Joe a significant look.

Nikki was baffled: what did it signify?

The policemen came into the room, nodding at the mayor, and saying hello to people they knew. Then with one smooth move, the captain took the carved wooden box from the mantelpiece and opened it.

Nikki's heart pounded hard. It was the box that held her immediate supplies: the cigarette papers, the roaches, and the plastic film canister in which she kept a few joints' worth of clean grass, "Now wait a minute," she began, while her guests, in silence, watched them.

The captain opened the canister and gave it a sniff, and said, "As I thought."

"Could we please have this conversation in another room?" Nikki asked.

The two policemen followed her to the kitchen, and she closed the door behind them.

The captain asked, "You are Nikki Elkins?"

She nodded.

The captain asked, "Where's the rest of the pot?"

"What are you talking about?"

"Someone who uses as much as you has more than this on hand," said the captain, putting the lid back on the canister and shaking it.

"I don't know where you get your information," said Nikki.

But suddenly, she did know. His unerring move to the carved wooden box, which she had kept in the same place for years, made it apparent that someone who knew her had told the police where to look. And only one person in the world hated her that much.

"We're going to search your house, starting with the living room," said the captain. "Do you really want all of your guests to witness that? Why don't you just tell us where the rest of it is and spare yourself the embarrassment?"

Through the closed door, Nikki could hear an excited buzz.

The timer went off, making Nikki jump. Quiana, whose ears were keen, opened the kitchen door. "Go back to our guests," said Nikki. "I'll take care of the oven."

"Mom, what's going on?"

"Tell you later. Now go!"

She put on her oven mitts and reached into the oven, removing a metal tray of tiny quiches. Then she took out a tray of cheese puffs.

"It will be easier on you and *for* you if you don't make us conduct a search," said the captain.

Jed had come back from vacation and had finally graced her with a visit, so Nikki had almost an ounce in the freezer. Would she go to jail?

"All right, Joe," said the captain. "Start looking in the freezer."

"Don't!" cried Nikki. "I'll cooperate."

"Good guess?" asked the captain.

Nikki blushed.

The captain said, "Smokers like to keep it fresh."

Nikki reached into the freezer and brought out a Tupperware storage container. She put it on the counter.

The captain opened the yellow plastic tub and sniffed the marijuana inside. "We're going to confiscate and weigh that," he said. "But it looks less than two ounces to me."

"Much less," said Nikki.

"Or else you'd be looking at jail time."

Cindy knocked at the kitchen door and poked her head in. She looked from Nikki to the policemen to the Tupperware container on the counter. "We were wondering if we should get started," she began. "The mayor has to leave soon."

"Yes, please go ahead," said Nikki.

"Do you need a lawyer?" asked Cindy. "The room's full of them."

"Do I need a lawyer?" Nikki asked the captain.

"No," he said. "You're a first offender. I'll give you a ticket and you'll just pay a fine."

Nikki said, "Go on, Cindy, tell the mayor to introduce you."

"What about you...?"

"You heard what he said," Nikki told her. "It's just a ticket. Now go please." Cindy left the kitchen.

Nikki asked the captain, "Do you mind my asking why you paid me this visit?"

"We got a tip," said the captain.

"And that's all you need to get a warrant and enter a premise?"

"Ma'am, you invited us in. We both heard you."

"And you went right for the box," said Nikki. "Someone told you about that, as well."

They didn't deny it. The captain said, "Here's the citation. You can appeal it at the Village Court or you can send us a check for $500."

She walked them to the door, aware of a silence in the living room as everyone stopped talking. People began asking her questions, but she said, "It's nothing," and retreated to the kitchen, where she placed the cheese puffs and quiches on serving platters.

George MacKenzie joined her in the kitchen.

"I'm so sorry about that," said Nikki. "Very bad timing."

"Not as far as he's concerned."

"How do you mean?"

"The captain's brother is running for Village Trustee against Cindy." He paused to let this information sink in. Then he asked, "What do you think—coinkidink?"

"You mean he wants to damage our campaign with a 'drug bust' at our fundraiser?"

"Exactly."

"Oh, God, I feel terrible," said Nikki.

"Listen, maybe I'm just being paranoid. Maybe it will all be fine. It's certainly not your fault," George said—which made her know he thought it was.

Three days later, the local paper, a weekly, featured the story on page 1: "Pot Seized at Dem Event." They illustrated the story with three photographs: one of Nikki's house, one of Cindy MacKenzie, and one of Nikki. Nowhere in the article did it mention her company, but Nikki knew that someone would bring a story like this to the attention of Lillian or Bethany. Everyone would know she was a doper now; she would never be taken seriously again—the stoner stigma would be hard to escape. Roberta had trashed Nikki's reputation in her very hometown.

Indeed, the next time Nikki went to the Italian deli for some fresh mozzarella, she saw the counter guys smile at each other as she came in. One of them pursed his lips and inhaled sharply, as if sucking a joint.

34
Nikki's Journal

October 15, 1998

*Embarrassed, ashamed, humiliated, mortified. Thank you so
much, Roberta. Oh, thank you for getting me busted in my own
hometown, thank you for the parents who won't let their children
come to Quiana's house, thank you for the snickers at the delicates-
sen and the frowns at the post-office, and thank you for my picture
in the paper. Thank you for outing me without asking me. Thank
you for helping a good candidate, Cindy MacKenzie, look suspicious. Thank you for making a mockery of my efforts to connect
to my community. While I'm at it, thank you for driving away the
man I adored. I really want to thank you, Roberta, for making my
life HELL, at home and at work.*

You're going to pay for this, you crazy drunk.

35

Roberta

April, 1999

Ever since Hevron had shown up at her apartment with a rose and a bottle of wine, Roberta had been deeply suspicious of email. She had changed her password that night, but if Nikki had obtained her password once, she could somehow get it again, so Roberta changed her password frequently and wrote only business mail from that address. Now that she had Internet access at home, all her personal email originated from that address, which she could also access from work. She didn't go as far as Cynthia, who continued to maintain that email made life more difficult, but one way or another (such as reading the collection of well-chosen jokes one of her clients sent daily), email took a lot of time.

She glanced at the bottom of her computer screen and noticed the envelope icon, signaling a new email. It was addressed to her, Nikki, and Lillian. Bethany wanted to see them in her office at 2:30. Some marketing matter, no doubt—but why wasn't Yvonne cc'd?

Roberta loathed being in close quarters with Nikki and hoped that they wouldn't have to sit side by side in Bethany's office. Roberta now found everything about Nikki offensive: her British intonation; her messy, curly hair; her flowery perfume; her confidence. Roberta was having a very good spring, but she was tormented by the thought that Nikki was having a better one. She tried getting information from Andy, but he had become adept at navigating the rocky waters between the two women, and Roberta could learn nothing from him.

Roberta got a call from a prospect at 2:27 (and, after all, how often did prospects call back?), so she was the last person at the meeting.

The others were seated around the small conference table in Bethany's office. "Sorry I'm late," Roberta said, sitting down at the opposite end of the table from Nikki. "I just got a call from Blossomgate Spa."

"Nice," said Lillian. "Very nice. Now close the deal! Bring them in!"

Advice like that was priceless.

"Ladies!" said Bethany. "First of all, I want to commend you. Our sales are up 23% this year."

"It was a great idea to expand into new counties, Bethany," said Lillian.

"Thank you, Lillian," she said. "I've relied on your good advice and good cheer for so many years. I don't know how we're going to do without you."

Roberta leaned forward. *What*?

Bethany continued. "I've called you reps here because this morning, with great reluctance, I accepted Lillian's decision to retire from the company. As you know, she's been with me from the beginning, ever since we worked out of my bedroom in Scarsdale. We have grown this company together! But there comes a time in everyone's life when she wants to slow down, smell the roses—and spend more time with her grandchildren. I've told Lillian that I understand, that maybe soon I'll retire myself. But in the immediate future, I need someone to manage the sales department." She paused to look from Roberta to Nikki and then back to Roberta again. She said, "I like to promote from within. I think only someone who's worked here a while and knows our culture should take on that responsibility. So it's come down to the two of you, ladies. In the next few months, I'm going to watch you closely, give you new challenges, and see who should head up this department. One of your first jobs as Vice President for Marketing will be to hire your replacement as a sales rep."

Roberta glanced at Lillian, whose face was slack. Roberta realized it had not been her idea to retire, although she was well past retirement age. Nor would she endorse this trial period that Bethany was suggesting. Lillian would surely feel that Roberta should get the promotion: she had been with the company longer, she had the highest sales figures, and she was a seasoned sales professional.

For shit sure, Roberta would never work under Nikki.

"I'll be watching you, ladies! Good luck." Bethany stood up, and the others did, too. "It's a great opportunity, I hope you agree."

Nikki asked, "What about Yvonne?"

"Oh, she stays, no matter what," said Bethany.

Damn! thought Roberta.

Nikki said, "No, I meant..." She left what she meant dangling in the air.

Bethany picked it up. "She's a fine rep, but I don't think she could handle the additional responsibility. No, ladies: it's going to be one of you."

Later in the day, Roberta entered Lillian's office and closed the door. She said, "Lillian, I'm so sorry you're leaving."

"I guess it's time," said Lillian without conviction. There were tears in her eyes.

Roberta found herself saying, "You've taught me so much! I'm going to miss you."

"Thank you, Roberta. You're our star."

"Make sure you tell Bethany that."

"I do, I always do."

"Remind her that this is Nikki's first job in sales. First job anywhere, for all I know."

"I'd make you sales manager in a shot, but it's not my decision."

"You should hear the things Nikki used to say about you! When I was still talking to her."

"Like what?"

"I don't want to hurt your feelings, Lillian."

"No, go on, tell me."

"This is what *she* said, not what I said."

"Spit it out!"

"She said you were 'ignorant and arrogant.' She said you were a dimwit."

"She did, did she?"

"And she'd smirk and roll her eyes when you were talking, as if you'd just said something foolish. You must have caught that."

"She's not a good person," said Lillian. "And I can't say I like her. But over the years she's become a good rep. She has good ideas."

"But she doesn't have the experience to head up a department."

Lillian said, "It's not my call, you know. A lot of things aren't my call."

"What will you do now?"

"I haven't had time to think about that," said Lillian. "This is all very sudden."

On the way home, Roberta read another article about the Columbine murders. What kind of country had America become, where students weren't safe in their schools, where social outcasts became killers? Roberta was sure that there'd be copycat killings at other schools. What if someday Benjamin witnessed a school shooting—or worse? But she had to stop this train of thought. When you're a parent, potential disaster lurks everywhere.

"Lillian's retiring," Roberta told Paul that night as she came through the door, carrying the mail. She laid the envelopes and magazines down on the mail table and kissed Benjamin, who was making a complete mess of the dinner Grisella was feeding him.

"That's good," said Paul.

"It might be *very* good. Bethany wants to promote from within. It's between me and the bitch."

"Uh-oh," said Paul, scooping up the mail. "Mud-wrestling time!"

"If Bethany chooses Nikki, I quit! I've got skills! I can go anywhere!" She walked toward the bedroom.

"Of course you can." He followed her to the bedroom and began sorting through the mail.

"Maybe I'll go to one of Bethany's competitors! I know the field and our weaknesses relative to theirs..."

"You'll get the promotion," said Paul. "Don't tie yourself up in knots. Why did Lillian leave?" He singled out an envelope to open.

"I think she's losing it. Last week at a convention, she told our biggest client she'd like to visit his office and convince him to try Bethany meals. He's been with us five years. Bethany herself had to jump in and smooth things over."

Paul took up the letter knife and inserted its tip into the flap of an official-looking envelope. Then he sliced it open. After reading the first few lines, he said, "Huh?" The blood drained from his face.

"Darling, what is it?" She took off her shoes.

"They're tripling our rent."

"What? How can they?"

"The rent board learned about our marriage." He sat down in a chair.

"And...?"

"Our household income is more than $250,000, so they can raise the rent to market rate."

"We'll fight it!" said Roberta, unzipping her skirt and stepping out of it.

"They'll ask for our tax documents," said Paul. "We'll lose."

"There must be some way," said Roberta, opening a drawer and taking out some jeans.

"We could get a divorce," said Paul. "That would be the only way."

She stared at him. Paul had loved his apartment a lot longer than he had loved her.

"Just kidding," he said quickly . "I wonder who could have told them."

"Well, I know," said Roberta, hanging up her skirt.

"You don't think Nikki..."

"Of course it was her. Who else would it be?"

"Maybe a neighbor..."

"Like who? Gloria, who adores me? Clarice, who likes you to be here for the girls? Trust me, it wasn't Clarice or a neighbor."

Paul just sat there shaking his head.

"Nikki's evil," said Roberta. "I told you that."

"At that kind of rent, we might as well buy something," said Paul. "Build some equity. Maybe we should look in Westchester."

"Yeah, but don't you want to kill her? Bash in her head? Like a snake!"

"It's hard to believe she'd report us to our landlord," said Paul. "After all, what have you ever done to her?"

At this, Roberta gave a little smile. She just couldn't help it.

"What?" asked Paul.

"Well," said Roberta with a certain pride, "I did get her arrested."

Paul's mouth dropped open "What do you *mean*?"

"I called the cops and told them to search her house for pot. And they found it! It totally ruined her fundraising event!"

"Are you kidding me?" Paul asked.

"No," said Roberta. "War is war, and I don't think that bitch should get away with her illegal habit."

"But she was your friend," said Paul.

"Was," said Roberta.

"It's just so vengeful. Like, if we have a quarrel are you going to report me to someone?"

"Depends on the quarrel," she said, trying to lighten things up.

He gave her a look.

"I'm *kidding*," said Roberta. "Besides, you don't do anything illegal, do you?"

"That's not the point," said Paul.

"So what's the point?"

He shook his head and left the room. She did not run after him. He was a reasonable man; by tomorrow he'd see things her way.

36

Nikki

August, 1999

Taylor met Nikki and Quiana at the airport, driving a small, immaculate canary-yellow truck. They put their bags into the open bed.

Quiana said, "Oh, Aunt Tay, this is awesome."

"My new toy," said Taylor with a grin. "You don't mind squashing in front?"

"No, it's cool," said Quiana. Nikki stuffed herself in beside her.

"It's a manual," said Taylor, "And it runs on veggie oil."

"So, like, no carbon emissions?" asked Quiana.

"That's right." Taylor changed gears, put her foot on the pedal, and the little truck surged ahead.

"It's so cold out," said Nikki. "What is it, like 50 degrees? In August?"

"'The coldest winter I ever spent was last summer in San Francisco,'" said Taylor. "Or so said Mark Twain."

Nikki said, "Well, about Mark Twain? Scholars have never been able to find that line in his writings. People just like to attribute anything droll to Mark Twain, in the hope of making it funnier."

"Maybe he said it but he didn't write it down," said Quiana. "You don't always write down everything you say."

"He was pretty good about memorializing himself and recycling his good lines," Nikki said. "And he wrote a huge autobiography."

Soon, they left the highway and began driving on local streets. Changing gears showily, Taylor zoomed to the top of the hill and raced down.

"Wheee!" said Quiana.

Nikki's stomach lurched. "I've heard about the hills here but I didn't think they were smack in the middle of the city."

"That's why I love this little truck," said Taylor. "The hills. And the color." She was wearing a matching yellow T-shirt.

They came to a parking garage. Taylor waved a pass and the wooden barrier shot up. She explained, "I get home so late, I don't have time to circle around."

They removed their bags from the truck and followed Taylor to the elevator. They took it to the fourth floor, where it opened directly onto an enormous loft with almost no furniture in it.

"You live here?" said Quiana. "I love it!"

"It's amazing," said Nikki, going to a bank of windows facing the Golden Gate Bridge. "Have you won the lottery?"

"In a way. It's my company—they gave me all these stock options, and now they're worth a lot. So I sold some back. Might as well enjoy life—in my few hours off."

"You can't go wrong buying real estate," said Nikki, who had seen the value of her Westchester house double in the previous ten years.

"That is so true," Taylor said.

Nikki noticed the fireplace, sheathed in slate. "We could have a fire."

Taylor said, "I don't have any wood."

Quiana said, "So what do you actually do at your company?"

"I write code."

"And they pay you so much to do that?"

"It's a very successful company," said Taylor. "And my role has expanded."

"So are you, like, a millionaire?"

Taylor nodded.

Quiana's eyes were enormous and admiring. What kind of values are those? thought Nikki. But she, too, was impressed.

"Like, how many millions?" asked Quiana.

"That's rude," said Nikki. "You don't ask things like that."

"Why not?" asked Quiana.

"It's one of those taboos. You never ask a woman how old she is, how much she weighs, or how much money she has."

"How many millions, Aunt Tay?"

Taylor flashed both hands, spreading her fingers wide.

"Ten million!" said Quiana. "Oh my God!"

"On paper, anyway."

"Jesus," said Nikki. "I had no idea. Your clothes..."

"Everyone wears jeans and T-shirts at work."

"Is everybody rich?"

"The people who were there at the beginning, yeah, we are, but we don't have time to enjoy it."

"You could quit," said Nikki. "Even Treasury Bills would throw off $300,000 a year, and who needs more than that?"

"But I like my job. It's exciting. We're bringing great things to the world."

"You're really lucky, Taylor. Not many people can say that." Nikki paced the loft and said, "Why don't we go shopping this afternoon? Get you some furniture. You need a table and chairs, some lamps, book cases, a desk..."

Taylor's cell phone rang and she flipped it open. After listening, she said into it, "Yes. I see. OK." She snapped it closed. "I'm sorry. There's a problem at work. I have to go in."

"Can I go with you?" asked Quiana.

"No, it's going to be a long night."

"When are you coming back?" asked Nikki.

"Late."

That was one good thing about Bethany Moore, thought Nikki: you never worked late. At five o'clock, the entire staff, except for the officers, rose as one. Except for Roberta, of course, who rose at 4:30, although that "baby" of hers must be in nursery school by now.

"What are you gonna do about dinner?" Quiana asked Taylor.

"They have this incredible cafeteria, with fabulous organic food— and it's free."

"Free?" asked Nikki.

"See, they want you to stay all the time, so they make it very pleasant. They have ping-pong tables and a gym. It's a whole new paradigm." Taylor planted a kiss on Quiana's cheek and gave Nikki the house-keys, a map, and a guidebook to San Francisco. Then she was out the door. In a few minutes, they heard her truck leave the garage.

"She is so cool," said Quiana. "And so rich!"

"In just a couple of years—it's amazing." Nikki tried to sort out her feelings. On the one hand, good for Taylor—what a coup! On the other hand, by comparison, Nikki, who had been quite pleased with her paychecks, now felt like a pauper.

On the third hand, if she actually became a pauper, she could always get help from Taylor. And photos of Taylor and her loft might be an interesting contrast to the other images in the women and houses book Nikki kept imagining.

Returning to New York after a week away was always a shock. JFK was squalid and confusing, and it was hard to find the taxi queue, where you waited too long for your cab. The highway took you through a depressing part of Queens, and you always had to explain to the cabbies (whose job it was, after all) about the correct way to price a trip to Westchester: full value of the meter until city limits, near the Conner Street exit, after which double from that point on—*not* double for the whole ride!

The house smelled musty, and there was a pile of mail beside the front door, all of it, seemingly, junk. In the week they'd been away she'd gotten a grand total of two phone calls. Quiana had gotten fifteen. The plants looked thirsty, and the milk had gone bad.

The next morning, when the radio clock awoke her at seven, Nikki felt she'd been fished from the bottom of the sea. Apparently, now that she was back in Westchester, she was finally on California time. She stumbled out of bed. Outside the air-conditioned bedroom, the upstairs was steamy, although it was cool enough downstairs. Sometimes she thought her personal comfort zone was just a few degrees, from 68 to 75. Already it was too hot for breakfast on the porch.

Nikki had recently read that most people have more or less the same thing for breakfast and lunch every weekday. She certainly had monotonous breakfasts: cereal with fruit. Perhaps she didn't like making choices so early in the morning. But she hadn't shopped, and there was no fruit or milk, so she got half a bagel from the freezer and put it in the toaster. She had her coffee black. She thought about Ian, who always had his coffee black. She had dated a few men in the past eighteen months, but she hadn't met anyone she liked nearly as much as Ian. Don't think about him, she told herself—several times a day. Thinking about Ian threw her into a vortex of loss and regret. Perhaps he would have forgiven her the photo if she had explained, really explained, the circumstances—or if, in his eyes, she hadn't been so wanton, dancing with the stranger in that market town. *Doudou.*

Nikki was still in a fog when she got to the office, so after she sat down and turned on the computer, at first she didn't get the significance of what she was seeing. The desktop displayed itself, but she couldn't find any folders to open. Even the shortcuts on her desktop were gone. Was her computer broken? It seemed to be operating fine, but where were her files, her directories? She opened her email to see if someone had sent an announcement about the computers. That's when she saw that her inbox contained only 4 messages, all received during the last hour, instead of the thousands she always left in there to establish a record.

"Hey, Cynthia," Nikki called. "Is your computer working okay?"

"It sure is," she said. "And yours?"

"Not really." Nikki glanced at Roberta, who didn't hide her interest and pleasure in this conversation.

Then the full implication hit Nikki. Her files had been destroyed. She kept clicking her mouse, but her computer had been thoroughly cleansed. Every one of her records, each carefully calibrated selling document and pitch, all her client and prospect information, so laboriously gained and recorded—gone. As well as her email. As she apprehended the enormity of her loss, she felt hollow and weak. No records at all, just when she needed everything to go right, with Bethany's eyes upon her. She felt her teeth grinding against each other as she thought of Roberta destroying her data—or, given Roberta's lack of tech skills, paying some hacker to do it. When Nikki looked away from the computer screen, the room was tinged red with her rage.

It was going to be tedious and demoralizing recreating her database, and while she was doing this, she'd be slipping behind in her sales.

Except... wait a minute. This was a commercial enterprise, and data was crucial. The computers were all networked; surely there were back-up tapes. She could feel Roberta watching as she walked toward the IT department.

Vlad, the tall young Russian, was staring at a screen when she entered his cubicle. He told her that they did indeed have back-up tapes. They'd made one on Friday: her files were safe. "And email?" she asked.

"That we don't save. But probably is on hard drive. We can restore for you."

"That's such a relief!" She said, "I could kiss you—but that would be harassment."

"No, no, no," Vlad said.

She wondered which this was: gallantry or the definitive kiss refusal? She asked hastily, "Could you find out who did it? Would there be digital clues?"

"Sometimes yes, sometimes no. Main thing: your informations is safe. Will get it back to you today."

"Wow, that's such a relief."

He'd turned back to his screen when Nikki asked, "Tell me something."

He looked up at her.

"Is there anything to all this Y2K stuff? Are all the computer chips in the world going to malfunction at midnight this New Year's?"

"Is theory," he agreed.

"I have friends who are planning to stay in Florida all January, in case the power plants and heating systems fail. They figure at least they'll be warm."

"Thousands people is working on Y2K. Billions spent. Maybe will work. Maybe not. Will be interesting, no, to find out?"

Nikki walked back to her desk and sat down with a smile on her face. She hoped Roberta saw it. God, that woman made her self-conscious, but she wouldn't have to deal with Roberta much longer, and that alone was reason to smile. Nikki knew that if Bethany chose her, Roberta would quit, which would be deliciously ironic now that Roberta had moved to Westchester—to a house with a pool, she had let it be known. Perhaps by ratting on Roberta to her former landlord, Nikki had inadvertently improved her circumstances. This was a disquieting notion.

What she really resented about Roberta, Nikki thought, not for the first time, was being brought down to her level. This insane office feud had brought out a vengeful side to herself she'd never suspected existed. With Roberta gone, she could go back to being her old self—or so she hoped. You can't just erase a demeaning experience, one that had gone on for years.

She reflected that her feud with Roberta had actually proved more degrading than that night with those guys in DC.

Nikki stood up. She'd drop in on Lillian and see what had happened during the week she'd been in San Francisco. The woman was always good for a laugh. Nikki got a perverse pleasure in seeing how Lillian tried to overcome her hostility with loud and awkward bonhomie and unwittingly hilarious turns of phrase. But Lillian's office was empty. Her books and photos and paperweights were gone; her bulletin board contained nothing.

Nikki turned in shock and caught Yvonne's eye. "Gone," said Yvonne, motioning her toward the kitchen. Nikki followed her in. Yvonne said, "Lillian said if she was going to go, it should be right away."

"Well, she *was* getting... *confused*."

"Roberta's telling everyone that Lillian left in a hurry so she could have her going away party at Lusardi's last Friday without you!"

"Really? You think Lillian hates me that much?"

Yvonne said, "How do you feel about her?"

"Let's just say I'm glad she's gone."

"I'm sure you are," said Yvonne.

There was an edge to her voice, and Nikki could tell Yvonne knew that either Roberta or Nikki would be promoted to Lillian's job. Nikki could end up being her boss—and that was the best of Yvonne's options.

Yvonne continued with false sympathy. "Poor Roberta! She's just lost her biggest fan."

"Yes," said Nikki with a grin. "There's always that."

"I like your blouse," said Yvonne. "The color. It matches your eyes."

"Thanks," said Nikki. Clothes were for women what sports were for men: a safe, absorbing topic of conversation. She remembered Ian deploring how hard it was for him, a Brit, to become friends with

American men because he couldn't talk to them about sports.

This was the second time she had thought about Ian today, and it wasn't eleven o'clock yet.

At lunchtime, she got a few things from the small store near her office and hurried home. An hour wasn't all that long when you had to shop and drive and make lunch and eat and drive back. Today, she had roast turkey and tomatoes and sliced avocado in her mesclun. She brewed herself fresh coffee in the one-cupper and went back to the garden, where she had exactly four minutes to lie on a chaise under the trees. On hot days like this, when she lay in the shade and not in the sun, she sometimes returned to the office with leaves and seeds in her hair. She'd have to check the mirror.

What would impress Bethany most: showing some high-level managerial skill or landing a big new client?

Big new client. Bethany was all about the money. Tomorrow morning, she and Andy would work on identifying her most likely big prospect. Andy was good, and he understood her job perfectly. He'd get it, too, if she was promoted, as she had told him before her vacation. "Roberta said the same thing," he'd replied, rather smugly, "so I'm good either way."

It was borderline annoying that Andy never indicated even tacitly that he was on Nikki's side in the feud, as any sane person would be.

When Nikki got back to work, she saw there was broken glass in her parking space, # 65, so she found another empty space. She hoped whoever usually parked in # 87 was on vacation and not still at lunch. She'd check with Cynthia when she got upstairs. When she walked into the building, she was already thinking of the afternoon ahead and whether her files had been restored. She pushed the button for the elevator.

Roberta entered the lobby. Seeing Nikki, she hesitated, as if considering taking the stairs. The women hadn't spoken to each other in more than two years.

Nikki broke the silence. She said, "What, scared to ride *alone with me in an elevator?*" Her voice dripped with scorn. The elevator door opened, and Nikki gave Roberta a challenging look. Roberta swept by her and entered the elevator, head high, face haughty. The door closed and they were alone in the metal box.

Nikki said, "Thanks for the glass in my parking space."

"I don't even know where your parking space is, you crazy bitch."

Perhaps that was true. Nikki was sorry she had brought up something so questionable and trivial when Roberta had done her so much real damage .

Suddenly, the elevator slowed, gave a shudder and stopped.

Roberta jabbed her finger against the "4" button again and again. Nothing happened.

Roberta muttered, "I don't believe this."

Nikki had to smile at her discomfort, even though she herself was starting to sweat. The elevator remained immobile and silent. Nikki couldn't even hear the motor.

Roberta said, "I *really* don't believe this!"

"Believe it," Nikki said coolly. She stared directly at Roberta. "You're stuck in an elevator with the person you hate most in the world. But there are quite a few people you hate, aren't there? Let's see, there's Yvonne, and that brother of yours, is it Kenny?"

"Shut up!" said Roberta. "I don't have to listen to this."

"Oh, yes you do! Because, guess what, we're stuck here together! It's worthy of Sartre, don't you think? Oh, I forget, I'd better not make you feel *intellectually insecure!* You just might get hysterical."

"No Exit," yelled Roberta. "And he's right! Hell *is* other people, other people like you!" And she hit the red alarm button, setting off a ring, like a very loud old-fashioned telephone, only it was just a single ring, sounding on and on. Then it was still. "Someone better come soon," she said darkly.

"Or... what, exactly?" asked Nikki. "You'll have a meltdown? You know, that's kind of losing its novelty."

"You are *such* a slime-ball," said Roberta. She opened her handbag and began fumbling inside it.

Nikki's heart plunged: what if she had a gun? After all, she got on MetroNorth at the 125th Street Station... But Roberta's hand emerged with her mobile phone.

Why were so many people getting these cellular phones, Nikki wondered once more. She could understand doctors having them, or Taylor, who was always on call, but salespeople like Roberta? Really, what was the point? When did interested clients need to get hold of you *at that very moment* or the deal would fall through? Anyway, the phones didn't even work half the time. She saw Roberta angrily snap hers closed and return it to her bag. Nikki concluded the elevator was—what did they call it?—a dead zone. So much for Roberta's stupid gizmo.

Nikki said, "*I'm* the slimeball? *You* sent Ian that photo. *You* wrecked our relationship—just for spite. I loved him, and you made him hate me."

"You made your own bed on that one, you slut."

"At least I like sex. You probably don't. I really pity your husband—he seems so nice. Cute, too."

"My husband's none of your fucking business," shouted Roberta. Once again, she hit the alarm, and once again the high sound rang for thirty seconds.

When the alarm ceased, the silence seemed sepulchral. "Someone will come now," muttered Roberta.

Nikki thought so, too. After all, it was the middle of a weekday afternoon in an office building: someone was sure to have heard the alarm.

A few seconds later, an intercom came on, and a man with a Hispanic accent said, "Hello. I'm the super. What's the problem?"

"The elevator's stuck between floors," said Nikki.

"Is anybody hurt?"

"No, we're okay."

"You are how many people?"

"Two ladies," said Roberta. "We work at Bethany Moore."

"I'll have my elevator guy get you out."

"When is that going to be?" asked Roberta.

"I'll call him right now." Only it sounded more like "rye now." The intercom was disconnected.

"Now we wait," said Nikki.

"Lovely," said Roberta.

"Oh, and by the way? If you think you destroyed my computer files, think again!"

"I don't know what you're talking about."

"*Dimwit*, we work in a company! They have back-up tapes! Vlad's restoring all my files and email even as we speak."

"Like I give a shit?"

"Spoken like the true lady you are," said Nikki. "Like, what you did was not only illegal, it was also *pointless!*"

"You're a fine one to talk about 'legal.' I'm surprised you're not in jail, where you belong."

"Oh, *that!*" said Nikki. "I forgot to thank you for my pot bust! That was really classy. But, guess what, birdbrain? You don't go to jail for small amounts of pot. I just got a small fine."

"I hear your name was in the local paper," remarked Roberta.

"I'm sure you showed Lillian and Bethany."

"They should have canned you there and then, you nitwit junkie!"

"Well, they didn't. And you know why? Because they can't afford to lose talent like me. You were the star here, *once*. Well, not any more!"

The intercom came on, and they heard the man with the accent again. "Hello, this is the super again. How you doing in there?"

Roberta said, "It's about time! We've been *stuck* in this miserable *box* for half an *hour*. How do you *think* we're doing?"

The super said, "We get you out soon."

"You goddamn better," shrieked Roberta.

Nikki said, "Excuse my colleague. I believe she's becoming hysterical."

Roberta gave an indignant yelp.

Nikki said calmly, "We're just wondering what the problem is and when it might be resolved."

Another voice reached them now. "Ladies? There are two of you, right?"

"Unfortunately," said Roberta, "I'm stuck here with this *bitch*."

The voice said soothingly, "I'm the emergency elevator repairman, and I'm going to find out what's wrong and fix it. I'll have you out of there in just a little while. Please stay calm and be patient. You're going to be fine."

"Thank you," said Nikki. "I'm glad you're working on the problem."

Roberta said, "I can't *believe* this is happening to me."

Nikki found herself laughing. "That is *so* typical," she said. "It's always all about *you*."

"Whatever," said the repairman, and he switched off the intercom.

"Alone again," said Nikki. "Just we two." To her own ears, it sounded like nothing in the world could make her happier. She said, conversationally, "So how's Hevron? Did Paul like him?"

Roberta swung back her arm and hit Nikki in the face with her handbag.

Nikki's jaw dropped open with surprise, but she quickly recovered herself and taunted, "Ooh, that really hurt. Maybe you need a *drink* to give you some strength!"

Roberta hit her again with the bag, this time hard to her stomach. She shouted, "Why don't you just leave me alone, you junkie bitch?"

The blow crumpled Nikki, who crouched a moment, gasping. Then from her low position, she made a rush at Roberta, grabbing her thighs and heaving her backwards, over her head. There was a thump as Roberta fell to the floor. Her bag flew open, and she made a grab for her keys, but Nikki wrestled them away, twisting Roberta's arm back until she let go. Then Roberta grabbed Nikki's earring and pulled. The pain was sudden and searing as her earlobe tore, and Nikki fell backwards against the elevator floor.

Roberta sat upon her, pounding her fists into Nikki's eyes and nose. "That's for reporting us to the rent board." Smash. "And that's for Hevron." Another smash. "And that's for the tax audit."

"I didn't get you audited, you lunatic!" Nikki clawed upward with the keys at Roberta's face, opening a red channel on her forehead. Feeling Roberta suddenly weakening, Nikki made a tremendous effort and unseated her. She pulled herself up by the rail.

Roberta stood up, too, on the opposite side of the elevator, blood raining down her face. Then, gasping and heaving, she made a rush at Nikki, who pushed back at her. But Roberta was larger, potent with rage, and she smashed Nikki against the elevator wall. Nikki's head hit the railing as she slid down, and then the air turned thick and gray, like smoke. Then she saw black.

37

Roberta

August, 1999

Roberta was on all fours, blood streaming from the cut on her forehead. She heard the loudspeaker go on. "Ladies, this is the elevator repairman, and I've got the problem fixed. The elevator's going to start going now." With a shudder and a clank, the elevator began to move again.

When the doors opened on the fourth floor, Roberta crawled toward the landing.

Most of the staff at Bethany Moore was waiting outside the elevator. When Roberta moved toward them, there was a gasp of horror.

"Call 911," said Bethany, and Vlad ran into the office.

Roberta collapsed onto the floor, and Cynthia, pulling off the scarf she was wearing, ran to her.

The elevator repairman, a middle-aged man with startlingly black hair, asked, "What happened? There shouldn't be any injuries. There wasn't a crash."

Andy looked inside the elevator and yelled in horror, "Somebody help me with Nikki!"

The elevator repairman was saying, "I heard all this thumping, and I couldn't figure it out."

Bethany walked into the elevator, and Andy bent down to move Nikki.

"My God," said Bethany. "Look how her head is twisted. Don't touch her, Andy."

Roberta heard him say, "I think she's dead," and for one little moment she was glad. Then she was incredulous.

"She isn't dead," said Roberta from the landing. "She's just pretending."

Cynthia was pressing her scarf into the gash on Roberta's forehead. She said, "Lord, child. What happened?"

"She kept taunting me," gasped Roberta. "And we had a fight." She started sobbing.

"Can you stand?" Cynthia held out her arm, and Roberta slowly rose to her feet. Her legs were trembling. Cynthia said, "Did you push Nikki?"

"I don't know," sobbed Roberta. "I have to see a doctor."

Cynthia said soothingly, "The ambulance will be here any minute."

"I'm not going to some random emergency room doctor!" shrieked Roberta. "She gouged my face! I need a plastic surgeon!"

Cynthia said, "You're going to wait right here until the medics evaluate your condition."

"I am *not*," said Roberta. "Get me a car service." And when nobody did anything, she pulled out her cell phone.

"Nikki may be *dead*," Yvonne was telling Cynthia. "Roberta can't just leave before the police arrive."

But Roberta was already speaking into the phone, giving the address of Bethany Moore. "Andy," she said. "Help me downstairs. I need to get to a plastic surgeon so I'm not scarred forever."

"But what about Nikki?"

"There's 911 for Nikki, but there's only Dr. Mandelbaum for me."

"You have to stay here," said Cynthia, but Roberta, aided by Andy, made her way to the staircase, and nobody saw fit to stop them.

Roberta kept Cynthia's scarf pressed into her forehead as she went down the stairs, with Andy holding her upper arm.

When they reached the first floor, the ambulance had arrived, and Roberta walked out the door, with Andy still holding her arm. A medic looked at them questioningly, and Andy said, "The emergency's on the fourth floor."

A black town car was pulling up by the building, and Roberta opened the door and got inside. "Do you want me to come with you?" asked Andy, but Roberta shook her head. She said to the driver, "428 Park Avenue in Manhattan." Then she took out her cell phone to tell Dr. Mandlebaum she was coming.

38

Nikki

September, 1999

Nikki was dreaming she was packed in a box, cushioned by white styrene foam. "It's for your own good," said the man, but she had to stay in one position hour after hour or forever. Then there was pain and the dark one entered and she dreamed of the grand room again, always marveling that it existed in her own house, accessible rarely and randomly. There it was, again: the huge room with the curved, ebony furniture, the bright Persian rugs and the crystal chandeliers, and she wanted to show someone this luxurious place, but she only could enter it when she was by herself. She dreamed Ian was at the foot of her bed, smiling tenderly at her and holding her foot through the thin blanket. She dreamed she was crying with joy and then crying that it was a dream and the dark one came in and adjusted the fluids in the bag. She was in a library, looking for Quiana, and then she dreamed she was waking up in a hospital. Then she *was* waking up in a hospital and she croaked, "Hello. Hello? Anybody there?" And she opened her eyes in this dream that was no dream and there was no one there, so she went back to the grand room, where she apparently owned a Renoir, which she approached in delight. She stayed for a while in the splendor of the room.

When she opened her eyes again, she saw, unmistakably, Ian in profile against the hospital window. She said, in wonder, "Ian, I dreamed you were here and now here you are."

He said, "I was here before, too. But you were mainly out of it."

"You held my foot," she said.

"I did."

"What day is it? What happened?"

"It's Thursday, darling."

She didn't know what surprised her more, hearing him calling her that or realizing she'd been out cold for three days. "Ian—tell me— what happened? Why are you here?"

"I missed you."

Nikki felt tears coming into her eyes. She touched the white foam collar that encircled her neck. "What's this?" She wiggled her toes; she wasn't paralyzed.

"They're stabilizing your neck. They want to keep you in that position for another few days. Do you remember what happened?"

"I was in an elevator with Roberta, and we were fighting, and she came at me..."

"Your head hit the elevator wall, and the rail knocked it into an odd angle and it stayed stuck there. And you were also concussed. They stabilized you, then they basically pulled and twisted your head back into place. You're going to be fine."

She remembered Roberta punching her face and asked, "Do I have a black eye?"

"Two," said Ian. "And a torn ear."

"Do I look grotesque?"

"Yes," he said, and kissed her, carefully, because of the collar. "Roberta quit her job."

Nikki closed her eyes in relief.

Ian said, "When Paul told me you were in the hospital, I had to come see you. Because I realized..."

"What, Ian?"

He just looked into her eyes. By now, he was sitting on the bed, holding her hand.

She said, "How do I know you're not just a dream?"

He pulled a paperback book from his pocket, turned it to the back, and said, "Read it."

She started reading the publisher's blurb about the book, which was about bioethics.

"Now read it over again."

She read the same lines to him. "You can't do that when you dream," said Ian. "The words always change, or the letters slide away or dissolve."

This was one of the things she had missed most about Ian: he had something interesting to say about almost everything.

A nursing assistant entered the room, a small African-American woman. "Good afternoon. I see you're awake," she said to Nikki.

"I'm trying to persuade her that she isn't dreaming," said Ian.

The nursing assistant slipped the blood pressure cuff on Nikki's arm and began inflating it. "Feel that pressure?"

Nikki nodded: her arm felt tight.

"You wouldn't feel that in a dream, just as you wouldn't feel a pinch."

Ian said, speculatively, "There must be some conservation mechanism to prevent the body from mobilizing itself against imagined pain, which is why we don't feel pain in our dreams."

The nursing assistant took off the blood pressure cuff and said, "I promise, Ms. Elkins, you're awake. You're not dreaming." She put a thermometer in Nikki's ear to take her temperature and gave the instrument a click. "Welcome back." She made some notes on the chart and left the room.

"How's Quiana?" Nikki asked Ian, who was now seated in an armchair by her bed.

"She's with your ex. They'll be here later on."

Nikki nodded.

They said at the same time, "That photo."

"Go on," he said.

"No, you."

"Well, I realize there's more to you than that one photo. We all make mistakes. I made a big mistake, too, letting one image outweigh everything else. Can you forgive me?"

Her eyes were welling again; she had missed him so much.

He said, "I was such an ass. A 'penultimate' ass."

Nikki smiled.

Ian said, "I have to make a confession."

"Go on."

"That photo..."

"Oh, leave it alone!"

"No, you have to know. I found that picture just *awful*—but also, kind of, arousing."

"Ian, I was drunk! They took advantage of me! I was their prey!"

He said, "I know all that. I'm really sorry. I just thought you should know, in case we start seeing each other again. I'm a beast."

"You are." Above the stiff white medical collar that kept her head in place, Nikki's smile was radiant. She patted the bed. "Come closer, beast."

39

Roberta

"Watch this," said Paul.

Roberta looked up from the chaise just in time to see Paul toss a beach ball to Benjamin, who was standing in the shallowest part of the pool. "We've been practicing this to surprise you."

Roberta was pleased to see that Benjamin actually caught the ball, but when he tried to throw it back to Paul, he held it over his head and tossed it backward.

They probably wouldn't use the pool much longer this year, but it certainly was great on this late September day. The move from their Manhattan apartment last May had been less painful than she'd imagined, and the pool was quite a plus. Since then, she had swum every evening, to relax after another tense day at Bethany Moore Meals.

Well, those days were over and done! Roberta had quit before they could fire her. Lillian had left, so she had no protector. Paul said Roberta should have waited to be fired, so she could qualify for unemployment insurance, but she pointed out they would claim she'd been fired for cause, considering she'd put Nikki in a the hospital. She was careful to hide her jubilation about this from that goody-goody Paul.

Dr. Mandelbaum had done his best, but he had warned Roberta that there might be a visible scar on her forehead for months. So for the first time in her life, Roberta started wearing bangs. It was important to look your best when you were job-hunting, and the bangs made her look a lot younger. Paul had learned from Ian that Nikki wasn't going to press charges. Well, why should she? She was getting her reward: she would be the new Vice President of Marketing at Bethany Moore. Exactly what the cunning bitch had always wanted.

Now by the pool, Roberta fished in her bag for her compact. She applied some lipstick, more for moisture than color. Benjamin and Paul were splashing each other at the shallow end of the pool. Boys. Roberta studied herself in the small, circular mirror. She should have cut bangs years ago—perhaps the only reason she hadn't was because Nikki wore bangs. What a relief it was to finally be done with Nikki's relentless presence, on the job and in her psyche! She should have quit long ago. Within three weeks of leaving, Roberta had found a sales position in medical supplies. The job was close to her new house and might end up paying her even more than she'd gotten before. As part of her job, she'd sometimes be making sales calls on old clients from Bethany Moore; she knew this was part of the reason she'd been hired. The other part? Well, she was a terrific salesperson. She was a star. That's why she made a lot of money. That's why she had such great clothes. And this nice house. And her kind, if sappy, husband. And her wonderful child. If she could only lose ten pounds, her life would be perfect. She sipped her glass of wine.

Her new job started the next day. Roberta would make a special effort to be nice to everybody, to get along, to blend in. Going to work shouldn't be like going to combat, and she was going to be agreeable to everyone. She wasn't going to have any fights, and she wasn't going to start any feuds. She was going to look for the good in people.

There was one sales rep at her new job who was very appealing, a woman of about forty with a Southern drawl and a ready smile. On her desk was a framed photo of two little boys around Benjamin's age. She wore diamond earrings and lived in the next village. Perhaps they would have a drink after work; perhaps they would be friends.

It would be great to have a good friend at work.

Acknowledgements

Thanks to publisher extraordinaire Naomi Rosenblatt. Thanks to my close writer friends, Jane Delynn, Sonia Pilcer, and Kathleen Rockwell Lawrence. Thanks to my mother, Glynne Hiller, and my sister, Colette Hiller, and my cousin, Jackie Shabot. Thanks to my wonderful husband, Mark Thompson.

About the Author

Catherine Hiller's most recently published book was the controversial *Just Say Yes: A Marijuana Memoir.*

She is the author of the novels *An Old Friend from High School, 17 Morton Street, California Time, Cybill in Between,* and *The Adventures of Sid Sawyer.*

John Updike wrote that her short story collection *Skin: Sensual Tales* was "good, brave, and joyful writing."

She has also written two children's books, *Argentaybee and the Boonie* and *Abracatabby.*

She is the co-producer of two hour-long documentary films: *Do Not Enter: The Visa War Against Ideas* and *Paul Bowles: The Complete Outsider.*

Catherine Hiller has a BA from Brooklyn College and a PhD from Brown University. The mother of three adult sons, she lives with her husband and their dog in Westchester County, New York.

Hooked, Lined & Single

Rashmi Kumar

Srishti
PUBLISHERS & DISTRIBUTORS

Srishti Publishers & Distributors
N-16, C. R. Park
New Delhi 110 019
editorial@srishtipublishers.com

First published by
Srishti Publishers & Distributors in 2014

To my grandparents
My childhood begins and ends with you both!

"Teach me to do thy will."

—Psalms 143:10

Acknowledgements

◆

As a new mother, it is easy for a woman to lose herself through the journey of nurturing, caring, feeding, changing diapers, waking up at odd hours and literally seeing your little one grow minute by minute. But there are those who made sure to remind me every now and then that I am also a woman, an individual, a writer and possess the special power of touching lives through my words. My readers, I owe this success to you. You never for once made me feel that my journey has come to an end. In fact, you always reminded me that I still have miles to travel.

My family, who never let success get into my head. They never truly stopped believing in me, no matter what. My friends in India, who make my life worth living each day. My friends in Canada, who helped me immensely to make this new country my new home. Team Srishti Publishers who have fulfilled my dream through this book.

Above all, thank you Lord, for not only loving me but also for being with me through some of the most challenging phases of my life. I hope I can continue to use your gift of writing to touch more lives.

Part - 1

The Beginning

or

101 Reasons why I Should Try Again

Mission Me a la Marriage

◆

With me, Ala

Myra told me it worked that way.

"It did. It did. It did..."

This is what I had to repeat to myself 140 times. This is what my female soulmate repeated to me 400 times, though I've mentioned it only three times for the readers' convenience. So, in all, there was a mental, social, spiritual and religious assault on me, some 540 times! But I took on the ravages of these numbers and decided to go for it anyway.

So there was a list of demands made by this woman I had grown up with for the last fifteen years and couldn't say no to:

- Number one: Get a tattoo – any part of the body would do – as long as it's big enough to be seen.
- Number two: Get a Brazilian wax – a must do.
- Number three: Get a hair makeover – do away with the unruly curls – they're out of fashion. *Ouch! Are they?*

I didn't want to get a tattoo done because it's painful. I didn't want to get a Brazilian wax done because it's even more painful. And I didn't want to get a hair makeover done because it's painfully painful (I am a huge fan of my curls). But Myra, for the sake of being herself, believed that all these must-dos would do me a world of good. Now you might wonder why a best friend would push me for such painful things, that too against my wish. Was she trying to make me a rebel? Did she see my short curlies jutting out of my knickers? Or did I have a bald patch that had to be covered with leftover hair? None of it. Myra just believed that a makeover – inside and outside – would do me good. And for some strange reason, I knew that it was going to work as well. *How, says who, really?*

Nevermind! Finally, in the squeaky little breathing space that Myra allowed me, I decided to do what I did best – write. Out of sheer compulsion, I started penning my thoughts in a tiny notepad. It was so tiny that Myra wouldn't have had the slightest suspicion.

And instead of enunciating thoughts that could vary from,

```
Dear Diary, today morning I woke up realising I
have missed my periods… in the afternoon I went
to see a doctor… evening I cried, night, I wanted
to be a mommie, etc…
```

to thoughts like:

```
Swimming, swimming, swimming in the middle of the
sea, certainly not winning, mind down on its knees…
```

which I thought were profanely boring…

I subscribed to penning down random words and phrases like,

```
Hebrew greeting on my shoulder blade... XYZ is a
mother fucker... (doodle of my name)
```

My notepad soon looked more like miniature graffiti on paper. *A writer should do better than that!* So I re-vamped. This time, I was more specific:

```
I am Alafia Singh...Though my name means peace and
blessings in the native African language, right
now, I have run out on both... I have neither peace
nor blessings; I am not even in Africa to change
my mood with some fantastic African lover! I need
resurrection, I need resurrection, I need resurrection,
I need resurrection, I need...
```

And while I wrote all that I didn't have and craved for, I began tearing up.

Wouldn't any girl who's 31 years *old* in India, desperately wanting to get married – well, okay, not desperately; almost desperately – tear up too? Having survived a mini marriage at 22, which lasted a whole of 11 months and 10 days, the pressure was immense and the loneliness, burdening. Deeply concerned relatives and various others I bumped into at festivals or weddings talked about the delay in my getting hitched, and that heightened my loneliness. They shamelessly sermonised: to not be so snobbish, or so narrow in my thinking. *How do they master the art of cornering the vulnerable kinds?* Some even claimed, again brazenly, that I was unreasonably high in my expectations, and that I had to learn to compromise, *if at all* I ever wanted to get married again. Then there were those who had already lost hope, because as per Indian standards, I was way beyond a decent marriageable age. *Did they see the first few grey hair peeping out?* Then there were those who strongly believed that extensive travelling and writing books had screwed up my mind. *How is it my problem if Indian men hate intellectual women!*

Oh, but hold on! If that sounded like I was all-lost-with-no-hope, you got it all wrong. Then again, before I went on to prove how-beautiful-life-is and 101-reasons-to-smile, I wanted to add another challenge that stared stark at me. Like when you stare at the lizard on the toilet door (if you're scared of one, you'll know what I mean!) just when you've shut it close. So now, you can neither pee in peace nor can you open the door after peeing, if at all (in peace). All you can do is wait for the lizard to dislodge. But in my case, the options were limited. Rather, I had none.

Although I was born into a Protestant Christian family, and grew up learning verses from the Psalms and Proverbs, I was never made to endorse the religion and wear it on my sleeve. So my name did not bear any anglicised lineage, nor did I look like a 'typical Christian girl'. Well, I still don't know what a typical Christian girl looks like, except that she might wear a cross around her neck, which again, I didn't. I didn't wear many cute little dresses, nor did I waltz around with a glass of wine, doing a 'hey man... yo man...' jig. *Who told people only Christian girls did all of that?*

Now, the good part: I was blessed with above-average looks and intellect that Myra was now trying to salvage. Men often asked me out on dates and even short holidays to get cosy for some quick fun. I've also made a decent career out of writing books, although many still feel it's a vocation, not an occupation.

But I wanted none of it. I didn't want to be a trophy wife to a lover whenever he came to India, and the prospect of taking expensive vacations with another lover didn't allure me either. Moreover, I often got seriously offended if a (prospective) lover were to even suggest, "Let's get humpy, beautiful one!" While any woman my age would triumph over such male attention, I squirmed as if someone had just shoved a cupful of tiramisu in my panties. So I would often accept/reject a proposal on the basis of my current state of mind. A holiday or a quickie in a hotel room/ your place or mine – Never! But a definite yes for a decent meal/ coffee/ promenade, etc., if the man was charming enough.

What I looked for, and perhaps wanted in every man was that soft corner that could be charmed by my dark brown eyes, the butter brown skin, or the sonority in my voice. I wanted to get married. I asked Myra if there was anything wrong with that, to which she declared with nonchalance, "Of course not, Ala... you deserve a companion too!"

"Then why am I not getting what I deserve? Am I bad enough or do I just move around with an invisible signboard around my neck that says: I am *just* a good fuck?" Myra often went numb with concern when I asked her those questions, fresh from another finding-Mr-Right-disaster. And there were way too many of them.

The latest one: the unfailingly attractive, divorced ship charterer from Singapore, ten years older to me. Things between me and Pervez Jehangir were turning to be straight out of a Bollywood movie. But like a majority of Hindi cinemas, this one was not going to have a happy end.

Later on how Pervez ruled my heart, he just did; and did it with such ferocity that mission post-mortem-Pervez left me even more vulnerable, unstable and craving for more.

Darling Vishesh Venkat and once an adorable boyfriend had often told me that I can't take no for an answer. "Ala, you're so used to a *yes* from everyone, every time that you have a problem with one small thing not going in your favour..." he would say, but very lovingly.

Of course I had a problem listening to a *no*, but when that *no* happened a little too often, you ended up looking like that exotic piece of art work, that lay hanging in a corner on the most obscure looking wall of an art gallery. The one that everyone admired and some even fell in love with, but no one really wanted to buy. And certainly not at any throwaway price like its counterpart that hung on a freshly-painted bright yellow wall.

Mission PJ

◆

Unaccomplished

Here's how it started.

I didn't want me and Pervez to kiss each other. But we did.

Later, I also let him remove a lock of hair from my face and that too with his finger which I knew would snake its way to other segments of my body, soon. It's another thing that he ridiculed my new hairdo, which I had put together specially for him. He thought I looked Bohemian. He didn't like the look. I loved it. Yet, I let him move the same finger on my lips now. The finger had its own mind. Rascal! It knew where it was going to head next. So it took a sharp right to caress my jaw line, feel its pointy edge and as if on an impulse, stopped and waited to make the next move. But my mind battled against that damned hungry rascal. Just a few minutes back Pervez had made a comment about how bad the hotel room was and how every Indian in the lobby gloated over him. *Because he was an NRI? My foot!*

But now the finger came with its other savage brethrens and they all knew what they were there for. So from my jaw line which they had abandoned long ago, they tickled my back to feel the bra hook.

"Ah, ok hang on. Can't we just talk about what we're here for?"

If these fingers were attached with mini daggers, they would stab my mouth for spoiling the moment for them.

"Hang on for what? Aren't you enjoying this moment?" shot back an irritated Pervez.

"I am, but let's talk commitment first, Pervez."

"Hey, take it easy. Let's get to know each other first."

"Yeah but..." I-don't-want-this was sucked out of my mouth by his.

So we kiss. My fears come true. For most part of the evening, I do everything that Pervez likes or wants. And for most part of the evening, he did not know me or trust me either, and yet sex was prime on his mind.

"How come you're not wearing the popular brand you kept talking about over the phone for hours? Your name doesn't even flash on Google's twelfth page!" he said while sinking his teeth into my neck with an urgency.

"Is that supposed to mean I am not worthy of you, Mr Jehangir?"

"No, that's just supposed to mean it's strange. Check my name; it's right there on page one," he said while taking another mouthful of my shoulder.

"Yay, Pervez. I am not a celebrity. Actually, I am not even half as well-known as my next door neighbour's dog."

"Come on! Don't be upset, I was just kidding. I came down all the way from Singapore just to be with you. I don't even know if I am with the same person I met online."

"And yet you sleep with the same person you don't know too well?"

What I said didn't matter at all. Pervez was busy working on my body and his lips were pressed against my belly button.

I did not stop him. I let him work his way on me. That was me, giving in too easily, giving in reluctantly.

After he had had his fill of Indian flesh, he separated himself from the embrace. We bathed together mechanically. I was hoping he'd at least talk the real talk now and he did.

Pervez and I had met through an online matrimonial portal; let's call it *mujhseshadikaro.com* (literally meaning marry me!). I liked him immediately. He looked almost childlike in his display photograph, earned well, lived a comfortable life in Singapore, and I instantly clicked on the 'Express interest in Pervez Jehangir' button. Another window popped and flashed, 'Congratulations Alafia Singh! You've successfully shown interest in Pervez Jehangir. If he accepts your interest, we'll intimate you.' I wondered how someone/ anyone can show interest *successfully*. And how rude of these online guys to tell me *if* he accepts my interest!

Surprisingly, his response was as instant as my 'interest'. I was happy. No, I was euphoric. Here's a good guy and if this materialises, I could be meeting ship charterers from all over the world, travelling with him every week, resting in a water-facing apartment and learning how to whip Singaporean cuisine – all for Pervez. I think I was overawed.

After two months of endless telephone conversations (I waited for his calls every day at 8 am sharp, and 9 pm sharper), we decided it was the right time for him to come down to India and meet me.

"So all set for the night, are we?" he asked flirtingly, almost suggesting that we could have another round of love making. But clearly my body and mind were not ready.

"Oh, so now you're going to sit that far, huh? Never mind," he was irritated and for what I wondered.

"We need to talk, Pervez."

"Sure, you always have lots to talk about. What is it with Indian women?"

"Well, you're an Indian too!"

"Yeah, an Indian who never lived in India."

"And are you proud about it? Anyway, Pervez, can we just talk about *us*?"

"Go on..."

"I have spent a whole day with you. I will soon be headed back home and flooded with questions from mom and dad about you and me."

"And so? What do you expect me to do?"

"Nothing! I just expect you to tell me what's on between us," I was almost desperate.

"I don't know you fully yet and you can't set a deadline on me."

"But we just made love, goddammit!"

"Can we not talk about this please?"

"And why shouldn't we talk about it? I spent two months chatting with you. I gave my heart and body to you. I have been honest with you about every fuckin' thing in my life and you turn around to instruct me on not talking about it?" I found myself yelling, because I *was* yelling.

"Hey hey hey... easy breezy girl. No one talks to me like that!"

"Well, let this be the first time then, mister!"

"Okay calm down, Alafia..."

He pulled me close to him. We got into his bed again and I sat down with my head on his chest. I moved my hands around his butter smooth thin skin and was filled with longing, but more than that I was filled with hope that Pervez was just taking time and that he would actually come around and marry me. As to how naive I was being was proof enough by the fervent hope I was clutching on to, while every part of me – the clever me – that evades me more often than not in matters of the heart, said, "My sugar, my honey, my darling little Alafia, Pervez just made a fool of you! He's a swinger. He just wanted to have fun and never commit, or maybe after screwing you, he felt that you were not the right girl for him!" And then, my mind immediately changed gears and made me feel more foolish by arguing on things like, "Why did you then allow him to screw you? Why did you go all out to be with this NRI stud? Should you have really allowed him to go that far if you knew you were going to get hurt emotionally?"

These thoughts gathered in my mind as tightly as Pervez's grip around my waist. He knows that I had easily been bought over by the beautiful side of the world he showed to me. Was I conned? Well, partly yes and partly no. For instance, during our phone conversations, when he said things like, "Gosh... Alafia, I am gonna have to make space to accommodate your fetish for bags." (I am habitual to buying handbags *where ever* I go). Or, saying things like, "You're gonna love Singapore and you're gonna love the house here. It fits into the picture of exactly what you want." And then he would smile and remain quiet and only speak after being nudged, to which he'd reply, "Oh! Ms Singh, I was lost with you in the house already, preferably the kitchen...what say?"

So his fault: He *did* show me dreams. My fault: I believed those dreams.

This continued for a while and we both seemed happy, or at least I assumed he was too. And why I don't feel conned is because he didn't force me to sleep with him the day he landed from Singapore, he didn't ask me to go all out to pick up expensive clothes to please him (lingerie included), he didn't even ask me to lie to my parents about his arrival in India, but I did all that anyway. And while Pervez sat fondling his member in bed with me, I became more and more clueless about what led me to do certain things which I knew were going to butcher me emotionally.

I had been doing regular rounds of *mujhseshadikaro.com* but had never before come this close to anyone. And just when I thought, I'd hit jackpot, I had damaged my sense of self even more, and all in the quest to marry? *Well, yes.*

Once again, I allowed myself to go with the flow. Pervez undressed me hurriedly and I gave in one more time, locking safely the plans of marriage and tossing away the keys carelessly amidst our clothes which were scattered on the carpeted floor.

This time it was pure sex. No tenderness or warmth that I badly wanted to feel. We behaved like duteous disciples of *Kamasutra* – the ancient Indian Hindu text widely considered to be the standard work on human sexual behaviour. And our sexual behaviour surely outlived all our fantasies the entire evening we spent pinned down to the bed.

When we finally woke up, Pervez was surprisingly tender, but he still didn't speak about whether he enjoyed being with me or whether he'd love to carry on with this largish libido that both of us shared, for the rest of his life, with me!

A distraught woman's shrieking voice in my mind told me that this was perhaps the last time I would ever see

Pervez. The woman was right – *I* was right. Pervez changed the minute we stepped out of his hotel room.

During the silent ride to my house, I just said one thing, "I wish you'd just told me clearly that I was not the one you were looking for. It'd have made handling this situation easier for me."

"But that's just not the case. I like you, Alafia. It's just that you cannot put a gun on my head and ask me to tell you right away if I will marry you or not."

He was right. And, I wasn't wrong too. I was only justified in knowing what he felt about us and where it was going to go beyond our sexual drive, of course.

We walked up to my sixth-floor apartment. I thought he would bend down to kiss me; he didn't.

"Good night, Alafia."

I said nothing and ran up to my room. It took me a staring down by my pink-painted room walls to realise that I was crying.

Mission Cry and Try

◦◦

Always accomplished

It was one of those nights when I curled up in a foetal position on a damp bed. The wet patch resembled a mini pool that rested right besides my head. The circle was caused due to incessant weeping and was going to look terribly discoloured the next morning. But I was getting more and more used to this colour and this pattern – cry the whole night, wash the sheet in the morning, cry the whole night, and wash the sheet in the morning. I endorsed it because that was the only way to relieve my pain.

Abhijeet, my suave lawyer friend, would almost kick my arse and say, "What pain? Just because you're not getting married? You were married once, so why do you want to go through that pain again?"

To which, I would angrily retort, "Yes, I was married but never lived a married life. You get that? Now shut up and let me get off the phone." But shouting at my dear Abhijeet didn't make me feel any better. In fact, I'd end up feeling more miserable.

During the short period that I was married, I didn't understand what it was to *be* married. And my ex-husband Ram and I were constantly getting into a situation where

16

both of us wriggled out only by hurting each other. We were persistently finding space to meet a common ground where we could nurture a loving relationship, but that ground was too often tread with suspicion, no communication and no sex.

My twenty-two-year-old mind did not know how to 'adjust' and 'compromise' without crying and Ram didn't know how to wipe those tears. He'd given up on me and I'd given up on the marriage. In one of those rare moments when we did change clothes in front of each other or he came out of the bath in just a pair of boxers or I in just a wrapped towel (and sometimes nothing at all and we still didn't have sex), he sat me down on the bed and said, "Alafia, I think divorce is the only way out for us."

"I think you're right."

"It's a living hell, and you and I don't have to suffer like this."

"True."

Before leaving the room, Ram did something unexpected. He clicked a quick picture of me and said, "You do look very pretty in wet hair." I smiled as the door in front of me closed. Ram was out of the room and I was left wondering how two lovely people can talk so amicably about separation and why is it that they fall short of expressing their concern, if not love, equally amicably?

But then there was no concern and no love. What Ram and I were doing was basic civility and this gesture transcended to the court room, as we hugged each other tightly to exchange goodbyes forever. Why didn't we ever hug each other with such passion while we were still married? I wonder, but never get the answer.

I continued having dreams about Ram, even long after we were divorced. And even after he got married again. I had a dream about his wife, although I'd never seen her and never met her. This *is* true of ex-spouses and ex-lovers: we continue dreaming about them and their lovers and spouses even long after we're married or in love again. They are always there. Either smiling wickedly at us on being cheated by a lover or crying angrily because of the pain you might have caused them.

Ram has been around too. I ask him to leave but he doesn't. And these days, he's coming back very often. Pervez's absence gives an easy access to his presence. And tonight, as I wait endlessly for Pervez's call, he's looking at me mockingly and saying, "You never waited for *me* that desperately? Let that Pervez guy teach you a lesson now."

And, I'd angrily ask Ram to go away again, "You're sitting smug with your new wife, am I not supposed to marry too? Get away. Let me be."

And surprisingly, Ram goes away, leaving me alone with aching thoughts of Pervez and painful memories of our love-making. I have learnt over the years, and specially after Pervez's experience, that your body should not be surrendered so easily, at least not if you are one of those who mix sex with emotions. Abhijeet can keep them disunited so easily, almost like keeping apples away from onions or garlic from pudding.

Anyway, the phone bell does finally ring, but it was not the standard 9 pm call. If my heart had ears, they would explode. Thank God, my organs are well positioned, unlike my relationships.

I wanted Pervez to say no to me as soon as possible because I could sense that coming. I didn't want to argue. I didn't want to fight. Pervez and I had realised that we belonged to different worlds. He was the calculative charmer, high on his career and scarred by his divorce. I was the dreamer who wrote books for a living and was happy with my divorce. Let's put it this way: my life was chai and samosa; his was caviar and champagne. While I was willing to kick in a dozen plateful of caviar topped with squids, octopuses, escargots, frog legs, eels, conches and *whatever* Pervez wanted, he was not willing to even take a cracking bite of my humble samosa. We were different and I knew it was the last phone call we'd ever share. It was.

"I can't work on deadlines, Alafia."

"You did tell me that... I understand..."

"Glad you do. You're not going to tear up, are you?"

"Don't worry. I won't."

"I suppose I needed more time to know you."

"But..." I wanted to blurt out things like you had sex with me you asshole, without knowing me? You just wanted sex? You're a swinger, who can never commit. But I swallowed my words as good as my tears.

"You come to Singapore, let's have fun."

"Yeah right." Again I bit my own tongue to chock my voice and suppress the surging anger caused by Pervez's frivolity of the whole situation.

For men, and most men, sex is a process of bodily pleasure. It could be true for women too, but in many cases, women like me surrender completely either to make their man feel good or because they're so blown away by the man's glamour, sagacity or rich (and at times wealthy) lineage, that what follows in order to balance out that fatal attraction is sex.

The worst part is, there have been times when I have strived to treat sex as sex – literally, as in just for the sake of gratifying the urge or the sexual instinct, but have failed as badly as the act itself. Essentially, because post-coition, I either got attached to the man I slept with or if he treated me as just a toy girl, it bruised my self-esteem and I would then come up with something like, "How could he lose interest in me so quickly? Am I that bad? I was simply used. All he ever wanted was sex…"

So at times, the man would be gentle enough to answer all these questions, and at times not; and the times when he was not would put me into depression once again.

But I wish I could shake these rascals up and tell them that all I ever really wanted was a nest where I could lay giant-sized eggs of a happy marriage.

Was marriage the only thing I wanted? *Yes*. Why not? If you don't have a job, wouldn't you want to get a new one? Or if you didn't have a house, you'd go hunting around for one too, right? I understand that marriage has a greater emotional value, but so does getting a house or a job!

Well, I could hardly muster the courage to tell Pervez all that I was feeling. I was such a cow in front of him that in the end, I could only squeak a goodbye, and in this case, moo one.

Mission Name Shame I

❖

Challenged

"It's high time. Aren't you going to think about your life?" demanded a concerned mother who had grown accustomed to my inability to find a perfect match for myself.

As always, I retorted by saying, "I am trying".

And, I *was* trying. I set deadlines. I looked for a potential groom in every single man I met. I crowded spaces on matrimonial websites and newspaper ads and even told a random uncle or aunt to search for a match for me. At first, I was met with assurances, followed by subtle hints that *now* I should find someone on my own. Why? Because I was married once (through an arranged set up, approved by parents and in which we Indians still strongly believe), and now I shouldn't let my parents go through the ordeal once again.

So I was determined not to let them go through it. I set out once again, and this time, I clicked a straight 'yes' to Kunnakudi Rathnam Thanthanadi Sastri. As to why I would even click in affirmation to a name like that, I don't know, but Kunnakudi looked good. He had a toothy smile that was so warm and genuine that I immediately wanted to get to know him better.

So, wise friend Onil – under whose scrutiny most proposals were accepted or rejected – approved that Kunnakudi was handsome; so handsome he was.

"But what about a terrible name like that, Onil?" I grunted.

"We'll manage that, trust me!" he smiled, while reassuring me from the comfortable confines of his New York-based law firm.

"If he loves you, really, he'll change his name," he laughed.

"Oh, shut up, you evil...!"

While I was trying to get out of Pervez's bitter-sweet memories, Kunnakudi's silent entry into my life would work two ways (or so I happily assumed): It was going to help me get out of the Pervez phase faster; and secondly, there was no harm trying, he just might be my man.

So I packed the suave ship charterer away to unpack this warm yet unrefined businessman.

We decided that Sunday afternoon was a good day to start our initial talks over the phone. I had finished editing the crucial plot of my new book, was feeling more confident and absolutely raring to go. Secretly, I was praying for a miracle.

"Allo... allo... allo, Ms Singh, ai (hi), Kunnakudi." (He stressed on Singh's 'gh' and Kunnakudi's 'Kunna' with such emphasis that I almost corrected him.

"Hi Kunnakudi! Yes, I am Alafia Singh."

He laughed and the laughter was so compressed that it almost seemed like someone had stepped on his groin and forced him to snort. I didn't get the reason behind the laughter anyway. It was either nervousness or plain joy of speaking to a new woman. So I paused to let him get hold of his words, which he'd clearly lost by now.

"So are you the same Alafia Singh who's making news these days?"

"Am I? Not that I am aware of!"

"Ah, come on, Ms Sin*gh*."

"Ok, you can call me Alafia."

"So, you are the same young, new-age author?"

"Well, I write for a living."

"But do you make money out of it?"

"Well, I make enough to sustain myself, Kunnakudi."

"But why are writers so frustrated then?"

"Who said they're frustrated? And if they're so frustrated, then they might as well look out for something different!"

He laughed again. This time, the groin was stepped upon harder, for the sound that came out was even more compressed.

"Hey, we've had enough of me. Can't we talk about you too?" I was still patient and hoping that he *is* the guy for me.

"Ah, wokay. You must be aware, I yam a businessman and supply computer parts to many Indian companies."

"Right. I know that."

"And I have lived in Hyderabad all my life and I love the city."

And almost suddenly he said, "So would you like to shift to Hyderabad, my city?"

"Sure, Kunnakudi, but first let's see where this goes."

Kunnakudi spoke so much in such heavily-accented English that often I had to skip listening to what he had to say, and he had lots to say. Most importantly, he'd already fallen in love with me, my voice, my photographs, my almost everything.

After over an hour's rambling about his life, my divorce, his bachelorhood (like Pervez, he was also ten years older), my 'pretentious' singlehood and comparisons between Delhi and Hyderabad, I decided it was time to give myself some rest.

In the end, what he said brought my newly-gathered determination to marry, completely down, "I am dying to mit you, Ms Sing*h*."

Next day onwards, Kunnakudi's calls started pouring in more frequently. First, he started with a good morning call and it gradually moved to – Have you had your fud? Have you had your tea? Have you finished your work? Are you back from the gym? Have you had your juice? Have you changed? Have you had your dinner? Are you about to sleep, fart, pee, burp, breathe-calls.

Yet, I didn't want to hurt this man. I could have easily turned him away, but just didn't have enough courage to slice someone apart who had nothing in him that I wanted in a man except honesty. Moreover, somewhere deep within, I wanted this to work. I was willing to ignore his never-ending name which he refused to abbreviate and forego his unending conversations which were often directed more towards him and hardly had me in it.

My mother told me that I *had to* go through the process if I seriously wanted to get married. And the process included: Looking your best, talking little and whenever you did, only your sweetest vocal cord should vibrate to produce the most effective sound. You should be willing to handle home and work equally efficiently and if you were divorced, you should preferably be the tormented one and not the tormenter. If you happened to be from the minority community, especially a Christian, then you should be ready to face queries like:

How come you have a Hindu name? How can you be of a Brahmin lineage? So both your parents are Christians? Do you go to the church every day? Do you speak any language other than English? Do you even wear anything other than short skirts?

There were times when I was patient with each question thrown at me and then there were times when I came back home and burst into tears. And those who did get married through the arranged marriage route always had unsolicited advice like: "Look, we also got married through the arranged route; it's not always so bad. Wonder why it's so tough for you." Some would even express their sympathy and say, "It's ok. Maybe you shouldn't have told them you're an author. You know, there's no harm in toning it down. Or maybe you can just tell them that one of your parents is a Christian. You can always reveal the truth after you're married!"

I agree. All this does work, but not for me. Not that I am the self-righteous, holier-than-thou flag-bearer; I cannot and will not marry someone I cannot feel for and definitely not on the shaky grounds of a lie or a hidden truth. Also, it took me many years to convince my close friends Onil, Abhijit and Myra about my being not too pushy, not too strong and not too choosey. Though my relatives continue to believe that I have a superiority defect that can never be rectified.

I don't answer them anymore. Proving a point can often take its own toll over your mental state. It had slowly started plaguing me.

All this while, Kunnakudi continued to call in spite of my subtle hints that things might never work out between us.

Mission Name Shame II

◆

Given up

So what happens when you have nowhere to go?

Read: Nothing between you and your ex-boyfriends ever materialised.

Read: You're constantly made to feel you're over the hill, even when you manage to look hotter than someone ten years younger to you.

Read: When you're craving to find the right man – with the right ingredients that suit your requirements – you're made to feel guilty.

Read: When the only next questions people pop, after a two-minute chat is – "So when are you getting married? Why don't you *seriously* find someone for yourself?"

So you start believing what's available is good enough, even if it's not right for you. And this is exactly what was happening to me. I knew Kunnakudi was a warm and honest person, but beyond five minutes, I failed at having a dialogue with him. One day I decided to be upfront, instead of dropping hints that he completely seemed to miss.

"We need to talk."

"Ah... Sure!"

"I have thought a lot about this, Kunnakudi, but there is a serious lack of compatibility between us."

"Oh really... but I like you!"

"Well, I like you too, but there's a gap that I feel cannot be filled, because you and I are so different."

"But I love you..."

"Now that! That is the problem..."

I wanted to go on and on but I decided to stop. I wanted to tell Kunnakudi that I had been there way too many times in the past and while being loved was a great idea, I had had enough men who had fallen in love with me over the phone, with my voice or with my photographs and then suddenly vanished.

To say that I looked ghostly was not true but I did come easy. I modified myself according to what my current man wanted. If French cuisine is what he loved, I learnt how to cook it; if his taste was international politics, I lapped up everything that was happening world over; if the man loved colouring his hair, my hair was coloured too; if he hated travelling, I submissively succumbed to his wishes. All in all, I became the man himself – the man whom I wanted to love me, make me belonged and who treated me like the sexiest woman who ever existed. I was so accommodating that whenever I started dating a new man, friends often joked, "So which language are you learning these days?" or "What's your latest hair-do?"

But with Kunnakudi, nothing like that ever happened. He had perhaps suffered the absence of a woman in his life so much that now he wanted to prove that he was the best. No matter how. No matter where. Like he poured out a detailed description about his meeting with a client and how he 'ripped' them apart even with his heavy accent. "I wore this crisp paant and talk-*ed* so boldly that the CEO could have kissed me." And on another occasion he almost convinced me that he was a writer too, with his talent just waiting to get out to the world.

"Ms Sin*gh*, don't think you're the only writer around! I have never told you this, but I write often. I know one day I will write a book too. But it would be a heavy literary piece."

Sure. I don't contest that. You could write a bestseller for all I care. Just that I can't be with a man who secretly starts comparing my life with his.

In spite of my rebuttal, Kunnakudi continued calling. Myra felt I had not been assertive enough to let him know how I felt. Well, was there more left even after I told him that things were not going to work out between us? Guess the poor guy with the nicest smile ever had to be told that I do not like his name, his accent, his I-am-the-best attitude and his stalking me day and night.

I did say it all. And Kunnakudi was too shocked to respond logically, "I think we can still continue being friends... You're so aggressive, are all Delhi girls like you... You have a funny name too, what the hell does Alafia mean anyway?"

I kept quiet and requested him to hang up. He did *not* relent. "Listen, Kunnakudi, I don't mean to insult you. But you're getting on my nerves now. I need to stop talking to you. Is that clear?"

"So which means we will never talk again?"

"No. Never. But good luck for your partner search."

"Okay bye... but..."

I did not wait for him to complete and hung up. I soon realised that just warm smiles were not going to work for me.

I needed more. But my heart still goes out for Kunnakudi Rathnam Thanthanadi Sastri.

I was exhausted.

The Mission Continues

⚫⟡

Myra minds

It was only later that summer that Myra got worried. I was exhibiting all traits over which I fussed and she vexed. The only thing that kept me going was my previous book's publicity tours across India and finding time to work on my third book. Other than these two activities, I had no social life, no calling, my head constantly ached, I had developed heavy bags under my eyes, my legs and my abdomen pained erratically due to the acute stress I had developed, and mission marriage consumed me like a war-ravaged soldier consumed by the quest of finding food and water.

So after Myra left for a cool, quaint little town, close to the city of Dehradun in the northern state of Uttarakhand, by the name of Landour, I finally did it! I did get the tattoo, the Brazilian wax and the hair makeover. I knew at first she was going to gape at me, then she was going to criticise the positioning of the tattoo or the length of the hair, and then she was going to declare that she loves it anyway.

Little did she know that these fancy indulgences did work on me, but only externally and were as short-lived as daylilies that spent the day sharing their beauty with the sun. But as soon as the sun set, it left these lovely blossoms withered and dead.

Myra had not seen me in months, but knew something was terribly wrong with me because on several occasions she had heard me pant heavily while climbing the stairs and I had to excuse myself for a breather while talking to her. On another occasion, in the middle of our conversation, I'd suddenly burst out crying and there was no way I was going to stop. Nothing she did or said comforted me.

But this beautiful girlfriend with a sensitive heart tried, and also tried to reason out my inability to find an interesting man during so many book promotional activities. "At least some guy, sweets... keep your options open," said Myra in a tone of desperation.

She was not to stop at that. "Okay. Some fan? Someone who's right for you?"

I almost giggled at her innocent anxiety to help me.

"Yeah baby, I know what you're saying but if I like someone, that someone has to like me too and if someone likes me, I have to like him too," I tried to explain to her in a similar tone of desperation.

And then Myra would suddenly give up, realising that she was pushing her already pushed friend of fifteen years a bit too far. She would turn around to say, "Okay, leave it Ala! It's all destiny, you know. It's karma!"

I believed in it – karma – but that it'd ever apply on me, I'd hardly imagined! During our long discussions on (my) karmic patterns, Myra often told me that in order to work with my karma, needed to acknowledge its presence. "Nothing happens by chance; it is your karma working to teach you what you need to experience," she said.

So that put another doubt in my mind. "Have I performed bad deeds in my current life? Did I perform bad deeds in my previous life, if at all I was privileged to one? Am I actually a bad person? If there is a repeated pattern of my actions or actions performed by others towards me. What was I getting from them, except hurt and pain?" I wondered.

With these thoughts in my mind and restlessness to pack my bags to escape the scorching Delhi heat, I left to be with Myra in Landour. Something in me said that this was the right thing to do. And Myra, who'd decided to unwind in a cottage here for six months – away from her husband Utsav – coaxed me to spend the last few weeks with her.

Other than reliving our girlie adventures, it was also time to heal my exhausted body and mind. That was the only way I could get back (to whatever I needed to) with zeal!

Myra had already been living at the Wilson's Cottage for the past five months. The cottage was huge, with carvings of deodar wood on the cupboards, doors, kitchen furnishing, and roof and even the floor. So much so that it gave me an instant smell of a polished jungle. But the smell was fresh and so calming that the moment I stepped inside the big dining room, I knew that I was going to get the much-needed mental spa.

We rushed to hug each other, Myra and I. And if women are known to talk endlessly, whoever has bestowed that honour, it's not off the mark. Because from the moment I dropped my bags on the beautiful wooden floor, we chatted endlessly. It was almost as if I didn't want to speak about marriage. It did not exist. Never existed. It suddenly didn't matter if I were divorced. Without a (committed) man, with (ample) sex, or whether I had a tattoo hanging out of my bosom, that I could so freely show now. Nothing really mattered. With Myra, I could just be. Breathe easy and pull back the lost strings of my life.

The sun was going to set soon. We both peeped out of the large French window and marvelled at the beautifully silhouetted Lower Western Himalayas, with its companion for the sturdy Himalayan oak trees shining golden against the slanting sun. The silent disappearance of the orange fireball would leave behind the tiny faces of the stars and a tempting breeze that would remind me of the absence of a loving partner to curl up with under a blanket.

But the thoughts were immediately brushed aside as Myra suggested a hot bath followed by some freshly cooked chicken stew, which we anticipated devouring because of our meal-less afternoon. But I knew the next day was going to be another day. Myra would dig deeper into my soul to try to deal with the spazzy effect caused by the recent emotional erosions.

Again over dinner, we chatted about everything but marriage. I knew she cleverly avoided looking at my dark circles, eye bags, permanent frown lines and patches of shining scalp despite the new hairdo. But I did catch her looking at me a little pensively. She didn't have to say it, but I knew—had Myra had her way, she'd perform a cosmetic surgery on me right away and charge only a smile in return.

In the thick of the night, the chicken stew and naans vanished as easily as our conversation.

The Mission and Me

●◆

With Myra

So my previous night's guess was right. After an early morning breakfast of home-made pizza topped with delectable chunks of Mozzarella cheese, mushrooms, bell peppers, onions and sliced ham, prepared specially by Rasheed, our young caretaker who looked more like someone who could break into a gangsta rap any moment due to his heavy influence from American street culture, we headed out to take a walk among the inviting old deodars.

Dressed in his trademark oversized T-shirt, low baggy jeans, a fitted baseball cap and a heavy silver-coloured chain, we saw Rasheed run towards us. This was the first time I was seeing him and my instant reaction to Myra was... "Wow! You've got someone interesting..."

Myra gave one quick wink to Rasheed and said, "Yo man!" We both laughed. And although Rasheed was an elementary school dropout, his flawed English was incomplete without *yo man... watdfuck... watdhell...*

"Hey man... you going out ain?" asked Rasheed inquisitively.

"Yes, Rasheed. We are going down for a walk. By the way, meet my friend Alafia." Myra smiled.

"Hey Alafia... your name good... man! Watdfuck does it mean?"

I giggled a bit at the unnecessary usage of 'watdfuck' and told him that in African language it meant peace and blessings.

"Wow... Africaan... I have so many Africaan friends in America. They love me, I love them!"

"Hey that's so cool! How did you reach America?"

Myra told me that Rasheed had worked at a restaurant in New York for four years before coming back to Landour to take care of his ailing mother. "And that's what explains the way he looks and talks!" we both laughed.

Apparently Rasheed did not understand the last sentence and chose to remain quiet. "Hey... you eat lunch here or out?" he enquired almost suddenly to hide his embarrassment.

"We will come back and eat here, Rasheed. Make sure you prepare something finger-licking, okay?" said Myra, winking at him again.

"Yo man yo...dontcha worry..." said Rasheed with determination to please us, and it seemed as if the menu was already there in his mind.

We took leave of this Indo-Afro-American man in his mid-thirties, who would have easily passed off as ten years younger had Myra not told me his age.

Just five minutes after zig-zagging our way into the narrow pathways, we could see the Kellogg's Church standing tall with its pristine white walls shining bright in the morning sun. For a long while we walked in silence, breathing in the fresh fragrance of the leaves along with the aroma of breakfast being made at the Tibetan settlement for foreign students who came to learn Hindi in Landour School of Languages.

And sensing as if this was the right time to speak, Myra broke in, "So Ala, what's this whole thing about getting married? Aren't you happy the way you are?"

I turned sideways to look at Myra, who stared back at me with her beautiful, big, brown eyes that shone browner in the golden sun. "I feel lonely, My. I need a companion."

"But you have everything going on for you, Ala. You have name, fame, respect, creative satisfaction, admiration from men... what else do you need?"

"Sure I have *all* of that, but I need steadiness in my relationships. I am sick of hopping from one relationship to the other, from the arms of one man to another. I am sick of it, My!"

Sensing my discomfort and looking at the frown on my forehead grow deeper, Myra decided to pause, but only for a few seconds, before she decided to take a different route to understand my problem all over again.

"Alright! How about not killing ourselves over the right guy, while trying to get one at the same time?"

"Isn't this what we're doing already?"

"No sweets, this is *not* what you're doing. Right now what you're doing is killing yourself. You're not giving life a chance to find the right person for you."

"Then what am I supposed to do? Everyone around me is married and I am *not...*"

"Sure, you're not. But that doesn't mean you'll continue not to be."

What Myra said made perfect sense. Of course, I needn't fuss over getting married and no one held me by the gunpoint to tie the quintessential knot either, but still I *needed* to be married. Needed to because I was sick of being alone, sick of making love to a man who I was not sure would be with me after six months. I wanted a partner who could understand me, love me, and fulfil his dreams with mine. One with whom I could go to Christmas parties, Diwali parties, book-promotion parties, house parties, and all sorts of parties – which now I went to all alone.

I couldn't tell this to Myra for the fear of being ridiculed at the prospect of finding a life partner only to attend parties. I know she didn't think that way, but somehow there are certain things inside a person's heart which are meant only for the self. There were many things I wanted to tell Myra, but couldn't. Like I wanted to tell her how coolly I *hizzit the skizzins* with a co-American author in Goa, when we both were there together to promote our books, or how I shacked up with Onil's friend (without his knowledge, of course!) at his own house and never saw the man again, or how I had been getting booty calls from Myra's own friend and I'd been refusing him on ethical grounds (no entertaining a girlfriend's male friend).

The sun was fully up by now but still playing hide-and-seek with the gigantic deodars that towered over its small frame. Myra and I spent our remaining time listening to the hum and moan of the wind bellowing through these pines. Somewhere in the distance, we also picked up the *tink-tonk tink-tonk* of cowbells and the song of the herdsman wafting up with the winds.

We must have walked a lot but it felt we could walk even further. I complimented the green scarf Myra had tied around her neck that went well with her white tank top and khaki-coloured harem pants and suddenly asked her, "So what should I do, My?"

"Nothing. Just don't stress yourself. Be happy. Be good," she stated quite simply. "See, Ala, a lot of times things don't happen because we need to keep learning from them. You gotta see what there is to learn from what's been happening with you."

She continued further and said, "I am talking about recognising your karmic pattern, Ala. Feel it! See it for yourself. Feel what you keep doing to draw the pain on you over and over again."

Myra was making a lot of sense and I knew what she meant by recognising one's karmic pattern. I made a mental note of it and knew I had a lot of work to do when I got back to Delhi.

We neared Wilson's where Rasheed was already waiting for us with his boyish smile and a shining baseball cap – a richer cousin of his humble headgear he wore in the morning. It was only midday but Myra and I were already hit with waves of hunger and couldn't even wait to wash up. Rasheed's stint with a food joint was evident as he laid the table immaculately with napkins, coasters and the works, and in the centre of it all, he had placed a brilliantly-carved, tall, wooden candle stand with an angel-shaped candle resting on it. The wax angel looked like it could fly on to our plates any moment, although one of its wings was chipped.

I gave Rasheed an appreciative smile, patted his back and removed the lids to see what we were going to devour in a few seconds. "This is cold potato salad, with herbs and diced egg," explained Rasheed. Next to it was Cauliflower au Gratin with the melted butter still glazing the beautifully-cut cauliflower florets. We were also served mushroom canapés that was freshly brought out of the pan and served with toasted bread.

Rasheed looked so pleased with his dishes that he couldn't stop smiling. "Hey man, I hope you like it."

"Of course, we'll love it, Rasheed!" I said.

"Hey man, you're partial. Just because Ala is here, you treat her with your best culinary preparation. You were not so generous with me in the last five months. Watdfuck huh..." Myra mocked at him, to which Rasheed smiled shyly and turned away to get extra spoonfuls of Cauliflower au Gratin.

The food tasted so good that I could have married Rasheed right away. But then, sometimes in life, we wish things were that easy and that uncomplicated!

I carefully observed this Landour-born, small-town boy who had big dreams. He wanted to open his own restaurant and marry an American, preferably a blonde. Life was so simple for him and his thoughts so uncluttered. For a moment I was jealous of this rascal of a caretaker. He might fulfil his dreams, he might not; he might marry a blonde or might end up marrying a Kumaoni; but he'd still be happy.

He would still continue to grin boyishly, live in a make-believe hip hop world and whip up delicacies for guests who'd come to stay at Wilson's Cottage.

The Mission Continues

•◇

Still with Myra

Soon I was spending most of my days just pigging on Rasheed's homemade epicurean fare that ranged from Indian to American, Kumaoni to Coorg. And he was bloody good at it. So Myra and I had composed an impromptu poem in this gangsta rapper-cum-cook's honour and each time he brought out tantalising goodies from his kitchen, we chortled, "I love Rasheed's food, I love Rasheed's food... It makes me feel really good... Yummy and nutritious food... Keeps me in a superb mood."

To this, Rasheed would smile, stuff us up a bit more and coyly protest, "Ya girls very naughty. Make fun of my food huh. I don't cook for you no more."

Three days there and I must have already gained five kilos. It might be true because I couldn't feel the sharp curve around my waistline anymore, or could I? I was busy checking myself out in the full-length mirror attached to the almirah that looked like the Narnian wardrobe through which kids transported themselves into a land of myth and fantasy. While I was determining the prospects of literally entering the dark wooden cupboard and deluding myself into what could happen next, Myra entered the room and announced that some spiritual guru was going to visit us. "So you better hurry. Stop drooling over your own body; I could get Rasheed over if you want," she winked at me and left me puzzled.

Did she say a spiritual guru? Now what was that supposed to mean? Am I not a devout Protestant who's only supposed to believe in the Gospel truth? Then who was this yogi? She didn't even tell me his name? "Listen, My! What is all this you're getting into? We don't need a matted hair, saffron-cloth draped sadhu baba, who smokes out of a chillum and chants, 'Chai, chillum, chapatti... chalo Parvati...'"

"Whoa! Where on earth did you learn that, Ala? How cool is that!"

"Oh just on my recent trip to Kasol in Himachal. But anyway, you chuck that. We seriously don't need to turn this haven into an ashram."

Myra smiled and my pleas went totally unheard. And the gypsy woman that she is, she looked so in sync for the occasion in a long russet skirt with such chunky and noisy jewellery, that the room resounded of one bad symphony in practice session.

Rasheed came announcing that 'she' had come. Ok, now who's *she*? The junkie paramour of our sadhu baba? I quickly draped a shawl around me, half-interested and half throwing profanities at Myra for killing the pleasure of our afternoon siesta.

My friend was already busy talking to a woman, who must have been in her early 30s and extremely attractive and fashionable by every standard. She definitely didn't look like a lovelorn paramour, nor did she sport the archetypal witch's beads hanging around her neck, bangles all over her arms and kohl touching her cheeks. She gave me a pleasant smile and extended her arm for a quick but gentle handshake. "Hi, I am Tara."

"Oh! Nice to meet you, Tara. I am Alafia."

"Wow, what a lovely name!"

"Thanks," I smiled and waited for Myra to introduce us further because it felt like Tara was *the* one waiting for me and I just walked into *her* territory. Now in a few minutes, she could even get up to offer me a cup of hot chocolate.

"So Ala, how did you like our sadhu baba?"

It dawned upon me that *she* could be the spiritual guru. This woman, a spiritual guru! Alright, then Rasheed could be a spiritual guru too, in his spiffy shoes, baggy sweat pants and the bling around his neck and arms.

"Hey, why don't you come and sit here?" Ok, so I sure *was* a stranger in this set up. I rolled my eyes and slumped next to her. It turned out that Myra had already planned this out. She'd given my detailed introduction to Tara. She could have even mentioned the number of times I had had orgasm(s), number of men I dated, or the number of buckets I filled with my tears and snot. I was so cross with Myra, it was beyond me. She could have been pushed down the hill and sent tumbling into the acres of forest in front of our cottage for all I cared. How dare she reveal my life to a stranger? And anyway, was I inflicted with some life-threatening disease where details of the ailment are hidden from the patient and everyone around wears a frozen smile in an effort to bring joy to the remaining days of the patient's life?

I was still seething when Rasheed brought three cups of ginger honey tea with some chocolate chip cookies. I wondered how this man always managed to fill our stomachs with the right food at the right time. As soon as he left,

Myra informed me that Tara was a certified spiritual healer (I don't know what that meant!), and if there was something she could do to deal with my situation in a better way, this was it. Was she asking me or telling me? I was touched by my friend's concern for me but baring it all out in front of a stranger made me feel utterly helpless and somewhat irritated.

"I understand your anxiety, Alafia, and you really don't have to tell me anything," said Tara smiling in between her sips of the fresh-as-dew tea. Oh! So, she sure was intuitive!

Yeah beautiful one, I don't have to tell you anything, because my closest pal has already spilled the beans (albeit out of concern). But I was actually too weak to handle this 'betrayal' of love by Myra. Was I hurt? No, not exactly. What bothered me was the fact that the girlfriend didn't think it was necessary to inform me that someone was going to lecture me on crisis management and how to handle men out of the blue or perform a step by step psychotherapy on me, till I discovered that I was either a male or even a homosexual in my last earthly incarnation, born somewhere in the territory of modern South of Latin America around the year 700 and I danced, sang and acted for a living (compensating my current earthly penchant for neither of the three).

Tara asked Myra to leave the room. This was scary, given that I cannot ever openly talk about my innermost feelings to a stranger. Tara *was* a stranger, although she made *me* feel like one.

"Okay, now let's focus, Alafia. You need not worry about anything. We know you've been through a hell lot of trouble in life and we're just trying to help you in some way. If this works for you, good; if it doesn't, nothing to lose."

I sat up in rapt attention and suddenly decided to give in, now that I was *caught*.

Tara continued talking about the theory of karma, somewhat close to what Myra had been telling me. "So I am going to take you back to your past life!" she declared (and lives in case I had lived many).

I smiled but remained sceptical. What could I uncover? Would I be in some drug-induced trance? Would I even remember what I saw, assuming of course that I would see something? Well, and Myra has to pay for it, moreover, if Tara was 'nuts' or 'phony', I'll find out soon enough and blame it all on Myra.

I sat in a reclining chair that Rasheed had managed to procure magically from somewhere. She then closed the blinds and darkened the room. Her soft voice combined with the ginger honey tea did put me at ease, almost making me sleepy (she'd already had five cups by now and I'd serious notions about this glutton of a woman). She lit a candle, and asked me to take a deep breath and begin to count back from one hundred. Part of me already wanted to leave, but I stayed on.

"100, 99, 98, 97, 96... 95... 9...4... 9...3..." I slowly said out loud till my voice started resembling someone who was as boiled as an owl.

"Go back to where it all began."

"I see nothing."

"Concentrate harder. Ask for God to reveal the secret lives that have long since faded from your conscious memory."

Still nothing happened. Maybe I just didn't have any past life! Maybe my sufferings were a result of my own stupidity/ (excess) wisdom.

I was still counting helplessly, "64, 63, 62, 61, 60, 59, 58, 57..." getting more and more exasperated and woozy with every count.

Suddenly, I threw up my hands in the air and covered my face with them. Something had hit my face. It was a tiny pebble and it had scrapped my face. More pebbles followed and now they were larger, heavier, sharper and they were darting at my body from all sides. I was covered in blood. My clothes getting wet with blood stains, I could feel the wetness. My knees bled. My hands bled. My legs, my stomach too. I hunched over, putting one arm in front of me, trying desperately to escape. I looked for shelter. After several minutes, I touched what seemed to be a wall. I followed the wall until I found an entrance. At the place where two walls joined I crouched down, putting my face on my knees and covering my head with my arms. Exhausted, I fell into a deep sleep.

The next morning, I woke up completely covered in blood. I couldn't move. It took me several minutes to realise I was still alive. I walked out of the building, shielded my eyes from the sunlight, and walked down a cobblestone street. I looked at my feet, clothing, and arms. Although every part of me was soaked in blood, I could see that I wore black shiny sandals and a white skirt with many sequins that could send the sun shying. I had fashionable gold arm bracelets, dozens on each arm, and a bright orange scarf that was not much blotched. The street looked deserted, yet I limped along in deep pain. I wanted to cover myself because my skirt was torn. I looked around but there was no one to help me. The sun was so bright that it turned my limping to a crawl. Silence filled the air. I called out but there was no answer.

I continued walking down the town's main street. I spotted some men in white turbans and called out to them, but they spat on my face and left looking disgusted. I walked further into a shop. I saw no one. On the wall, a mirror hung. I looked into the mirror. I saw myself: black hair, about forty years old, and had an olive complexion, but I could see mostly red. I left the shop and continued walking. The town looked familiar.

Finally, I saw some women standing and exchanging a joke, perhaps, because they were laughing. When I asked them for some food and clothes, they pushed me aside and ran indoors. Why was everyone so angry? I made my way further and came upon a wealthy nobleman's home – only a nobleman could have lived in such a large house. The front porch had four Corinthian style pillars. Huge slabs of blue marble carved the ground in the front of the building – obviously a fresco at one time. I walked nimbly and entered what must have been the foyer. The walls bore mosaic tiles that had pictures of blue dolphins. Several yellow fish also emerged. One tile mentioned, "Welcome to all who venture into these premises. Here lies the house of a great nobleman, Sinan Yahudi, ruler of this town, who's also a fair judge and physician."

"No, it can't be!" I cried out.

Tears started rolling from my eyes. I kissed the tile and touched the letterings written in Turkish. "He was my master...my guide." I wanted to be embraced by him.

A month earlier I had married Suleiman, my ninth husband. My master had asked me not to, but I disobeyed him. Suleiman had loved me and was even willing to accept my child I had from Latafat, an ex-husband. But I swung freely from the arms of one man to another. My first husband was Farhat, then I fell in love with Ilyas, then Ekrem, then...

But I had to find them, find all my husbands. I was still weeping. I ran out of Sinan Yahudi's house and rushed to find Suleiman's house. Maybe he'd give me some food and clothes! But I had little strength, so I collapsed on one of the front porch steps and cried. After what seemed like half-an-hour, I thought of Latafat. I couldn't remember where he lived.

I was exhausted. Several hours later, I was suddenly being shaken. I woke up.

"Fatma, get up! Don't worry, I'm here to help you," said Sinan Yahudi. I jumped up, threw my arms around him, and sobbed.

"What happened?" I asked. "Why is everyone so angry with me? Why am I soaked in blood?"

"You were stoned by the villagers on account of being dishonest with all your husbands. I'm so sorry, Fatma, but they all loved you so much! Poor Ediz and Koray... you left them to die!"

"Are they dead?" I asked.

"Yes."

"And Suleiman?"

"Dead as well. He loved you the most."

"What's to become of me now? I have no one left in this entire world except for you," I said.

"Don't worry. I'll take care of you. I have a chariot waiting for us. I knew that you would come here. The sun will soon be setting. It's a long journey. Come, my girl, there's nothing here anymore for you. Let's leave."

I walked out with Sinan Yahudi. At the edge of the city, we boarded his chariot. I looked back as the chariot left Izmir. I knew that I would never return. A new life awaited me somewhere.

"One, two, three," a woman yelled out. It was Tara. At the count of three, she snapped her fingers.

"Where am I?" I asked.

"In your lovely cottage," she smiled.

"What happened? I must have briefly dozed off for a minute," I said.

"You must have tapped into one of your past lives."

"That's impossible. I would know if something like that happened. Let's continue with the session."

"Continue? With what?" asked Tara.

"It's only 2 pm. The session has hardly begun. I'm still waiting to be put under. But mind you, I'm sceptical."

"It's 5.30 pm, Alafia."

"What happened?"

"You tell me! By the way, who is Suleiman? You mentioned him several times throughout the afternoon and showed special interest in him."

For a moment I felt stunned, like I had just emerged

from a deep sleep. Three-and-a-half hours of my life had disappeared and I had no clue. That scared me. And to scare me more, slowly my recollection of my visit to Izmir in Turkey returned. What I had experienced felt so real: the white-turbaned men, the marble columns at the ruler's house, and the harsh sun that had shone upon me. For a moment the thought crossed my mind that either I had gone temporarily mad or Tara and Rasheed had connived and slipped a narcotic into my tea. I didn't know what to believe. Unlike a normal dream which I would forget upon waking up, this experience seemed etched in my memory. Everything had been so vivid, like a grandiose episode filmed in Technicolor, with myself in the lead role. The intensity of the experience captivated me; no ordinary drug or drink could induce such an experience. I had crossed into another dimension, tapped into the unknown, and lived to tell about it.

Tara smiled at me reassuringly.

She analysed my experience, telling me that my present problems were a repeat of my previous problems back in Turkey. Her explanation sounded absurd, yet it rang true. "But how?" I asked slightly irritated and exhausted.

"You cheated on every man who loved you and gave his life for you. You have carried the same free spirit in this life too," she explained.

"So am I supposed to feel guilty for what I did in my past life?"

"No Alafia, that's the trick. Once you have rung the bell, you cannot go back and un-ring it! The past is done and cannot be changed. Yet what is important is to heal the past through love and forgiveness and then... move on."

I was still dazed, yet intrigued.

"Let's put it this way. You *have to* forgive all those who stoned you and humiliated you, and express gratitude for the one who saved you. You get me"

"But I was a woman with loose sexual morals. I cheated on every man who loved me." Did I really believe I did that, given my one-man-motto in the last 31 years during my current existence on earth?

Tara sported the smile of someone who just found a lost key by accident, just as she was about to hammer the lock down.

"Alafia, my dear, forgiveness also means letting go of *your own* guilt, shame, sorrow, anger, and other negative emotions that are keeping you from forgiving people, events, situations, and the past in general."

This was perhaps the first time since afternoon that I was taking Tara seriously. Not just that, I carefully listened to every word she mouthed.

"If you are truly sorry, if you have learned from your mistakes, and if you are committed to never repeating them, then you have corrected the past to the extent possible. You need to forgive yourself, forgive others, and forgive the situation so that the unforgiving attitude does not keep you in the past."

I was quiet. What Tara said made so much sense. Perhaps, I had always been a little too hard on myself. I kept looking at her face. Flashes of my 'visit' to Izmir shadowed her visage. As she ordered for some more ginger honey tea, I tried to remember every detail as though I had been there in person.

Tara caught me dabbing my face and examining my arms, legs and neck. She smiled again, but I turned away still dizzied.

The Mission-ary Pause

◆

Just me

Yes! I did feel light and unburdened. Whether I still believe in the mystery of what happened to me, I am unsure. But it did feel like I really wanted to *let go*. Forgive myself and let go of my past life husbands/lovers (Oh! Wasn't I such a fille de joie), or some child I'd left behind, a master I didn't listen to or those who didn't provide me with food and clothes. Was there a way I could do it? Yes and no. Like Tara, I didn't possess the supernatural qualities and it'd be rather spooky to evoke the spirits of these lovable people from some previous birth. And then there were also those I needed to forgive from this lifetime.

Now if I were to go down on my knees and say sorry to each one of them, would they find me a man to marry? Okay, perhaps this might not be all that persuasive, but what might work is the way I said sorry to Sister Jonas in high school! 'Sorry' was written anywhere between 500 and 5,000 times, depending on the severity of the mischief and Sister Jonas' mood. There were other ways to express this important feeling – standing in the sun the whole day, standing on the bench in front of the class, standing with one's 'hands up' or simply standing outside the classroom, while other students guffawed at you and carried out chores with an air of superiority. By the way, why do most punishments require standing, couldn't we say sorry sitting down?

So it clearly meant I had to take an apologetic stand, *standing*.

This was my last day in Landour and Myra and I decided to make the most of it. The previous night we'd asked Rasheed to pack an entire day's meal for us and undoubtedly this was his moment of glory. But in the morning he surprised us by declaring, "I am gonna bunk off the food for ya girls today."

"Wha...wha...what do you mean Rasheed?" Myra panicked.

"Well, to peace out with Alafia, I am gonna come with ya girls," he grinned, dressed in his best gangsta accoutrements.

"That's superb, Rasheed. We'd love to have you over." Myra winked at me.

This happy soul was ready with a handy cooking stove, logs of wood, a bottle of kerosene, cutlery and the works. Wow, so he was fully prepared for an impromptu kitchenette that included a runny stream, along with a canopy of tall trees.

So we all decided to explore this tiny town on foot. And didn't John Muir say, "In every walk with nature one receives far more than he seeks."

So we walked. Three of us were quiet and lost in our own little worlds as if we were trying to discover something, anything. Myra was happily married to Utsav for the past four years and though she never spoke about anything other than her happy state of marital mind, I could feel her need to want more out of life. Maybe she wanted to be a famous theatre artiste but couldn't because she chose marriage over her career!

Rasheed, on the other hand, had busied himself whipping delicacies for tourists, but maybe he had a desire to go back to America, open a stuffy little restaurant and earn lots of money. Then he could practice hip hop music by the night and even buy real gold bling!

As for me, I needed a man and a man to marry, but then maybe I didn't need anyone. For now, maybe I just needed solitude and like Tara had said, "A willingness to let go."

We walked across the magnificent trees that graced the hillside. Occasionally, three of us would smile at each other and share a word or two about the mighty old deodars or the mating call of a jet black jungle crow. But at other times Rasheed would don the hat of a persuasive guide and fill us in on, "Hey… ya girls know the Landour bazaar? You get cheap stuff, good stuff there. You buy, you go there. So you buy?"

And many more such touristy information would follow, to which we'd turn a deaf ear and say, "Thanks Rasheed. Next time." This makeshift scout knew that we needed to be left alone.

So after this idle banter, we would regain our walk and pause only to have a closer look at some large residences built during the British era and perched so tightly on a hill top that even a French chateau would be put to shame. Moreover, the massive mansions almost always looked like they had no living occupants other than burst of colourful flowers, fluffy clouds and tall deodars as loyal sentinels. This 'walk of life' was also suddenly interrupted whenever Myra cried out loud in delight to watch the dramatic play between these superstars of the nature, wherein the chief characters were being played by the sun, trees, clouds and hills. Those in the second lead were the birds, and herds of cows or monkeys. One of the main characters (superstar sun) also handled the stage lighting, while the background score was provided by an erratic drizzle and local kids who shouted happily whenever they saw visitors, and of course the walking trio of Myra-Rasheed-Alafia filled up the spectators' gallery. The direction and production was handled by the Mr Almighty One.

"Look, Ala, the sun is behind that tree; doesn't it look like the whole damn thing is on fire?"

"Yes, My! And now look there! The sun's gone. The naughty little cloud has hidden it inside its tummy…"

"Watdfuck man… this sun is bloody good actor. He now hide behind hill and stand up again."

This continued till we settled for an instant meal of baked fish fillet served with juicy raw tomatoes, onions and olive oil. Not to forget that Rasheed even managed to cook some hot rice for us and beautifully served the two dishes in bone china crockery! And if I ever decided to fall in love with this man, *this* was the moment. He poured two glasses full of cranberry juice for us that was sprinkled with some freshly crushed black pepper corns. To say that the food tasted like manna would be a humble encouragement for our darling Rasheed.

I knew this was my moment, so I excused myself and decided to spend some time alone. I could see Myra and Rasheed watch me merge with the trees on a grassy patch of a hillock, but I didn't turn around to look at them. I knew that no one other than Myra could understand my need to be left alone at that hour. The grass had become slippery with the sporadic drizzling and one slip of the foot could send me rolling down into the valley, so all I could hear of Myra from a distance was a muffled, "Take care, Ala…"

Then I did something unusual. I chose a wise old deodar to talk to. Anyone who decided to stop by and have a closer look at me would think that I was a freaky-deaky who needed a check up from the neck up! But like Rasheed would say, "Watdfuck!"

"OK, I know that Tara is right and I need to let go, will you please help me let go?" The tree's trunk did not respond, but somewhere I felt a raindrop slip on my nose from its leaf (and this resembled Bollywood style affirmation when a flower mystically falls from a deity's head onto a devotee's palms, confirming that the prayer has been answered).

"I want to let go of Ram. I hurt him. I couldn't be a good wife to him. I want to let go of the several men I have betrayed. I want to let go of the guilt. I also want to forgive those who have wronged me." I suddenly remembered the Bible verse that says, "Forgive them for they do not know what they do." But it wasn't like I was being persecuted (although my emotional trauma ensured that I could be only ten steps short of entering a loony bin!)

The old deodar heard me patiently. Isn't that the only thing you need sometimes? And then I continued, "See, I also want to say sorry to Suleiman, Latafat, Ediz and Koray." (Remember them?) And, then I was feeling literally like a bobo because I just asked for pardon from the husbands of my past life. But I *had* to!

"All that I really want is to marry the right person. Please help me get one... Oh! But you're not a god, yeah but you probably lived as long as a modern god. So can you..."

And tears started trickling down my cheeks that had regained its flesh because of Rasheed's finger-licking food. "Well, I know you can't wipe my tears and you probably shouldn't... I just want you to know that everyone who's possibly done *any* wrong to me is forgiven. I have released my pained paramours right now into this valley and you are witness to it. The clouds, the sun, the birds... they all are witness to it."

After this self-customised ritual, I sat in silence for a few minutes. I could virtually feel each negative setback buried deep within fly out of me and away into the valley, like a dry leaf. I would have preferred to imagine a crumpled paper ball but for nature's sake, a dry and brown leaf would do fine!

Rasheed welcomed me back with chocolate chip cookies and ginger honey tea. I knew its relevance in the scheme of things.

PART - 11

The in-between and reaching
the shore without oars.

Mission Resumed

◆

No stopping now

The holidays were over and I survived. But the thing about Post Holiday Depression or PHD as it is clinically known is that even the sweetest memory about your holiday leaves you in tears. Right, it should make you happy and all charged up to take your usual life head on, but it doesn't. So right now, I am faced with a situation where even if someone is listening to hip hop and eating vegetable au gratin at the same time, I have to leave the room in distress.

So I took out my little graffiti notepad and doodled,

Chilly air. Open air. Urge to fly, hibernate. Is this my true self? The lost woman I once was, the woman I am today. Thanks deodar tree. Thanks Rasheed. Thanks Myra. Thanks Sinan Yahudi. Thanks everyone for accepting me as I am.

I closed the diary. Took a deep breath and was ready to pole vault into another sphere. I knew that that sphere would throw challenges at me once again. Once again, someone might question my integrity because of my fatal divorce; another man might even want to try sex first (to get a feel of the most abused word called *connection*), some parent might actually want to get my divorce papers cross-checked and in some cases the mother, father, the son (my potential partner), his sibling and sibling's spouse might even come home and decide to never revert, if they found the match not suitable.

But I could be ready to face these, what my mother calls, ritualistic arranged marriage procedures, without letting myself run over by emotional upheavals that were a result of doubt, self-pity, fear, anger, rejection and at times a raging desire to blow a potential partner's skull apart. I also find the term 'potential partner' (often used by my mother again) very amusing because someone has clearly decided without any validation that the person in question has some potential, I wonder for what! And whatever makes one call a person 'partner' in the first meeting itself, even if he is not fit enough to take your dog out for a walk.

So *mujhseshaadikaro.com* figured on my to-do list with a feverish determination. Mom and dad subscribed to matrimonial ads for me in the best news dailies. After Sunday church service, each morning we followed our own self-devised service order at home: Get the regular breakfast of butter-toast and tea, sit on the bed cross-legged or as you like it, open the matrimonial section of the newspaper, encircle the match most suitable for me, note down their contact details and start calling them one by one.

And, in case someone wanted to express interest in me after elaborately going through the 'Brides Wanted' section, the situation would be far more chaotic because these expressions of interest by various men through phone calls, would often end up in arguments and extremely engaging (by all means!) brain-wracking sessions like, "You shouldn't have told them your real age, you should have been a little more courteous, you have got to overcome your attitude problem, perhaps your father shouldn't have been so aggressive with that poor guy, perhaps your mother shouldn't have called them home."

I was still a Ph.D. pupil, but a more patient one this time.

And mister, where did you come from? I saw Ram standing right there. Arms crossed, crisply pressed and dressed, with that same smug smile and all. My expression at him was anywhere between 'did you just step on my poodle's paw?' to 'did you just say I have grown nine-inch long strands of hair on my buttocks?'

"What are *you* doing here?"

"Well, wouldn't I be happy to see my ex-wife happy?"

"Hey mister, why can't you just be with your current wife and let me be. I have forgiven you. I have let go of you."

"That easily? I am your friend. I am here to protect you and tell you that marriage is a terrible thing...the spouse sucks, didn't I?"

"Oh, Ram! Stop it...I think marriage is great. Just because things didn't work out between us doesn't mean they won't now."

"But what about your freedom?"

"Watdfuck!" *Thanks Rasheed.*

"You would make such a terrible mistake; you don't even know how to handle your own husband in a bedroom!"

"But that was past and it's gone."

"Well, the fact is once a divorcee, always a divorcee."

I turned away from Ram and cupped my ears. Memories from the past were churning my stomach and I felt sick.

But, I stood up, told myself and Ram (who had vanished by now–the viper!), "I have let go of my past. I have been forgiven and I have forgiven. I am ready to move on."

I was ready to meet Amartya Banerjee the next day.

Mission Religion

●◆

And I thought it didn't exist!

"Wow author...so will I get to marry an author?"

"What is so great about marrying an author?

"And what is not? I will get to stand behind you as you sign copies for your fans."

"Don't you know that you should never date or marry an author because she'll fictionalise everything? She'll write about things you have done to her, or things you never did for her."

"Like what, my beautiful one?"

"Well, she'll turn around and tell the reader you never bought her flowers. Not once, while you always did. She'll also tell the reader how you said it's not that you didn't love her but you couldn't be with her and that it's your fault and not hers, except she'll tell it much more compellingly."

He stood still and then laughed. "You are funny, Alafia."

Amartya Banerjee and I were bonding well. And with every little thing he did, I could tell he was perfect husband material. A glossy only-for-girls magazine carried a ready reckoner on "How to Know if He's a Husband Material" and I was going to make use of it right away.

Was Amartya sensitive and reliable? – Don't know.

Was Amartya a hard worker? – Yes or, so his appearance said.

Does Amartya see you as a part of his future? – Don't know. Weren't we there to explore that?

Is Amartya genuinely interested in being part of your life and that of your family? – Don't know. Too early to say.

Does Amartya feel that he knows the depths of the real you? – Don't know. Ask him.

Is Amartya your true best friend? – No way. We've known each other for exactly twenty minutes.

Damn the girlie mag. I could tell it from the guy's face that he was falling for me and could even turn out to be sensitive and reliable, someone who'd be genuinely interested in being part of my life and that of my family. Someone who could know the depths of the real me and be a true friend too. All that was fine, but I had my little concerns. Abhijeet says, don't call any concern little, a concern is a concern.

Amartya, this 32-year-old private wealth manager and a divorcee, had obviously never seen a gym in his existing life, words like *diet, health food, vitamin supplements, exercise* and *weight loss*, never figured in his scheme of things. So what I saw in front of me was someone puffed up with straw and probably in need of assistance in waddling his way out of the door to the parking lot.

Moreover, while I was married for 11 months and 10 days, Mr Bean Bag was married for 10 days. Ten days, did I hear that right? I wonder how that equation worked… they looked at each other for an hour, sort of liked one another, by the time one week was up, they had already made out, bathed, dressed, slept and ate together and on the eighth day they were ready to scratch out each other's eyeballs? In marriages that last for a duration of 55 hours to 12 days, either something goes fundamentally wrong with the spouse or the marriage, or both or you could be blasted while exchanging vows or suffering from partial dementia/amnesia only to realise next morning that you wanted to marry Ms Chiyo from Japan but ended up marrying Ms Chipo from Africa. And sorry for calling Mr Bag 'Mr Bag', there's no way I cannot do that.

So Mr Bag and I exchanged those glances that were suggestive of: Yeah, we're getting to like each other. And what's with some extra weight? I could get him to lose that any day, provided we were married first. And he called me up as soon I reached home after that first meeting at a plush café in Hauz Khas Village. Sure signs of good times to come.

The next day, my mother spoke to Mr Bag's father and then his mother spoke to my father, then they both spoke to me and then my parents spoke to him. So yes, we were all bonding well, person to person, family to family. Finally, there was going to be *one* man in my life. And since I didn't want anything to go wrong this time, I seriously chewed over the idea of mugging up the region's history (to impress the parents who still lived in Kolkata). I could tell Mr Bag's parents that the word Bangla or Bengal has been derived from the Dravidian-speaking tribe Bang/Banga that settled in the area around 1000 BC. This would certainly knock out any Bengali parent and how proud they'd be to get a well-researched daughter-in-law home.

Now Mr Bag had also started missing me and I had started imagining how good he'd actually look even if he knocked off a mere 15 kilos. So one day our conversation went something like, "My colleagues spotted me humming the other day…"

"Wow… so you sing?"

"Well, only when I am too happy!"

I knew where the dialogue was heading and didn't I want it that way too? So I asked him what he waited to be asked. "And why are you so happy?"

"One is when one finds joy…"

"And who or what is your joy spot, mister?"

"Is that difficult to guess?"

"No."

"It's you, Alafia… you have brought so much happiness to my life that I have actually started wearing coloured clothes."

"Oh! How sweet. You really are getting colourful!" I cracked a bad one.

We both laughed and realised that it was not such a bad *connection*, after all. Men and connections do go hand in hand. Onil and Abhijit (I can even tell these male friends that the size of a man's member is not appealing enough to turn me on!) feel that a man could connect to a woman's personality or if you're a little more esoteric, soul-wise. "However, that bond doesn't mean he has to be tolerant of intolerable or frequent bad behaviour," adds the latter and the smarter one as a word of caution. There's another thing about connection and men. They like to *connect* with a woman on their own terms and conditions (read: women who don't scare them with things like feelings, emotions, meanings, relationships and commitment and most of all… marriage). But Mr Bag was not like that. He was ready to commit and marry, or else why would he put up his name in the matrimonial ad?

So we met again. The second time was better than the first one and the third time was even better than the one before. He even held my hand and told me each time we met, how gorgeous I looked. Yes, I had started looking better. The colour of my skin was improving, turning a great mocha that I always wanted. The new hairdo also sort of adjusted itself to my face and I was gathering healthy fat at the right places.

Then I noticed that Mr Bag wore so many rings and that freaked me out. It was also the first time I noticed his pudgy fingers touch mine. So the fat sausage sticks were decked with sapphire, garnet, diamond, pearl, ruby and so many other colourful gemstones that he might as well set up a fly by night kiosk and sell all those psychedelic stones to make a fortune. "Do you believe in these stones?"

"No, I don't, but mom does."

"And if *she* does, why are *you* wearing them?"

"Mom really wants me to wear them; you know how it is with mothers. I don't live with her, so she constantly worries about my safety."

"But they look gross, Amartya."

"Oh! Do they? You don't like them?"

I wanted to tell Mr Bag that not only did I not like them, I had a good mind to wriggle them out of the longer and linger and in this case the shorter and shabbier. And while I was staring hard at his rings, he decided to drop another bombshell.

"Alafia, I have something to ask you."

"Sure, you don't need my permission."

"Mom wants to know your blood group."

"*Mom* wants to know? Alright, it's O+ve. But why?"

"No, it's like this – I am AB+ve so she wanted to know the chances of us having a baby in future."

"What?"

"Yeah, I am sorry but you know how it is with mothers!"

"No, I don't. This is pretty annoying, you see. Is your mother also going to ask me if I lose hair daily, and if I lose 127 strands of hair per day, and not 227, I might not be able to raise a child properly because I lose more than I can sustain!"

"Hey, no Alafia! That's how mothers are. Just relax, my love."

Did he just say 'my love' and did he again voice for his mother?

I could breathe the scent of a mama's boy. Yes I could. I could imagine Mr Bag making goo-goo eyes at his mother or sucking his thumb in her awesome presence. Yeah, he could even sit at her feet and press them as an added feature. My fantasy took a leap as I looked at Mr Bag's fingers, and I saw him as one who could even regress to the extent of adopting a baby-voice and indulging in childish prattle whenever the mother was in the vicinity.

The bad part of the evening was: mother-messing-up-man's-moment. The good part of the evening was: Mr Bag's patience and some great caramel custard after lunch.

While I drove back home, I made a mental list of everything that could be/should be discussed with Mr Bag. I was too scared of the mother's omnipresence. Divorced? Yes. Author? Yes. Good cook? Yes. Travel? Yes. Prone to getting hurt? Definitely yes, yes. And even blood group…

well yes. Religion? No. Did I just say I didn't tell him about my religion. Did my parents? I almost made it sound like I had a pet cobra that refused to sleep anywhere except on my pillow or that sometimes snuggled with me under the quilt.

So early the next morning, I picked up the phone and asked Mr Bag casually, "Hey Amartya, you do know that I am Christian, right?"

There was a stammer and then a pause and then the voice spoke, "No. Yeah, I mean, so what?"

"Oh thank god! I knew that with your kind of intellect, religion hardly mattered."

"Yeah yeah, of course."

So it was great for me. This man actually loved me, but apparently not enough because next morning dad received a call from senior Mr Bag saying that they were no longer interested in the alliance.

Did Charlie Brown say that, "Sometimes I lie awake at night, and I ask god, 'Where have I gone wrong?' Then a voice says to me, 'This is going to take more than one night.'?"

Mission Poetic Stethoscope

◆

Your lips are like rose petals

Thank god mom empathised. It was one of those rare times when she was truly convinced that it wasn't my fault. Sometimes it's important to get a kind of a go-ahead from your loved ones to feel better but it's also unnerving when your life has a resemblance of everyone's thoughts, right from how they think that the length of your skirt could have been slightly longer to how most single women end up being psychotic and volcanic in the absence of a partner (this is a belief carried by most Indian households).

So while I was down, I was not out. You can never be 'out' after you have undergone a rigorous soul-cleansing spa, where you take out some precious moments to forgive, forget and be forgiven and forgotten in return. Now the thought of poking fun at Tara made me smile and roll my eyes in embarrassment. Her warm mannerism and radiant smile had only ensured that I glided smoothly from one life to another.

Another good thing happened. Mr Bag's presence and sudden absence didn't have a larger than life impact on me. So, I didn't experience euphoria while he was around and I didn't get all spazzy even after he was not. I mightn't have been cool as a cucumber, but I was cool enough to maintain my sanity and resume my search on *mujhseshaadikaro.com*. And there was one Dr Ashish Rampal who caught my attention next, my first time with a doc!

The process was usual; tried and tested: Exchange a few mails, share your likes and dislikes, reasons for divorce, reasons for being single, splash it with some compliments, show him you might be genuinely interested and voila...the voice you are hearing could actually end up being the father of your babies one day!

Now I must clarify that this exercise is not as easy as it seems. Picking up weights double your size at the gym might be easier, but no, not this one. While it sounds like you've been thrown open with opportunities to meet various men, date them, dine with them (often at their expense), and at times even have sex with them, the deal can be pretty exhaustive. Let me explain why and how. If you meet Mr Springy and you like him, it is not always necessary that Mr Springy ends up liking you too. There are also chances that you're meeting Mr Springy, Mr Milky-Skinned, Mr Fine-Limbed, Mr Handsome, Mr Boyish, Mr Naughty at the same time and might end up liking all of them, so while you're spoilt for choices, you really want to know if Naughty is better than Handsome. There are also times when none of them show interest in you (it *is* possible); so if you're still bearing the flag of "this happens in arranged marriages," you will go right out and resume your search and might end up finding Mr Mature, Mr Reliable, Mr Dependable, Mr Dickhead, Mr Horny, all of them or none of them. And what could possibly happen with women like us is that we could emotionally attach ourselves to each one of them, go all out and experience an explosion of the heart if all of them or some of them turn around to say no, after they give you hope: *My mother will be your fan. This house deserves only you, honey. Where were you all these years? So let's decide the honeymoon!*

There are also chances that many of them can con you knowing that you're the "vulnerable type" which is translated into a hard-nosed woman with a soft heart, who has survived bad relationship(s)/marriage(s) but is now willing to change the course of her life by accommodating a man she believes will adore her even when she offers lettuce for dinner and tolerates her pre-menstrual tantrums.

So I opened my heart for Ashish with a new-found determination that I was not going to allow myself to get hurt.

This doctor, who specialised in geriatrics, was divorced with a year-long marriage and looked at least five times older than his age. Even at 34, his hairline had completely receded, but like mom said, "You're not going to marry his hair... hair can always grow back, good men don't!" I thought hard. Perhaps she was right. So I was turning a blind eye to issues like obesity or baldness. After all, marriage *was* beyond all this. Moreover, I didn't want a horde of all those concerned for me to turn around and say, "See, you've always been too picky, so we know why finding a groom for you is tough."

Now the only twist to the doctor and my dealings was that we never spoke; we only messaged or exchanged mails. Weird! But I kept telling myself that it takes all kinds to make this world. Give yourself some time, Ala... When are you ever going to stop jumping the gun?

So our first mail was more on the lines of what I do, what he does and our basic expectations from a partner. Great so far because I was impressed with Ashish's language which was hinted with good humour that I immediately heard myself say, "Doctors can write stuff too!" Our second mail was more on the lines of our individual reasons for getting divorced and what we expect out of life now and so with every mail we were making steady progress. I looked forward to his mails because ever since I turned 14, I had stopped writing letters. And while this was nothing compared to the weekly postcards I wrote to my grandfather while he was alive, the feeling of drafting a letter was exciting and somewhat nostalgic.

Onil called that night and I told him that life was finally falling back in place. "I didn't cry after Mr Bag, I don't seem to mind that Ashish is bald and that he prefers communication only through mails."

"Ala... are you sure this guy is not dumb or suffers from some serious speech disorder?"

"I don't know, Onil. I am just playing it by the ear!"

"Well, you got to find that one out, and sooner the better."

I decided to take Onil's suggestion seriously and wrote back a mail telling Ashish that we NEED to talk, to which I got the most insipid reply, "We will, Alafia. We will." And this mail was followed by another one, which read:

```
Dear Alafia,

Do we need to talk loved one?
Can't we wait till we see the sun?
Harsh words and violent blows
Hidden secrets nobody knows
Eyes are open, hands are fisted
Deep inside I'm warped and twisted…
```

```
Do we need to talk loved one?
Can't we wait till we see the sun?

Yours only
Ash.
```

I was touched by this poem because maybe I had been harsh and apologised to this poet in the making profusely. But maybe the doc was on another tangent, because what I got next was:

```
A heart is torn open,
A love is broken,
A life is empty,
With few words spoken...
```

It took me another ten days to realise that this poet was *only* interested in composing poems and his agenda of marriage seemed more and more cluttered by the eulogy of my beauty he'd now started throwing at me.

"Your sound is that of a Lark's song in the morning when mist covers life and I feel forlorn..."

To which I stupidly replied, "But you've not even heard my voice yet, mister!"

And this was followed by another one:

```
Dear Alafia,

Lord Byron says, She walks in beauty, like the night
Of cloudless climes and starry skies;
And all that's best of dark and bright
```

Meet in her aspect and her eyes:
Thus mellowed to that tender light
Which heaven to gaudy day denies.

Isn't this how you are my loved one?

Yours only
Ash.

I was still trying to understand which of the two I was more: livid or frustrated. I was both and pleaded with this jerk to never write to me again. I pleaded because I knew he would not stop. He didn't.

But I was also happy that we never spoke because his last mail read:

My love,

Your lips are like rose petals that whisper words
I love to hear so much,
Your breasts hold me captive
Within my prisoned wish
Thighs that draw me near them,
Soft enough to kiss.
I could make love oh so cataclysmic
And drive you orgasmic…
Only yours…till death.

Did I say I was cool enough to maintain my sanity and resume my search?

Mission Submission

◆

Destiny, karma, picky... or what?

It would be well for a wise man to take a break before testing the rough waters again. And I definitely deserved one too. But the word *marriage* was fixated on my forehead like a unicorn's horn. This mythical animal's tusk is said to be a very powerful antidote for poison and I believed that my horn too would cure me of the poison of singletude.

I told Myra what had happened between me and the doctor and she burst out laughing, "Ala, at least someone is so eager to give you orgasms, it's been arid as the Sahara here for the last six months."

"Listen, really My, you can't find humour in this. It's not funny... the bloody motherfucker!"

"I don't want to say this but wonder how you manage to pick on the biggest dickheads ever born in the history of this planet."

"Well you know what, My, I tell them that I am a pussyhead. Dead funny, ain't it?"

Myra was on a laughter riot by now. I could almost imagine her covering her mouth and nose and doing some girly *tee-hee hee, woo-hoo hoo...* But soon I began to find my situation funny too. Often when sorrow or deep longing for something overrides other emotions, it transforms into humour, so I tickled my own belly to join Myra's riot. I also wondered if the repeated pattern had anything to do with the way I conducted myself or just an extended stroke of bad luck.

I was getting accustomed to loving these breaks between groom-search and its culmination thereafter. The intervals were getting more and more infused with short trips out of Delhi, wild parties with friends or indulging in a short fling, replete with the hope that between these aphrodisiacal moments I would still manage to find *the* man, *my* man.

Ali and Shehnaz called that day after their six months hiatus in Paris and insisted that their come-back party would be incomplete without my attendance. Although I was immediately tempted by the trademark Khan household mutton biryani and mutton kebabs, I decided to play the helpless girl struck with sorrow and declined the invitation. "Ala sweetheart, just park those jerks elsewhere, dress in your sexiest best and come," commanded a flirtatious Ali.

"Yeah, but I really cannot have fun like this. I am on a mission, Ali," I tried to be funny with a serious tone.

"Sure. Ok how about I introduce you to Avirook Sengupta?"

"A who?"

"Avirook Sengupta!"

"Well, not another Bengali for me, please."

"My hot lady-wolf, don't behave like a deer in the headlights. Take charge. Here's your chance to meet new guys, have fun and enjoy life. Who knows you might find your Mr Right, munching away on some of our kebabs?"

Ali did know how to touch the weakest chord, so I agreed.

The Khans have been married for the last 15 years, have consciously decided to remain childless and most part of their married life is spent travelling together to the most exotic locales around the world. While Shehnaz exhibits the no-nonsense, and talk-less air, Ali is the flirtatious types who has mastered the art of inane talking, that's often laden with innuendoes, but seriously committed to Shehnaz in front of whom he behaves like the most obedient, hen-pecked husband. And it would be foolishness to believe that the serious Shehnaz has no idea of her husband's many liaisons. I often asked Ali about how he managed to strike that perfect balance between an amorous lover and a dutiful husband. "Tres simple mademoiselle... just don't mix the two! I still continue to have sex with my ex-girlfriend. She's married and so am I, but how does it matter. Or does it?"

I was too stunned to answer. Not that I wanted to behave like I am straight out of a mother's womb, but these things just didn't fit into my mental space anymore. One thought said that these situations were best avoided and another thought prodded me into feeling that I had been there myself. I had been the other woman, the wife, the seductress, the hunter and the hunted. But still when you see someone else in the same situation, your moral flag droops a bit and you get all judgmental. I have done that too often and said things like, "No wonder he's divorced because he is so and so, or no wonder she can't find a guy because she's done this and that." And then I had a good laugh about being bitchy because *I was* also so and so and had done this and that.

So after much deliberation, I decided to pick the sexiest dress in my wardrobe. And on Ali's instructions, it had to be a little black dress. "You want to knock the headlights out of this guy Avirook, don't you, my wolfie?"

"NO, I don't want to knock anything off anyone, Ali. Give me a break. I am in no mood to date, alright."

"Easy honey. Just be yourself. Sounds fine?"

"Yeah, it does."

I was ready to look like a femme fatale after being off the socialising scene for a long time. The dress covered my ass in a dignified way and offered a plenteous display of my thighs. And this was also perhaps the first time, I was going to show off my Hebrew boob tattoo in public.

But still my mind was on Mr Bag and also on how editing my profile information a bit on *mujhseshaadikaro.com* might pull in some more interest. I had already mentally pruned the portion I wanted to stress upon while choosing the fancy jewellery to go with my look, "Only those truly interested in marriage should show interest. NO TIME FOR TIME WASTERS." Also changing the profile picture into a more traditional-looking avatar might garner more interest. Maybe the one in a sari or salwar kameez...

Just then, Ali's driver had started ringing the door bell incessantly. There was no choice but to rush downstairs while barely managing to pick the right footwear because driver Rizwan, who was more revered than Ali's own father, was a stickler for time and known to put people in their place if they didn't follow what he loved to follow – time.

There was a stoic silence in the car as Rizwan drove me to Ali's plush bungalow in Nizamuddin. The only verbal-time-please we ever had was when he enquired if the AC was too strong. Other than that, Rizwan shot fleeting glances at me through the rearview mirror in an almost enviable manner because out of Ali's many friends, I was the only privileged one who always got a ride to and fro.

"Hope Rizwan chacha's eyes are not squinting in your bright light, honey?" Ali called me up.

"Not yet," I smiled.

"Okay. Come soon. Avirook is here already. I have told him all good things about you."

"Oh boy! Stop it."

The Khans' welcome bash was yet to begin. I was among the early birds.

Intermission I

❧

Easy come easy go

The Khans' parties are known for their extravagance and although the guests were asked to come without a dress code, after seeing the dazzling Arabian night theme set up, I wished I had at least worn a gold bra with plenty of gold jewellery or maybe some false eyelashes for extra glamour.

Ali spotted me at once and came running with open arms. "Beautiful beautiful... you look beautiful, my lady-wolf."

"Thanks but stop calling me a wolf for god's sake, Ali!"

"Anyway, come meet my best pal Avirook."

While Avirook and I exchanged pleasantries, our eyes locked for a few seconds. "So an author meets an author. Hope you guys make each other comfortable. Khuda hafiz." With that Ali vanished into a controlled burst of thick, white artificial smoke.

We looked at each other and were about to speak when Shehnaz suddenly appeared. She looked like a complete antithesis of her husband: bland, serious and disinterested. "So good to see you, how was Paris?"

"Oh yeah, not bad eh!... Hope you're enjoying yourself?"

"Yes, just about getting to."

"Do try out the olive stuffed rolls, they are out of the world."

Shehnaz enquired about Avirook too, who in his non-verbal reply put his arm around her shoulder and left me on my own. This put me in a situation where I wasn't sure if sulking or bitching about this pleasant-looking person was a better option. I was the hotter one, I was single and we were just going to start a conversation, but Avirook left. He just *left*! So I decided to be alone for the rest of the evening. It was a status I was used to by now, so no one even bothered asking me to get a 'close' friend or a boyfriend along – they knew the faces changed but the status remained the same.

I noticed that the terrace was dotted with tiny tents draped with red and gold chiffon adorned with twinkle lights. These little hideouts looked like mouth-watering shinning invitations for couples who needed privacy to cuddle up. There were enchanting metal lamps suspended from artificial palm trees that also served as a prop to cover a portion of peeling wall paint. The trees and other walls were covered with swags of gold and plum gossamer.

More guests started flowing in and I could only see their shadowy silhouettes from the thick smoke that had suddenly started smelling of apple, or maybe I was already one Long Island Ice Tea down. I could spot a couple who looked married, or maybe not, but the sound track of a flute and drums and cymbals (along with my drink) could easily have led me to deception. These guests were followed by more guests and then more guests till the entire terrace looked like an edited scene from Arabian Nights.

And then there was a realisation that hit me as hard as the drum beats: Other than Avirook, I was the only 'single' in this party. But he'd found his interest elsewhere and I tried to camouflage my loneliness by pretending to observe most insignificant object so closely that any passerby would let me be for the fear of breaking my intense relational meditation on whatever they saw me stare at at that moment. Spiced chicken, salads, kebabs, fish tikkas had started making rounds and I found further recluse in them. But then for how long could one sit in an isolated corner, pretending to be wowed by a silly Arabic theme (which was beautiful but when you're not comfortable being alone, everything seems silly!).

"Hope you're having a good time."

Someone tapped my shoulder.

"Oh yeah, it can't get better!" I look pathetic when I lie through my teeth.

"Sorry, Shehnaz and I had some important things to discuss."

"Oh sure. You don't even have to tell me."

"Right so, so... tell me a bit about your last book."

Okay. At least he realised that he'd left me alone, but he was not apologetic that he left *me* alone.

"So my book was all about..."

"Brilliant! Another drink to that?"

"Sure." Tonight I was not going to say no to get blotto.

Avirook was deeply into spiritualism, was separated from his wife of ten years and awaited his divorce in two months. Moreover, he had brilliant eyes which could set any heart on fire.

I was three drinks down and was smiling endlessly, putting in an extra effort to show off my dimple which becomes prominent only when I smile really hard. In fact, I had started flirting with Avirook and to discover that I could still manage the fine art of seduction was bringing back my lost confidence. For a change I was also the one doing most of the talking. But we had decided to throw anything 'intense' out of the window that spelled: our divorces, break-ups, being single, pressure to marry etc. During our conversation I did, however, discover that Avirook was in no mood to marry and although that disappointed me a bit, I knew I couldn't tie a stone around his neck and throw him into a running river if he didn't.

I was so hammered that I couldn't remember if we exchanged a kiss, but we certainly held hands the whole time we were together. So god is not that unkind. My need to have a companion that evening was taken care of. Then we decided to duck into one of those little tents that had seemed out of my radar of consideration just an hour ago... but now, I was all jumpy and doe-eyed to get inside one of them. Then I couldn't remember the rest of the evening, except that I felt light and euphoric.

My only concern was how I was dropped home. I know Avirook accompanied me, while Rizwan drove us towards my house.

Intermission II

●◆

Sex is in the mind. Really?

That both Avirook and I were on fire was quite evident from the fact that we couldn't wait to meet. As to what exactly we did the previous night inside the Arabic tent at Ali's is still unclear to me. And obviously getting on top of each other in public wouldn't have been the best thing to do in an Indian home, no matter how modern the occupants were, so Avirook fed in my mind that "he and I just held hands and sat really close. That's it!"

He came to pick me up the next day. We decided to watch a movie together but watched it in silence without showing any signs of intimacy like playing with each other's fingers or leaning our bodies against one another. So, I would say we were practicing body and mind control because neither of us wanted to come across as needy or desperate. And the movie was not even a rom com; on the contrary it was filled with violence and devoid of sex. But even that came to an end; now what?

"Dinner and drinks?" Avirook announced more as a decision than an option.

"Drinks? No way. Dinner definitely yes." I couldn't afford another round of being Miss Hammer Head.

"OK. If you insist, Alafia, but remember cold kills cold, iron cuts iron?"

He stared directly in my eyes now, almost as if he held me captive with them, as if the eyes guided me to make my next move, speak out my next word.

"So home? I mean, let's go home?"

I wanted to say no, and blurt out things like, "We've just known each other for a day, why home? Why not a nice sit out? It's maybe too early for..." But I heard myself say,

"Yes, let's go home."

We were at his place in Noida and we ordered pizzas the moment we stepped in. He was trying to build the perfect ambience but what for? By now I was playing dumb, like I was caught in a hunter's net unaware. But the truth was that I had enticed the hunter to catch me in his net and do with me whatever he felt like; or to be precise, make him do to me what I wanted him to do. Women are smart at that game. We set the trap and once we are caught in the trap that has been masterminded by us, we act like the naive victims. The men on the other hand, don't get this womanly quirk at all. A man who's spent a gorgeous night with a woman who's all confident and flirty would wake up to see the same woman turn into a marshmallow prototype or is already begging for him to *explain* the previous night's happenings to her. Now, this would often make the woman look like a burning train and the man – the sole survivor who's trying to run to save his dear life. So most men run away from women like these and most men run away from me for the same reason (assessment based on the last 11 years of knowing men closely).

Alright, so back to the ambience. Surprisingly, Avirook's taste in music was bad because creative people are known to have evolved musical tastes, so you'll always find them following a genre of music that makes them sound intelligent and talk intelligent. If romanticism was not his flavour for the day, it showed. He played a Punjabi song, known for its loud beats and catchy rhythm and lyrics which can take years to mature into your system if you're not used to pace and pulse, but yes, it was great if you wanted to break into a dance. And you could do it instantly even if you were a native of Sub-Saharan Africa.

"So is this good for you? You like it?"

"Well, I was hoping for something more romantic."

"You know what happens when you get separated?"

"Sure mister, tell me about it."

"Yes right, things between you and your spouse get scattered. So you still have to deal with the leftovers that belong to your wife. Sometimes you realise that her clothes still share space in your cupboard or her old pictures are still buried in one of your drawers or better still that over-used toothbrush still yawns at you every morning from its exotic Italian holder – also bought by your wife."

"Well a lot of my stuff is still with my ex-husband."

And, I know exactly what Avirook was talking about because half a dozen of my clothes, wedding and honeymoon photographs, and toiletries were still at Ram's place; it's another thing that before getting his new wife home, he would have disposed *all* of it. And, this happens especially when your separation/divorce is not phased out or planned.

"So, *she* took away a large part of my music collection. Have you heard of any Bong who doesn't follow Pink Floyd or Metallica?"

"And she left you with Punjabi songs?"

"Well, yeah, maybe she wanted me to dance through our divorce."

We both laughed at the bad joke, but the tension between us was growing. We wanted to touch each other, but neither one of us initiated it.

Avirook turned off the music and offered me a glass of wine almost immediately. There was something odd about his house too. Each artefact was layered with old newspapers that had acquired the shape of a rectangle on the wall, or an oval shape on the side wall or some cylindrical shape on the dining table, which was covered with heaps of *Hindustan Times* and *The Times of India* too. Sensing my puzzled look, he started narrating the inconsequential details about how his mother had covered even the furniture in plastic and paper sheets because they have gone to the US to visit his... and will be back.

Thankfully Avirook noticed that I was bored out of my skull and had finished my drink. He poured me another one and sat next to me as he rolled his joint. With each puff he was transcending into another world. Now he gawked at me as if he was about to say something but rolled the words into ringlets of smoke. But he said them anyway. "Has anyone ever told you how terribly attractive you are!"

"Yes, many."

"Do you want to...get inside the...bedroom maybe?"

He held my hand (that was our first touch since the previous day) and led me to the bedroom, which was thankfully not covered in heaps of newspapers. The only thing striking in the bland-room were two magnets stuck on the iron almirah. One had an image of Abraham Lincoln saying, "Stand with anybody that stands right." The other one had Beethoven's, "I shall seize fate by the throat."

Avirook had started kissing me. My eyes were still open and reading Lincoln's quote that I must have read eight times by now. But he was such a terrible kisser. You don't need rocket science to distinguish a bad one from a good one. His mouth was closed and so rigid and dry that with closed eyes I could have easily mistaken his lips to be two thin pieces of chalk.

"You have to open your mouth a bit, Avirook."

"Oh! I am sorry...I have not done this in years. It's almost like I have forgotten how to kiss."

I was trying my best but Avirook's progress was slow, although desperate.

We had undressed each other. His body looked far more attractive without clothes. When he told me he'd not tasted a woman's flesh in a long long time, he was right because he was eagerly working on my back and then suddenly turning me over with a jerk, licking my stomach and back with long strokes as if the meat pieces would vanish into some unknown animal's mouth, if not lapped up urgently.

He took out a packet of unused condoms. Oh! So he was prepared for it and that suddenly made me lose interest in what we were going to do.

"Condoms? Had you planned this?"

"No! They have been here since my wife left... untouched, unused."

I smiled. But, I also wanted to believe Avirook.

Having a perfect knack to say things when they should *not* be said, I asked him "Why?"

"Why what, Alafia?"

"Why are we doing this?"

"Doing what? You have got to trust me on that condom thing, girl!"

"Okay, I trust you on that one but are we going to have sex just because we want to have sex? I mean do we even have feelings for each other?"

"Wow...but you'd the whole evening to think about it, did you have to think about it just now?"

"Yeah."

"But we *are* attracted to each other, aren't we? And... and...I do like you."

"But my priorities are different...I want to marry and settle down!"

Right. Now I was speaking my mind but maybe I should have not led the man this far. The keep-it-real stand that I took just when he was going to pull out a condom from the packet should have been done earlier. But maybe things could work too. If he really wanted to have sex with me and I laid down the condition of marriage, maybe just maybe, he would agree and we could wait to get his formal divorce and this moment might be forgotten as one of our first funny dates.

So with an erect pud and condom in one hand, he sized up my naked body. Perhaps he felt like stuffing that little piece of rubber in my mouth, but the truth was told. But I just went by what Lincoln said, "Stand with anybody that stands right." So wasn't I right? I just spoke the truth. I just wanted to marry and Avirook didn't. So why did I entice him? Maybe I will ask Myra about that but for now Avirook had to rush to the toilet to help himself.

I was still lying naked after he returned. Like a salivating puppy, who was still hungry, he asked me, "Did you enjoy doing that to me?"

"Hell no, I just wanted to speak my mind out."

"There were other times, we could have...anyway, leave it," he said as he stood naked, with his member looking half its earlier size.

Intermission III

◆

Tips. Tips. Tips. Tips.

Now this is how I screwed up. Avirook might go and tell Ali and Shehnaz all about the play between me and him and I cannot even begin to imagine what these friends would think about me or how they might never leave me alone with any of their male friends for the fear of seducing them and dumping them, especially right before 'the act' with an erect Mr Jimmy. Nothing could hurt a man's ego more than this and I knew Avirook was hurt, and a hurt man is an angry man. So I called up the SOS numbers one by one. Myra was the first one and perhaps the only one on the planet who still believes that Mr Right is on his way to meet me. Let's call him Mr Invisible for now, shall we?

"Mess... it's a complete mess," I cried over the phone.

I recounted the entire episode to her. And did she do the obvious? Of course she did. She cracked up once again. Now was this best girl friend also giving up hope on me? Just few months back she was so concerned about my health: physical and mental and mouthed each word with such caution and now, even before I complete a sentence, she cackles.

"Hey baby, don't mean to hurt you but imagine the poor guy's plight. If he was angry, he wasn't wrong."

"When did I say he was wrong? My, all I am saying is I fudged it all up!"

"And how do you think you messed up, baby?"

"Well, haven't I? We could have been good friends first, known each other better and then..."

"Maybe you would have been married?"

"Well... yeah maybe."

"And maybe not."

"Why?"

"Let's turn around the tale a bit: If he really wanted to get to know you better, he wouldn't have proposed the idea of having sex on your first date. Secondly, even if you had let him know your intentions in all honestly and if he really didn't want to have sex, he would have respected your point of view and tried to know you better, as a friend."

"Yeah, that's an intelligent assumption, My."

"But then, these are just assumptions, sweets, so maybe you need to be clear about your intentions at the very beginning."

"So are you trying to tell me I should tell a man that I want to marry him even before he touches my finger? By that logic, I would remain single for the rest of my life!"

"Every equation works differently. You just need to know what works best for you. Use your wisdom, Ala."

Yes, you see, I will use my wisdom. However, the point is if I had any wisdom of handling men, I wouldn't have made that panic call to you! And it's all about finding *the* man, not any man. The Holy Grail must be easier to find. But then I live in India where people interpret being friendly as sexually-liberated. The funny thing is I did not regret not having sex with Avirook because I genuinely wanted/ needed someone for whom having sex was not like having your glucose biscuit: dunk and dump.

Abhijit, the more irritating one out of the two was my last option, so the second SOS call was made to Onil.

The same story was retold with every detail and same emotions. His reaction?

"Take it easy."

Does he mean I should be easy to have sex or not have sex? Well, as it turned out, he meant that I should take life easy.

"What's the harm in enjoying life and getting plenty of sex while it lasts?"

"Yeah, actually you're right."

But something in me was not convinced. However a part of me did worry about ageing all alone in a cubicle and then even if I screamed for sex, I wouldn't get it.

Alright, so this was typically a man's perspective on sex: Seize it while you please it.

So Onil's parting words were, "See the other side of the grass is always greener. You run after the thing that you don't have but often ignore what you do. So value what you have and stop running behind what you don't."

Wow! So much for a sermon but I didn't know how to counter that. In a more practical way, what he said made perfect sense. But in a more convoluted way, I just wanted him to understand what I was doing and why I was doing what I was doing. But perhaps Onil would never because he was lucky to marry the girl he loved and still continues to love from the deepest core of his heart. I wish this would someday be replicated in my life, but till then, thank god for loving friends, who might not necessarily understand you but love you despite your nuttiness.

And finally Abhijit's tip was just the same, "You were married once, so why worry about marriage again?" And no matter how much I tried to convince him, it wouldn't work. He was convinced that once married is married forever or there can only be one marriage, rest is compromise.

But I have another tale to tell Abhijit.

Mission Mush and Back

◆

Trying isn't everything

After the Avirook sex debacle, I was terribly guilty.

What happens is when you are constantly reminded that you need a man in your life and that *you* are solely responsible for his absentia, you start wondering if you really are. There must be something terribly wrong you might have done to not enjoy the sweet fruit of a stable companionship.

While I have already mentioned what others think about you if you are single or were once married, wanting to marry again, or were never married and wanting to marry, you pretty much think about yourself not very differently from what they think about you. You undergo this whole pitiable process of self-doubt and low self-esteem. So when your mom says "you can't adjust," you really believe it more than a prankster who'd turn around to say that the colour of your eyes has changed from black to blue. When your cousin says "you are stubborn," you start remembering the last time you rolled on the floor and threatened to give up on food because all you wanted to eat was candy floss for dinner. When your neighbour tells you, "you need to lower your sails," you wonder how, because there were such big holes on them, that they needed repair, not lowering. They do.

And with each passing birthday, as the number of candles increase on your chocolate truffle cake, you can feel it within your gut that your confidence has taken an equally sharp dive. You get more and more known for high-sounding, gob-smacking, bamboozling attributes like overtly ambitious, hot-headed, stuck up, selfish and those with a tender heart feel nothing but sorry for you. You feel sorry for yourself too. I want to add another attribute here – desperate.

So after all that had happened, I shouldn't have called up Avirook, right? Any self-respecting, sensible, logical person wouldn't, yes, any person with *these* traits wouldn't, but I went right ahead and called him up.

"I think we need to meet."

"No, I think we need to get lessons on respecting people."

So this day he needed to write his book, on another day he had an aunt to meet, yet on another occasion, he'd just rolled a joint and needed solitude.

"Should I say you are trying to avoid me?"

"Get a grip over your life, Alafia."

"That can wait. First let's get some nice dinner together."

He relented.

"So what's your problem, do you have to insult me again?"

"Man, look at you, Avirook. So angry, huh?"

"Shouldn't I be?"

"Sure, should definitely be."

"Then?"

"Then… we connected so well…"

Our plateful of Sole came sizzling on the platter. The butter ran in tiny rivulets across the baked carrots, beans and cauliflower florets. The French fries looked just as pounceable with a fresh sprinkle of salt and black pepper resting on the fried pale yellow hill.

In between the juicy morsels, Avirook shot a glance at me through his bloodshot eyes. It was not difficult to tell that the hashish was playing up in his blood now. But he still looked attractive. There was a certain charm about him: the intellectual raw charm of a sensitive heart and sharp mind. I lifted his index finger and started rubbing it with my thumb – a suggestion that I was *ready* – though truth be told, I still wasn't.

"Have you mastered the art of hurting a man where it hurts him the most?"

And have men mastered the same art to turn around and hurt me even more? "Come on. I thought we were over it."

"Are all women as funny as you?"

"How can I vouch for my other sisters?"

"Now what is it that you want?"

"I just want us to give it another try."

After the dinner and two portions of Peach Turned-Upside Down smeared with caramel custard, we walked towards the car in the thick of the night that was yellow due to the newly erected tall neon street lamps.

We got inside the car and even before the engine fired, I grabbed Avirook by the neck and began to kiss him. It was the same kiss – dry and lifeless. They were the same lips – contrite and emotionless. Through years of dedicated indulgence in the practice of smacking, I have realised that these lips have a mind of their own. They know exactly when to command the tongue (its best friend) to roll itself over and make them look glossier, in an attempt to attract someone's attention. They also know when to twitch, curl up and purse to avoid that same attention.

While Avirook's facial expressions turned into a little school boy's who was punished one minute and praised soon after for helping the teacher wipe the blackboard clean of its complicated mathematical algebra, I was still not convinced if I should really go ahead with what I was seducing him for.

I lifted his hand to keep it on my breast. Even in the shadow of the yellow light, the parking attendant could guess that sir and madam were up to something really naughty, so he let us be and didn't come running after the car to get his ten rupee *baksheesh*.

This red-eyed dragon threw another look at me and relieved me of all the impending agony. "We don't have to do this."

"We don't?"

"No, Alafia, we don't."

From somewhere a mosquito came and glided on my arm. In the hazy beam, I noticed its tiny wings and piercing apparatus that would leave a red blotch on my skin. I began scratching the affected area. Avirook looked at me and the red dot. "Nothing will ever go to Ali and Shehnaz. Nothing has. Okay?" My forced attempts towards seduction were put to rest.

Nice man, this Avirook, I still wish he could kiss better.

Oh! Mission

◆

And she never gives up, she never gives in, she just changes her mind

There were seventeen members waiting for their proposals to be accepted. Some five had already rejected the interest I had shown in them and some seven had sent me a personal mail with more photographs other than the ones already on their profile. *Mujhseshaadikaro.com* at this rate was busier than a local vegetable market. It was almost as if a groom/ bride could be bargained on the same scale as your favourite produce. Cabbage, small or big? No, medium-sized and slightly dark green. Tomatoes? Yes, red big juicy ones. Ginger and garlic? Yes. Enough to last a week. Leek? What's that?

The best thing about this marriage portal was that you could customise anything and everything to suit your preference. So if you wanted someone from the business community there were enough options for you to choose from. If a white-collared NRI was your preference, you had an obscene number of choices right from Hawaii to Alaska. And then there were all types and sizes – Tamilian widower settled in Washington DC looking for hardworking and fun loving girl who believes in family values, a Hindu Brahmin boy from Haryana looking for a simple person, who is good-natured, smart and friendly, Sunni Muslim from Mumbai who's very cool and likes spicy dishes looking for a jovial and caring girl – everything was available. Even grooms who threw in messages like:

I am intrast by buttiful girl fr marriage, I am a simple friendly comedian, I am looking for a matching girl, I like traveling, watching movies, shoping, eating out, enjoy with frnds, surfing net, I want to marry with that girl which is same to same, I want to good girl who love me lots n care me lot n trust n honest girls, I am a cool person to hang out with...my friends call me Mr Cool.

So you see, there was no dearth of men. They were *there*, right there. I just needed to pick and choose and click on the 'I accept' button. Later, I even upgraded myself to the platinum membership, where I was assured, I would only meet, 'the most elite and well-educated.' No, I am not downsizing the importance of *mujhseshaadikaro.com*, and I have friends who got married through this classic, tried and tested Indian route to matrimony.

After my now-friends-now-lovers dilemma came to an abrupt halt with Vishesh (remember the ex-boyfriend who said I had a problem handling rejection?), he went right ahead, found a suitable Tamilian girl who sang Carnatic music and made excellent dosas and 'took the plunge with her,' as he had stated before marrying her. And mom keeps mentioning a friend's daughter who found her right match at 35 and who's so happy today that she tears up with the very thought of leaving her warm abode, her husband and in-laws and pet cats, behind to spend a weekend with her mother.

And if others can, so can I. After all, the stars were in my favour, as told by Vishesh's astrologer who had predicted he would marry in September (and he did). So I was supposed to get married by the end of last year, I didn't. Never mind, "the stars would be favourable till the end of next year," the *swamiji* had foretold. So, I had a whole year of groom-hunting and that was an awful lot of time, given that in Indian arranged marriages, you don't spend too much time dating. You are not supposed to, because the families are involved and if one proposal doesn't work out, other options are always available.

So the entire year was packed. And while I will not mention the details of one date a week, I was surely on a marathon and some deserve a quick mention.

Anup Tandon
Divorced
32
Doctor

We met, with both families present. I loved them instantly, not because they cut a sorry figure of a family deprived of the simple joys of life writ large on their faces, but because they were so humble. So simple these people were, especially the boy, even baby lamb must not have listened to its mama as much as he did.

"We love Christianity. Christians build so many churches, they so gentle people," stated the father to my mother.

"My wife work in Christian hospital. She matron there."

I bowed my head and tried to look at the boy who was so shy that were he to be told about my exploits (sexual, mental, spiritual), he would drown his face in his mummyji's lap and remain there forever.

"So you an author, child? Anup loves to read. His room is filled with Sidney Sheldons and who's that other guy... Coel... Coelh... something..."

"Paulo Coelho, uncle."

"Yes yes, that same author."

"So what books you read, child?"

"Uncle, I follow—"

"Okay leave that... how you divorce?"

My father salvaged the situation and narrated the whole story. Ram reappeared standing right behind the senior Mr Tandon, but thank god, he disappeared as quickly as the bland vegetable Tom Yum Soup. This Chinese restaurant was now playing the instrumental version of the popular Indian ghazal *Chupke Chupke*.

The mother was quiet all along and only spoke when spoken to.

"So what do you think, Mr and Mrs Singh?"

"What should we say, Mr Tandon, it's all up to Alafia."

Thank you mom for being so helpful!

"Okay, you notice something on Anup's body?"

"No, we don't."

"Roll up your sleeves son."

The son obeys.

"Now show them son. See, we didn't want to hide anything. Anup has a small defect. That is not disease, not illness. He is normal."

Anup had small rough bumps on the skin of his arms. "There is no cure for it. This is hereditary, my father had it. I didn't. Anup have it now. But not to worry, this is no disease."

My heart ached for this gentle-looking soul. I wish I could give him all my love, but that's the least I could do.

Ryan Peters
Divorced
32
Voice and accent trainer

Ryan and I were introduced through our church pastor, who vouched for this god-fearing man's zealous devotion to Jesus. When Ryan and I met for the first time he had reached the place 45 minutes before time and when I sat next to him, I saw that he had made three circles on the tissue paper which looked tortured.

"Hey Ryan!"

"Praise the Lord, Alafia."

"Well! So, what are you scribbling?"

"Thought I would show you something."

"Go on."

I was actually competing against the crumpled piece of paper for attention.

"See, this circle represents the Father, this the Son and the last one is the Holy Spirit. So all three together form a trinity."

"But why are you telling me all this?"

"Because we need to form a trinity if we were to marry. You, I and Jesus."

"Yes. That's great. We will. All three of us together."

"Look, I can already feel the Holy Spirit moving. Can you feel it?"

I looked everywhere, but could only spot some spirited collegians who cackled loudly.

Then Ryan proceeded to give me a tiny sermon on how important it was to be godly. I loved his spirit but I had still not connected with the other spirit he now saw standing behind me. The experience was scary because I lacked the capacity of dealing with supernatural beings and didn't know how I would react if that benign spirit were to tap on my shoulder and say, "Hello there, lovely lady, care for some more coffee?"

Ryan was about to draw some more circles.

I saw Ram stand there and laugh. The rascal always appeared when he knew he could laugh at my expense.

"Go and spend some time with your wife, you jerk."

For the first time he turned around to say something sensible. "Run, Alafia. Run!"

I did.

Arun Kapoor
Single
31
Businessman

He came in his luxury sedan and the first question he asked me was why I didn't drive one! The moment we set our eyes on each other we knew we were as different as ice cream is from lemon pickle.

"So it's okay if you're a *divorcee*. Such women have gone on to do so much in life."

"Really? How much?"

"Don't you know? Mallika Sherawat is a divorcee."

Arun was on a diet because making muscles was his only ambition in life, other than counting wads of notes. "I will only stick to some Greek salad, if you don't mind. You can eat whatever you want. But honestly, if you ask me, you should go for some salad too. You should lose some weight."

I sucked my teeth at him in a forced attempt.

"So how many countries have you travelled to?"

"OK, chuck it. What's your basic, CTC?"

"Where do you party every Saturday night?"

"America is the only way for you, what are you doing in India?"

Then he showed me his latest acquisition of a watch worth a few millions. "But, we spend that kind of money every day. It's normal."

And I spoke exactly five words since we had met ("hi" inclusive).

Now if this dining place had been empty, if the chef and his staff had fallen into a deep slumber and if other guests were given a magic potion to lose their senses, I would grab all the knives in the kitchen, gather all the glass plates, tuck the fork in my jeans pocket and jab each instrument inside Mr Rich Flesh with such precision and brutality that leave aside marriage, at that moment I wanted to leave him incapable of even getting an erection in the leftover years of his loaded life.

Don't come back, Ram. Please. This was my worst so far.

Have mercy. I was your ex-wife, and now a D.I.V.O.R.C.E.E.

Demission I

❖

Next strategy

"Ala, I am getting married."

"What? I mean when? I mean how? I mean to a guy?"

You cannot expect me to be all sorted at three am, when it's dark and I have had yet another fanciful night of imagining a man's body over mine and more. But when this call comes from a sister, who's cute, plump, eight years younger and in love for the last four years and who suddenly announces her plans to marry, you certainly end up behaving like your hair colour has been painted green without your knowledge.

Anushka is 24 and chose Japan to be her home since she was 14. So yes she's proficient in Japanese and also resembles one. And although I am a semi-decade ahead of her, she has been my hero throughout our growing up years. I never had many chances of sistering/mothering her because Anushka grabbed my hand (since she was 11) and helped me cross the road and she even exerted her right over the kind of clothes I wore. No short or skimpy for her. "Ala, you've to wear something sober or else you don't step out of the house."

"Excuse me?"

"Yes. You got that right."

That's how she was, my younger sister.

But now that she was going to get married and that too in four months, my mind underwent the scariest roller coaster ride ever.

Now technically in an Indian society, the elder sibling always marries first. Right, so I was married first. But even when the sibling decides to remarry, the elder one again gets the first chance second time around. In fact, in some families, the younger sibling could end up waiting for years before the elder one finds a groom/bride. We know of a family where the younger sister got married at 48, because the older one got married at 50. And I hardly doubt that Anushka would wait for 24 more years to marry. So did that mean I had precisely *four* months to find Mr Right? Or could there be a possibility that she and I could get married the same day? There was another possibility: Anushka delaying her marriage to save her sister the embarrassment. The last hope was divine intervention. I could pray to all the gods of the world to help me bump into someone who could at least stand next to me while certain wedding ceremonies were being performed and which needed 'only married' couples to solemnise it. There was another way of escaping the whole situation: fake illness, fake work, fake wedding or fake anything that was reasonably buyable.

And while I was still working on the solutions to avoid or overcome my misery, the preparations had already begun. The sister had decided to quit her meaty job in Japan to settle in India with the love of her life. He was an Indian, his home was in India.

Anushka was in India and she was home with me, mom and dad.

PART - III

You sing. I sing.
But where's the melody?

Demission II

∞

Saturn is heavy on you

I was left to the care of Mintoo's aunt's aunt who'd started the auspicious evening with inauspicious news. "But why is this guy named Mintoo? Couldn't you find another person with a better name to marry you?"

"Oh shut up, Ala. You just listen to what this old one has to say."

I looked at the aunt's aunt who looked at my astrological chart with such alacrity that I knew at once that this woman took her job seriously. "Child, the planetary position of your Saturn according to the astrological chart is the weakest right now."

I looked at Anushka once again who was busy fixing up the time with some henna artists. No Indian wedding is complete without henna tattooed over the arms and legs of the bride. And this bride wanted to tell the Krishna-Radha love story through her intricate design that would turn anywhere between deep orange to rust red after being washed. So even while accepting the challenge of covering her arms and feet with gooey sticky henna artwork, she chose to be secular. As a child too, she had uniquely modelled herself to visit a gurudwara, church, mandir and masjid the same day and if it's not the same day, the holy voyage would not take place at all!

"So how do I make this Saturn powerful, happy?"

"See, child it's very simple. Feed a black stray dog, or donate any food grain that weighs as much as you do to crows or wear a 14-faced rudraksha string."

"But someone had told me that I don't have any planetary plotting."

The aunt's aunt looked livid. It were as though I had just challenged her intense devotion towards the solar system and made them appear not more than science class diagrams that I too followed with equal devotion as a gawky school kid. But there was some concern as I could sense the air around this devoted planet pupil go thin. "Child, you *really* need to do something to appease *Shani Devta* (Saturn God)."

Sure I could. But the solutions were tricky. Not that finding stray animals was rare in this country, but finding a black one and befriending it so that it would not bite into my flesh but the stale flatbread I bought for it would surely be a tough task. My ass already looked the size of Spain so searching for hungry crows and throwing away an entire country-sized goody for them was again so unreal. And was I going to sit and count the number of faces my desired *rudraksha* had? What if I were conned for 13? Did I want to get unlucky with this one too?

Anushka drummed a steel plate with her finger nails (fake ones – she got them as soon as she landed in India) and announced that the henna artists would be there the next day at 4 pm sharp. "So all those who are interested, please show up on time."

Then she walked over to me for some suggestions that meant life and death to her. Sure, you could challenge Saturn against henna designs.

"Ala, what's better – Radha-Krishna love story, *Mahabharata* or *Ramayana?*"

"Nativity scene!"

"Shut up, Ala. I might as well ask a wall for help."

From behind, mom who was busy supervising the kitchen work for the guests who had arrived/soon to arrive, shouted, "Is that how you talk to a sister who's eight years older than you. Aren't you supposed to call her *didi*? You have forgotten all your manners back in Japan, but in India we still call our elder sister *didi*. Understand?"

Anushka rolled her eyes and winked at me, "So, *didi?*"

"Rub it in, you bitch."

Mintoo's cousin who was busy feeding her toddler who refused to eat anything other than the crumbed biscuits from the carpet, looked in my direction with a startle, as if her mother, not I were eight years older than my sister.

"You are *eight* years older than Anu?"

"Yes, I am."

She probably must have mumbled something in her mouth and left to look after her toddler who was now licking and scraping the rough wool threads off the carpet.

The electrician with strings of fairy lights had just arrived, followed by his two helpers. The little light bulbs would be suspended through the entire terrace and balcony – a sure sign of a big occasion in the house. The walls were freshly painted bright white, the potted plants were given a muddy russet, and extra cooks, drivers, and house helps were hired to cater to the special needs of each and every relative. Extra mattresses, pillows, mosquito nets, bed spreads, towels and so on were also brought out from the buried piles of old and excess clothes and upholstery that were neatly tied up in cloth bundles with crunched cloves to keep them away from moths, tucked away in wooden closets or iron trunks shoved under the beds or on top of cupboards.

The house now definitely looked like it had many years ago. The same events stood right in front of me again, and again there was the same joy and mirth my parents had experienced then.

I noticed Anushka after the aunt's aunt finally relieved me with a promise that I would definitely take corrective measures to make friends with the angry Saturn god. In a couple of hours she'd drive down to Chandni Chowk or Dariba Kalan to get extra shiny rolls of golden netted cloth, wrapping paper and other items that would be used to decorate presents for Mintoo's family members. She preferred driving down to these crowded market places all by herself instead of visiting the next door middle-class markets of Lajpat Nagar or Sarojini Nagar, all for cheaper rates for the same products. How confident, how undeterred she was, my sister.

Perhaps she was always like this, right from the time she was born. And maybe she never pooped without a diaper. Time took me back to those days when as a 12-year-old she turned around to ask me one day, "Ala, do you know what dating is?

I was 20 then and just about tasted many of those first kisses. "Sure I do."

"So when you date someone, that's your boyfriend right?"

"Well, yes."

"So you have a boyfriend?"

I remember how she had stumped me for words because the mention of words like a girlfriend or boyfriend was still not acceptable in the family. "Of course I don't have any boyfriend, Anu."

"Oh! Come on. You're lying. Who's that boy who comes to drop you home every day from college?"

I hushed her and rolled my eyes in mock disgust only to be stoked by her again. "Look, I am going to marry the only boy I date."

And Mintoo was her first and last boyfriend. While I had gone on to date many and marry the one I had never dated.

Upstairs, the electricians had placed their tools to fix up the lights that would brighten up the whole house for another week or so. It was a laborious job. One helper stood on the balcony while the other stood downstairs and caught hold of the suspended string aimed in his direction. The head electrician directed them.

Mom was losing her patience over some servants who had not fed the fresh batch of relatives who'd arrived all weary from a train journey. Dad was looking up angrily at the clouds that were bursting against each other as a forewarning for heavy rains which meant running the fresh paint off the walls, delay in fixing up lights, and traffic snarls that would further delay the pick-up of more batches of relatives yet to arrive. All this would mean more money and time spent. If dad had his way he'd point a boot towards the playful clouds that in turn may mock at him with the face of a joker or a naughty boy.

This house was surely the house of a wedding now.

Thoughts of what the aunt's aunt had said raced back at me with the sound of thunder in the background. This was the same place where I once belonged. This was a familiar zone, only the characters were different.

And this feeling is strange and only the one who's gone through it knows what it means to belong there. Every wedding that you witness is a reminder of your own – no matter how bitter it was. So it is not exactly living the past, like many might think, but what happens is that you are constantly aware of how all this was a part of you once and while it is not a part of you any more, you want all this and more back in your life and in a better way. And while you don't have it right now, the absentia of a partner has not been such a rosy time either. So you are in this spazzy sphere – oscillating between feeling happy for a loved one who's found her true love to how and why this journey has been so difficult for you.

Thank god, it didn't rain. The clouds fooled my father again, but he was happy playing the dud singing the popular Hindi film song, *rimjhim gire saawan...*

From the terrace I watch Anushka's tiny figure followed by two cousins dash hurriedly towards the car. It's already late and brides-to-be are not supposed to step out of the house, but this is tradition and that's Anushka.

She looked up and shouted out right from where she was. "Ala, Chinky, Rimpy and Tanu will be there any moment. Be sure you are around. Okay?" I nodded back and shouted, "Don't worry."

I was going to be the household *didi*.

Mission Bells Ring

My sister's wedding

The first ones to arrive that morning were Chinky, Rimpy and Tanu. These were Anushka's three best friends since her school days. While two of them, Chinky and Tanu, were ordinarily good-looking like any girl that age, the third one in the trio was so pretty that if we lived in a jungle and men were animals, she could be hung from a tree as a bait to catch them. And with their presence, the house had turned into a minicamp for NCC cadets who ate together, slept together, shared fantasies about their young boyfriends and often bathed together.

The next to arrive were the cousins – some recently married and younger than me and some my age with infants in their arms. While the brothers' new wives made extra efforts to please the elders, the sisters' husbands drew extra attention as the new male members of the extended family. The older ones had of course established themselves well within the unit and proven their mettle. There was another cousin who had divorced and married immediately the month after, so I was the only aberration. Everyone was either in a good or bad marriage and those left had not attained the marriageable age yet.

The batch after this was followed by the parents of these cousins who were either our parents' real brothers or sisters or distant cousins who were as old as them.

The final and more distinct batch belonged to the ancient bearers of the family name: Our parents' parents, uncles, aunts and older cousins, who were at times as old as our grandparents. This mostly happened as in those days the mother and daughter often underwent labour pain in opposite rooms.

The house where only three residents resided till a few days back now wore the look of a refugee camp. Women got dressed in one room, men in the other, while servants ran errands to get them tea, water, safety pins, *chappals*, combs, polythene bags and anything they required at that particular hour.

"*Didi!* When are you going to get ready? It's already 5."

"Yeah Rimpy, I know. I should run. Thanks for the reminder."

In the midst of the drone of human voices that mixed from high octave to tenor, I completely lost track of time and rushed into my room to see that it was already occupied with a dozen women who were mostly standing there in their petticoats, either circling the sari around or doing their hair and then waiting to wear the sari. Anushka was given a separate room to dress up.

Before we all were to head out to the wedding, there was a traditional family ceremony to be performed, where a red *tilak* would be placed on the bride's forehead, as a mark to keep away the evil eye. This was a hurrah moment for me because Anushka looked so angelic that I leapt to put that red dot on her forehead. "Not you, not you, this ceremony is only performed by those married," shouted an aunt from behind. I sucked my teeth at Anushka and left the plate full of red paste into some relative's hands.

And this girl, this little girl who was brought up along with me for the last so many years was suddenly made to be so distant because of a custom that didn't allow me to touch her first, that restricted me from doing anything to fight the evil eye. I thought I had tears welling up in my eyes. And if a distant aunt noticed, she loudly remarked, "Alafia must be so jealous and frustrated this time. Poor girl. It's hard to see a younger sister getting married in front of your own eyes, while yours ended years ago."

"Yes, no wonder she looks so sad all the time," said another one.

"People get divorced and get married so early. This girl has very high rates, you see."

"It's all her fault. Look at Anushka, how quickly and smartly she got married. Alafia just lacks the knack."

If I had the courage to turn around and scream at each one of them, I would; but I didn't. My legs suddenly became too weak to even stand on one foot. Past images of this very ceremony had started swirling around me. Had I known I would be single again one day, I'd have set a new rule that very day – apply the *tilak* only if everyone was allowed to do so, irrespective of one's marital status.

Ram had reappeared. But this time he was not mocking. He was indifferent. He saw my struggle to get up and walk briskly towards the terrace because that was the only area without any human interference. He followed me there too.

"Why Ram, why don't you leave me alone? I had let go of you, remember?"

"But I don't chase you. You keep calling me back."

"Do you see what I am going through, how I am segregated? Do you see that?"

He was quiet and I thought he was more interested in looking at the fairy lights which were lit up even as the sun had an hour to go down.

"Why couldn't you just be a little more loving towards me? I was so young and naïve."

To my surprise Ram was quiet and somewhat pensive.

"*Didi... didi...* where are you, *didi*?" I think it was one of the three best friends shouting out for me.

"Coming, coming!" I shouted out while wiping my tears and carefully dabbing them with a tissue so as to not smudge the mascara.

I ran downstairs with the aunts' words still throbbing in my ears. Now it had started stinging my temples too. Mom was at her frantic best, "These girls will kill me one day. The younger one thinks she's still in Japan and the older one keeps disappearing."

"Where were you, child? Okay let it be. Now let's step out quickly."

The relatives were dressed in the best – covered with bling and sequins. While on our way, some had forgotten their clutches, some struggled with their hairpins, some had their saris coming off and some palpitated without their handkerchiefs, the others threw orders at their new daughters-in-law.

☛

The church looked like a well-furnished piece of art work, perfectly decked for a wedding ceremony. Was I walking down the aisle? No you fool. It's Anushka, your sister. See, she's coming... there she goes. How angelic, how fairy-like in that white dress. Your rouge was a little too bright, remember? Yeah! This rouge is just perfect, sitting on Anushka's white cheeks like cherries on cream sauce.

Wait, wait! Your wedding march is too fast, Anu. And you bloody fool, you cried during your entire march. How silly you looked in that wedding video!

Ram peeped at me again. "What the hell are you doing at the altar now? Come down."

"So you remember everything, do you?"

"Yes."

"Do you also remember how the wedding ring just wouldn't go down your finger? It was so tight."

I smiled.

Anushka looked at me from the altar in surprise because she caught me smiling to myself. She rolled her eyes in the typical manner and turned to the pastor who had started solemnising the wedding.

"And thank god we didn't have the Hindu wedding. I hate the tedious ceremonies, Alafia."

"Yes and because of which your family hates us till today." I remember how anxious my parents were to get me married in a non-Christian family. But with Anushka they had left everything to destiny.

The wedding was over. The church gong rang out loud, *thongh thongh thongh.*

Everyone congratulated one another.

While Anushka left the church with her now official husband, she beamed; while mom and I teared up and smiled in intervals.

And when I went to catch the bouquet to be thrown by Anushka outside the church, the many contenders, including the three best friends, made space for me as reverence to a *didi* though secretly wondering if I was seriously eligible for this fun game. But I so badly needed that bouquet – that bunch of flowery good luck – literally caught from a new bride by a wannabe bride. So if you carefully watch the bride's aim and catch that flying bouquet, chances are you'd be the next in line to get married. But if you don't, you are bound to keep attending weddings, till you reach the experienced age of 40. But perhaps I was *didi* Alafia here too, as people took that role seriously, while internally I was still a little big girl. And then, someone did stab that wannabe spirit again.

"Alafia! Not you, child. This game is only for those who were never married. The younger ones deserve a chance… come come!" I smiled as I looked straight through Anushka and then the bunch of water lilies and orchids she was just about to fling.

Mission Fission

❖

Do you need a psychiatrist?

Do I? So I brought out my writing pad after many days and wrote everything that had happened during the wedding. Every word that had coiled around me like a vicious snake. So there was no other way to unwrap this black viper but to cut it into little letters and words and sentences onto my private pages.

> *Anu looked beatific no... But the little bitch didn't cry, no she didn't. ~~Angry, irritated~~, no... what did they say... desperate, frustrated. LOL. Never mind... let them say whatever they want. Rasheed... what is that word he uses? Yeah, watdfuck! But do I really give a fuck? And I had forgiven everyone so why is it that someone or the other keeps coming back to say nasty things to me? Yeah, I am man-less, marriage-less... does that qualify me to see a psychologist. Dunno. But let's try shall we Alafia? Yeah at least I don't need medicines. Thank you god.*

I fixed up the date for the first week of the coming month, which meant I had two weeks to go before I could start my therapy and since I had never taken these sessions before, I wanted to brace myself to get a complete sense of what I was getting myself into. I was going to be 32 the coming week – a reason strong enough to sober down, look inside my life a little more seriously and not feel ashamed to seek for any help that might come along.

Ali called up with the usual gusto in his voice that was welcoming and annoying. "Lady wolf... Ready for some fun on your birthday?"

"Stop calling me a wolf, will you?"

"Alright done. I don't call you wolf and you come and show me that terrific face of yours soon. Okay?"

"Okay. Do you ever leave people with options?"

"No. But I have an option for you. Either you see me every day till Saturday or you see me on Saturday."

"Latter."

What goes on in the mind of a woman is difficult to tell. But what goes on inside the mind of a woman who is single, divorced and still has some words of praise throbbing in her ears is even more difficult to tell. She can be predictable and just when you start believing in her predictability, she might turn right around to give you a shock that totally knocks you off your chair. The worst part is she can end up shocking herself. So just when I think this evening was going to be all happy dinner and happy drinks, it turns out to be 'happy' something else.

We head to a club in GK where everything is tailor-made to up my spirits quite literally. Ali is at his flirtatious best with his hands slipping down over my hips and breasts every now and then. My resistance doesn't work on this strongly-built man who on any given day is quite capable of lifting me with one hand, even though I have shown no signs of losing an ounce of flesh since my Landour trip.

"Ali, you will have to stop it or else I am going to tell Shehnaz."

"You know how attractive I find you Alafia."

After which Ali didn't touch me the whole evening. So if this meant going around thanking each hottie in the room personally, I would do it. Even with a thank you card delivered personally after a thank you speech for each one of them. Ali was distracted most of the times, either pointing out Miss Big Boobs or Miss Fleshy Thighs. Shehnaz's all-women's trip to Venice had given him the chance to indulge in his favourite activities and an unbarred license to flirt with any woman.

I was mostly quiet. Seated in one corner of the room, I wanted to flirt too but some strange energy of thoughts within stopped me. There were exceptionally good-looking men and so many of them all around but my mind and body were still tired with the thought of getting close to any man, for anything.

It was a quarter after two when I decided to head home. And as if destiny had its own way of playing games with me, who should call Ali, but Avirook.

"Yes, yes, yes, buddy. Don't worry I also have the lovely lady with me."

"So we are headed towards your house. Get some more drinks in place, will you?"

"Who was it, Ali? Where are we going?"

"My little wolfie, don't you worry. It was Avirook."

"*What?* I mean what are you saying?"

"Don't sound so shocked darling. He just wants us to come over."

"Us? And who does this *us* mean?"

"Us is you and I."

"Does he know *I* am with you?"

"*Ya Khuda*...how does it matter, Alafia?"

"Matter? Of course it matters."

"How?"

Ali is the kind of man who's seen the entire world and its people so he is much more than someone who'd normally pass off as street smart. He's world smart, human smart, space smart.

"Is something cooking between the two of you?"

"Two who?"

"You and Avirook, darling."

"Of course not. You know I don't fancy his types."

"Then why are you reacting so strangely with the mere mention of his name?"

"Ali, That's because it's so late. We need to head home, and my home, not his!"

"Just ten minutes there and we're sorted, okay?"

I hated the thought of bumping into Avirook again. Although we both had parted ways amicably, there was a certain uneasiness about all that had happened and all that could happen *now*. I wondered how he'd react after seeing me at the door. Would he throw me out of his house, the same house that had stood witness to his humiliation? Or he would be all nice in front of Ali and the moment we were left alone, he'd ask me to get out of his house on some pretext. Or he might be normal and forgiving.

The door opened.

"And look who's here! *Tat tat dhan... dhan dhan dhan...*" Ali mocked the welcoming sound of a drum while pulling me from behind his back and presenting me in front of Avirook, the emperor.

Avirook's instant reaction was his heart coming to his mouth. He looked like his life had actually been sucked out of him.

"So, should we come in buddy?"

"Oh! Of course of course, you *both* are so welcome."

We exchanged some unpleasant smiles.

Ali and Avirook got chatting while I downed myself with some more drinks. I nudged Ali to get up and get out but the conversation between them had now moved from last vacation they took together to some real estate deal where they were planning to invest jointly. So I quietly crept out of the room to make space in the balcony through which I could see the entire vista of Noida's famous Oakland Apartments, where most lights by now had been turned off and the ones which were on, belonged to foreign students who were revelling on a Saturday night.

Someone hugged me from behind. It was Ali. I knew that strong touch. I wriggled out of his grip partly because I didn't want it, and partly because I didn't want Avirook to see us like this. Ali took me by the arm and led me towards Avirook. "Look at this shy girl!"

"Yeah, what a shy girl."

And then everything happened so quickly as if we had rehearsed this so many times earlier. Almost by a push or some guided force, I hugged Avirook. Ali hugged me from behind.

Before I knew it, I was sandwiched between the two. Here I was between two men. I didn't have a future with either, yet I wasn't entirely unhappy.

I mumbled, "Ali, I do need a psychologist."

Transmission Failed

◆

Blanked out

The next morning, I was groggy. I felt like a wrestler who was tossed around gently but with no major injuries. That was physically. Mentally, I felt so confused.

While my already flagging morals had sunk to their lowest, I had this whole new set of problems knocking, rather banging on my mind's door. Was sex so dominant in my mind for me to go all humpy with any man, even if I were not attracted to him?

So my heart said, *No way. This is not who you are.*

My mind said, *This is just sex. Plain sex and you need it right now, baby. These men are safe; you are not going to get into any trouble so go for it.*

My heart again said no. *Don't do this. You are not even attracted to them. Don't do something you don't like, baby.*

And then like it always happens, you often let your mind rule over your heart at a wrong place and time, and that's exactly what I did. I told myself that this was purely sexual and that I might as well have some fun with it. Life's blind curves are worse. You have not only a speeding truck, but a speeding car, a speeding bike, a herd of cows, a family of two infants balancing on a bicycle... all round the blind curve and the worst part is, from a distance the road looks so clear and the sounds, so muted that you have absolutely no idea what is around that bend.

The three of us decided to spend a day at Ali's place. It had all been planned out really well by him. The best thing was that Rizwan had been let off for a week and the other servants had been lured for a movie outing.

We were immediately taken inside Ali's guest bedroom. The air of tension between me and Avirook had also almost naturally dissipated because suddenly we were thinking alike. Feeling alike. We were finally on the same page after all that heart burn. In fact, he looked like a washed pink baby and brimming with joy. Ali on the other hand looked like the mini effigy of a He Man in his pair of blue tight shorts and a yellow vest. The room smelled of incense or *itar*, I couldn't tell. One wall was covered with pictures of Mecca and Medina and the other had framed photographs of the last trip the husband and wife had taken to Paris.

But my mind was suddenly swirling around like a top that got so nervous of being spun around that it forgot how to stop. I had some weird thoughts rolling into my mind just then: What would Myra be up to? How would she react? Would she be nonchalant or shocked? Anushka would be leaving for her honeymoon anytime now. Why hadn't she called, and would she wear the lingerie I gave her? Would

Shehnaz divorce Ali and murder me in public view if she knew?

We toyed around with each other. One man vied for my attention, while the other proved that earlier rejection was forgotten.

We took a break. Yes we did. Gorged on some mutton kebabs Ali had asked the cook to prepare, had some exotic raspberry-flavoured vodka he had got from Russia and chatted about the most inane things in life.

But I don't know if I was shocked or relieved when Ali informed me that he and Shehnaz had not had sex in the last five years. "And what about Shehnaz, what does she do?"

"Well, wolfie, I don't know. I think she knows what I do, though!"

"And she doesn't mind it?"

"See, I obviously don't romance a woman in front of her. But it's sex you see, wolfie. It's hunger. Now look, you had the hunger too. Do you feel bad about fulfilling it? No one gets hurt, and no one gets emotional."

Yes it's true. No one gets hurt. I was guilty as hell because I had sex with men I didn't love; it's true that I cannot have sex with someone unless I feel it but what I realised while looking at these men who had resumed talking about their investment plans in a property is that no one got hurt in the end really. No one.

For the last time I had had sex was with a man I liked and wanted to marry, but only ended up getting hurt.

Psychic Emission

•◆

Delving deep down

So sex is important. Period. And I don't want to hide or run away from it by faking that I can do without sex. I can't. But do I want to experience more of what I did before the weekend of my birthday, I would say no. I am not the moral propagator of high value systems within Indian society. I am also not the one to preserve my body as a holy shrine for the right man to worship it, but what I had come to realise after that night was that sex cannot be forced and that it has to come easily and not for the sake of having sex, but for the sake of celebrating the body, the mind, the person, the emotions with the sex.

And sex and age has a natural co-relation too. When you're 32, the prospects of you ending up rubbing the member of every man you think is attractive start becoming slim. Now reverse the numbers. When you're 23, you have all the chances, but if you're really stupid at 23, may the gods save you. Not only do you miss out on men, you miss out on good men and end up with the wrong ones. So I was a stupid 23 and now a stupid 32, but if you truly acknowledge your dumbness (albeit the age) and work your way around it, you would have won half the battle.

131

So normally what happens is that on my birthday, I tear up. And while it's still unclear to me as to why I end up sobbing privately or publicly, another little wise birdie sat on my shoulder and told me, "You expect too much. You expect everyone to wish you, surprise you, thrill you, amuse you."

"But you stupid birdie, don't we all expect that on our birthdays?"

"I don't know about everyone ma'am, but I am your birdie. Don't I come every time you call me?"

"I don't call you every time, you little monster. I don't even know you, we haven't even met before!"

"Think about it, ma'am. I was always there; flapping my wings noisily for your attention but you never glanced at me, ma'am."

"Okay, whatever. And what's your name you said?"

"*Wisdom*. The Proverbs in the Bible is dedicated to me, ma'am."

"Okay. So will you come again when I need you?"

"I am always around. You just have to open your eyes and mind to see me."

"Oh! Shut up and off you fly."

Wisdom flapped its little wings and away it flew with a promise to come back soon.

It had been pouring heavily since morning and the slush gathered at the end of the road was making it difficult for the residents to cross the block without dipping the tip of their jeans or sari or pyjama in the muddy overflowing gutter water. The white coat of paint now looked a hazy off-white and dad looked only too relieved that it had not run off during or before the wedding. The bright red paint on the pots, however, bled so profusely that in the most abject way it seemed that the whole garden was on a mass menstrual cycle. The extra house help was let off, the mattresses, pillows, mosquito nets were also tucked away with crushed cloves and naphthalene balls. Mom was not shouting as much and breathing rather easy and dad soon had no reason to point a shoe towards the sky. Although at the back of their minds, they thought endlessly about my life and my future – with or without a man.

And I am 32 finally – without a man. And I choose to spend the day with my parents who showered me with blessings and presents (their favourite blessing asking god to give me the best husband). Mom whipped up my favourite Indian delicacies that I had grown up eating, right from *puri bhaaji, sheera, kheer* and vegetable *pulao* which I still believe has only my mother's copyright since no one can perfect it as she can.

That aside, other than the mouth-watering culinary fare spread out generously on the dining table, Indian family meal times are also the crucial hours to discuss important issues and what could be a better time than a birthday to rake up something as relevant as marriage plans.

"So child, what next?"

"Another book, mom. Am already working on it, you forgot?"

"No, Ala. About your future, marriage, etc."

"But we've tried looking for someone on that website and through newspaper ads."

"Yes. Perhaps we should try harder."

I looked at dad who was digging a hole into a hot *puri* to let the steam out of its fat belly.

"And look at you. Busy eating that *puri*. Do you want to get your daughter married or not?"

This was mom's chance.

"Kids younger than her have started getting married. Half of them will have children after a few years. Do you still want to keep your daughter home?"

"I am trying. I am trying."

Myra's call salvaged the situation for me.

"Till now I haven't cried, My."

"Yeah Ala. This year I haven't cry as well."

And we burst into shrill giggles over a joke only she and I could relate to.

"So all set for tomorrow, are we?"

"Well yeah. Let's see how it goes. I am not sure how this is going to help."

"Don't worry. Like I said, just don't fret over anything. Go easy, okay?"

So finally my date with the psychoanalyst arrived. I was going to open my heart in front of a complete stranger who looked gentle, patient and so understanding that I wondered if she was single, and if she were, how did she cope with it. And if she was not single and her marriage was anything like Ali and Shehnaz's, how did she manage that puzzling no sex marriage, infidelity and 'good' husband who didn't go around thrashing or slandering his wife, providing her with all the comforts, with the only exception of sex and emotions.

So we started with what got me to her. A chaotic mind of course!

"So tell me, how can I help you, Alafia?" She asked me in a manner that had warmth and firmness.

"Help me get married doctor, please," is what I'd have loved to answer.

"I think I am losing my mind. Feels like I have no control over it." And then I started doing the talk, the real talk. I told her things I had never told myself or anyone ever.

"So what makes your mind so chaotic, Alafia?"

"Marriage, stability, companionship, love. That's all that I ever wanted and that's all that eludes me."

She looked at me and smiled. The kind of smile she must have flashed at every patient every hour and yet I needed that smile just as much as I needed sex.

"So would you like to talk about the last relationship you had and why it was good and bad for you?"

I told her everything. Right from the first time I was kissed to how deeply Anushka'a marriage had affected me. Remarks people made during the wedding which still resounded in my ears.

"I got married at... I had sex at the age of... I want to marry because... I need a companion because..."

It seemed like time had stopped by to take a walk in the rains. There was so much more I wanted to tell her, ask her.

Suddenly thoughts of Tara crossed my mind. She was as gentle, but in a spiritual way. And just when I was picturing myself in that heady past life Tara had introduced me to, I heard this same firm voice in the room say, "Your time is up for today, Alafia, but when you come back the next time, let's talk about why you really need a man."

Honestly, I don't know. The answer, I was convinced would be same in every session, and session after session.

Mission M

◆◆

Why do we need men?

Asking why I need a man is like asking me, "Who taught you how to kiss. Did you take tutorials on how to see with your eyes? Or did someone teach you to cry tears when hurt?" No one did, right? So, just as the mechanism of kissing, seeing and crying is unexplainable, answering why a woman needs a man is probably as unthinkable, unanswerable.

I can't remember a situation or an age or time when I have needed a man for just one thing. I have needed him in totality. If I like Mr Sexy's great body, but he doesn't treat me well, I would probably move over to Mr Courteous. Now I like this gentleman but if I cannot have a conversation with him for more than two minutes, I would go ahead and consider Mr Intelligent, but if this guy is a motor mouth with no moolah, Mr Money is what I would look for next. And if Mr Money is all show, my immediate bet would be Mr Unassuming. And while the list can go on and one quality or several others could draw me to a man, why I need him with all or none of these attributes, I cannot tell.

And while the word 'men' starts with the letter M, it's no mystery that its corresponding items like marriage, maternity, menstruation, menopause and mess up start with 'M' too.

And how tactically these words make sense when put in the same chronology is something to think about! So other than men and marriage, maternity is an issue that could have great relevance for a woman of my age and background. Had Ram and I decided to get passionate even once during our marriage, I would have been a mother today, and while I couldn't have thought about acquiring this status *then*, I feel my body clock ticking away every minute now. Just seeing a happy haloed mother grabbing her child's finger makes me want to have one of my own and do everything the infant makes her do, right from changing nappies to undergoing sleepless nights. Also, I am told that with advancing age, your chances of conceiving become rare, so from a menstruating fertile female, you could soon be struggling with an issue like menopause, as early as 35 (I have only read and heard these stories, but have no physical evidence to prove it). What could be the aftermath of this 'M' tragedy is how inexplicably it could lead to a mess up even before you realise it.

So when my psychoanalyst asked me why I need a man, I answered rather plainly, "I need a man because I need a man."

"But why is it that you *need* a man?"

"I *need* a man because there is a need to need him."

"Mmm. And where does that need come from, Alafia?"

Jesus Christ! How am I supposed to know that? If I did, I would have been in your chair, lady.

"I don't know really."

"Think about it a little hard."

I pause to think really hard. I do come up with answers that might be slightly convincing, but not totally up to the mark.

"Okay let's restructure this: What is it in a man that you think will fulfil that void in your life?"

"May... b...e... the void of loneliness. It's good to have a companion, you know."

"Most definitely. But how does a man fill up that void?"

"Mmm, I really don't know."

She paused for me to speak. The room was silent with only the sound of the AC blasting cold air that covered my skin with goose bumps.

While looking at the AC in disgust, I suddenly answered, "A man fills up that void by providing me with security, love and companionship. He can also fulfil my need to be a mother, my need to nurture and nourish. And all this will only come true if and when I marry someone."

I was making illogical statements that only a woman who is desperate can. But I was desperate. After revelation number one that I need sex, this was my revelation number two.

And then this experienced shrink hit the nail on its head.

"But haven't most of your relationships been unfulfilling and unrewarding for you, where you have ended up giving much more than you deserved to get?"

"Yes, that's true."

"And still you have gone looking around for more hurt?"

"No one goes around looking for hurt, doctor."

Although I know that in the weirdest way, I like to don the hat of the one who is victimised, I am aware that I suffer from martyr's syndrome. But it's equally true that whenever I do enter a new relationship, I give love a new hope, a new dimension, with a fervent promise that *this* time, it will work out.

"See, a man helps me find the beauty in me. I think my whole world becomes the man. If I don't have a man around, my life is nothing."

"So, Alafia, *you* can't help yourself?"

And then the session moved on to the innermost layers of buried memories: The time I was a child, an adolescent, a teenager, and a young adult, and how I fared emotionally in each one of these phases. It was unbelievable how much I had buried within me. There was one layer of debris piled up over the other that was slowly being unwrapped and unfolded right before this stranger – the details of which I will avoid getting into.

However, before we closed in on the one-hour session, my therapist gave me homework. Homework? Okay. I wanted to smile and tell her that I was an author, who travelled the world and knew a thing or two about life, but I shut up, because I was no one in here, in this room, which was witness to many of my secrets week after week. Secrets which were long forgotten, and supposedly long forgiven.

"So Alafia, your homework is to figure out how *you* can help yourself, without the presence of a man. Okay?"

Well, I knew the answer already and like the bright front-bencher I wanted to raise my hand and impress the teacher even as she wrote the questions on the blackboard. So sexually it was simple, I only had to indulge in the master of all indulgences – masturbation or masterbation as I love to call it. Three to four times in a week, or at times even every day, and you are all set. Emotionally, I wasn't sure. So I reframed the question to suit my convenience. "So Alafia, your home work is to know how *you* can help yourself *emotionally*, without the presence of a man. Okay?"

And my immediate answer again would have been, "Go for another man, and another man, and another man... till you end up finding the right one."

Man Shun Not

●◆

Doing without a man

Alright so we get back to the same point: Why I need a man and how I can do without one. Honestly, I think I would acquire nirvana if I were to wake up one morning to find myself turned into a *boho* one day or to be precise a *bole* (bohemian lesbian). And while I am also aware that the possibility of this miracle is as bleak as bleak can be, the idea is not only alluring, but compelling too. So kissing a girl has figured in my dreams, yes it has, but it lacks the innate capacity of translating itself into reality.

So this option is blindly crossed out and only finds space in my private dreams over which I have no control, and thankfully no man does either. Then is it possible for me to spend the rest of my life without the presence of male species and therefore sex? And while the answer has already been figured out earlier, what needs to be explored now is how I can go on without emotionally anchoring my desolate ship to any man. Truth be told, even the thought of some dude turning his face away from me sends my confidence spiralling down. Not been spoken to, admired, hugged, kissed or even fussed around when jealous, insecure or in love, can have the effect on my moral similar to the effect melted cheese has on a hot pizza.

In fact, I do not remember the last time I was without a man. A man, some man, was always around, so I never explored the possibility of being emotionally independent or mentally secure on my own. And while I could have given past wounds sufficient time to heal, what I did was to band-aid them, let's say man-aid them, and move right ahead into a new relationship blindly. So logically, relationships left me with little or no time to know who I really was or what I was truly capable of. There were chances that I could end up feeling loved, confident and assured even without a man, but for now, that seemed like a distant possibility.

But it's not like I have always been gutted in the absence of one. In fact, with every new phase, the man changed. He changed with every book promotional tour, with every new habit picked up, old ones dropped, weight gained, weight lost, emotions sunk or emotions heightened, and the funny part is that while I witnessed the altering face of every man, I tucked myself conveniently behind the façade of love-no love, commitment-no commitment, marriage-no marriage and remained just as I was: insecure, lonely and with acute low self-esteem that stopped me from challenging myself or trying to know who or what the real person inside me was. And while these traits of a lonely sad *didi* Alafia were nothing to gloat over, I knew they needed immediate attention. But the question remained, how?

According to a survey carried by one of those self help magazines, most people who are lonely turn to religion. But to me, religion was a way of life that society followed because that was what they were taught to do as children. So coming from a middle-class Christian family what our parents tutored me and Anushka was just the same. We went to the Sunday

School and sang hymns from the Bible. Later we attended the church service as grown-ups, listened to sermons even if we thought the preacher had no clue what he was talking about, and yet continued doing this year after year. Our lives remained unchanged and so did our belief system.

So while it was a great idea to turn to religion to find answers to unsolved mysteries about life, I doubt if any religion offered prospects of overcoming a single person's life into a prosperous, fulfilled, companion-rich life. Moreover, my analytical mind needed more. It needed me to dig deep down, drill out the emotional debris and excavate the ancient memories to fill it up with newfound understanding of who I could possibly be, without a man.

It was worth a try and at the most, I'd end up feeling worse. And in case I did, I had the choice of getting back to older options and even finding new ones. Come on, we all are capable of wooing someone or the other who is willing to go to bed with us!

So what was I going to do next? Unfortunately, neither Myra, nor Onil, Abhijit, or Vishesh was in a position to answer that for me. I had to find my own answers.

The bloody winged nuisance came along and perched right on top of my shoulder, that wisdom birdie. "And what on earth are you doing here?"

"I thought you remembered me, ma'am."

"Well, did I?"

"Yes you did, remember?"

"Okay, whatever. Hey! wait a minute, wis...d...om or whatever your name is, has my ex-husband sent you here to spy on me? He is in a habit of reappearing every now and then."

The birdie looked sad and tweeted something as if mumbling profanities at me.

"Okay okay – don't go all puppy eyes – you're a bird."

The little rascal suddenly looked happy and chirped shrilly into my ears.

"Ma'am, you might like to spend some time alone."

"Really? Like how?"

"Like maybe going on a holiday."

"Again? Are you crazy? Who will look after the publicity of my next book and how will it help anyway?"

"My job was to only make a suggestion, ma'am. Anyway, when have you ever listened to me?"

"Listen, wisdom, you talk too much. Fine, I relent. I will take a holiday. Fine?"

And as if this was the only right decision I had ever taken in my life, wisdom birdie did a little jig for me by raising its bright golden and blue wings and lowering its magnificent red crown that wobbled like a jelly inside a bowl as it tilted downwards.

So after this precious little unprecedented suggestion, I did think it was a good idea for me to get away for a while.

But then I had another doubt that I almost gave up the grand plan. Was I running away from what I couldn't handle? Was I being an escapist? Abhijit said yes I was. Maybe I was. I had the choice to stay back and pay regular visits to my psychologist who was professionally determined to help me, while I was personally determined to be helped. Actually I didn't want to run away. I wanted to stay right there.

I even indulged in the fancy idea of renting a flat in Goa or begging a friend in Kerala to lend me her studio apartment for a month. None of these worked out. Many friends and well-wishers came forward to help me with their own houses, but darlings, I was not houseless. I had a mom and a dad and a house that was capable of accommodating a small portion of neighbourhood at any given day.

I took this as a divine indication and was just about to let go of the idea when I got a call.

"Hi, Miss Alafia?"

"This is she."

"Hi Alafia. Raghunath Murthy here."

"Raghu...nath. I am afraid, I can't recall this name."

"Alafia, you remember you had taken part in a contest called Travellers Quest on our website?"

"Yes. But that was several months ago."

"Yes, you are right and we're calling to inform you that you are the winner of this contest."

"Oh! Thanks. That's brilliant."

"As a winner you are entitled to a month's complimentary stay at our resort. You could choose to cut down on your stay time. But we'd like you to stay on at this prestigious property for..."

This man and his words and the offer blended into the stillness of a sunny afternoon after the previous day's heavy downpour. It couldn't be true. It couldn't be true... I said this to myself with the spirit of a woman who'd experienced excitement and disbelief at the same time.

"Hello, hello, Alafia, are you there?"

"Yes yes, Murthy, I am here."

"So would you like to accept your prize?"

More than anything else, mister!

Mansions without Men

•✦

Define a weirdo

A family had decided to descend into the swimming pool, which was right next to the table where I take my daily cup of espresso – a habit I completely blame Myra for. In an introspective mode, I allowed myself to be distracted by this quartet – a stereotype of the typical Indian family where the husband plays the pivotal role of a bread winner and the dedicated wife looks after the children who might someday go to foreign universities to acquire expensive degrees and end up getting even more expensive suitors for themselves.

The pot-bellied father in his mid-thirties didn't tire of calling his tiny daughter 'princess' each time she dipped her tiny feet into the swimming pool. The mother who entered the pool in a rundown *kurta* pyjama proudly looked at the chubby son whenever he completed the breadth. The father-mother peeped at me in intervals from behind the instruction board and would encourage their kids to do better each time they noticed me looking at them, "See people are looking child, do the laps faster. Very good, princess, dip your feet one more time."

This continued for a good two hours till my mind swapped places and I imagined myself beaming at the same son with

145

a sense of pride and picking up the husband's and children's wet clothes and shoes when it was time to go inside the room and take a shower.

While I could hardly call this a meditative-espresso-break, my attention was diverted to a bunch of 20 school kids who, albeit the sunny morning, were running around with sweaty bodies and red faces around the entire resort to find some hidden treasure. And suddenly six of them came charging towards their teacher in a jubilant manner, managing to find what was hidden behind one of the bushes laden with honey-coloured wild flowers.

A few other families had checked in at the resort as well, and while I had totally lost track of what I was thinking about, I did what I have often enjoyed doing with Myra – eavesdrop. From what I heard, the family of five lived in Old Delhi's Chandni Chowk because this location figured in their conversation at the end of almost every sentence. The grandfather admired his granddaughter even as she threw pebbles at the passersby who pinched the child's milky white cheeks.

"Talking and running childrens look good. The childrens who are quiet suffer problem. Look at our Shivi, she always talk, always run. Come come my child, come here to dadaji…" declared the grandfather, while the grandmother, father and mother looked at their four-year-old with an equal sense of wonder. I imagined their jaws literally dropping each time she just breathed.

I had already spent a week at the resort, and other than doing 'my stuff' I also developed the good or bad habit of poking my nose into other people's business – imaginatively. Good because people act as inspiration for writers and bad because I was supposed to mind my own business and focus on the only person I was here for – *me*. But I could afford that break once every now and then because just thinking about *your* life, *your* past, present, future, *your* happiness, sadness can not only get taxing for the pretty brains, it can be extremely exhausting for one's body and mind.

So, out of all the options I was earlier contemplating, here I was at the Jim Corbett National Park situated in the foothills of the Himalayas in Uttaranchal. The school kids had begun a game of tug of war and shouted out animatedly each time a team either won or lost. I have another three weeks to go and I decide to dive deep within myself, among other things.

My mind wanders off to these families I had been observing over the passage of a few days. What they form is a unit that is affiliated by consanguinity, affinity and co-residence. Anthropologists too vouch for a traditional family set up in a society that forms a primary economic unit, while partaking in its political functions too. So what does that leave me with? Other than my parents and a sister, I have no immediate family that is close to me, so which means when I am sick or suffering, they are the only people I can call upon. Therefore, anthropologically speaking, it also implies that I do not form a part of my country's economic or political unit. And adding some garnish to my further incompetence, I might end up having no children to nurse and no grandchildren to pet.

So do I really want to marry because the society demands that I do? Yes and no. In Indian society most things come with a shock value, so what happens over and over is what happened during Anushka's wedding. We Indians are *used to* seeing a woman in her early thirties *at least* married if not with kids. While this is a situation my body and mind has got accustomed to, I have to deal with stares from families and school kids, accompanied with a "she is such a weirdo" expression that I find amusing with every passing day. So I was least surprised when one of the school kids actually came up to me and asked, "Ma'am, why do you sit alone all the time?" To which I smiled back and said, "Sweetie, why are you in a group all the time?"

She just chuckled and backed off, ascertaining that *this* woman certainly needed help. Yes, we are used to seeing foreigners, especially Caucasians who often come to India in search of their true selves. It is ironical that Myra asked me to move out of India in search of my true self, where she believed I'd end up finding more like me. So till that time, I was trying to discover my magic spot or let's call it the Buddha land, where I was struggling to connect with the person within me. Honestly, I have never believed in these spazzy spiritual connection theories but I had too much time at hand to not give it one full-throated attempt.

So what really works for me other than the privacy of my breathtakingly beautiful cottage number three (a VIP room that also serves as a honeymoon suite) is the bank of the Kosi river that runs proximate to the Park. My first impression of the tiny rivulet that flowed beside the resort was that since it was strewn with so many boulders, its flow looked erratic and I wondered if it resembled my life uncannily. So this was my 'connection spot' and there couldn't be a better deal, because none of the patrons ever came here. They'd see the dull river with its slippery boulders and practically no bank, and would speedily zip away.

One morning, as I was sitting on a flat stone that must get covered by the waters of the Kosi during the monsoons, I try to shut out thoughts of my divorce. It doesn't help because I would still be termed as someone who either walked out on her marriage or was forcibly thrown out. But then I struggle to rationalise it and I know that before I move ahead with any other issue, *this* needs to be addressed more than anything else. True, that I had performed a self-customised ceremony where I had forgiven everyone, but had I forgiven myself? Not really. I still held myself responsible and so guilty that if Ram gazed inside my mind through a crystal ball, he'd be the happiest man alive.

September 26

I take this pledge in the most unfashionable manner.

If I were not doing this and if I were not in this hot (rocky) seat, I would count myself as a complete weirdo or a complete freaky show-off. However, like Myra said, "Stop bothering about what people think. Just do what *you* think is right."

I decide to numb my sensibilities to the surroundings and place this dumb, under-confident girl right in front of me.

"Hi, know me?"

"Yeah I see you every day. But don't really know you."

"I know it."

"So enjoying yourself?"

"Yeah it's lovely… this jungle."

"Hey listen… Can we come straight to the point if you don't mind?"

"Mmm."

"Listen, Alafia, I just want to tell you that *I forgive you. You are not responsible for your divorce.*"

"But..."

"Yeah I know you would turn around to give me ten reasons as to why you were responsible... But it's gone. I forgive you. *You are free.*"

"So aren't you going to charge me... for... this... divo...?"

"No. You have suffered enough. Now it's time for you to go out and enjoy yourself freely – without any fear, without any guilt."

"Really?"

"Yes. Really."

"Everyone else has forgiven you except your own self."

"Mmm."

"So what are you waiting for? You are not a sinner. You are just someone whose marriage hasn't worked out."

I start tearing up as I watch the tiny river bird dive straight into the Kosi and come out with its wings shaking off the excess water. And then it flies away so swiftly as if it just attained moksha.

Yes! Forgiving is as easy as that.

"You are free. You are forgiven. You get that, Alafia?"

"I do."

"So jump up in joy. This is who you are. This is not what defines you."

I don't quite jump but dip my feet into the cool muddy Kosi and look up at the clear sky with a triumphant smile and shout out, "I am free now. Do you hear that?"

Permission Granted

◆◆

Anything that works for you, works well

It's not an overnight exercise, this forgiving thing. It's not even like the well-promised organic facial where your skin starts glowing in thirty minutes. So just by doing a mock little theatrical role play, you don't instantly start believing that you are forgiven. No matter how easy it is to say sorry, it is really most difficult to feel it and then express it from the innermost nerve of your inner thigh. So *feeling* that I have forgiven myself is going to take a lot more effort than I imagined. It is a ritual I must follow every day until I reach a stage where I believe and know for certain that I am free. That I am forgiven.

Interestingly, we talk about forgiving others all the time. I am also often advised on how I should forgive Ram or anyone who has caused any grief to me. Now I wonder why no one ever bothered to find out if *I* had forgiven myself. But for this realisation I would take the credit as solely mine. It had finally dawned upon me after all these years that I was not only hard on myself, but also quite unforgiving. So I punished myself, felt sorry, felt small and held myself totally responsible for any goof up whatsoever.

I was also eight sessions old with my psychotherapist and had realised that other than talking too much, I hadn't really done anything. But what I had done and that had the most significant bearing on my life is that I had started dealing with a side of me that I knew existed but was lost. I had managed to retrieve it before it died. I had also come face to face with a side of me that was tucked away in some corner of my heart or mind or liver. I don't know, but it certainly resembled a narrow tunnel that was endless and one that no man would ever want to enter.

September 27:

In this luscious forest reserve, I decided not to take any of those safaris that tourists flock to this sanctuary for, year after year. Instead, I spent my time looking at a family of monkeys that greeted me outside my cottage every morning. They swung from one tree to the other so playfully and so forcefully that to a tourist it would seem like they were fighting with each other over which branch they should choose for their afternoon siesta or debating over what's better for dessert: bananas or watermelons. So often those passing that route ran away in fear, while the brave ones mumbled the *gayatri* mantra, for some courage. After watching this run and play drama the entire morning, I decided go on my favourite walk to the connection spot. (I nicknamed it 'conspot' for my convenience. A great name to undo my mental conning!) The rock that I chose to sit on was half submerged in water and the other half so slippery that it seems like someone had glued soft brown mud on its edges. I sit with my one foot dipped in the water and the other one folded on the rock. I focused and told my mind that it was okay to feel hopeless, fearful and lonely. "It is fine because I am with you right now. If you're hopeless, I will give you hope; if you're fearful, I will make you strong; if you're lonely, I will give you company."

The mind looked at me meekly, with sweat beads of disbelief glistening across its forehead. I know it wanted to say that you are too weak to take care of me.

"I know I am weak and there will be times when I will still be harsh on you. I might subject you to some torture once again but I hope you will forgive me during such times. Won't you?"

"I have already forgiven you, remember?"

"And I am also just trying. So let's just do this together, shall we?"

The mind told me how scared it is to be ridiculed by me again.

"I know. I know. I know, honey. I know how terribly I have wronged you. But can we start trusting each other please?"

"Sure. Let's give it a try."

"Thanks so much darling. I will try my best. There will be moments when I might feel so lonely and terrible again, but bear with me. Know that I *am* trying to deal with it."

The mind smiled and gave me a big mindful hug.

"I love you."

"I love you too, darling. We will work this out together. I promise."

I told my heart the same thing. But it looked far more dejected than the mind. So I had more convincing to do.

"Hurt no?"

The heart gave me that crooked smile suggesting that it didn't matter! You don't care after all.

"Very hurt, no?"

"Just by adding superlatives you can't change me, Alafia. You have hurt me so much."

"I know, my love, I have hurt you. But trust me, I never wanted to."

"Then how did you manage to, Alafia?"

"That hurt has been caused by others, my love."

"Oh! Shut up will you. There were times when *you* chose to get hurt."

"Yes. I accept that. You are right. But you know that I am trying to change it."

"Anyway, Alafia. It's too late. I am too butchered already. Excuse me, but I cannot be of no help to you henceforth."

"Please don't say that, darling. I will be nothing without you."

The heart seemed resolved.

I didn't know how to take this ahead. But I was persuasive.

"You know I am already very weak and I know you are very lonely and tired too. I know you don't trust me anymore, but can we please give this one chance? Please."

"What's the guarantee I will not be broken again?"

"Listen, my love, there is no guarantee. We might face painful situations again. But let us just determine to deal with it."

"I promise, this time around it will be different."

"Okay. I will trust you, Alafia."

"Thanks."

Heart seemed wary but a little hope gleamed in his eyes.

Then I did something I would have never imagined doing. What I did was rather cheesy and I didn't dare to share this with Myra, Onil or Abhijit. Friends have the innate capacity of poking so much fun at you that they can make your most serious act seem like the most popular scene from a comical movie. So this was my secret Holy Communion. Before reaching conspot, I had cut pieces of papers into tiny squares and addressed them to the people who were my enemies. And to reinforce that thought, I wrote their names on the chits and lit them up one by one. So up in smoke went insecurity, then fear was set ablaze, and then loneliness turned into black soot and dissipated against the harsh light of the sun.

Then I cupped my hands together and scooped up the ashes and silently immersed them in the noisy Kosi, and repeated the act till there was no ash left on the small flat stone on which I had lit up these human-devils.

According to Hindu rituals, the ashes of a deceased's body are immersed in the Ganges because it is easier for ghosts or negative energies to gain control of the ashes and misuse them, but by immersing the sediments in water, they are dispersed and hence unavailable to the ghosts in a collected form to gain control of. Also, scientifically, water is also all-assimilating and absorbs the distressing vibrations from the body of a person alive or dead. What I did was a well-thought out and well-researched strategy to let go of what I had held within me for the last many years. This act also reinstated that ghosts of my past were never going to come back to gain control over me.

The phantoms of fear must be laughing behind my back for all I care, but at that very moment, I did feel like a huge load had suddenly been lifted from my back. So this self-customised ritual did work for me.

As I watched a thin line of the river quickly gulp down the black burned paper inside its vast forgetful belly, Dinesh, one of my favourite stewards called out to me. "Ma'am Mr Murthy is here. He wanted to know if you're free to have lunch with him today."

Though I had never seen this Murthy guy and wanted to humbly refuse, I said yes. "Thanks, Dinesh. Please tell him I will see him around 2 pm at the Grill House." The Kumaoni with butter-coloured skin gave me a puzzled look and left.

I was used to that look and smiled as I watched his taut young body stride past the rocks. Then I looked at my foot that looked spongy under the water and simultaneously made mental notes of what I wanted to scribble in my diary after getting back to my room.

`"Ashes were immersed… Much more to do…"`

Transcription Reconnected

••

Looking for yourself

This Murthy guy was nothing like I had expected. He didn't come across like the typical resort manager who looked nervous in a necktie, white shirt and black trousers. Murthy spoke with the lilt of a young man in his early 20s and appeared charming just like one.

Our lunch was formal and interspersed with many questions like, "Hope you are enjoying your stay here, would you like to go on a safari over the weekend, where did you study?" And of course the most important one, "Are you married?"

Being married in India is so important that you could sacrifice a day's meal just to sit with someone and chew the endless possibilities of the victim's singlehood. So the question chased me again, even in the midst of my so called solitude, but I was so used to this Indian inquisitiveness that now it hardly mattered anymore.

"So, Mr Murthy, it was a pleasure meeting you and in case I do change my mind about the safari, I know who to call," I smiled.

"You are an author, Ms Singh, and entertaining you is our honour," he said while sizing me up, not in a lascivious way but rather checking out a 'bold' Indian girl who doesn't seem to give a damn to whether she has a partner by her side or not, and seems oblivious to the fact that that's the only one thing her outrageous hormones demand.

"I will not be seeing you too often, Ms Singh. I understand that at a place like this, you might like to enjoy being by yourself."

I could hear myself breathing a sigh of relief for I really needed my 'me time' and there was no way I was going to have that if this reasonably attractive man came to look after my well-being every three hours. Alright, not that I minded and not that I wanted to have any distractions by the means of attraction, but I was too busy trying to figure out the likelihood of taking a solo trip to heaven and wondering how it'd be up there – would they have a special singles table? Would they have dating options too? Would God personally come and tell each one from my sisterhood that they could now pick *any* man of their choice because the dead had privileges over the living?

But I was alive.

I was snapped back to reality when Dinesh, the young server came in with a lemon sorbet that was a great a palate cleanser.

September 28:

So it was a great start. The mind and heart were in total control now. After a lot of persuasion, they were finally *mine*. But I couldn't help feel a tad melancholic. I cocked my head to one side and ran my index finger across my lower lip. And as if my brain storming came from scratching my lip, I instantly knew what I'd been desperately trying to gauge. I blinked rapidly as I went back to that vital question: "Why do I need a man?"

I planted myself again on *the* soft rock, to collect myself and grasp a coherent thought.

So I began by rationalising and the first thought that came to my mind was: certainly not to get laid. So is it because I couldn't hold myself up like a bone marrow and was softer than a marshmallow? Or because I would not feel good unless a man tells me that *I am* good. Or was it out of sheer habit to track down a suit in the hope of *working* things out. And then, what was with this *working things out* anyway? Couldn't I go on without even trying to *work* things out? It works better for the men and might work better for me in the longer run.

Around 1980, there was a bumper sticker that read "A woman needs a man like a fish needs a bicycle." After 40 years of the feminist movement (and greatly increased male-bashing), is this sentiment still growing? But I had the answer to my self-doubt. I might not need a man to help me breathe and live and eat and sleep. *But I did need him.*

I looked at the wide Kosi. It was so noisy and yet so calm. It was almost as if its calmness got permeated through the cool air into the body, mind and heart. One moment I wanted to be the river I was jealous of and the next moment I wanted to be me. But who was *me*? Just an insecure, fearful, shy person? I was trying to be what I was not; I was trying to fit where I couldn't. And with no prospects in sight, there was one man who refused to leave me alone and he was there again.

I smiled at him.

He smiled too.

I stared at him.

He stared too.

"Good to see you here too."

"Wow. And is this Ms Alafia Singh talking to me?" Ram's mouth remains open.

I smile again.

"What makes you so kind to me – the river, the hotel manager or that waiter?"

"Whoa whoa whoa... Don't look so hurt, Ram. Honestly, I think I was missing you."

"It's good to know that," he smiled, revealing his uneven line of teeth that I never liked but which suited him well.

"So tell me what this is about?" Ram knew something had been going on in my mind for a long time. Oh! This bloody ghost of a human!

"I am scared to be alone," I murmured.

Ram didn't say much. He disappeared just as quickly as the sun behind the clouds.

I didn't say goodbye to him because I knew he'd come back soon. At this point, he knew I needed to be alone.

So, to be clear, I didn't really need a man, I wanted him. I think men were wild and crazy, industrious and whimsical, predictable and mysterious. Oh wait...so were women. Although, really, men are no different. So was he really the unicorn to my Pegasus? Chuck it because I would never quite understand why I needed, err...wanted a man. Besides, I didn't want to figure this out anymore; it was not my job. And for me, having this knowledge was enough.

Part - IV

On my own and in no Hurry.

Continuing Me Mission

❧

Still looking around

Even if I were alone, I was not quite alone. Calls from Myra were consistent. She wanted to know every detail of how I was faring. And there was no way I could escape this girlfriend's persistence, concern and the oh-so-natural girlie curiosity. "Is he cute? Do you like him?"

"Come on My, not every good-looking man has the right to be in my bed."

Myra had been flooding me with questions about Murthy, but after that introductory lunch we'd not even so much as said hello to each other.

"So what exactly do you do the whole day, Ala?"

And she was not the only one to ask me that question. Everyone wanted to know if I was in my right senses to spend that kind of time alone, without friends and without civilisation (the working of phone lines and internet was solely dependent on the weather forecast!). But Myra knew that I was happy, or at least I sounded happy; and it's all that mattered to her.

"Alright, Ms Singh. Shoot with your itinerary," presses on the pushy woman.

"My, I don't follow a schedule. I just go with the flow. The whole idea is to spend that kind of time where I can."

"Where you can understand the miseries of your life better?"

"Well thanks honey, at least you recognise it as misery!"

"Oh no, Ala, I didn't mean to sound insensitive. I know you've been through a lot."

There was silence at the other end. I knew Myra was waiting to word the right kind of sentences, lest she falters with her choice of words again.

"But now you deserve happiness, with or without a man. You get that, right?"

I didn't have an option but to say yes because this is precisely what I was determined to find out. Women like me can sometimes be so hung up on titles; we want to label everything and especially our status in the relationship. So who am I really? Am I your girlfriend, fiancée, keep or wife? In Indian homes, while growing up we were taught to be good wives and mothers in that specific order. We were never taught that single and happy are synonymous with one another. We were taught to stand by our man even if he pales in comparison. And the reason why I have struggled with so many is because of my utmost emphasis on *we* instead of me. I learned a lot about myself and I was not putting it to use. Now I have raised the bar on loving me first and foremost and not out of insecurity but a gradual belief that like naiveté, desperation is not cute. Let's face facts: I am past my easy-going stage of twenties when I had time to bounce back from dumb mistakes. My rebound game is not that good anymore and I have lost my elasticity to nonsense a long time ago. What I am convinced about is that I cannot have a man because right now I need him and I need to want him.

September 29

Today I decide to have a night session. I visit conspot later in the evening and try to look for my favourite and overused rock where I have perched up every day like a sinner and tried to wash away every stupid "sin" from the past. I have never taken Biblical teaching too seriously; until now when this verse from chapter Mark screamed from a distance in my memory and my mother made me parrot it at an age I didn't even know how sin was spelt. "And when you stand praying, if you hold anything against anyone, forgive him, so that your Father in heaven may forgive you your sins." I knew as a certainty that I didn't hold anything against anyone, anymore.

I finally dip my feet into the night river. The water is cold and although I have not seen a single fish so far, I imagine the touch of tiny Mahseer all over my toes. I don't mind it and laugh it off as a natural fish pedicure. I know I am scared and thrilled at the same time. When am I ever going to get a chance to sit under the stars, feeling fresh water on my skin while the majestic Kumaon hills chaperone me?

Dinesh comes running with two lanterns and one bamboo stick. I feel slightly embarrassed as I gape at him again and cock my head on one side to have a full glance of his taut body and cream-coloured skin. Oh! He had that raw innocence which made my hormones do double backflips. I wish I could just grab him by his hair, bend him over, pull open his fly and do Alafia a la dominatrix right there and then. "Ma'am... m... ma... ma'am, excuse m... ee..."

"Oh Dinesh, y... e...e...s, did you want something?"

"Ma'am I came to put these lanterns for you. Murthy sir didn't want you to sit alone in the dark."

"Yeah yeah, why not! Go ahead and do whatever you want here." He gave me a careful smile but looked away soon after. May be he was scared of his seniors, maybe he was scared of my aura, and maybe he was trying to suggest that this was not the right time and place for your naughty thoughts ma'am.

He placed the lanterns on the sand right next to the rock on which I was now seated in a lotus position and thrust the bamboo stick between two tiny rocks and hung another lantern on its head. "Anything else you *want* ma'am?"

Yes my darling, ma'am could want many more things but she's more a chicken than a woman right now. She could easily have you under her quilt right now and have you for breakfast, lunch and dinner and even dessert but good lord, no. I have just learned to differentiate sanity from insanity and I was going to cling on to the former with a renewed zeal.

"Nothing else Dinesh, you may leave now." And I smile as he looks at me with puzzled eyes and leaves obediently.

I peel my eyes off Dinesh and look straight ahead. I see nothing but darkness and a faint silhouette of the green hills that are radiating gray by now. Up above the stars looked like they could be plucked a handful into my palms. All I had to do was jump and pluck, jump and pluck.

The river had turned noisier and perhaps secretly even instructed me to get back to my room, read a nice book, and get some hot chocolate and sleep.

But I was not going to listen to anyone. Not *right* now. I was alone or maybe even lonely or whatever you want to call it, but I had never felt this peaceful in my solitude. I had never enjoyed my own company this thoroughly. I felt so radiant, so close to nature.

Was this all I ever wanted in my life? To sit by a shore, gaze at some old hills and muddy river and frightening stars and *feel good*?

The answer is, surprisingly, yes.

Ram comes back and flashes a grin. He stares at me in the eye while his face looks yellow in the reflection of the glow from the lanterns. I think he moves his thumb on my cheek or am I hallucinating? I don't know.

He doesn't talk to me that night and leaves without even turning to look back or mock at me or even crack a joke. I know this is his final goodbye.

"Have a *happy* life Ram."

I smile the smile of freedom.

Ready for Readmission?

◆

Grapes are not sour. I have just learnt to deal with the lack of them.

Something in me was buoyant and ready to take life on with full zeal. I am not saying that not having a man was liberating; all I am saying is that I have simply adjusted to the fact that I always needed a man in my life to fulfil my own insecurities and inabilities. If you want to guffaw at this revelation, so be it! Alright, now I am not being all up-in-arms. I still believe in the story when a prince will come along and whisk me away. My foot will pop up on that magical first kiss. He'll know exactly what to do and what to say and he'll buy the most perfect, thoughtful, extravagant gifts. He will never look at porn, have no interest in strippers, he will pick up his socks, and not be friends with any of his exes. He'll love me for me, exactly as I am. But for now, I wanted to love me.

I had exactly a week more left before I left Corbett and thereafter headed to Mumbai to promote my book. For a change, I had no holiday hangover. I knew I was going to be fine even as I would soak myself in a run around busy schedule in Delhi once again. So I had started spending more time at conspot and wrote in my diary more regularly. But most of what I scribbled still made very little sense. There were still loosely connected words strung together. So the pages looked something like:

> Happy. Marriage? No fret. Relationships? No fret. Good girl. Hot Dinesh, hot dinner. Deprived of both. Need to lose wait? Hell, no. Need to lose weight? As hell! Will miss these companions. Will the trees, hills, river and stars miss me too? Will they come to my rescue once again?

In the midst of these ridiculous thoughts and an even more ridiculous writing, the phone buzzes exactly after three days. And it's Abhijit. "Where the fuckin' hell have you been Ala?"

"In the fuckin' heaven Abhi," I giggle.

I can imagine him with a straight face and grim lips.

"Ok sorry. You know the connectivity issue here, right? I had no internet, no phone. Nothing for the last three days. Yours is the first call to come."

"And how many days more till you get out of that jungle?"

"Oh dear! I am not going to be here forever. By the way, you know what? I have decided to give this search-for-Mr-Right some break."

"Thank god for some wisdom, Ala! How the hell did you acquire it at this age?"

"Shut up, devil!"

"Listen, you were married once and I always told you that this marriage thing is not meant for you. You're just beyond all this Ala. But you've been so eager to…"

"Abhi, we're not going there again. I have told you that I didn't want to remarry for the heck of it. I wanted it because I wanted it!"

"Anyway, it's better late than never. I am just happy that that insane I-want-to-get-married addiction is finally out of your head. Just have sex. Have fun. Date. Enjoy."

"Wow! You don't get it Abhi, do you? Why do all our conversations have to end in a fight? It's so not about sex and dates, you moron."

"Jeez Ala, you're one hell of a complicated woman. You don't want to marry. You don't want to date. You don't want to have sex. Well, only you know what you really want. Or I am assuming you do."

"Abhi, do you know that you're capable of angering even the fuzziest teddy bear with the cutest red bow?"

By now, Abhijit's voice was quivering with laughter and I had already had enough of this close friend too, so the call ended with a promise to call him back soon. And which I will, irrespective of how much the man irritates me. I still love him, in spite of himself. He has been my best buddy for years and I knew that his way of showing love was different, even if it bordered on annoyance.

So am I bitter or better off? No one seems to know. I don't seem to know this either. I was forking at a pink salmon along with some best wine I had specially ordered that day (to celebrate the end of a "streak") when this reasonably attractive *gora* (white man) came along and sat at a table next to me. He didn't look at me. Oh no! Not at all, but I noticed him from a distance because of his immaculate spikes. When you've decided to be individualistically happy or happily individualistic, I guess you exude the typical pheromones that instantly give out signals like: Stay away, not available, too busy, bugger off, commitment ONLY. So men who catch this negative chemical secretion either run away/stop looking at you/show no interest, not even in sex, by the way.

And just as I was busy doing these recalculations (as a theory to convince myself for not being noticed) I hear a voice that demands something of me. "I know this is ridiculous, but my name is Ethan Miller and can I please borrow your phone for exactly five nanoseconds?"

I look up dazed and I can't speak a word because my jaw has just dropped hard on the cold stone floor. I can only manage to hear five nanoseconds, the dictionary meaning of which I am tempted to find out immediately.

"Hey, I know this is rude. But my phone has no connectivity. None of the phone lines are working here and the closest phone booth is an hour's drive from the resort."

I finally find my lost speech back. "Sorry, wh... what did you say?"

"Well lady, I am sorry I have to ask for your phone so shamelessly. You know you might think this is funny, but... ok, take this. This is my business card. I manage an art gallery in Toronto and right now I have an urgent call to make."

"Ok. Wait." I carefully look at his business card with his name on it and the name of his gallery that read: Pink. Why pink? I wonder. That's such an odd name for any gallery. Is he gay? Is he creating awareness about breast cancer? Is he really a woman in a man's body? Or is it just creativity? But there is nothing creative about the word "pink." Even "ink" and "kink" are slightly artistic, but pink? "So you need my phone?"

"I do need your phone and I will pay you in cash right away."

"Pay me? For what?"

"For using your phone eh! The bill."

I smile at him. The desperation in his voice is clear and so are his intentions.

"Sure. Here it is. Go ahead and make your important call."

He grabbed the cell phone even before I could hand it over to him.

"Ethan. Ethan Miller," he smiled and left for a secluded corner. When he came back, he was smiling, looked relieved and handed me my cell phone with a $ 20 bill.

"What is this?" I asked him puzzled.

"Well, I told you I'd pay you back."

"Don't be silly. It's fine. You were in need and had it not been for me, someone else would have helped."

"I know. But I would really appreciate if you take this."

I looked into his blue eyes which were shining earnest with gratitude. On any other day, I would have bounced with glee, but I was not quite ready to handle this emotion, not yet. "Hey, you know what? I am fine. You don't have to pay me."

He nods at me and stares straight into my eyes with a look of rejection.

"How about we share a meal together?"

I smile at him serenely and look again into his eyes which are beautiful and yes, other than blue, they are captivating and intelligent too.

"Some other time. But for now, I gotta go. And by the way, my name is Alafia Singh."

"Meal," he orders again. "And by the way, nice to meet you Alafia Singh."

I scuttle off to my room and my mind sharply tells me, "Get into bed."

I do as I am told.

Redemption

◆

Residual melancholy

Light fills the room, coaxing me from deep sleep to wakefulness. It's early morning and the monkeys outside are at their playful best. The park looks beautiful at any time of the day. Even when it's raining non-stop for five days, or when an angry gang of mosquitoes decides to attack you, or even when a hungry predator like a snake, wild bear, wolf or fox comes out openly in the night in search of prey. It's this unpretentious rawness that has driven me for the last month, where I have never woken up to witness a single dull moment – even when I have sat staring at the sky or have walked aimlessly next to the river.

I took a quick shower and indulged in some expensive figs and leaves soap loaded with aloe vera, coconut and, of course, figs. I even find myself humming an old Hindi song (to which we Indians often turn to in a happy state of mind or after a peg or two). And since the big girl in me was going back to her carefree self of her former days, I decided to dress up in something just as casual. I got into the shortest flaming orange shorts and wore a cool white tee, applied a generous amount of kohl and mascara on the eyes, softened my wet skin with some lavender moisturiser and smoothened out my hair with a leave in conditioner and voila!

Outside, Mr Murthy greeted me with a big smile. This was the third time I had seen him since our lunch together. Once again he surprised me by dressing up in the most un-manager-like manner with a cotton button-down shirt, brown loafers and faded jeans. But I was more than happy that our conversation didn't last beyond ten minutes.

I headed out straight to get a hearty breakfast of South Indian and continental dishes. The sight of steaming *idlis*, fresh *dosas* and the delectable spread of cereals, porridge, boiled eggs, bacon, grilled fish, sausages and fried mushrooms served with toast filled me with joy.

Dinesh and his other colleagues eyed me carefully. They knew that there was something different about me and they threw stolen glances in my direction which made me a little conscious about my appearance and I felt a little flattered too. And just when I was revelling in this Miss-Sexy-Thing spell that I had successfully cast on everyone, a voice shouted out right from the corner table. "Hey there... Good morning!" I turned around to see Ethan – attractively dressed in his khakis and a white cotton shirt walk towards me.

"Good morning," I smile.

"It's a beautiful morning, isn't it?"

"Indeed, it is."

"I will be going on a safari this morning. Would you like to accompany me?"

"Oh! Thanks. My morning is going to be fairly busy. But where are you headed?"

"I will be travelling to Jhirna and will try my luck at spotting a tiger," he laughed while exposing his perfectly aligned white teeth.

"You bet!"

I could have continued this friendly chat, but instead, I chose to head straight towards an empty table. So I smiled and left this Canadian wondering if I was ruder or more shy or both or none.

"Hey, seems like you're in a bit of a hurry, eh?"

"I am just so hungry. I better grab a bite before my system collapses."

"Great. I have twenty minutes before I leave for the safari. Can I join you? I don't want to come across as forcing myself on you but you know, two is better than one," he laughed again and this time I was aware of his white teeth contrasted to my yellowing ones.

He already sat at a table and I didn't have much of a choice than to smile. For the last one month I had become so accustomed to eating alone that this felt odd and even intrusive, but I wasn't absolutely sure because there was some pleasantness about the way he talked. Although we had never spoken much, there was warmth in his voice along with a certain sense of peace and confidence. He was one of those men who know they have a natural charm but don't feel the need to throw it around, especially to impress a woman. He was himself. That was evident.

And while he went on rambling about this and that, my mind wandered to familiar territory and that terrain was certainly not a happy one. I had been there, fought enemies, survived battles and had come out a winner in my own eyes. So I didn't want to get back there. Not *now*. Maybe never. Or wait, maybe I would because I was not the live-life-without-love kinds. But at that moment, I simply wanted to revel in the glory of hoisting up a winner's flag. "Hey, are you alright, young lady?"

"Of course! Do I look like I am in the middle of sprouting two horns from my head?"

"Oh no. That's not what I meant. You looked so lost."

"I am lost eating," I giggled for no apparent reason in an attempt to cover my own embarrassment of not paying attention to Ethan's soliloquy about how he ended up here and also with the realisation that my mind was once again *there* – over thinking, over analyzing – drawing conclusions out of *what may not be*.

"Alright then, I better get going. Remember you've promised me a meal," he smiled and left.

What was this? What was happening? Was I getting attracted to this man? Was he getting attracted to me? But then there was no novelty in this feeling. It had happened before, and at least half a dozen times. And now I didn't want to get laid. Because that was exactly how it had happened in the past: romantic dinner, stolen glances, suggestive moves, *the* calculated move and then it all ends up with moving on top of each other.

After breakfast, I spent most of my day reading at the conspot. What this place did to me was something like a lazy muzak for the soul. Going there could be oddly depressing but also utterly self-involving. It's funny how redemption waits to happen. When I was looking at the floating clouds again, I instantly knew I was never again going to be this happy in my life.

It Is Me, Finally

◦◇

Commitment is not always commitment

Finally, Ethan persuaded me to have dinner with him. Why does it always have to be *dinner* with someone you're attracted to? Maybe it was the darkness that gave you the chance to hide what you wanted to hide and reveal just the right amount.

We had a simple meal, but it was the only romantic one I'd had in months. Together we decided on asparagus cream soup and devilled eggs that were meticulously stuffed with a creamy shrimp and green onion filling. Ethan floored me by wearing a *kurta pyjama* in which he looked like some exotic prince. And that was the magic of being attracted to someone. When you're going to fall into a mousetrap (in this case maletrap), you know it. How and what makes you so sure about your double flipping pheromones, is immaterial.

The good thing about Ethan was that he talked just the right amount. Not less, not more but just well enough to leave silent gaps to brood over and take in every word. But after years of travelling around the country for book promotions, meeting various people who tell you that your writing is crap and they can write better and, of course after years of being in the dating business, with an ex-husband and a divorce as an attachment, you just learn how to talk – even with those who are naturally the less social types and leave you with an awkward pause after every sentence.

But with Ethan, these little quiet interruptions were easy. They came with an opportunity to blush, observe Dinesh (who'd turned red) and admire my companion's good looks on the sly. And so I surely feared what might occur post the gastronomic delight. It is inevitable in many cases, but in my case, I wanted to make sure that I wasn't wrongly paired once again. And the chances of us doing horizontal bop seemed more and more likely because:

a) He was not a gay. Pink gallery was named 'Pink' because according to Ethan, it was the only colour capable of separating those who can from those who cannot.
b) He was not championing any women's cause which made him an easy-going person. But did he know that in less than 48 hours I'd be headed straight to this city called Mumbai. And once I was there, its vastness would compel me to dive head on into a busy life allowing me to breathe in only traces of my beautiful days at Corbett.

Also, at that very moment, a thought suddenly struck me – I would not be this happy in my life ever again. I might get happier, but *this happy*, no.

"So do you suddenly start thinking about your boyfriend when you look lost?" My soup fell on my shirt when I heard those words.

I managed a crooked smile and started wiping the green on my white dress.

Was this his way of finding out whether I was dating someone or not?

"Well, what about your girlfriend? Is she some nice Canadian blonde with a heady Scottish and Ukrainian bloodline?"

"I don't have a girlfriend."

This time the loaded devilled egg fell right into the soup. Because c) and most importantly, *he had no girlfriend!*

"Are you really alright, Alafia?"

"Of course I am. Do I look like I am mad as a hatter and no longer in charge of my cognitive skills?"

"You do talk a lot when caught off guard!" he smiled and cocked his head upwards to look straight into my eyes.

"Okay. Whatever. Do you know that my stay in Corbett comes to an end tonight?" By now, I was conscious about the way he was looking at me. But soon, his white skin changed from red to yellow.

"But why so early?"

"Early? I have been here for almost a month now."

"So are we running out of time?"

"I don't know what your question means."

He took a pause so he could weigh his words properly and then he seemed to have decided that he didn't need to explain anything to me after all.

The sun was down and the cresset placed right next to our table was emitting flames which seemed to dance its way into the nippy air. I was suddenly reminded of how Vishesh loved to see any light reflect on my face – brake light, lamp post light, cell phone light – for him it wasn't ghastly, it was beautiful. For Ethan, light would mean light. Or maybe he was better than that, but there was no way of knowing because I was soon going to leave behind a trail of these moments. It had no future. Ethan and I only meant one fascinating date. Period.

"Care for a walk?"

"Sure, it is rumoured that a snake makes rounds in the evenings here."

"Are you scared?"

"For sure."

I expected him to say something but he didn't. He quietly looked at me and thankfully didn't come up with any of those corny lines that I feared would put me off. There was no: I will hold your hand, I will crush the snake or I will be your snake charmer shit! Ethan conveyed his words most effectively through his eyes and better through his silence. And for some strange reason I was reminded of Paul Overstreet and Don Schlitz's hit country song, *You say it best when you say nothing at all.*

"Well, I think you're going to be in for a shock, but I think I like you, Alafia."

I was so not prepared for this moment. It had happened so many times in the past – these so-called 'special moments', so however much I would have liked it, I didn't feel the novelty. It seemed stale, repetitive and boring. I was disgusted at my emotional impotence but when there's been an action replay of the same story with different characters, I didn't know what the best thing to do was.

I shrugged.

"Aren't you going to say anything at all?"

"What do you expect me to say?"

"Just something, anything."

"Ethan, how well do I know you to have this conversation with you? Or how well do you know me?"

"What's there to know? All I said is that I like you."

Even this desperate exchange of dialogues seemed familiar. In the past, I too had given away my heart a little too easily, almost all the time and even to those who didn't deserve it. But this time for a change I was being offered this hollow muscular organ by someone who was not eager to please me and who genuinely possessed some inherent qualities which were definitely a turn on.

"I am not too sure how I can handle this. I will be gone tomorrow. I don't intend on sleeping with you, you'd go back to Canada or where ever you come from and moreover, isn't it unnatural for you to like me in just one date?"

"Eh...there she goes again. She talks because she's cornered. Blah blah blah blah blah..."

The air was getting cooler and I felt like putting an end to our walk. Ethan knew I was cold because he saw me hug myself and shiver.

"How about we get some hot chocolate at The Den?" he suggested.

The Den was a makeshift bar and coffee shop. On days when the resort made bulk bookings from various corporate houses around Delhi, this watering hole served booze till three in the morning and on days when only one or two customers were left in the resort, it offered some great coffee with warm bread and little butter cubes. This was that odd day when other than Ethan and I, a few workers and chefs were the only occupants here. Dinesh was nowhere to be seen, maybe he had decided to not stay the night after getting totally cheesed off with me.

We grabbed a comfortable couch. It wasn't placed in a secluded corner or under the dimmest of lights; in fact, we were sitting right at the entrance. So this proved a point to me again: This man was not even looking for a cosy moment with me. I had already assumed that he liked my company and I was not totally off-course.

There were two servers inside who didn't hide their annoyance of being invaded upon. Had we not showed up, they would have probably had a swig or two and snoozed under their tattered blankets.

"Two regular coffees, please."

After placing the order, Ethan took a straight dive into my eyes once again. What's with this looking deep into the eyes routine?

"Now listen, Alafia. I know that you're going away and I know that you can stay back but I will not ask you to."

Only if he did.

"But all I am saying is that I like you. I don't believe in love at first sight, but I do believe that people can click instantly. There can be immediate sparks. And between you and me, I could feel those sparks."

I so wanted to tell him about my bad divorce, bad relationships and the time and effort it had taken me to become strong and healthy once again. But I didn't say any of those things.

"I have seen relationships die and I am not willing to witness another death."

There was silence between us once again. No one spoke. The servers were almost glaring at us, hoping that we'd leave early. They also looked quite nonplussed about how this madam who had spent a month without a companion was suddenly with this *gora*, who had apparently stolen their madam from them.

After feeling that I was being too hard on Ethan, I decided to help him.

"Okay, here's what it is, Ethan. I like you too. In fact, I was attracted to you the moment I saw you but other than that, I don't have anything else to say. You look like a nice man and any woman would be lucky to have you."

"Oh, Alafia! That's more praise than I can handle."

"It's just the way I feel about you. And this is not the first time I have been so quick and easy with my praises for a man, but..."

I almost bit my tongue for saying such stupid things. I was killing my own prospects, if there were any.

"And yes, I do not have a boyfriend."

The night felt safe with this man. There were no pressing issues like sex, commitment, mush, separation. He was not intimidated that I was an author or that I was bold enough to stay away from my family in a jungle for a month. The best thing about Ethan was his acceptance of me just as I was, without any frills. It was pure liking. No ifs, not buts.

The dawn was beginning to crack. This was the longest and my last night at Corbett.

Strong, Secure

꘎

Balancing act

So there I go again. Sitting on top of a decision I am yet to make. But in the past, I had rested my mind too much to allow it to think, feel or process anything and dived head on without measuring the risks. As a result, my heart was broken too many times. Agreed that a broken heart means you tried but a healing heart means you were not willing to try again soon.

As promised to my heart and mind, I was not willing to explode them again with romance and pain. So what if there was a *nice* man willing to love me? Nothing was at stake, but me. I could once again waltz into a man's arms, but hey, was I ready?

The *me* is a big thing. The more you talk about it, the more you risk being called individualistic. But most people forget that if the individual part in me is not alright, can I really expect to keep someone else happy?

So yes, Ethan and I did exchange a passionate kiss. Our lips locked and our eyes shut as we melted in each other's warm breath.

That night was surreal, and had to find space in one of my books. I know I was going to remember this man forever. But this time, I was going to let loose this intense emotion that in the past had led me to an unending cycle of balance and imbalance. Well, I didn't even know where I stood, whether I should endorse *balance* as my best buddy or just dump her for being a fine-weather friend.

I packed my bags and called the reception for the cab. The goodbyes were exchanged without much fanfare. My imagination went berserk as I imagined the young men (mostly the servers and Dinesh) standing in a line to see their favourite madam leave. Whom would they check out on such regular basis now? But nothing happened. Life does move on, doesn't it? People come and people go. I was now learning to move along with them. Getting stuck with the good and bad times you shared with someone in your past can really screw your present. I am not saying that you forget all about the pain and pleasure and stop remembering someone, I am just saying, you have to allow a free entry to new emotions too.

Ethan came right into my room after his shower. He looked radiant in a white long sleeve button-down cotton shirt with comfortable chinos. I had a burning desire to grab him by his collar and make love to him right there and then. But lying under someone is the easiest and the most difficult thing to do.

"So all packed, are we?"

"Do I have an option?"

"You do. Provided you exercise it."

"Every option is not to be exercised, mister."

Once again the room was filled with silence.

"Well, I will miss you."

I looked at his intense eyes. They were ready to suck me in once again, but I moved over to make another call to the reception for my cab.

"Ethan, I will miss you too."

I don't know when I peeled away from his embrace. It seemed like ages had gone by. Although I wish we stood still for eternity, it was time for me to go.

Hastily, I took out my notepad and began to scrawl,

Someday when I am somewhere and maybe someone's, I am gonna look back on this moment of my life as a time of immense happiness. This happiness came from the depths of my sadness. A brutal time of grieving... mourning. But a time that was changing my life and me...

I had finally written something in my notepad after a long time and it was something that had made sense to me for the first time.

"Hey, what are you doing in the washroom?"

"Nothing... Just gathering a few moments of my leftover time!"

He kissed me again. "I think I am falling in love with you, Alafia. Don't go. I think I do love you. Okay, let me put it this way... I like..."

"Don't say anything," I smiled.

I knew he was falling in love. I know when a man is. And I wish I could do something to bail him out of this situation.

My cab started moving. I turned back to see a faint though still attractive figure of Ethan. He looked in my direction and I thought he waved at me.

I smiled and I looked ahead. Isn't that what life was all about?